D1177446

THE MODERN LIBRARY
of the World's Best Books

Two Novels

by

Bernard Malamud

*The publisher will be pleased to send, upon request,
an illustrated folder listing each volume in*

The Modern Library

TWO NOVELS

THE NATURAL
&
THE ASSISTANT

Bernard Malamud

The Modern Library

New York

THE MODERN LIBRARY

is published by

RANDOM HOUSE, INC.

BENNETT CERF   •   DONALD S. KLOPFER

Manufactured in the United States of America

Contents

The Natural   3

The Assistant 211

The Natural

For My Father

Pre-game

IIIIIIIIIIIIIIIIIIIIIIIIIIIIIIIIIIIIIIIIII

Roy Hobbs pawed at the glass before thinking to prick a match with his thumbnail and hold the spurting flame in his cupped palm close to the lower berth window, but by then he had figured it was a tunnel they were passing through and was no longer surprised at the bright sight of himself holding a yellow light over his head, peering back in. As the train yanked its long tail out of the thundering tunnel, the kneeling reflection dissolved and he felt a splurge of freedom at the view of the moon-hazed Western hills bulked against night broken by sprays of summer lightning, although the season was early spring. Lying back, elbowed up on his long side, sleepless still despite the lulling train, he watched the land flowing and waited with suppressed expectancy for a sight of the Mississippi, a thousand miles away.

Having no timepiece he appraised the night and decided it was moving toward dawn. As he was looking, there flowed along this bone-white farmhouse with sagging skeletal porch, alone in untold miles of moonlight, and before it this white-faced, long-boned boy whipped with train-whistle yowl a glowing ball to someone hidden under a dark oak, who shot it back without thought, and the kid once more wound and returned. Roy shut his eyes to the sight because if it wasn't real it was a way he sometimes had of observing himself, just as if this dream he could never shake off—that had hours ago wakened him out of sound sleep—of him standing at night in a strange field with a golden baseball in his palm that all the time grew heavier as he sweated to settle whether to hold on or fling it away. But when he had made his decision it was too heavy to lift or let fall (who wanted a hole that deep?) so he changed his mind to keep it and the thing grew fluffy light, a white rose breaking out of its hide, and all but soared off by itself, but he had already sworn to hang on forever.

As dawn tilted the night, a gust of windblown rain blinded him—no, there was a window—but the sliding drops made him thirsty and from thirst sprang hunger. He reached into the hammock for his underwear to be first at breakfast in the dining car and make his blunders of ordering and eating more or less in private, since it was doubtful Sam would be up to tell him what to do. Roy peeled his gray sweatshirt and bunched down the white ducks he was wearing for pajamas in case there was a wreck and he didn't have time to dress. He acrobated into a shirt, pulled up the pants of his good suit, arching to draw them high, but he had crammed both feet into one leg and was trapped so tight wriggling got him nowhere. He worried because here he was straitjacketed in the berth without much room to twist around in and might bust his pants or have to buzz the porter, which he dreaded. Grunting, he contorted himself this way and that till he was at last able to grab and pull down the cuff and with a gasp loosened his feet and got the caught one where it belonged. Sitting up, he gartered his socks, tied laces, got on a necktie and even squirmed into a suit coat so that when he parted the curtains to step out he was fully dressed.

Dropping to all fours, he peered under the berth for his bassoon case. Though it was there he thought he had better open it and did but quickly snapped it shut as Eddie, the porter, came walking by.

"Morning, maestro, what's the tune today?"

"It ain't a musical instrument." Roy explained it was something he had made himself.

"Animal, vegetable, or mineral?"

"Just a practical thing."

"A pogo stick?"

"No."

"Foolproof lance?"

"No."

"Lemme guess," Eddie said, covering his eyes with his long-fingered hand and pawing the air with the other. "I have it—combination fishing rod, gun, and shovel."

Roy laughed. "How far to Chicago, Eddie?"

"Chi? Oh, a long, long ways. I wouldn't walk."

"I don't intend to."

"Why Chi?" Eddie asked. "Why not New Orleans? That's a lush and Frenchy city."

"Never been there."

"Or that hot and hilly town, San Francisco?"

Roy shook his head.

"Why not New York, colossus of colossuses?"

"Some day I'll visit there."

"Where have you visited?"

Roy was embarrassed. "Boise."

"That dusty sandstone quarry."

"Portland too when I was small."

"In Maine?"

"No, Oregon—where they hold the Festival of Roses."

"Oregon—where the refugees from Minnesota and the Dakotas go?"

"I wouldn't know," Roy said. "I'm going to Chicago, where the Cubs are."

"Lions and tigers in the zoo?"

"No, the ballplayers."

"Oh, the ball—" Eddie clapped a hand to his mouth. "Are you one of them?"

"I hope to be."

The porter bowed low. "My hero. Let me kiss your hand."

Roy couldn't help but smile yet the porter annoyed and worried him a little. He had forgotten to ask Sam when to tip him, morning or night, and how much? Roy had made it a point, since their funds were so low, not to ask for anything at all but last night Eddie had insisted on fixing a pillow behind his back, and once when he was trying to locate the men's room Eddie practically took him by the hand and led him to it. Did you hand him a dime after that or grunt a foolish thanks as he had done? He'd personally be glad when the trip was over, though he certainly hated to be left alone in a place like Chicago. Without Sam he'd feel shaky-kneed and unable to say or do simple things like ask for directions or know where to go once you had dropped a nickel into the subway.

After a troublesome shave in which he twice drew blood he used one thin towel to dry his hands, face, and neck, clean his razor and wipe up the wet of his toothbrush so as not to have to ask for another and this way keep the bill down. From the flaring sky out the window it looked around half-past five, but he couldn't be sure because somewhere near they left Mountain Time and lost—no, picked up—yes, it was lost an hour, what Sam called the twenty-three hour day. He packed his razor, toothbrush, and pocket comb into a chamois drawstring bag, rolled it up small and kept it handy in his coat pocket. Passing through the long sleeper, he entered the diner and would gladly have sat down to breakfast, for his stomach had contracted into a bean at the smell of food, but the shirt-sleeved waiters in stocking caps were joshing around as they gobbled fried kippers and potatoes. Roy hurried through the large-windowed club car, empty for once, through several sleepers, coaches, a lounge and another long line of coaches, till he came to the last one, where amid the gloom of drawn shades and sleeping people tossed every which way, Sam Simpson also slept although Roy had last night begged him to take the berth but the soft-voiced Sam had insisted, "You take the bed, kiddo, you're the one that has to show what you have got on the ball when we pull into the city. It don't matter where I sleep."

Sam lay very still on his back, looking as if the breath of life had departed from him except that it was audible in the ripe snore that could be chased without waking him, Roy had discovered, if you hissed scat. His lean head was held up by a folded pillow and his scrawny legs, shoeless, hung limp over the arm of the double seat he had managed to ac-cuire, for he had started out with a seat partner. He was an expert conniver where his comfort was concerned, and since that revolved mostly around the filled flat bottle his ability to raise them up was this side of amazing. He often said he would not die of thirst though he never failed to add, in Roy's presence, that he wished for nobody the drunkard's death. He seemed now to be dreaming, and his sharp nose was pointed in the direction of a scent that led perhaps to the perfumed presence of Dame Fortune, long past due in his bed. With dry lips puckered, he smiled in expectation of a spectacular kiss though he looked less like a lover than an old scarecrow with his comical, seamed face sprouting prickly stubble in the dark glow of the expiring bulb overhead. A trainman passed who, seeing Sam sniff in his sleep, pretended it was at his own reek and humorously held his nose. Roy frowned, but Sam, who had a moment before been getting in good licks against fate, saw in his sleep, and his expression changed. A tear broke from his eye and slowly slid down his cheek. Roy concluded not to wake Sam and left.

He returned to the vacant club car and sat there with a magazine on his knee, worrying whether the trip wasn't a mistake, when a puzzled Eddie came into the car and handed him a pair of red dice.

"Mate them," he said. "I can't believe my eyes."

Roy paired the dice. "They mate."

"Now roll them."

He rolled past his shoe. "Snake eyes."

"Try again," said Eddie, interested.

Roy rattled the red cubes. "Snake eyes once more."

"Amazing. Again, please."

Again he rolled on the rug. Roy whistled. "Holy cow, three in a row."

"Fantastic."

"Did they do the same for you?"

"No, for me they did sevens."

"Are they loaded?"

"Bewitched," Eddie muttered. "I found them in the washroom and I'm gonna get rid of them pronto."

"Why?—if you could win all the time?"

"I don't crave any outside assistance in games of chance."

The train had begun to slow down.

"Oh oh, duty." Eddie hurried out.

Watching through the double-paned glass, Roy saw the porter swing himself off the train and jog along with it a few paces as it pulled to a stop. The morning was high and bright but the desolate station—wherever they were—gave up a single passenger, a girl in a dressy black dress, who despite the morning chill waited with a coat over her arm, and two suitcases and a zippered golf bag at her feet. Hatless, too, her hair a froth of dark curls, she held by a loose cord a shiny black hat box which she wouldn't let Eddie touch when he gathered up her things. Her face was striking, a little drawn and pale, and when she stepped up into the train her nyloned legs made Roy's pulses dance. When he could no longer see her, he watched Eddie set down her bags, take the red dice out of his pocket, spit on them and fling them over the depot roof. He hurriedly grabbed the bags and hopped on the moving train.

The girl entered the club car and directed Eddie to carry her suitcases to her compartment and she would stay and have a cigarette. He mentioned the hat box again but she giggled nervously and said no.

"Never lost a female hat yet," Eddie muttered.

"Thank you but I'll carry it myself."

He shrugged and left.

She had dropped a flower. Roy thought it was a gardenia but it turned out to be a white rose she had worn pinned to her dress.

When he handed it to her, her eyes widened with fascination, as if she had recognized him from somewhere, but when she found she hadn't, to his horror her expression changed instantly to one of boredom. Sitting across the aisle from him she fished out of her purse a pack of cigarettes and a lighter. She lit up, and crossing her heartbreaking legs, began to flip through a copy of *Life*.

He figured she was his own age, maybe a year or so older. She looked to him like one of those high-class college girls, only with more zip than most of them, and dressed for 6 A.M. as the girls back home never would. He was marvelously interested in her, so much had her first glance into his eyes meant to him, and already felt a great longing in his life. Anxious to get acquainted, he was flabbergasted how to begin. If she hadn't yet eaten breakfast and he could work up the nerve, he could talk to her in the diner—only he didn't dare.

People were sitting around now and the steward came out and said first call for breakfast.

She snubbed out her cigarette with a wriggling motion of the wrist—her bracelets tinkled—picked up the hat box and went into the diner. Her crumpled white rose lay in the ashtray. He took it out and quickly stuck it in his pants pocket. Though his hunger bit sharp he waited till everyone was maybe served, and then he entered.

Although he had tried to avoid it, for fear she would see how unsure he was of these things, he was put at the same table with her and her black hat box, which now occupied a seat of its own. She glanced up furtively when he sat down but went wordlessly back to her coffee. When the waiter handed Roy the pad, he absently printed his name and date of birth but the waiter imperceptibly nudged him (hey, hay-

seed) and indicated it was for ordering. He pointed on the
menu with his yellow pencil (this is the buck breakfast) but
the blushing ballplayer, squinting through the blur, could
only think he was sitting on the lone four-bit piece he had in
his back pocket. He tried to squelch the impulse but something forced him to look up at her as he attempted to pour
water into his ice-filled (this'll kill the fever) glass, spilling
some on the tablecloth (whose diapers you wetting, boy?),
then all thumbs and butter fingers, the pitcher thumped the
pitcher down, fished the fifty cents out of his pants, and after
scratching out the vital statistics on the pad, plunked the
coin down on the table.

"That's for you," he told the (what did I do to deserve
this?) waiter, and though the silver-eyed mermaid was about
to speak, he did not stay to listen but beat it fast out of the
accursed car.

Tramping highways and byways, wandering everywhere bird
dogging the sandlots for months without spotting so much
as a fifth-rater he could telegraph about to the head scout of
the Cubs, and maybe pick up a hundred bucks in the mail as
a token of their appreciation, with also a word of thanks for
his good bird dogging and maybe they would sometime
again employ him as a scout on the regular payroll—well,
after a disheartening long time in which he was not able to
roust up a single specimen worthy to be called by the name
of ballplayer, Sam had one day lost his way along a dusty
country road and when he finally found out where he was,
too weary to turn back, he crossed over to an old, dry barn
and sat against the haypile in front, to drown his sorrows
with a swig. On the verge of dozing he heard these shouts
and opened his eyes, shielding them from the hot sun, and
as he lived, a game of ball was being played in a pasture by
twelve blond-bearded players, six on each side, and even from
where Sam sat he could tell they were terrific the way they
smacked the pill—one blow banging it so far out the fielder
had to run a mile before he could jump high and snag it
smack in his bare hand. Sam's mouth popped open, he got

up whoozy and watched, finding it hard to believe his eyes, as the teams changed sides and the first hitter that batted the ball did so for a far-reaching distance before it was caught, and the same with the second, a wicked clout, but then the third came up, the one who had made the bare-handed catch, and he really laid on and powdered the pellet a thundering crack so that even the one who ran for it, his beard parted in the wind, before long looked like a pygmy chasing it and quit running, seeing the thing was a speck on the horizon.

Sweating and shivering by turns, Sam muttered if I could ketch the whole twelve of them—and staggered out on the field to cry out the good news but when they saw him they gathered bats and balls and ran in a dozen directions, and though Sam was smart enough to hang on to the fellow who had banged the sphere out to the horizon, frantically shouting to him, "Whoa—whoa," his lungs bursting with the effort to call a giant—he wouldn't stop so Sam never caught him.

He woke with a sob in his throat but swallowed before he could sound it, for by then Roy had come to mind and he mumbled, "Got someone just as good," so that for once waking was better than dreaming.

He yawned. His mouth felt unholy dry and his under-clothes were crawling. Reaching down his battered valise from the rack, he pulled out a used bath towel and cake of white soap, and to the surprise of those who saw him go out that way, went through the baggage cars to the car between them and the tender. Once inside there, he peeled to the skin and stepped into the shower stall, where he enjoyed himself for ten minutes, soaping and resoaping his bony body under warm water. But then a trainman happened to come through and after sniffing around Sam's clothes yelled in to him, "Hey, bud, come outa there."

Sam stopped off the shower and poked out his head.

"What's that?"

"I said come outa there, that's only for the train crew."

"Excuse me," Sam said, and he began quickly to rub himself dry.

"You don't have to hurry. Just wanted you to know you made a mistake."

"Thought it went with the ticket."

"Not in the coaches it don't."

Sam sat on a metal stool and laced up his high brown shoes. Pointing to the cracked mirror on the wall, he said, "Mind if I use your glass?"

"Go ahead."

He parted his sandy hair, combed behind the ears, and managed to work in a shave and brushing of his yellow teeth before he apologized again to the trainman and left.

Going up a few cars to the lounge, he ordered a cup of hot coffee and a sandwich, ate quickly, and made for the club car. It was semi-officially out of bounds for coach travelers but Sam had told the passenger agent last night that he had a nephew riding on a sleeper, and the passenger agent had mentioned to the conductor not to bother him.

When he entered the club car, after making sure Roy was elsewhere Sam headed for the bar, already in a fluid state for the train was moving through wet territory, but then he changed his mind and sat down to size up the congregation over a newspaper and spot who looked particularly amiable. The headlines caught his eye at the same time as they did this short, somewhat popeyed gent's sitting next to him, who had just been greedily questioning the husky, massive-shouldered man on his right, who was wearing sun glasses. Popeyes nudged the big one and they all three stared at Sam's paper.

WEST COAST OLYMPIC ATHLETE SHOT

FOLLOWS 24 HOURS AFTER SLAYING OF
ALL-AMERICAN FOOTBALL ACE

The article went on to relate that both of these men had been shot under mysterious circumstances with silver bullets from a .22 caliber pistol by an unknown woman that police were on the hunt for.

"That makes the second sucker," the short man said.

"But why with silver bullets, Max?"

"Beats me. Maybe she set out after a ghost but couldn't find him."

The other fingered his tie knot. "Why do you suppose she goes around pickin' on athletes for?"

"Not only athletes but also the cream of the crop. She's knocked off a crack football boy, and now an Olympic runner. Better watch out, Whammer, she may be heading for a baseball player for the third victim." Max chuckled.

Sam looked up and almost hopped out of his seat as he recognized them both.

Hiding his hesitation, he touched the short one on the arm. "Excuse me, mister, but ain't you Max Mercy, the sportswriter? I know your face from your photo in the articles you write."

But the sportswriter, who wore a comical mustache and dressed in stripes that crisscrossed three ways—suit, shirt, and tie—a nervous man with voracious eyes, also had a sharp sense of smell and despite Sam's shower and toothbrushing nosed out an alcoholic fragrance that slowed his usual speedy response in acknowledging the spread of his fame.

"That's right," he finally said.

"Well, I'm happy to have the chance to say a few words to you. You're maybe a little after my time, but I am Sam Simpson—Bub Simpson, that is—who played for the St. Louis Browns in the seasons of 1919 to 1921."

Sam spoke with a grin though his insides were afry at the mention of his professional baseball career.

"Believe I've heard the name," Mercy said nervously. After a minute he nodded toward the man Sam knew all along as the leading hitter of the American League, three times winner of the Most Valuable Player award, and announced, "This is Walter (the Whammer) Wambold." It had been in the papers that he was a holdout for $75,000 and was coming East to squeeze it out of his boss.

"Howdy," Sam said. "You sure look different in street clothes."

The Whammer, whose yellow hair was slicked flat, with tie and socks to match, grunted.

Sam's ears reddened. He laughed embarrassedly and then

remarked sideways to Mercy that he was traveling with a slam-bang young pitcher who'd soon be laying them low in the big leagues. "Spoke to you because I thought you might want to know about him."

"What's his name?"

"Roy Hobbs."

"Where'd he play?"

"Well, he's not exactly been in organized baseball."

"Where'd he learn to pitch?"

"His daddy taught him years ago—he was once a semipro— and I have been polishin' him up."

"Where's he been pitching?"

"Well, like I said, he's young, but he certainly mowed them down in the Northwest High School League last year. Thought you might of heard of his eight no-hitters."

"Class D is as far down as I go," Mercy laughed. He lit one of the cigars Sam had been looking at in his breast pocket.

"I'm personally taking him to Clarence Mulligan of the Cubs for a tryout. They will probably pay me a few grand for uncovering the coming pitcher of the century but the condition is—and Roy is backing me on this because he is more devoted to me than a son—that I am to go back as a regular scout, like I was in 1925."

Roy popped his head into the car and searched around for the girl with the black hat box (Miss Harriet Bird, Eddie had gratuitously told him, making a black fluttering of wings), and seeing her seated near the card tables restlessly thumbing through a magazine, popped out.

"That's him," said Sam. "Wait'll I bring him back." He got up and chased after Roy.

"Who's the gabber?" said the Whammer.

"Guy named Simpson who once caught for the Brownies. Funny thing, last night I was doing a Sunday piece on drunks in baseball and I had occasion to look up his record. He was in the game three years, batted .340, .260, and .198, but his catching was terrific—not one error listed."

"Get rid of him, he jaws too much."

"Sh, here he comes."

Sam returned with Roy in tow, gazing uncomfortably ahead.

"Max," said Sam, "this is Roy Hobbs that I mentioned to you. Say hello to Max Mercy, the syndicated sportswriter, kiddo."

"Hello," Roy nodded.

"This is the Whammer," Max said.

Roy extended his hand but the Whammer looked through him with no expression whatsoever. Seeing he had his eye hooked on Harriet, Roy conceived a strong dislike for the guy.

The Whammer got up. "Come on, Max, I wanna play cards."

Max rose. "Well, hang onto the water wagon, Bub," he said to Sam.

Sam turned red.

Roy shot the sportswriter a dirty look.

"Keep up with the no-hitters, kid," Max laughed.

Roy didn't answer. He took the Whammer's chair and Sam sat where he was, brooding.

"What'll it be?" they heard Mercy ask as he shuffled the cards. They had joined two men at one of the card tables.

The Whammer, who looked to Sam like an overgrown side of beef wrapped in gabardine, said, "Hearts." He stared at Harriet until she looked up from her magazine, and after a moment of doubt, smiled.

The Whammer fingered his necktie knot. As he scooped up the cards his diamond ring glinted in the sunlight.

"Goddamned millionaire," Sam thought.

"The hell with her," thought Roy.

"I dealt rummy," Max said, and though no one had called him, Sam promptly looked around.

Toward late afternoon the Whammer, droning on about his deeds on the playing field, got very chummy with Harriet Bird and before long had slipped his fat fingers around the back of her chair so Roy left the club car and sat in the sleeper, looking out of the window, across the aisle from where Eddie slept sitting up. Gosh, the size of the forest. He thought they had left it for good yesterday and here it still was. As he watched, the trees flowed together and so did the hills and clouds. He felt a kind of sadness, because he had lost the feeling of a particular place. Yesterday he had come from somewhere, a place he knew was there, but today it had thinned away in space—how vast he could not have guessed —and he felt like he would never see it again.

The forest stayed with them, climbing hills like an army, shooting down like waterfalls. As the train skirted close in, the trees leveled out and he could see within the woodland the only place he had been truly intimate with in his wanderings, a green world shot through with weird light and strange bird cries, muffled in silence that made the privacy so complete his inmost self had no shame of anything he thought there, and it eased the body-shaking beat of his ambitions. Then he thought of here and now and for the thousandth time wondered why they had come so far and for what. Did Sam really know what he was doing? Sometimes Roy had his doubts. Sometimes he wanted to turn around and go back home, where he could at least predict what tomorrow would be like. Remembering the white rose in his pants pocket, he decided to get rid of it. But then the pine trees flowed away from the train and slowly swerved behind blue hills; all at once there was this beaten gold, snow-capped mountain in the distance, and on the plain several miles from its base lay a small city gleaming in the rays of the declining sun. Approaching it, the long train slowly pulled to a stop.

Eddie woke with a jump and stared out the window.

"Oh oh, trouble, we never stop here."

He looked again and called Roy.

"What do you make out of that?"

About a hundred yards ahead, where two dirt roads crossed, a moth-eaten model-T Ford was parked on the farther side of the road from town, and a fat old man wearing a broad-brimmed black hat and cowboy boots, who they could see was carrying a squat doctor's satchel, climbed down from it. To the conductor, who had impatiently swung off the train with a lit red lamp, he flourished a yellow telegram. They argued a minute, then the conductor, snapping open his watch, beckoned him along and they boarded the train. When they passed through Eddie's car the conductor's face was sizzling with irritation but the doctor was unruffled. Before disappearing through the door, the conductor called to Eddie, "Half hour."

"Half hour," Eddie yodeled and he got out the stool and set it outside the car so that anyone who wanted to stretch, could.

Only about a dozen passengers got off the train, including Harriet Bird, still hanging on to her precious hat box, the Whammer, and Max Mercy, all as thick as thieves. Roy hunted up the bassoon case just if the train should decide to take off without him, and when he had located Sam they both got off.

"Well, I'll be jiggered." Sam pointed down about a block beyond where the locomotive had halted. There, sprawled out at the outskirts of the city, a carnival was on. It was made up of try-your-skill booths, kiddie rides, a freak show and a gigantic Ferris wheel that looked like a stopped clock. Though there was still plenty of daylight, the carnival was lit up by twisted ropes of blinking bulbs, and many banners streamed in the breeze as the calliope played.

"Come on," said Roy, and they went along with the people from the train who were going toward the tents.

Once they had got there and fooled around a while, Sam stopped to have a crushed cocoanut drink which he privately spiked with a shot from a new bottle, while Roy wandered over to a place where you could throw three baseballs for a dime at three wooden pins, shaped like pint-size milk bottles and set in pyramids of one on top of two, on small raised platforms about twenty feet back from the counter. He changed the fifty-cent piece Sam had slipped him on leaving the train, and this pretty girl in yellow, a little hefty but with a sweet face and nice ways, who with her peanut of a father was waiting on trade, handed him three balls. Lobbing one of them, Roy easily knocked off the pyramid and won himself a naked kewpie doll. Enjoying the game, he laid down another dime, again clattering the pins to the floor in a single shot and now collecting an alarm clock. With the other three dimes he won a brand-new boxed baseball, a washboard, and baby potty, which he traded in for a six-inch harmonica. A few kids came over to watch and Sam, wandering by, indulgently changed another half into dimes for Roy. And Roy won a fine leather cigar case for Sam, a "God Bless America" banner, a flashlight, can of coffee, and a two-pound box of sweets. To the kids' delight, Sam, after a slight hesitation, flipped Roy another half dollar, but this time the little man behind the counter nudged his daughter and she asked Roy if he would now take a kiss for every three pins he tumbled.

Roy glanced at her breasts and she blushed. He got embarrassed too. "What do you say, Sam, it's your four bits?"

Sam bowed low to the girl. "Ma'am," he said, "now you see how dang foolish it is to be a young feller."

The girl laughed and Roy began to throw for kisses, flushing each pyramid in a shot or two while the girl counted aloud the kisses she owed him.

Some of the people from the train passed by and stayed to watch when they learned from the mocking kids what Roy was throwing for.

The girl, pretending to be unconcerned, tolled off the third and fourth kisses.

As Roy fingered the ball for the last throw the Whammer came by holding over his shoulder a Louisville Slugger that he had won for himself in the batting cage down a way. Harriet, her pretty face flushed, had a kewpie doll, and Max Mercy carried a box of cigars. The Whammer had discarded his sun glasses and all but strutted over his performance and the prizes he had won.

Roy raised his arm to throw for the fifth kiss and a clean sweep when the Whammer called out to him in a loud voice, "Pitch it here, busher, and I will knock it into the moon."

Roy shot for the last kiss and missed. He missed with the second and third balls. The crowd oohed its disappointment.

"Only four," said the girl in yellow as if she mourned the fifth.

Angered at what had happened, Sam hoarsely piped, "I got ten dollars that says he can strike you out with three pitched balls, Wambold."

The Whammer looked at Sam with contempt.

"What d'ye say, Max?" he said.

Mercy shrugged.

"Oh, I love contests of skill," Harriet said excitedly. Roy's face went pale.

"What's the matter, hayfoot, you scared?" the Whammer taunted.

"Not of you," Roy said.

"Let's go across the tracks where nobody'll get hurt," Mercy suggested.

"Nobody but the busher and his bazooka. What's in it, busher?"

"None of your business." Roy picked up the bassoon case.

The crowd moved in a body across the tracks, the kids circling around to get a good view, and the engineer and fireman watching from their cab window.

Sam cornered one of the kids who lived nearby and sent him home for a fielder's glove and his friend's catcher's mitt. While they were waiting, for protection he buttoned underneath his coat the washboard Roy had won. Max drew a batter's box alongside a piece of slate. He said he would call the throws and they would count as one of the three pitches only if they were over or if the Whammer swung and missed.

When the boy returned with the gloves, the sun was going down, and though the sky was aflame with light all the way to the snowy mountain peak, it was chilly on the ground.

Breaking the seal, Sam squeezed the baseball box and the pill shot up like a greased egg. He tossed it to Mercy, who inspected the hide and stitches, then rubbed the shine off and flipped it to Roy.

"Better throw a couple of warm-ups."

"My arm is loose," said Roy.

"It's your funeral."

Placing his bassoon case out of the way in the grass, Roy shed his coat. One of the boys came forth to hold it.

"Be careful you don't spill the pockets," Roy told him.

Sam came forward with the catcher's glove on. It was too small for his big hand but he said it would do all right.

"Sam, I wish you hadn't bet that money on me," Roy said.

"I won't take it if we win, kiddo, but just let it stand if we lose," Sam said, embarrassed.

"We came by it too hard."

"Just let it stand so."

He cautioned Roy to keep his pitches inside, for the Whammer was known to gobble them on the outside corner.

Sam returned to the plate and crouched behind the batter, his knees spread wide because of the washboard. Roy drew on his glove and palmed the ball behind it. Mercy, rubbing his hands to warm them, edged back about six feet behind Sam.

The onlookers retreated to the other side of the tracks, except Harriet, who stood without fear of fouls up close. Her eyes shone at the sight of the two men facing one another.

Mercy called, "Batter up."

The Whammer crowded the left side of the plate, gripping the heavy bat low on the neck, his hands jammed together and legs plunked evenly apart. He hadn't bothered to take off his coat. His eye on Roy said it spied a left-handed monkey.

"Throw it, Rube, it won't get no lighter."

Though he stood about sixty feet away, he loomed up gigantic to Roy, with the wood held like a caveman's ax on his shoulder. His rocklike frame was motionless, his face impassive, unsmiling, dark.

Roy's heart skipped a beat. He turned to gaze at the mountain.

Sam whacked the leather with his fist. "Come on, kiddo, wham it down his whammy."

The Whammer out of the corner of his mouth told the drunk to keep his mouth shut.

"Burn it across his button."

"Close your trap," Mercy said.

"Cut his throat with it."

"If he tries to dust me, so help me I will smash his skull," the Whammer threatened.

Roy stretched loosely, rocked back on his left leg, twirling the right a little like a dancer, then strode forward and threw with such force his knuckles all but scraped the ground on the follow-through.

At thirty-three the Whammer still enjoyed exceptional eyesight. He saw the ball spin off Roy's fingertips and it reminded him of a white pigeon he had kept as a boy, that he would send into flight by flipping it into the air. The ball flew at him and he was conscious of its bird-form and white flapping wings, until it suddenly disappeared from view. He heard a noise like the bang of a firecracker at his feet and Sam had the ball in his mitt. Unable to believe his ears he heard Mercy intone a reluctant strike.

Sam flung off the glove and was wringing his hand.

"Hurt you, Sam?" Roy called.

"No, it's this dang glove."

Though he did not show it, the pitch had bothered the Whammer no end. Not just the speed of it but the sensation of surprise and strangeness that went with it—him batting here on the railroad tracks, the crazy carnival, the drunk catching and a clown pitching, and that queer dame Harriet, who had five minutes ago been patting him on the back for his skill in the batting cage, now eyeing him coldly for letting one pitch go by.

He noticed Max had moved farther back.

"How the hell you expect to call them out there?"

"He looks wild to me." Max moved in.

"Your knees are knockin'," Sam tittered.

"Mind your business, rednose," Max said.

"You better watch your talk, mister," Roy called to Mercy.

"Pitch it, greenhorn," warned the Whammer.

Sam crouched with his glove on. "Do it again, Roy. Give him something simular."

"Do it again," mimicked the Whammer. To the crowd, maybe to Harriet, he held up a vaunting finger showing there were other pitches to come.

Roy pumped, reared and flung.

The ball appeared to the batter to be a slow spinning planet looming toward the earth. For a long light-year he waited for this globe to whirl into the orbit of his swing so he could bust it to smithereens that would settle with dust and dead leaves into some distant cosmos. At last the unseeing eye, maybe a fortuneteller's lit crystal ball—anyway, a curious combination of circles—drifted within range of his weapon, or so he thought, because he lunged at it ferociously, twisting round like a top. He landed on both knees as the world floated by over his head and hit with a *whup* into the cave of Sam's glove.

"Hey, Max," Sam said, as he chased the ball after it had bounced out of the glove, "how do they pernounce Whammer if you leave out the W?"

"Strike," Mercy called long after a cheer (was it a jeer?) had burst from the crowd.

"What's he throwing," the Whammer howled, "spitters?"

"In the pig's poop." Sam thrust the ball at him. 'It's drier than your granddaddy's scalp."

"I'm warning him not to try any dirty business."

Yet the Whammer felt oddly relieved. He liked to have his back crowding the wall, when there was a single pitch to worry about and a single pitch to hit. Then the sweat began to leak out of his pores as he stared at the hard, lanky figure of the pitiless pitcher, moving, despite his years and a few waste motions, like a veteran undertaker of the diamond, and he experienced a moment of depression.

Sam must have sensed it, because he discovered an unexpected pity in his heart and even for a split second hoped the idol would not be tumbled. But only for a second, for the Whammer had regained confidence in his known talent and experience and was taunting the greenhorn to throw.

Someone in the crowd hooted and the Whammer raised aloft two fat fingers and pointed where he would murder the ball, where the gleaming rails converged on the horizon and beyond was invisible.

Roy raised his leg. He smelled the Whammer's blood and wanted it, and through him the worm's he had with him, for the way he had insulted Sam.

The third ball slithered at the batter like a meteor, the

flame swallowing itself. He lifted his club to crush it into a universe of sparks but the heavy wood dragged, and though he willed to destroy the sound he heard a gong bong and realized with sadness that the ball he had expected to hit had long since been part of the past; and though Max could not cough the fatal word out of his throat, the Whammer understood he was, in the truest sense of it, out.

The crowd was silent as the violet evening fell on their shoulders.

For a night game, the Whammer harshly shouted, it was customary to turn on lights. Dropping the bat, he trotted off to the train, an old man.

The ball had caught Sam smack in the washboard and lifted him off his feet. He lay on the ground, extended on his back. Roy pushed everybody aside to get him air. Unbuttoning Sam's coat, he removed the dented washboard.

"Never meant to hurt you, Sam."

"Just knocked the wind outa me," Sam gasped. "Feel better now." He was pulled to his feet and stood steady.

The train whistle wailed, the echo banging far out against the black mountain.

Then the doctor in the broadbrimmed black hat appeared, flustered and morose, the conductor trying to pacify him, and Eddie hopping along behind.

The doctor waved the crumpled yellow paper around. "Got a telegram says somebody on this train took sick. Anybody out here?"

Roy tugged at Sam's sleeve.

"Ixnay."

"What's that?"

"Not me," said Roy.

The doctor stomped off. He climbed into his Ford, whipped it up and drove away.

The conductor popped open his watch. "Be a good hour late into the city."

"All aboard," he called.

"Aboard," Eddie echoed, carrying the bassoon case.

The buxom girl in yellow broke through the crowd and

threw her arms around Roy's neck. He ducked but she hit him quick with her pucker four times upon the right eye, yet he could see with the other that Harriet Bird (certainly a snappy goddess) had her gaze fastened on him.

They sat, after dinner, in Eddie's dimmed and empty Pullman, Roy floating through drifts of clouds on his triumph as Harriet went on about the recent tourney, she put it, and the unreal forest outside swung forward like a gate shutting. The odd way she saw things interested him, yet he was aware of the tormented trees fronting the snaky lake they were passing, trees bent and clawing, plucked white by icy blasts from the black water, their bony branches twisting in many a broken direction.

Harriet's face was flushed, her eyes gleaming with new insights. Occasionally she stopped and giggled at herself for the breathless volume of words that flowed forth, to his growing astonishment, but after a pause was on her galloping way again—a girl on horseback—reviewing the inspiring sight (she said it was) of David jawboning the Goliath-Whammer, or was it Sir Percy lancing Sir Maldemer, or the first son (with a rock in his paw) ranged against the primitive papa?

Roy gulped. "My father? Well, maybe I did want to skull him sometimes. After my grandma died, the old man dumped me in one orphan home after the other, wherever he happened to be working—when he did—though he did used to take me out of there summers and teach me how to toss a ball."

No, that wasn't what she meant, Harriet said. Had he ever read Homer?

Try as he would he could only think of four bases and not a book. His head spun at her allusions. He found her lingo strange with all the college stuff and hoped she would stop it because he wanted to talk about baseball.

Then she took a breather. 'My friends say I have a fantastic imagination."

He quickly remarked he wouldn't say that. "But the only thing I had on my mind when I was throwing out there was that Sam had bet this ten spot we couldn't afford to lose out on, so I had to make him whiff."

"To whiff—oh, Roy, how droll," and she laughed again.

He grinned, carried away by the memory of how he had done it, the hero, who with three pitched balls had nailed the best the American League had to offer. What didn't that say about the future? He felt himself falling into sentiment in his thoughts and tried to steady himself but couldn't before he had come forth with a pronouncement: "You have to have the right stuff to play good ball and I have it. I bet some day I'll break every record in the book for throwing and hitting."

Harriet appeared startled then gasped, hiding it like a cough behind her tense fist, and vigorously applauded, her bracelets bouncing on her wrists. "Bravo, Roy, how wonderful."

"What I mean," he insisted, "is I feel that I have got it in me—that I am due for something very big. I have to do it. I mean," he said modestly, "That's of course when I get in the game."

Her mouth opened. "You mean you're not—" She seemed, to his surprise, disappointed, almost on the verge of crying.

"No," he said, ashamed. "Sam's taking me for a tryout."

Her eyes grew vacant as she stared out the window. Then she asked, "But Walter—*he* is a successful professional player, isn't he?"

"The Whammer?" Roy nodded.

"And he has won that award three times—what was it?"

"The Most Valuable Player." He had a panicky feeling he was losing her to the Whammer.

She bit her lip. "Yet you defeated him," she murmured.

He admitted it. "He won't last much longer I don't think—the most a year or two. By then he'll be too old for the game. Myself, I've got my whole life ahead of me."

Harriet brightened, saying sympathetically, "What will you hope to accomplish, Roy?"

He had already told her but after a minute remarked, "Sometimes when I walk down the street I bet people will say there goes Roy Hobbs, the best there ever was in the game."

She gazed at him with touched and troubled eyes. "Is that all?"

He tried to penetrate her question. Twice he had answered it and still she was unsatisfied. He couldn't be sure what she expected him to say. "Is that all?" he repeated. "What more is there?"

"Don't you know?" she said kindly.

Then he had an idea. "You mean the bucks? I'll get them too."

She slowly shook her head. "Isn't there something over and above earthly things—some more glorious meaning to one's life and activities?"

"In baseball?"

"Yes."

He racked his brain—

"Maybe I've not made myself clear, but surely you can see (I was saying this to Walter just before the train stopped) that yourself alone—alone in the sense that we are all terribly alone no matter what people say—I mean by that perhaps if you understood that our values must derive from—oh, I really suppose—" She dropped her hand futilely. "Please forgive me. I sometimes confuse myself with the little I know."

Her eyes were sad. He felt a curious tenderness for her, a little as if she might be his mother (That bird.) and tried very hard to come up with the answer she wanted—something you said about LIFE.

"I think I know what you mean," he said. "You mean the fun and satisfaction you get out of playing the best way that you know how?"

She did not respond to that.

Roy worried out some other things he might have said but had no confidence to put them into words. He felt curiously deflated and a little lost, as if he had just flunked a test. The worst of it was he still didn't know what she'd been driving at.

Harriet yawned. Never before had he felt so tongue-tied in front of a girl, a looker too. Now if he had her in bed—

Almost as if she had guessed what he was thinking and

her mood had changed to something more practical than asking nutty questions that didn't count, she sighed and edged
closer to him, concealing the move behind a query about his
bassoon case. "Do you play?"

"Not any music," he answered, glad they were talking about
something different. "There's a thing in it that I made for myself."

"What, for instance?"

He hesitated. "A baseball bat."

She was herself again, laughed merrily. "Roy, you are
priceless."

"I got the case because I don't want to get the stick all
banged up before I got the chance to use it."

"Oh, Roy." Her laughter grew. He smiled broadly.

She was now so close he felt bold. Reaching down he lifted
the hat box by the string and lightly hefted it.

"What's in it?"

She seemed breathless. "In it?" Then she mimicked,
"—Something I made for myself."

"Feels like a hat."

"Maybe a head?" Harriet shook a finger at him.

"Feels more like a hat." A little embarrassed, he set the box
down. "Will you come and see me play sometime?" he asked.

She nodded and then he was aware of her leg against his
and that she was all but on his lap. His heart slapped against
his ribs and he took it all to mean that she had dropped the
last of her interest in the Whammer and was putting it on
the guy who had buried him.

As they went through a tunnel, Roy placed his arm around
her shoulders, and when the train lurched on a curve, casually
let his hand fall upon her full breast. The nipple rose between
his fingers and before he could resist the impulse he had
tweaked it.

Her high-pitched scream lifted her up and twirling like a
dancer down the aisle.

Stricken, he rose—had gone too far.

Crooking her arms like broken branches she whirled back

to him, her head turned so far around her face hung between her shoulders.

"Look, I'm a twisted tree."

Sam had sneaked out on the squirming, apologetic Mercy, who, with his back to the Whammer—he with a newspaper raised in front of his sullen eyes—had kept up a leechlike prodding about Roy, asking where he had come from (oh, he's just a home town boy), how it was no major league scout had got at him (they did but he turned them down for me) even with the bonus cash that they are tossing around these days (yep), who's his father (like I said, just an old semipro who wanted awful bad to be in the big leagues) and what, for God's sake, does he carry around in that case (that's his bat, Wonderboy). The sportswriter was greedy to know more, hinting he could do great things for the kid, but Sam, rubbing his side where it pained, at last put him off and escaped into the coach to get some shuteye before they hit Chicago, sometime past 1 A.M.

After a long time trying to settle himself comfortably, he fell snoring asleep flat on his back and was at once sucked into a long dream that he had gone thirsty mad for a drink and was threatening the slickers in the car get him a bottle or else. Then this weasel of a Mercy, pretending he was writing on a pad, pointed him out with his pencil and the conductor snapped him up by the seat of his pants and ran his free-wheeling feet lickity-split through the sawdust, giving him the merry heave-ho off the train through the air on a floating trapeze, ploop into a bog where it rained buckets. He thought he better get across the foaming river before it flooded the bridge away so he set out, all bespattered, to cross it, only this queer duck of a doctor in oilskins, an old man with a washable white mustache and a yellow lamp he thrust straight into your eyeballs, swore to him the bridge was gone. You're plumb tootin' crazy, Sam shouted in the storm, I saw it standin' with me own eyes, and he scuffled to get past the geezer, who dropped the light setting the rails afire. They wrestled in the rain until Sam slyly tripped and threw him, and helter-skeltered for the bridge, to find to his crawling horror it was truly down and here he was scratching space till he landed with a splishity-splash in the whirling waters, sobbing (whoa whoa) and the white watchman on the embarkment flung him a flare but it was all too late because he heard the roar of the falls below (and restless shifting of the sea) and felt with his red hand where the knife had stabbed him . . .

Roy was dreaming of an enormous mountain—Christ, the size of it—when he felt himself roughly shaken—Sam, he thought, because they were there—only it was Eddie holding a lit candle.

"The fuse blew and I've had no chance to fix it."

"What's the matter?"

"Trou-ble. Your friend has collapsed."

Roy hopped out of the berth, stepped into moccasins and ran, with Eddie flying after him with the snuffed wax, into a darkened car where a pool of people under a blue light hovered over Sam, unconscious.

"What happened?" Roy cried.

"Sh," said the conductor, "he's got a raging fever."

"What from?"

"Can't say. We're picking up a doctor."

Sam was lying on a bench, wrapped in blankets with a pillow tucked under his head, his gaunt face broken out in sweat. When Roy bent over him, his eyes opened.

"Hello, kiddo," he said in a cracked voice.

"What hurts you, Sam?"

"Where the washboard banged me—but it don't hurt so much now."

"Oh, Jesus."

"Don't take it so, Roy. I'll be better."

"Save his strength, son," the conductor said. "Don't talk now."

Roy got up. Sam shut his eyes.

The train whistled and ran slow at the next town then came to a draggy halt. The trainman brought a half-dressed doctor in. He examined Sam and straightened up. "We got to get him off and to the hospital."

Roy was wild with anxiety but Sam opened his eyes and told him to bend down.

Everyone moved away and Roy bent low.

"Take my wallet outa my rear pocket."

Roy pulled out the stuffed cowhide wallet.

"Now you go to the Stevens Hotel—"

"No, oh no, Sam, not without you."

"Go on, kiddo, you got to. See Clarence Mulligan tomorrow and say I sent you—they are expecting you. Give them everything you have got on the ball—that'll make me happy."

"But, Sam—"

"You got to. Bend lower."

Roy bent lower and Sam stretched his withered neck and kissed him on the chin.

"Do like I say."

"Yes, Sam."

A tear splashed on Sam's nose.

Sam had something more in his eyes to say but though he tried, agitated, couldn't say it. Then the trainmen came in with a stretcher and they lifted the catcher and handed him down the steps, and overhead the stars were bright but he knew he was dead.

Roy trailed the anonymous crowd out of Northwest Station and clung to the shadowy part of the wall till he had the courage to call a cab.

"Do you go to the Stevens Hotel?" he asked, and the driver without a word shot off before he could rightly be seated, passed a red light and scuttled a cripple across the deserted street. They drove for miles in a shadow-infested, street-lamped jungle.

He had once seen some stereopticon pictures of Chicago and it was a boxed-up ant heap of stone and crumbling wood buildings in a many-miled spreading checkerboard of streets without much open space to speak of except the railroads, stockyards, and the shore of a windy lake. In the Loop, the offices went up high and the streets were jampacked with people, and he wondered how so many of them could live together in any one place. Suppose there was a fire or something and they all ran out of their houses to see—how could they help but trample all over themselves? And Sam had warned him against strangers, because there were so many bums, sharpers, and gangsters around, people you were dirt to, who didn't know you and didn't want to, and for a dime they would slit your throat and leave you dying in the streets.

"Why did I come here?" he muttered and felt sick for home.

The cab swung into Michigan Avenue, which gave a view of the lake and a white-lit building spiring into the sky, then before he knew it he was standing flatfooted (Christ, the size of it) in front of the hotel, an enormous four-sectioned fortress. He hadn't the nerve to go through the whirling doors but had to because this bellhop grabbed his things—he wrested the bassoon case loose—and led him across the thick-carpeted lobby to a desk where he signed a card and had to count out five of the wallet's pulpy dollars for a room he would give up as soon as he found a house to board in.

But his cubbyhole on the seventeenth floor was neat and private, so after he had stored everything in the closet he lost his nervousness. Unlatching the window brought in the lake breeze. He stared down at the lit sprawl of Chicago, standing higher than he ever had in his life except for a night or two on a mountain. Gazing down upon the city, he felt as if bolts in his knees, wrists, and neck had loosened and he had spread up in height. Here, so high in the world, with the earth laid out in small squares so far below, he knew he would go in tomorrow and wow them with his fast one, and they would know him for the splendid pitcher he was.

The telephone rang. He was at first scared to answer it. In a strange place, so far from everybody he knew, it couldn't possibly be for him.

It rang again. He picked up the phone and listened.

"Hello, Roy? This is Harriet."

He wasn't sure he had got it right. "Excuse me?"

"Harriet Bird, silly."

"Oh, Harriet." He had completely forgotten her.

"Come down to my room," she giggled, "and let me say welcome to the city."

"You mean now?"

"Right away." She gave him the room number.

"Sure." He meant to ask her how she knew he was here but she had hung up.

Then he was elated. So that's how they did it in the city. He combed his hair and got out his bassoon case. In the elevator a drunk tried to take it away from him but Roy was too strong for him.

He walked—it seemed ages because he was impatient— through a long corridor till he found her number and knocked.

"Come on in."

Opening the door, he was astonished at the enormous room. Through the white-curtained window the sight of the endless dark lake sent a shiver down his spine.

Then he saw her standing shyly in the far corner of the room, naked under the gossamer thing she wore, held up on her risen nipples and the puffed wedge of hair beneath her white belly. A great weight went off his mind.

As he shut the door she reached into the hat box which lay open next to a vase of white roses on the table and fitted the black feathered hat on her head. A thick veil fell to her breasts. In her hand she held a squat, shining pistol.

He was greatly confused and thought she was kidding but a grating lump formed in his throat and his blood shed ice. He cried out in a gruff voice, "What's wrong here?"

She said sweetly, "Roy, will you be the best there ever was in the game?"

"That's right."

She pulled the trigger (thrum of bull fiddle). The bullet cut a silver line across the water. He sought with his bare hands to catch it, but it eluded him and, to his horror, bounced into his gut. A twisted dagger of smoke drifted up from the gun barrel. Fallen on one knee he groped for the bullet, sickened as it moved, and fell over as the forest flew upward, and she, making muted noises of triumph and despair, danced on her toes around the stricken hero.

Batter Up!

|||||||||||||||||||||||||||||||||||||

I shoulda been a farmer," Pop Fisher said bitterly. "I shoulda farmed since the day I was born. I like cows, sheep, and those hornless goats—I am partial to nanny goats, my daddy wore a beard—I like to feed animals and milk 'em. I like fixing things, weeding poison oak out of the pasture, and seeing to the watering of the crops. I like to be by myself on a farm. I like to stand out in the fields, tending the vegetables, the corn, the winter wheat—greenest looking stuff you ever saw. When Ma was alive she kept urging me to leave baseball and take up farming, and I always meant to but after she died I had no heart for it." Pop's voice all but broke and Red Blow shifted nervously on the bench but Pop didn't cry. He took out his handkerchief, flipped it, and blew his nose. "I have that green thumb," he said huskily, "and

I shoulda farmed instead of playing wet nurse to a last place, dead-to-the-neck ball team."

They were sitting in the New York Knights' dugout, scanning the dusty field, the listless game and half-empty stands.

"Tough," said Red. He kept his eye on the pitcher.

Removing his cap, Pop rubbed his bald head with his bandaged fingers. "It's been a blasted dry season. No rains at all. The grass is worn scabby in the outfield and the infield is cracking. My heart feels as dry as dirt for the little I have to show for all my years in the game."

He got up, stooped at the fountain and spat the warm, rusty water into the dust. "When the hell they going to fix this thing so we can have a decent drink of water? Did you speak to that bastard partner I have, like I said to?"

"Says he's working on it."

"Working on it," Pop grunted. "He's so tight that if he was any tighter he'd be too stiff to move. It was one of the darkest days of my life when that snake crawled into this club. He's done me out of more dough than I can count."

"Kid's weakening again," Red said. "He passed two."

Pop watched Fowler for a minute but let him stay. "If those boy scouts could bring in a coupla runs once in a while I'd change pitchers, but they couldn't bring their own grandmother in from across the street. What a butchering we took from the Pirates in the first game and here we are six runs behind in this. It's Memorial Day, all right, but not for the soldiers."

"Should've had some runs. Bump had four for four in the first, and two hits before he got himself chucked out of this."

Pop's face burned. "Don't mention that ape man to me—getting hisself bounced out of the game the only time we had runners on the bases when he come up."

"I'd've thrown him out too if I was the ump and he slid dry ice down my pants."

"I'd like to stuff him with ice. I never saw such a disgusting screwball for practical jokes."

Pop scratched violently under his loosely bandaged fingers. "And to top it off I have to go catch athlete's foot on my hands. Now ain't that one for the books? Everybody I have ever heard of have got it on their feet but I have to go and get it on both of my hands and be itchy and bandaged in this goshdarn hot weather. No wonder I am always asking myself is life worth the living of it."

"Tough," Red said. "He's passed Feeber, bases loaded."

Pop fumed. "My best pitcher and he blows up every time I put him against a first place team. Yank him."

The coach, a lean and freckled man, got nimbly up on the dugout steps and signaled to the bullpen in right field. He sauntered out to the mound just as somebody in street clothes came up the stairs of the tunnel leading from the clubhouse and asked the player at the end of the bench, "Who's Fisher?" The player jerked his thumb toward the opposite side of the dugout, and the man, dragging a large, beat-up valise and a bassoon case, treaded his way to Pop.

When Pop saw him coming he exclaimed, "Oh, my eight-foot uncle, what have we got here, the Salvation Army band?"

The man set his things on the floor and sat down on a concrete step, facing Pop. He beheld an old geezer of sixty-five with watery blue eyes, a thin red neck and a bitter mouth, who looked like a lost banana in the overgrown baseball suit he wore, especially his skinny legs in loose blue-and-white stockings.

And Pop saw a tall, husky, dark-bearded fellow with old eyes but not bad features. His face was strong-boned, if a trifle meaty, and his mouth seemed pleasant though its expression was grim. For his bulk he looked lithe, and he appeared calmer than he felt, for although he was sitting here on this step he was still in motion. He was traveling (on the train that never stopped). His self, his mind, raced on and he felt he hadn't stopped going wherever he was going because he hadn't yet arrived. Where hadn't he arrived? Here. But now it was time to calm down, ease up on the old scooter, sit still and be quiet, though the inside of him was still streaming through towns and cities, across forests and fields, over long years.

"The only music I make," he answered Pop, patting the

bassoon case, "is with my bat." Searching through the pockets of his frayed and baggy suit, worn to threads at the knees and elbows, he located a folded letter that he reached over to the manager. "I'm your new left fielder, Roy Hobbs."

"My what!" Pop exploded.

"It says in the letter."

Red, who had returned from the mound, took the letter, unfolded it, and handed it to Pop. He read it in a single swoop then shook his head in disbelief.

"Scotty Carson sent you?"

"That's right."

"He must be daffy."

Roy wet his dry lips.

Pop shot him a shrewd look. "You're thirty-five if you're a day."

"Thirty-four, but I'm good for ten years."

"Thirty-four—Holy Jupiter, mister, you belong in an old man's home, not baseball."

The players along the bench were looking at him. Roy licked his lips.

"Where'd he pick you up?" Pop asked.

"I was with the Oomoo Oilers."

"In what league?"

"They're semipros."

"Ever been in organized baseball?"

"I only recently got back in the game."

"What do you mean got back?"

"Used to play in high school."

Pop snorted. "Well, it's a helluva mess." He slapped the letter with the back of his fingers. "Scotty signed him and the Judge okayed it. Neither of them consulted me. They can't do that," he said to Red. "That thief in the tower might have sixty per cent of the stock but I have it in writing that I am to manage this team and approve all player deals *as long as I live.*"

"I got a contract," said Roy.

"Lemme see it."

Roy pulled a blue-backed paper out of his inside coat pocket.

Pop scanned it. "Where in blazes did he get the figure of three thousand dollars?"

"It was for a five thousand minimum but the Judge said I already missed one-third of the season."

Pop burst into scornful laughter. "Sure, but that entitles you to about thirty-three hundred. Just like that godawful deadbeat. He'd skin his dead father if he could get into the grave."

He returned the contract to Roy. "It's illegal."

"Scotty's your chief scout?" Roy asked.

"That's right."

"He signed me to a contract with an open figure and the Judge filled it in. I asked about that and Scotty said he had the authority to sign me."

"He has," Red said to Pop. "You said so yourself if he found anybody decent."

"That's right, that's what I said, but who needs a fielder old enough to be my son? I got a left fielder," he said to Roy, "a darn good one when he feels like it and ain't playing practical jokes on everybody."

Roy stood up. "If you don't want me, Merry Christmas."

"Wait a second," said Red. He fingered Pop up close to the fountain and spoke to him privately.

Pop calmed down. "I'm sorry, son," he apologized to Roy when he returned to the bench, "but you came across me at a bad time. Also thirty-four years for a rookie is starting with one foot in the grave. But like Red says, if our best scout sent you, you musta showed him something. Go on in the clubhouse and have Dizzy fit you up with a monkey suit. Then report back here and I will locate you a place on this bench with the rest of my All-Stars." He threw the players a withering look and they quickly turned away.

"Listen, mister," Roy said, "I know my way out of this jungle if you can't use me. I don't want any second pickings."

"Do as he told you," Red said.

Roy rose, got his valise and bassoon case together, and headed into the tunnel. His heart was thumping like a noisy barrel.

"I shoulda bought a farm," Pop muttered.

The pitcher in the shower had left the door wide open so the locker room was clouded with steam when Roy came in. Unable to find anybody he yelled into the shower room where was the prop man, and the one in the shower yelled back in the equipment room and close the door it was drafty. When the steam had thinned out and Roy could see his way around he located the manager's office, so labeled in black letters on the door, but not the equipment room. In the diagonally opposite corner were the trainer's quarters, and here the door was ajar and gave forth an oil of wintergreen smell that crawled up his nose. He could see the trainer, in a gray sweatshirt with KNIGHTS stenciled across his chest, working on a man mountain on the rubbing table. Catching sight of Roy, the trainer called out in an Irish brogue who was he looking for?

"Prop man," Roy said.

"That's Dizzy—down the hall." The trainer made with his eyes to the left so Roy opened the door there and went down the hall. He located a sign, "Equipment," and through the window under it saw the prop man in a baseball jersey sitting on a uniform trunk with his back to the wall. He was reading the sports page of the *Mirror*.

Roy rapped on the ledge and Dizzy, a former utility pitcher, hastily put the paper down. "Caught me at an interesting moment," he grinned. "I was reading about this catcher that got beaned in Boston yesterday. Broke the side of his skull."

"The name's Roy Hobbs, new hand here. Fisher told me to get outfitted."

"New man—fielder, eh?"

Roy nodded.

"Yeah, we been one man short on the roster for two weeks. One of our guys went and got himself hit on the head with a fly ball and both of his legs are now paralyzed."

Roy winked.

"Honest to God. And just before that our regular third base-man stepped on a bat and rolled down the dugout steps. Snapped his spine in two places." Dizzy grimaced. "We sure been enjoying an unlucky season."

He came forth with a tape measure and took Roy's measurements, then he went back and collected a pile of stuff from the shelves.

"Try this for size." He handed him a blue cap with a white K stitched on the front of it.

Roy tried it. "Too small."

"You sure got some size noggin there."

"Seven and a half." Roy looked at him.

"Just a social remark. No offense meant or intended." He gave Roy a size that fitted.

"How's it look?" Roy asked.

"A dream but why the tears?"

"I have a cold." He turned away.

Dizzy asked him to sign for the stuff—Judge Banner insisted. He helped Roy carry it to his locker.

"Keep anything you like inside of here but for goodness' sakes no booze. Pop throws fits if any of the players drink."

Roy stood the bassoon case in upright. "Got a lock for the door?"

"Nobody locks their doors here. Before the game you deposit your valuables in that trunk there and I will lock them up."

"Okay, skip it."

Dizzy excused himself to get back to his paper and Roy began to undress.

The locker room was tomblike quiet. The pitcher who had been in the showers—his footsteps were still wet on the floor —had dressed rapidly and vanished. As he put his things away, Roy found himself looking around every so often to make sure he was here. He was, all right, yet in all his imagining of how it would be when he finally hit the majors, he had not expected to feel so down in the dumps. It was different than he had thought it would be. So different he almost felt like walking out, jumping back on a train, and going wherever people went when they were running out on something. Maybe for a long rest in one of those towns he had lived in as a kid. Like the place where he had that shaggy mutt that used to scamper through the woods, drawing him after it to the deepest, stillest part, till the silence was so pure you could crack it if you threw a rock. Roy remained lost in the silence till the dog's yapping woke him, though as he came out of it, it was not barking he heard but the sound of voices through the trainer's half-open door.

He listened closely because he had the weird impression that he knew all the voices in there, and as he sorted them he recognized first the trainer's brogue and then a big voice that he did not so much recall, as remember having heard throughout his life—a strong, rawboned voice, familiar from his boyhood and some of the jobs he had worked at later, and the different places he had bummed around in, slop joints, third-rate hotels, prize fight gyms and such; the big voice of a heavy, bull-necked, strong-muscled guy, the kind of gorilla he had more than once fought half to death for no reason he could think of. Oh, the Whammer, he thought, and quickly ducked but straightened up when he remembered the Whammer was almost fifty and long since retired out of the game. But what made him most uneasy was a third voice, higher than the other two, a greedy, penetrating, ass-kissing voice he had definitely heard before. He strained his ears to hear it again but the big voice was talking about this gag he had pulled on Pop Fisher, in particular, spraying white pepper in Pop's handkerchief, which made him sneeze and constantly blow his beak. That commenced an epidemic of base stealing, to Pop's fury, because the signal to steal that day was for him to raise his handkerchief to his schnozzle.

At the end of the story there was a guffaw and a yelp of laughter, then the trainer remarked something and this other voice, one that stood on stilts, commented that Bump certainly got a kick out of his jokes, and Bump, he must have been, said Pop wouldn't agree to his release, so if he was going to be stuck in this swamp he would at least have a little fun.

He laughed loudly and said, "Here's one for your colyum, kid. We were in Cincy in April and had a free day on our hands because this exhibition game was called off, so in the Plaza lobby that morning we get to bulling about players and records, and you know Pop and this line of his about how lousy the modern player is compared to those mustached freaks he played with in the time of King Tut. He was saying that the average fielder nowadays could maybe hit the kangaroo ball we got—he was looking at me—but you couldn't count on him to catch a high fly. 'How high?' I ask him, innocent, and he points up and says, 'Any decent height. They either lose them in the sun or misjudge them in the wind.' So I say, 'Could you catch the real high ones, Pop?' And he pipes up, 'As high as they went up I could catch them.' He thinks a minute and says, 'I bet I could catch a ball that is dropped from the top of the Empire State Building.' 'No,' I says, like I was surprised, and 'Yes,' he says. So I say, 'We have nothing on for today, and although there isn't any Empire State Building in Cincinnati, yet I do have this friend of mine at the airport who owns a Piper Cub. I will give him a National League baseball and he will drop it at the height of the building if you will catch it.' 'Done,' he says, as perky as a turkey, so I call up this guy I know and arrange it and off we go across the bridge to the Kentucky side of the river, where there is plenty of room to move around in. Well, sir, soon this yellow plane comes over and circles a couple of times till he has the right height, and then he lets go with something that I didn't tell Pop, but which the boys are onto, is a grapefruit so that if it hits him it will not crack his skull open and kill him. Down the thing comes like a cannonball and Pop, in his black two-piece bathing suit, in case he has to go a little in the water, and wearing a mitt the size of a basket, circles under it like a dizzy duck, holding the sun out of his eyes as he gets a line on where it is coming down. Faster it falls, getting bigger by the second, then Pop, who is now set for the catch, suddenly lets out a howl, 'My Christ, the moon is falling on me,' and the next second, bong—the grapefruit busts him on the conk and we have all we can do to keep him from drowning in the juice."

Now there was a loud cackle of laughter in the trainer's room. The voice Roy didn't like—the frightening thought dawned on him that the voice *knew* what he was hiding—it changed the subject and wanted to know from Bump if there was any truth to the rumor about him and Pop's niece.

"Naw," Bump said, and cagily asked, "What rumor?"

"That you and Memo are getting hitched."

Bump laughed. "She must've started that one herself."

"Then you deny it?"

The door was shoved open and Bump waltzed out in his shorts, as husky, broadbacked, and big-shouldered as Roy had thought, followed by the trainer and a slightly popeyed gent dressed in an expensive striped suit, whose appearance gave Roy a shooting pain in the pit of the stomach—Max Mercy.

Ashamed to be recognized, to have his past revealed like an egg spattered on the floor, Roy turned away, tucking his jersey into his pants.

But Bump paraded over with his hairy arm outstretched. "Hiya, buster, you the latest victim they have trapped?"

Roy felt an irritable urge to pitch his fist at the loudmouth, but he nodded and shook hands.

"Welcome to the lousiest team in the world, barring none," Bump said. "And this is ol' Doc Casey, the trainer, who has got nobody but cripples on his hands except me. And the hawkshaw with the eyes is Max Mercy, the famous sports colyumist. Most newspaper guys are your pals and know when to keep their traps shut, but to Max a private life is a personal insult. Before you are here a week he will tell the public how much of your salary you send to your grandma and how good is your sex life."

Max, whose mustache and sideboards were graying, laughed hollowly. He said to Roy, "Didn't catch the name."

"Roy Hobbs," he said stiffly, but no one seemed to think it mattered very much.

.   .   .

The game was over and the players hoofed through the tunnel into the locker room. They tore out of their uniforms and
piled into the showers. Some stayed in only long enough to
wet their skins. Wiping themselves dry, they tumbled into
street clothes. Their speed, however, did them no good, for
Red, after courteously asking Mercy to leave, posted himself
and Earl Wilson, the third base coach, at the door and they
let nobody else out. The players waited nervously, except
Bump, who slapped backs and advised everybody to cheer
up. A few of the boys were working the strategy of staying in
the showers so long they hoped Pop would grow sick and
tired and leave. But Pop, a self-sustaining torch in the shut
managerial office, outwaited them, and when he got the quiet
knock from Red that the lobsters were in the pot, yanked
open the door and strode sulphurously forth. The team
shriveled.

Pop stepped up on a chair where for once, a bald, bristling
figure, he towered over them. Waving his bandaged hands
he began to berate them but immediately stopped, choked
by his rage into silence.

"If he coughs now," Bump boomed, "he will bust into
dust."

Pop glared at him, his head glowing like a red sun. He
savagely burst out that not a single blasted one of them here
was a true ballplayer. They were sick monkeys, broken-down
mules, pigeon-chested toads, slimy horned worms, but not
real, honest-to-god baseball players.

"How's about flatfooted fish?" Bump wisecracked. "Get it,
boys, fish—Fisher," and he fell into a deep gargle of laughter
at his wit, but the semi-frozen players in the room did not
react.

"How's he get away with it?" Roy asked the ghost standing
next to him. The pale player whispered out of the corner of
his mouth that Bump was presently the leading hitter in the
league.

Pop ignored Bump and continued to give the team the
rough side of his tongue. "What beats me is that I have spent

thousands of dollars for the best players I could lay my hands on. I hired two of the finest coaches in the game. I sweat myself sick trying to direct you, and all you can deliver is those goddamn goose eggs." His voice rose. "Do you dimwits realize that we have been skunked for the last forty-five innings in a row?"

"Not Bumpsy," the big voice said, "I am terrific."

"You now hold the record of the most consecutive games lost in the whole league history, the most strikeouts, the most errors—"

"Not Bumpsy—"

"—the most foolishness and colossal stupidities. In plain words, you all stink. I am tempted to take pity on those poor dopes who spend a buck and a half to watch you play and trade the whole lousy lot of you away."

Bump dropped down on his knees and raised his clasped hands. "Me first, Lawdy, me first."

"—and start from scratch to build up a team that will know how to play together and has guts and will fight the other guy to death before they drop seventeen games in the cellar."

The players in the locker room were worn out but Bump was singing, "Many brave hearts are asleep in the deep."

"Beware," he croaked low in his throat, "bewaaare—"

Pop shook a furious finger at him that looked as if it would fly off and strike him in the face. "As for you, Bump Baily, high and mighty though you are, some day you'll pay for your sassifras. Remember that lightning cuts down the tallest trees too."

Bump didn't like warnings of retribution. His face turned surly.

"Lightning, maybe, but no burnt out old fuse."

Pop tottered. "Practice at eight in the morning," he said brokenly. But for Red he would have tumbled off the chair. In his office behind the slammed and smoking door they could hear him sobbing, "Sometimes I could cut my own throat."

It took the Knights a while to grow bones and crawl out

after Bump. But when everybody had gone, including the coaches and Dizzy, Roy remained behind. His face was flaming hot, his clothes soaked in sweat and shame, as if the old man's accusations had been leveled at his head.

When Pop came out in his street clothes, a yellowed Panama and a loud sport jacket, he was startled to see Roy sitting there in the gloom and asked what he was waiting for.

"No place to go," Roy said.

"Whyn't you get a room?"

"Ain't got what it takes."

Pop looked at him. "Scotty paid you your bonus cash, didn't he?"

"Two hundred, but I had debts."

"You shoulda drawn an advance on your first two weeks' pay from the office when you came in today. It's too late now, they quit at five, so I will write you out my personal check for twenty-five dollars and you can pay me back when you get the money."

Pop balanced his checkbook on his knee. "You married?"

"No."

"Whyn't you ask around among the married players to see who has got a spare room? That way you'd have a more regular life. Either that, or in a respectable boarding house. Some of the boys who have their homes out of town prefer to stay at a moderate-priced hotel, which I myself have done since my wife passed away, but a boarding house is more homelike and cheaper. Anyway," Pop advised, "tonight you better come along with me to the hotel and tomorrow you can find a place to suit your needs."

Roy remarked he wasn't particularly crazy about hotels.

They left the ball park, got into a cab and drove downtown. The sky over the Hudson was orange. Once Pop broke out of his reverie to point out Grant's Tomb.

At the Midtown Hotel, Pop spoke to the desk clerk and he assigned Roy a room on the ninth floor, facing toward the Empire State Building. Pop went up with him and pumped the mattress.

"Not bad," he said.

After the bellhop had left he said he hoped Roy wasn't the shenanigan type.

"What kind?" Roy asked.

"There are all sorts of nuts in this game and I remember one of my players—seems to me it was close to twenty years ago—who used to walk out on the fifteenth floor ledge and scare fits out of people in the other rooms. One day when he was walking out there he fell and broke his leg and only the darndest luck kept him from rolling right overboard. It was beginning to rain and he pulled himself around from window to window, begging for help, and everybody went into stitches at his acting but kept their windows closed. He finally rolled off and hit bottom."

Roy had unpacked his valise and was washing up.

"Lemme tell you one practical piece of advice, son," Pop went on. "You're starting way late—I was finished after fifteen years as an active player one year after the age you're coming in, but if you want to get along the best way, behave and give the game all you have got, and when you can't do that, quit. We don't need any more goldbrickers or fourflushers or practical jokers around. One Bump Baily is too much for any team."

He left the room, looking wretched.

The phone jangled and after a minute Roy got around to lifting it.

"What's the matter?" Red Blow barked. "Don't you answer your telephone?"

"I like it to ring a little, gives 'em a chance to change their mind."

"Who?"

"Anybody."

Red paused. "Pop asked me to show you around. When are you eating?"

"I am hungry now."

"Meet me in the lobby, half past six."

As Roy hung up there was a loud dum-diddy-um-dum on

the door and Bump Baily in a red-flowered Hollywood shirt breezed in.

"Hiya, buster. Saw you pull in with the old geezer and tracked you down. I would like for you to do me a favor."

"Roy is the name."

"Roy is fine. Listen, I got my room on the fourth floor, which is a damn sight classier than this mouse trap. I would like you to borrow it and I will borrow this for tonight."

"What's the pitch?"

"I am having a lady friend visit me and there are too many nosy people on my floor."

Roy considered and said okay. He unconsciously wet his lips.

Bump slapped him between the shoulders. "Stick around, buster, you will get yours."

Roy knew he would never like the guy.

Bump told him his room number and they exchanged keys, then Roy put a few things into his valise and went downstairs.

Coming along the fourth floor hall he saw a door half open and figured this was it. As he pulled the knob he froze, for there with her back to him stood a slim, redheaded girl in black panties and brassiere. She was combing her hair before a mirror on the wall as the light streamed in around her through the billowy curtains. When she saw him in the mirror she let out a scream. He stepped back as if he had been kicked in the face. Then the door slammed and he had a splitting headache.

Bump's room was next door so Roy went in and lay down on the bed, amid four purple walls traced through with leaves flying among white baskets of fruit, some loaded high and some spilled over. He lay there till the pain in his brain eased.

At 6:30 he went down and met Red, in a droopy linen suit, and they had steaks in a nearby chophouse. Roy had two and plenty of mashed potatoes. Afterwards they walked up Fifth Avenue. He felt better after the meal.

"Want to see the Village?" Red said.

"What's in it?"

Red picked his teeth. "Beats me. Whatever they got I can't find it. How about a picture?"

Roy was agreeable so they dropped into a movie. It was a picture about a city guy who came to the country, where he had a satisfying love affair with a girl he met. Roy enjoyed it. As they walked back to the hotel the night was soft and summery. He thought about the black-brassiered girl in the next room.

Red talked about the Knights. "They are not a bad bunch of players, but they aren't playing together and it's mostly Bump's fault. He is for Bump and not for the team. Fowler, Schultz, Hinkle, and Hill are all good pitchers and could maybe be fifteen or twenty game winners if they got some support in the clutches, which they don't, and whatever Bump gives them in hitting he takes away with his lousy fielding."

"How's that?"

"He's just so damn lazy. Pop has thrown many a fine and suspension at him, but after that he will go into a slump on purpose and we don't win a one. If I was Pop I'da had his ass long ago, but Pop thinks a hitter like him could be a bell cow and lead the rest ahead, so he keeps hoping he will reform. If we could get the team rolling we'd be out of the cellar in no time."

They were approaching the hotel and Roy counted with his eyes up to the fourth floor and watched the curtains in the windows.

"I read Scotty's report on you," Red said. "He says you are a terrific hitter. How come you didn't start playing when you were younger?"

"I did but I flopped." Roy was evasive.

Red cringed. "Don't say that word around here."

"What word?"

"Flopped—at least not anywhere near Pop. He starts to cry when he hears it."

"What for?"

"Didn't you ever hear about Fisher's Flop?"

"Seems to me I did but I am not sure."

Red told him the story. "About forty years ago Pop was the third sacker for the old Sox when they got into their first World Series after twenty years. They sure wanted to take the flag that year but so did the Athletics, who they were playing, and it was a rough contest all the way into the seventh game. That one was played at Philly and from the first inning the score stood at 3-3, until the Athletics drove the tie-breaker across in the last of the eighth. In the ninth the Sox's power was due up but they started out bad. The leadoffer hit a blooper to short, the second struck out, and the third was Pop. It was up to him. He let one go for a strike, then he slammed a low, inside pitch for a tremendous knock.

"The ball sailed out to deep center," Red said, "where the center fielder came in too fast and it rolled through him to the fence and looked good for an inside-the-park homer, or at least a triple. Meanwhile, Pop, who is of course a young guy at this time, was ripping around the bags, and the crowd was howling for him to score and tie up the game, when in some crazy way as he was heading for home, his legs got tangled under him and he fell flat on his stomach, the living bejesus knocked out of him. By the time he was up again the ball was in the catcher's glove and he ran up the baseline after Pop. In the rundown that followed, the third baseman tagged him on the behind and the game was over."

Red spat into the street. Roy tried to say something but couldn't.

"That night Fisher's Flop, or as they mostly call it, 'Fisher's Famous Flop,' was in every newspaper in the country and was talked about by everybody. Naturally Pop felt like hell. I understand that Ma Fisher had the phone out and hid him up in the attic. He stayed there two weeks, till the roof caught fire and he had to come out or burn. After that they went to Florida for a vacation but it didn't help much. His picture was known to all and wherever he went they yelled after him, 'Flippity-flop, flippity-flop.' It was at this time that Pop lost his hair. After a while people no longer recognized him, except on the ball field, yet though the kidding died down, Pop was a marked man."

Roy mopped his face. "Hot," he said.

"But he had his guts in him," Red said, "and stayed in the game for ten years more and made a fine record. Then he retired from baseball for a couple years, which was a good thing but he didn't know it. Soon one of Ma's rich relatives died and left them a pile of dough that Pop used to buy himself a half share of the Knights. He was made field manager and the flop was forgotten by now except for a few wise-egg sportswriters that, when they are too drunk to do an honest day's work, would raise up the old story and call it Fisher's Fizzle, or Farce, or Fandango—you wouldn't guess there are so many funny words beginning with an f—which some of them do to this day when the Knights look foolish. The result is that Pop has the feeling he has been jinxed since the time of his flop, and he has spent twenty-five years and practically all of his pile trying to break the jinx, which he thinks he can do by making the Knights into the world champs that the old Sox never did become. Eight times he has finished in second place, five in third, and the rest in fourth or fifth, but last season when the Judge bought into the club and then took advantage of Pop's financial necessity to get hold of ten per cent of his shares and make himself the majority stockholder, was our worst season. We ended up in the sewer and this year it looks like a repeat."

"How come?"

"The Judge is trying to push Pop out of his job although he has a contract to manage for life—that's what the Judge had to promise to get that ten per cent of stock. Anyway, he's been trying everything he can think of to make things tough for Pop. He has by his sly ways forced all sorts of trades on us which make money all right but hurt the team. It burns me up," Red said, "because I would give my right arm if I could get Pop the pennant. I am sure that if he took one and the Series after that, he would feel satisfied, quit baseball, and live in peace. He is one helluva white guy and de-

serves better than he got. That's why I am asking you to give
him the best you have in you."

"Let him play me," Roy said, "and he will get the best."

In the lobby Red said he had enjoyed Roy's company and
they should eat together more. Before he left he warned Roy
to be careful with his earnings. They weren't much, he knew,
but if in the future Roy had a chance to invest in something
good, he advised him to do so. "There is a short life in baseball and we have to think of the future. Anything can happen
to you in this game. Today you are on top and tomorrow
you will be on your way out to Dubuque. Try to protect your
old age. It don't pay to waste what you earn."

To his surprise, Roy answered, "To hell with my old age.
I will be in this game a long time."

Red rubbed his chin. "How are you so sure?"

"It wasn't for nothing it took me fifteen years to get here.
I came for more than the ride and I will leave my mark
around here."

Red waited to hear more but Roy shut up.

Red shrugged, "Well, each to their choice."

Roy said good night and went upstairs. Entering Bump's
room, he picked up a gilt hairpin from the carpet and put it
into his wallet because some claimed it brought luck. For a
while he stood at the window and watched the lit Empire
State Building. It was a great big city, all right. He undressed, thinking of Pop's flop that changed his whole life,
and got into bed.

In the dark the bed was in motion, going round in wide,
sweeping circles. He didn't like the feeling so he lay deathly
still and let everything go by—the trees, mountains, states.
Then he felt he was headed into a place where he did not
want to go and tried urgently to think of ways to stop the bed.
But he couldn't and it went on, a roaring locomotive now,
screaming into the night, so that he was tensed and sweating
and groaned aloud why did it have to be me? what did I do
to deserve it? seeing himself again walking down the long,
lonely corridor, carrying the bassoon case, the knock, the crazy
Harriet (less and more than human) with the shiny pistol,

and him, cut down in the very flower of his youth, lying in a red pool of his own blood.

No, he cried, oh no, and lashed at his pillow, as he had a thousand times before.

Finally, as the sight of him through the long long years of suffering faded away, he quieted down. The noise of the train eased off as it came to a stop, and Roy found himself set down in a field somewhere in the country, where he had a long and satisfying love affair with this girl he had seen in the picture tonight.

He thought of her till he had fallen all but deep asleep, when a door seemed to open in the mind and this naked redheaded lovely slid out of a momentary flash of light, and the room was dark again. He thought he was still dreaming of the picture but the funny part of it was when she got into bed with him he almost cried out in pain as her icy hands and feet, in immediate embrace, slashed his hot body, but there among the apples, grapes, and melons, he found what he wanted and had it.

At the clubhouse the next morning the unshaven Knights were glum and redeyed. They moved around listlessly and cursed each step. Angry fist fights broke out among them. They were sore at themselves and the world, yet when Roy came in and headed for his locker they looked up and watched with interest. He opened the door and found his new uniform knotted up dripping wet on a hook. His sanitary socks and woolen stockings were slashed to shreds and all the other things were smeared black with shoe polish. He located his jock, with two red apples in it, swinging from a cord attached to the light globe, and both his shoes were nailed to the ceiling. The boys let out a bellow of laughter. Bump just about doubled up howling, but Roy yanked the wet pants off the hook and caught him with it smack in the face. The players let out another yowl.

Bump comically dried himself with a bath towel, digging deep into his ears, wiping under the arms, and shimmying as he rubbed it across his fat behind.

"Fast guesswork, buster, and to show you there's no hard feelings, how's about a Camel?"

Roy wanted nothing from the bastard but took the cigarette because everyone was looking on. When he lit it, someone in the rear yelled, "Fire!" and ducked as it burst in Roy's face. Bump had disappeared. The players fell into each other's arms. Tears streamed down their cheeks. Some of them could not unbend and limped around from laughing so.

Roy flipped the ragged butt away and began to mop up his wet locker.

Allie Stubbs, the second baseman, danced around the room in imitation of a naked nature dancer. He pretended to discover a trombone at the foot of a tree and marched around blowing oompah, oompah, oompah.

Roy then realized the bassoon case was missing. It startled him that he hadn't thought of it before.

"Who's got it, boys?"—but no one answered. Allie now made out like he was flinging handfuls of rose petals into the trainer's office.

Going in there, Roy saw that Bump had broken open the bassoon case and was about to attack Wonderboy with a hacksaw.

"Lay off of that, you goon."

Bump turned and stepped back with the bat raised. Roy grabbed it and with a quick twist tore it out of his sweaty

hands, turning him around as he did and booting him hard
with his knee. Bump grunted and swung but Roy ducked.
The team crowded into the trainer's office, roaring with delight.

But Doc Casey pushed his way through them and stepped
between Roy and Bump. "That'll do, boys. We want no
trouble here. Go on outside or Pop will have your hides."

Bump was sweaty and sore. "You're a lousy sport, alfalfa."

"I don't like the scummy tricks you play on people you have
asked for a favor," Roy said.

"I hear you had a swell time, wonderboy."

Again they grappled for each other, but Doc, shouting for
help, kept them apart until the players pinned Roy's arms and
held on to Bump.

"Lemme at him," Bump roared, "and I will skin the
skunk."

Held back by the team, they glared at one another over the
trainer's head.

"What's going on in there?" Pop's shrill blast came from inside the locker room. Earl Wilson poked his grayhaired, sun-
burned head in and quickly called, "All out, men, on the
double." The players scurried past Pop and through the tunnel. They felt better.

Dizzy hustled up a makeshift rig for Roy. He dressed and
polished his bat, a little sorry he had lost his temper, because
he had wanted to speak quietly to the guy and find out
whether he was expecting the redhead in his room last night.

Thinking about her made him uneasy. He reported to Pop
in the dugout.

"What was that trouble in there between Bump and you?"
Pop asked.

Roy didn't say and Pop got annoyed. "I won't stand for any
ructions between players so cut it out or you will find yourself
chopping wood back in the sticks. Now report to Red."

Roy went over to where Red was catching Chet Schultz, today's pitcher, and Red said to wait his turn at the batting
cage.

The field was overrun with droopy players. Half a dozen

were bunched near the gate of the cage, waiting to be pitched to by Al Fowler, whom Pop had ordered to throw batting practice for not bearing down in the clutches yesterday. Some of the men were at the sidelines, throwing catch. A few were shagging flies in the field, a group was playing pepper. On the line between home and first Earl Wilson was hacking out grounders to Allie Stubbs, Cal Baker at short, Hank Benz, the third baseman, and Emil Lajong, who played first. At the edge of the outfield, Hinkle and Hill, two of the regular starters, and McGee, the reliefer, were doing a weak walk-run-walk routine. No one seemed to be thoroughly awake, but when Roy went into the batting cage they came to life and observed him.

Fowler, a southpaw, was in a nasty mood. He didn't like having his ears burned by Pop, called a showboat in front of the other men, and then shoved into batting practice the day after he had pitched. Fowler was twenty-three but looked thirty. He was built rangy, with very light hair and eyelashes, and small blue eyes. As a pitcher he had the stuff and knew it, but all season long he had been erratic and did a great amount of griping. He was palsy with Bump, who as a rule had no friends.

When Roy came up with Wonderboy, he hugged the plate too close to suit Fowler, who was in there anyway only to help the batters find their timing. In annoyance Fowler pitched the ball at Roy's head. Roy hit the dirt.

Pop shrieked, "Cut that out, you blasted fool." Fowler mumbled something about the ball slipping. Yet he wanted to make Roy look silly and burned the next one in. Roy swung and the ball sailed over the right field fence. Red-faced, Fowler tried a hard, sharp-breaking curve. Roy caught it at the end of his bat and pulled it into the left field stands.

"Try this one, grandpa." Fowler flung a stiff-wrist knuckler that hung in the air without spin before it took a sudden dip, but Roy scooped it up with the stick and lifted it twenty rows up into the center field stands. Then he quit. Fowler was scowling at his feet. Everybody else stared at Roy.

Pop called out, "Lemme see that bat, son."

Both he and Red examined it, hefting it and rubbing along the grain with their fingers.

"Where'd you get it?" Pop asked.

Roy cleared his throat. He said he had made it himself.

"Did you brand this name Wonderboy on it?"

"That's right."

"What's it mean?"

"I made it long ago," Roy said, "when I was a kid. I wanted it to be a very good bat and that's why I gave it that name."

"A bat's cheap to buy," Red said.

"I know it but this tree near the river where I lived was split by lightning. I liked the wood inside of it so I cut me out a bat. Hadn't used it much until I played semipro ball, but I always kept it oiled with sweet oil and boned it so it wouldn't chip."

"Sure is white. Did you bleach the wood?"

"No, that's the true color."

"How long ago d'you make it?" Pop asked.

"A long time—I don't remember."

"Whyn't you get into the game then?"

Roy couldn't answer for a minute. "I sorta got sidetracked."

But Pop was all smiles. "Red'll measure and weigh it. If there's no filler and it meets specifications you'll be allowed to use it."

"There's nothing in it but wood."

Red clapped him on the back. "I feel it in my bones that you will have luck with it." He said to Pop, "Maybe we can start Roy in the line-up soon?"

Pop said they would see how it worked out.

But he sent Roy out to left field and Earl hit fungos to him all over the lot. Roy ran them down well. He took one shot over his shoulder and two caroming off the wall below the stands. His throwing was quick, strong, and bull's eye.

When Bump got around to his turn in the cage, though he did not as a rule exert himself in practice, he now whammed five of Fowler's fast pitches into the stands. Then he trotted out to his regular spot in the sun field and Earl hit him some long flies, all of which he ran for and caught with gusto, even those that went close to the wall, which was unusual for him because he didn't like to go too near it.

Practice picked up. The men worked faster and harder than they had in a long time. Pop suddenly felt so good, tears came to his eyes and he had to blow his nose.

In the clubhouse about an hour and a half before game time, the boys were sitting around in their underwear after showers. They were bulling, working crossword puzzles, shaving and writing letters. Two were playing checkers, surrounded by a circle of others, and the rest were drinking soda, looking at the *Sporting News*, or just resting their eyes. Though they tried to hide it they were all nervous, always glancing up whenever someone came into the room. Roy couldn't make sense of it.

Red took him around to meet some of the boys and Roy spoke a few words to Dave Olson, the squat catcher, also to the shy Mexican center fielder, Juan Flores, and to Gabby Laslow, who patrolled right field. They sidestepped Bump, sitting in front of his locker with a bath towel around his rump, as he worked a red thread across the yellowed foot of a sanitary sock.

"Changes that thread from sock to sock every day," Red said in a low voice. "Claims it keeps him hitting."

As the players began to get into clean uniforms, Pop, wearing halfmoon specs, stepped out of his office. He read aloud the batting order, then flipping through his dog-eared yellow-paged notebook he read the names of the players opposing them and reminded them how the pitchers were to pitch and the fielders field them. This information was scribbled all over the book and Pop had to thumb around a lot before he had covered everybody. Roy then expected him to lay on with a blistering mustard plaster for all, but he only glanced anxiously at the door and urged them all to be on their toes and for gosh sakes get some runs.

Just as Pop finished his pep talk the door squeaked open and a short and tubby man in a green suit peeked in. Seeing they were ready, he straightened up and entered briskly, car-

rying a briefcase in his hand. He beamed at the players and
without a word from anybody they moved chairs and benches
and arranged themselves in rows before him. Roy joined the
rest, expecting to hear some kind of talk. Only Pop and the
coaches sat behind the man, and Dizzy lounged, half open-
mouthed, at the door leading to the hall.

"What's the act?" Roy asked Olson.

"It's Doc Knobb." The catcher looked sleepy.

"What's he do?"

"Pacifies us."

The players were attentive, sitting as if they were going to
have their pictures snapped. The nervousness Roy had sensed
among them was all but gone. They looked like men whose
worries had been lifted, and even Bump gave forth a soft
grunt of contentment.

The doctor removed his coat and rolled up his shirtsleeves.
"Got to hurry today," he told Pop, "got a polo team to cheer
up in Brooklyn."

He smiled at the men and then spoke so softly, at first they
couldn't hear him. When he raised his voice it exuded calm.

"Now, men," he purred, "all of you relax and let me have
your complete attention. Don't think of a thing but me." He
laughed, brushed a spot off his pants, and continued. "You
know what my purpose is. You're familiar with that. It's to
help you get rid of the fears and personal inferiorities that tie
you into knots and keep you from being aces in this game.
Who are the Pirates? Not supermen, only mortals. What have
they got that you haven't got? I can't think of a thing, absolutely not one. It's the attitude that's licking you—your own,
not the Pirates'. What do you mean to yourselves? Are you a
flock of bats flying around in a coffin, or the sun shining calmly
on a blue lake? Are you sardines being swallowed up in the sea,
or the whale that does the swallowing? That's why I'm here,
to help you answer that question in the affirmative, to help
you by mesmerism and autosuggestion, meaning you do the
suggesting, not I. I only assist by making you receptive to your
own basic thoughts. If you think you are winners, you will be.
If you don't, you won't. That's psychology. That's the way

the world works. Give me your whole attention and look straight into my eyes. What do you see there? You see sleep. That's right, sleep. So relax, sleep, relax . . ."

His voice was soft, lulling, peaceful. He had raised his pudgy arms and with stubby fingers was making ripples on a vast calm sea. Already Olson was gently snoring. Flores, with the tip of his tongue protruding, Bump, and some of the other players were fast asleep. Pop looked on, absorbed.

Staring at the light gleaming on Pop's bald bean, Roy felt himself going off . . . way way down, drifting through the tides into golden water as he searched for this lady fish, or mermaid, or whatever you called her. His eyes grew big in the seeking, first fish eyes, then bulbous frog eyes. Sailing lower into the pale green sea, he sought everywhere for the reddish glint of her scales, until the water became dense and dark green and then everything gradually got so black he lost all sight of where he was. When he tried to rise up into the light he couldn't find it. He darted in all directions, and though there were times he saw flashes of her green tail, it was dark everywhere. He threshed up a storm of luminous bubbles but they gave out little light and he did not know where in all the glass to go.

Roy ripped open his lids and sprang up. He shoved his way out from between the benches.

The doctor was startled but made no attempt to stop him. Pop called out, "Hey, where do you think you're going?"

"Out."

"Sit down, dammit, you're on the team."

"I might be on the team but no medicine man is going to hypnotize me."

"You signed a contract to obey orders," Pop snapped shrilly.

"Yes, but not to let anybody monkey around in my mind."

As he headed into the tunnel he heard Pop swear by his eight-foot uncle that nobody by the name of Roy Hobbs would ever play ball for him as long as he lived.

He had waited before . . . and he waited now, on a spike-scuffed bench in the dugout, hidden from sky, wind and weather, from all but the dust that blew up from Knights Field and lodged dry in the throat, as the grass grew browner. And from time ticking off balls and strikes, batters up and out, halves and full innings, games won and (mostly) lost, days and nights, and the endless train miles from Philly, with in-between stops, along the arc to St. Louis, and circling back by way of Chi, Boston, Brooklyn . . . still waiting.

"C'mon, Roy," Red had urged, "apologize to Pop, then the next time Knobb comes around, join the boys and everything will be okay."

"Nix on that," said Roy, "I don't need a shyster quack to shoot me full of confidence juice. I want to go through on my own steam."

"He only wants everybody to relax and be able to do their best."

Roy shook his head. "I been a long time getting here and now that I am, I want to do it by myself, not with that kind of bunk."

"Do what?" Red asked.

"What I have to do."

Red shrugged and gave him up as too stubborn. Roy sat around, and though it said on his chest he was one of the team, he sat among them alone; at the train window, gazing at the moving trees, in front of his locker, absorbed in an un-tied shoe lace, in the dugout, squinting at the great glare of the game. He traveled in their company and dressed where they did but he joined them in nothing, except maybe batting practice, entering the cage with the lumber on his shoulder glistening like a leg bone in the sun and taking his chops at the pill. Almost always he hammered the swift, often murderous throws (the practice pitchers dumped their bag of tricks on him) deep into the stands, as the players watched and mut-tered at the swift flight of the balls, then forgot him when the game started. But there were days when the waiting got him. He could feel the strength draining from his bones, weakening him so he could hardly lift Wonderboy. He was unwilling to move then, for fear he would fall over on his puss and have to crawl away on all fours. Nobody noticed he did not bat when he felt this way except Pop; and Bump, seeing how white his face was, squirted contemptuous tobacco juice in the dust. Then when Roy's strength ebbed back, he would once again go into the batters' cage and do all sorts of marvelous things that made them watch in wonder.

He watched *them* and bad as he felt he had to laugh. They were a nutty bunch to begin with but when they were losing they were impossible. It was like some kind of sickness. They threw to the wrong bases, bumped heads together in the outfield, passed each other on the baselines, sometimes batted out of order, throwing both Pop and the ump into fits, and cussed everybody else for their mistakes. It was not uncommon to see them pile three men on a bag, or behold a catcher on the opposing team, in a single skip and jump, lay the tag on two of them as they came thundering together into home plate. Or watch Gabby Laslow, in a tight spot, freeze onto the ball, or Allie Stubbs get socked with it in the jaw, thrown by Olson on a steal as Allie admired a lady in the stands. Doc Knobb's hypnotism cut down their jitters but it didn't much help their coordination, yet when they were left unhypnotized for a few days, they were afflicted with more than the usual number of hexes and whammies and practiced all sorts of magic to undo them. To a man they crossed their fingers over spilled salt, or coffee or tea, or at the sight of a hearse. Emil Lajong did a backward flip whenever he located a cross-eyed fan in the stands. Olson hated a woman who wore the same drab brown-feathered hat every time she showed up. He spat through two fingers whenever he spotted her in the crowd. Bump went through his ritual with the colored threads in his socks and shorts. Pop sometimes stroked a rabbit's foot. Red Blow never changed his clothes during a "winning streak," and Flores secretly touched his genitals whenever a bird flew over his head.

They were not much different from the fans in the patched and peeling stands. On weekdays the stadium usually looked like a haunted house but over the weekend crowds developed. The place often resembled a zoo full of oddballs, including gamblers, bums, drunks, and some ugly crackpots. Many of them came just to get a laugh out of the bonehead plays. Some, when the boys were losing, cursed and jeered, showering them—whenever they came close enough—with rotten cabbages, tomatoes, blackened bananas and occasionally an eggplant. Yet let the umpire call a close play against the Knights and he became a target for pop bottles, beer cans, old shoes or anything that happened to be lying around loose. Surprisingly, however, a few players were chosen for affection and even admiration by their fans. Sadie Sutter, a girl of sixty-plus, who wore large flowered hats, bobby sox, and short skirts, showed her undying love for Dave Olson every time he came up to the plate by banging with all her might on a Chinese gong she dragged into the stadium every day. A Hungarian cook, a hearty man with a hard yellow straw hat jammed tight on his skull, hopped up on his seat and crowed like a rooster whenever Emil Lajong originated a double play. And there was a girl named Gloria from Mississippi, a washed-out flower of the vestibules, who between innings when her eyes were not on the game, lined up a customer or two for a quickie later. She gave her heart to Gabby, yelling, "Get a move on, Mo-lasses," to set him in motion after a fly ball. Besides these, there had appeared early in the present season, a pompous Otto P. Zipp, whose peevish loudspeaker could be heard all over the park, his self-chosen mission to rout the critics of Bump Baily, most of whom razzed the big boy for short legging on the other fielders. The dwarf honked a loud horn at the end of a two-foot walking stick, and it sounded as if a flock of geese had been let loose at the offenders, driving them—his purple curses ringing in their ears—to seek shelter in some hidden hole in the stands or altogether out of the ballpark. Zipp was present at every home game, sitting at the rail in short left field, and Bump made it his much publicized business, as he trotted out to his position at the start of the game, to greet him with a loud kiss on the forehead, leaving Otto in a state of creamy bliss.

Roy got to know them all as he waited, all one if you looked long enough through the haze of cigarette smoke, except one . . . Memo Paris, Pop's redheaded niece, sad, spurned lady, who sat without wifehood in the wives' box behind third base. He could, if she would let him, find her with his eyes shut, with his hands alone as he had in the dark. Always in the act of love she lived in his mind, the only way he knew her, because she would not otherwise suffer his approach. *He* was to blame, she had wept one bitter midnight, so she hated his putrid guts. Since the team's return to the city (the phone banged in his ear and she ripped up his letters when they were delivered) whenever he got up from his seat in the hotel lobby as she stepped out of the elevator, to say how sorry he was for beginning at the wrong end, she tugged at her summer furpiece and breezed past him in greeneyed scorn, withering in the process Bump at the cigar stand, who had laughed aloud at Roy's rout. ("Honeybunch," he had explained, "it was out of the pity of my heart that I took that shmo into my room, because they didn't have one for him and I was intending to pass the night at the apartment of my he cousin from Mobile. How'd I know you'd go in there when you said you weren't speaking to me?" He swore it hadn't been a gag—had he ever pulled one on her?—but Memo punished him in silence, punishing herself, and he knew it because she still came every day to see him play.) She walked out of the lobby, with her silver bracelets tinkling, swaying a little on her high heels, as if she had not too long ago learned to walk on them, and went with her beautiful body away, for which Roy everlastingly fried Bump Baily in the deep fat of his abomination.

It was for her he waited.

On the morning of the twenty-first of June Pop told Roy that as of tomorrow he was being shipped to a Class B team in the Great Lakes Association. Roy said he was quitting baseball anyway, but that same day, in answer to an angry question of Pop's as to why the team continued to flop, Doc Knobb said that the manager's hysterical behavior was undoing all the good he had done, and he offered to hypnotize Pop along with the others without hiking his fee. Pop shrilly told the psychologist he was too old for such bamboozlement, and

Knobb retorted that his attitude was not only ridiculous but stupid. Pop got redfaced and told him to go to perdition with his hocus pocus and as of right then the doctor was canned.

That afternoon the Knights began a series with the second-place Phils. Instead of falling into a swoon when they learned there was to be no further hypnosis, the team played its best ball in weeks. Against superior pitching, in the sixth they bunched three singles for a run, and though Schultz had already given up five hits to the Phils, they were scattered and came to nothing. The Phils couldn't score till the top of the eighth, when with two out Schultz weakened, walking one man and handing the next a good enough throw to hit for a sharp single, so that there were now men on first and third. Up came Rogers, the Phils' slugger, and hit a fast curve for what looked like no more than a long fly ball, a routine catch, to left center. Now it happened that Bump was nearer to the ball than Flores, who was shifted to the right, but he was feeling horny in the sun and casting about in his mind for who to invite to his bed tonight, when he looked up and noticed this ball coming. He still had time to get under it but then saw Flores going for it like a galloping horse, and the anguished look on the Mexican's face, his black eyes popping, neck like a thick rope, and mouth haunted, fascinated Bump so, he decided to let him have it if he wanted it that bad. At the last minute he tried to take it away from the Mex, risking a head-on collision, but the wind whipped the ball closer to the wall than he had bargained for, so Bump fell back to cover Flores in case he misplayed it.

The ball fell between them, good for a double, and scoring two of the Phils. Pop tore at what was left of his gray hair but couldn't grip it with his oily, bandaged fingers so he pulled at his ears till they were lit like red lamps. Luckily the next Phil smothered the fire by rolling to first, which kept the score at 2-1. When Bump returned to the dugout Pop cursed him from the cradle to the grave and for once Bump had no sassy answers. When it came his time to go out on deck, Pop snarled for him to stay where he was. Flores found a ripe one and landed on first but Pop stuck to his guns and looked down the line past Bump. His eye lit on Roy at the far end of the bench, and he called his name to go out there and hit. Bump turned purple. He grabbed a bat and headed for Roy but half the team jumped on him. Roy just sat there without moving and it looked to everyone like he wouldn't get up. The umpire roared in for a batter to come out, and after a while, as the players fidgeted and Pop fumed, Roy sighed and picked up Wonderboy. He slowly walked up the steps.

"Knock the cover off of it," Pop yelled.

"Attention, please," the P.A. man announced. "Roy Hobbs, number forty-five, batting for Baily."

A groan rose from the stands and turned into a roar of protest.

Otto Zipp jumped up and down on his seat, shaking his furious little fist at home plate.

"Throw him to the dogs," he shouted, and filled the air with his piercing curses.

Glancing at the wives' box, Roy saw that Memo had her head turned away. He set his jaw and advanced to the plate. His impulse was to knock the dirt out of his cleats but he refrained because he did not want to harm his bat in any way. Waiting for the pitcher to get set, Roy wiped his palms on his pants and twitched his cap. He lifted Wonderboy and waited rocklike for the throw.

He couldn't tell the color of the pitch that came at him. All he could think of was that he was sick to death of waiting, and tongue-out thirsty to begin. The ball was now a dew drop staring him in the eye so he stepped back and swung from the toes.

Wonderboy flashed in the sun. It caught the sphere where it was biggest. A noise like a twenty-one gun salute cracked the sky. There was a straining, ripping sound and a few drops of rain spattered to the ground. The ball screamed toward the pitcher and seemed suddenly to dive down at his feet. He grabbed it to throw to first and realized to his horror that he held only the cover. The rest of it, unraveling cotton thread as it rode, was headed into the outfield.

Roy was rounding first when the ball plummeted like a

dead bird into center field. Attempting to retrieve and throw,
the Philly fielder got tangled in thread. The second baseman
rushed up, bit the cord and heaved the ball to the catcher
but Roy had passed third and made home, standing. The
umpire called him safe and immediately a rhubarb boiled.
The Phils' manager and his players charged out of the dugout
and were joined by the nine men on the field. At the same
time, Pop, shouting in defense of the ump, rushed forth with
all the Knights but Bump. The umpire, caught between both
teams, had a troublesome time of it and was shoved this way
and that. He tossed out two men on each side but by then
came to the decision that the hit was a ground rules double.
Flores had scored and the game was tied up. Roy was ordered back to second, and Pop announced he was finishing
the game under protest. Somebody then shouted it was raining cats and dogs. The stands emptied like a yawn and the
players piled into the dugouts. By the time Roy got in from
second he was wading in water ankle deep. Pop sent him into
the clubhouse for a change of uniform but he could have
saved himself the trouble because it rained steadily for three
days. The game was recorded as a 2-2 tie, to be replayed later
in the season.

In the locker room Pop asked Roy to explain why he
thought the cover had come off the ball.

"That's what you said to do, wasn't it?"

"That's right," said Pop, scratching his bean.

The next day he told Roy he was withdrawing his release
and would hereafter use him as a pinch hitter and substitute
fielder.

The rain had washed out the Phils' series but the Knights
were starting another with the seventh-place Redbirds. In
batting practice, Roy, who was exciting some curiosity for his
freak hit of yesterday, looked tremendous but so did Bump.
For the first time in a long while Roy went out to left field to
limber up. Bump was out there too and Earl swatted fungos
to both.

As they were changing into clean uniforms before the start

of the game, Bump warned Roy in front of everybody, "Stay
out of my way, busher, or you will get your head bashed."

Roy squirted spit on the floor.

When Pop later handed the batting order to Stuffy Briggs,
the plate umpire, it had Bump's name scribbled on it as usual
in the fourth slot, but Pop had already warned him that if he
didn't hustle his behind when a ball was hit out to his field, he
would rest it a long time on the bench.

Bump made no reply but it was obvious that he took Pop's
words to heart, because he was a bang-up fielder that day. He
accepted eight chances, twice chasing into center field to take
them from Flores. He caught them to his left and right, dove
for and came up with a breathtaking shoestringer, and running as if on fire, speared a fantastic catch over his shoulder.
Still not satisfied, he pounded like a bull after his ninth try,
again in Flores' territory, a smoking ball that sailed up high,
headed for the wall. As Bump ran for it he could feel fear
leaking through his stomach, and his legs unwillingly slowed
down, but then he had this vision of himself as the league's
best outfielder, acknowledged so by fans and players alike,
even Pop, whom he'd be nothing less than forever respectful
to, and in love with and married to Memo. Thinking this way
he ran harder, though Zipp's geese honked madly at his back,
and with a magnificent twisting jump, he trapped the ball in
his iron fingers. Yet the wall continued to advance, and
though the redheaded lady of his choice was on her feet
shrieking, Bump bumped it with a skull-breaking bang, and
the wall embraced his broken body.

Though Bump was on the critical list in the hospital, many
newspapers continued to speculate about that ball whose
cover Roy had knocked off. It was explained as everything
from an optical illusion (neither the ball nor the cover was
ever found, the remnant caught by the catcher disappeared,
and it was thought some fan had snatched the cover) to a feat
of prodigious strength. Baseball records and newspaper files
were combed but no one could find any evidence that it had

happened before, although some of the older scribes swore it had. Then it leaked out that Pop had ordered Roy to skin the ball and Roy had obliged, but no one took that very seriously. One of the sportswriters suggested that a hard downward chop could shear off the outer covering. He had tried it in his cellar and had split the horsehide. Another pointed out that such a blow would have produced an infield grounder, therefore maybe a tremendous upward slash? The first man proved that would have uncorked a sure pop fly whereas the ball, as everyone knew, had sailed straight out over the pitcher's head. So it had probably resulted from a very very forceful sock. But many a hitter had plastered the ball forcefully before, still another argued, and his idea was that it was defective to begin with, a fact the company that manufactured the ball vigorously denied. Max Mercy had his own theory. He wrote in his column, "My Eye in the Knot Hole" (the year he'd done the Broadway stint for his paper his eye was in the key hole), that Roy's bat was a suspicious one and hinted it might be filled with something a helluva lot stronger than wood. Red Blow publicly denied this. He said the bat had been examined by league authorities and was found to be less than forty-two inches long, less than two and three-quarters inches thick at its fattest part, and in weight less than two pounds, which made it a legal weapon. Mercy then demanded that the wood be X-rayed but Roy turned thumbs down on that proposition and kept Wonderboy hidden away when the sports columnist was nosing around in the clubhouse.

On the day after the accident Pop soberly gave Roy the nod to play in Bump's place. As Roy trotted out to left, Otto Zipp was in his usual seat but looking worn and aged. His face, tilted to the warming rays of the sun, was like a pancake with a cherry nose, and tears were streaming through slits where the eyes would be. He seemed to be waiting for his pre-game kiss on the brow but Roy passed without looking at him.

The long rain had turned the grass green and Roy romped in it like a happy calf in its pasture. The Redbirds, probing his armor, belted the ball to him whenever they could, which was often, because Hill was not too happy on the mound, but

Roy took everything they aimed at him. He seemed to know
the soft, hard, and bumpy places in the field and just how
high a ball would bounce on them. From the flags on the stadium roof he noted the way the wind would blow the ball,
and he was quick at fishing it out of the tricky undercurrents
on the ground. Not sun, shadow, nor smoke-haze bothered
him, and when a ball was knocked against the wall he estimated the angle of rebound and speared it as if its course had
been plotted on a chart. He was good at gauging slices and
knew when to charge the pill to save time on the throw. Once
he put his head down and ran ahead of a shot going into the
concrete. Though the crowd rose with a thunderous warning,
he caught it with his back to the wall and did a little jig to
show he was alive. Everyone laughed in relief, and they liked
his long-legged loping and that he resembled an acrobat the
way he tumbled and came up with the ball in his glove. For
his performance that day there was much whistling and applause, except where he would have liked to hear it, an empty
seat in the wives' box.

His batting was no less successful. He stood at the plate
lean and loose, right-handed with an open stance, knees relaxed and shoulders squared. The bat he held in a curious
position, lifted slightly above his head as if prepared to beat a
rattlesnake to death, but it didn't harm his smooth stride into
the pitch, nor the easy way he met the ball and slashed it out
with a flick of the wrists. The pitchers tried something different every time he came up, sliders, sinkers, knucklers, but he
swung and connected, spraying them to all fields. He was,
Red Blow said to Pop, a natural, though somewhat less than
perfect because he sometimes hit at bad ones, which caused
Pop to frown.

"I mistrust a bad ball hitter."

"There are all kinds of hitters," Red answered. "Some are
bucket foots, and some go for bad throws but none of them
bother me as long as they naturally connect with anything
that gets in their way."

Pop spat up over the dugout steps. "They sometimes make
some harmful mistakes."

"Who don't?" Red asked.

Pop then muttered something about this bad ball hitter he knew who had reached for a lemon and cracked his spine.

But the only thing Roy cracked that day was the record for the number of triples hit in a major league debut and also the one for chances accepted in the outfield. Everybody agreed that in him the Knights had uncovered something special. One reporter wrote, "He can catch everything in creation," and Roy just about proved it. It happened that a woman who lived on the sixth floor of an apartment house overlooking the stadium was cleaning out her bird cage, near the end of the game, which the Knights took handily, when her canary flew out of the window and darted down across the field. Roy, who was waiting for the last out, saw something coming at him in the low rays of the sun, and leaping high, bagged it in his glove.

He got rid of the bloody mess in the clubhouse can.

When Bump died Memo went wild with grief. Bump, Bump, she wailed, pounding on the wall. Pop, who hovered over her at first, found her in bed clutching strands of red hair. Her cheeks were scratched where the tears rolled down. He was frightened and urged her to have the doctor but her piercing screams drove him away. She wept for days. Clad in black pajamas she lay across

the white bed like a broken candle still lit. In her mind she
planted kisses all over the corpse and when she kissed his
mouthless mouth blew back the breath of life, her womb stirring at the image of his restoration. Yet she saw down a dark
corridor that he was laid out dead, gripping in his fingers the
glowing ball he had caught, and that there were too many
locked doors to go through to return. She stopped trying to
think of him alive and thought of him dead. Then she really
hit the wall.

She could not stop weeping, as if the faucet were broken.
Or she were a fountain they had forgotten to turn off. There
was no end to her tears. They flowed on as if she had never
wept before. Wherever she turned she cried, the world was
wet. Her thoughts dripped on flowers, dark, stained ones in
night fields. She moved among them, tasting their many dark-
nesses, could not tell them from the rocks on the ground. His
shade was there. She saw it drifting before her and recognized
it by the broken places. Bump, oh Bump, but her voice was
drowned in water. She heard a gurgle and the bubbles breaking and felt the tears go searing down a hurt face (hers) and
though she wanted always to be with him she was (here)
weeping.

After unnumbered days she dragged herself out of bed, disturbed by all the space, her bare feet with lacquered nails, her
shaky presence among changeless things. She sought in the
hollow closet souvenirs of him, an autographed baseball "to
my Honey from her Bump" (tears), a cigarette lighter shaped
like a bat, click-open-light. She blew it out and searching further found an old kewpie doll he had won for her and a
pressed, yellowed gardenia, but couldn't with her wept-out
nose detect the faintest odor; also a pair of purple shorts she
herself had laundered and placed in the drawer among her
soft (and useless) underthings. Going through her scrapbook,
only rarely could she find menus (Sardi's, Toots Shor, and
once the Diamond Horseshoe) or movie ticket stubs (Palace,
Paramount, Capitol) and other such things of them both that
one could paste in, but most were pictures she had clipped
from the sports pages, showing Bump at bat, on the basepaths,

and crossing the plate. She idly turned the pages, sighed deeply and put the book away, then picked up the old picture album, and here was her sadeyed mother, and the torn up, patched together one was of Daddy grinning, who with a grin had (forever) exited dancing with his dancing partner, and here she was herself, a little girl weeping, as if nothing ever changed . . . The heartbreak was always present—he had not been truly hers when he died (she tried not to think whose, in many cities, he had been) so that she now mourned someone who even before his death had made her a mourner. That was the thorn in her grief.

When the July stifle drove her out of her room she appeared in the hotel lobby in black, her hair turned a lighter, golden shade as though some of the fire had burned out of it, and Roy was moved by her appearance. He had imagined how she would look when he saw her again but both the black and red, though predictable, surprised him. They told him with thunderclap quickness what he wanted to be sure of, that she, despite green eyes brimming for Bump, was the one for him, the ever desirable only. Occasionally he reflected what if the red were black and ditto the other way? Here, for example, was this blackhaired dame in red and what about it? He could take her or leave her, though there was a time in his life when a red dress would excite his fancy, but with Memo, flaming above and dark below, there was no choice—he was chosen so why not admit it though it brought pain? He had tried lately to forget her but had a long memory for what he wanted so there was only this to do, wait till she came in out of the rain.

Sometimes it was tough to, even for one used to waiting. Once a hungry desire sent him down to knock at her door but she shut it in his face although he was standing there with his hat in his embarrassed hands. He thought of asking Pop to put in a good word for him—how long was life anyhow?—but something told him to wait. And from other cities, when the team was on the road, he sent her cards, candies, little presents, which were all stuffed in his mailbox when he returned. It took the heart out of him. Yet each morning when she came out of the elevator he would look up at her as she walked by on her high heels, although she never seemed to see him. Then one day she shed black and put on white but still looked as if she were wearing black, so he waited. Only, now, when he looked at her she sometimes glanced at him. He watched her dislike of him fade to something neutral which he slowly became confident he could beat.

"One thing I hafta tell you not to do, son," Pop said to Roy in the hotel lobby one rainy morning not long after Bump's funeral, "and that is to blame yourself about what happened to Bump. He had a tough break but it wasn't your fault."

"What do you mean my fault?"

Pop looked up. "All I mean to say was he did it himself."

"Never thought anything but."

"Some have said maybe it wouldn't happen if you didn't join the team, and maybe so, but I believe such things are outside of yours and my control and I wouldn't want you to worry that you had caused it in any way."

"I won't because I didn't. Bump didn't have to go to the wall for that shot, did he? We were ahead in runs and the bases were clear. He could've taken it when it came off the wall without losing a thing, couldn't he?"

Pop scratched his baldy. "I guess so."

"Who are the people who said I did it?"

"Well, nobody exactly. My niece said you coulda wanted it to happen but that don't mean a thing. She was hysterical then."

Roy felt uneasy. Had he arranged Bump's run into the wall? No. Had he wished the guy would drop dead? Only once, after the night with Memo. But he had never consciously hoped he would crack up against the wall. That was none of his doing and he told Pop to tell it to Memo. But Pop was embarrassed now and said to drop the whole thing, it was a lot of foolishness.

Though Roy denied wishing Bump's fate on him or having been in any way involved in it, he continued to be unwillingly concerned with him even after his death. He was conscious that he was filling Bump's shoes, not only because he batted in the clean-up slot and fielded in the sun field (often watched his shadow fly across the very spot Bump had dived into) and became, in no time to speak of, one of the leading hitters in the league and at present certainly the most sensational, but also because the crowds made no attempt to separate his identity from Bump's. To his annoyance, when he made a hot catch, the kind Bump in all his glory would have left alone, he could hear through the curtain of applause, "Nice work, Bumpsy, 'at's grabbin' th' old apple," or "Leave it to Bump, he will be where they drop." It was goddamn stupid. The same fans who a month ago were hissing Bump for short legging on the other fielders now praised his name so high Roy felt like painting up a sandwich sign to wear out on the field, that said, ROY HOBBS PLAYING.

Even Otto Zipp made no effort to distinguish him from his predecessor and used the honker to applaud his doings, though there were some who said the dwarf sounded half-hearted in his honking. And Roy also shared the limelight with Bump on the sports page, where the writers were constantly comparing them for everything under the sun. One of them went so far as to keep a tally of their batting averages— Roy's total after his first, second, and third weeks of play, as compared with Bump's at the beginning of the season. One paper even printed pictures showing the living and dead facing each other with bats held high, as white arrows pointed at various places in their anatomies to show how much alike their measurements and stances were.

All this irritated Roy no end until he happened to notice Memo walk into the lobby one night with a paper turned to the sports page. From having read the same paper he knew she had seen a column about Bump and him as batsmen, so he decided there might be some percentage to all these comparisons. He came to feel more kindly to the memory of Bump and thought he was not such a bad egg after all, even if he did go in for too many screwball gags. Thinking back on him, he could sort of understand why Memo had been interested in him, and he felt that, though he was superior to Bump as an athlete, they were both money players, both showmen in the game. He figured it was through these resemblances that Memo would gradually get used to him and then come over all the way, although once she did, it would have to be for Hobbsie himself and not for some ghost by another name.

So he blazed away for her with his golden bat. It was not really golden, it was white, but in the sun it sometimes flashed gold and some of the opposing pitchers complained it shone in their eyes. Stuffy Briggs told Roy to put it away and use some other club but he stood on his rights and wouldn't. There was a hot rhubarb about that until Roy promised to rub some of the shine off Wonderboy. This he did with a hambone, and though the pitchers shut up, the bat still shone a dull gold. It brought him some wondrous averages in hits, runs, RBI's and total bases, and for the period of his few weeks in the game he led the league in homers and triples. (He was quoted in an interview as saying his singles were "mistakes." And he never bunted. "There is no percentage in bunts." Pop shook his head over that, but Red chuckled and said it was true for a wonderful hitter like Roy.) He also destroyed many short-term records, calling down on his performance tons of newspaper comment. However, his accomplishments were not entirely satisfying to him. He was gnawed by a nagging impatience—so much more to do, so much of the world to win for himself. He felt he had nothing of value yet to show for what he was accomplishing, and in his dreams he still sped over endless miles of monotonous rail toward something he desperately wanted. Memo, he sighed.

Pop couldn't believe his amazed eyes. "Beginner's luck," he muttered. Many a rookie had he seen come out blasting them in the breeze only to blow out in it with his tail between his legs. "The boy's having hisself a shower of luck. Usually they end up with a loud bust, so let's wait and see," he cautioned. Yet Roy continued on as before, by his own efforts winning many a ball game. The team too were doubtful he could go on like this, and doubtful of their doubt. They often discussed him when he wasn't around, compared him to Bump, and argued whether he was for the team or for himself. Olson said

he was for the team. Cal Baker insisted no. When asked for a
reason he could give none except to say, "Those big guys are
always for themselves. They are not for the little guy. If he
was for us why don't he come around more? Why does he
hang out so much by himself?" "Yeah," answered Olson, "but
we're outa the cellar now and who done that—the wind?
That's what counts, not if he sits around chewin' his ass with
us." Most of them agreed with Olson. Even if Roy wasn't actively interested in them he was a slick ballplayer and his example was having a good effect on them. In the course of three
weeks they had achieved a coordination of fielding, hitting
and pitching (Fowler and Schultz were whipping the opposi-
tion, and Hinkle and Hill, with an assist here and there from
McGee, were at least breaking even) such as they had not for
seasons known. Like a rusty locomotive pulling out of the
roundhouse for the first time in years, they ground down the
tracks, puffing, wheezing, belching smoke and shooting sparks.
And before long they had dislodged the Reds, who had been
living on the floor above them since the season started. When,
near the end of July, they caught up with the Cubs and,
twelve games behind the league-leading Pirates, took possession of sixth place, Pop rubbed his unbelieving eyes. The players thought now that the team is on its way up he will change
his crabby ways and give us a smile once in a while, but Pop
surprised them by growing sad, then actually melancholy at
the thought that but for his keeping Roy out of the line-up for
three weeks they might now be in first division.

A new day dawned on Knights Field. Looking down upon
the crowds from his office in the curious tower he inhabited
that rose on a slight tilt above the main entrance of the ball
park, Judge Goodwill Banner was at first made uneasy by
what he saw, for every rise in attendance would make it more
difficult for him to get Pop to give up the managerial reins, a
feat he hoped to accomplish by next season. However, the
sound of the merry, clicking turnstiles was more than he
could resist, so, although reluctantly, he put on extra help to
sweep the stands and ramps and dust off seats that hadn't
been sat in for years but were now almost always occupied.

The original Knights "fans," those who had come to see them suffer, were snowed under by this new breed here to cheer the boys on. Vegetables were abolished, even at the umps, and the crowd assisted the boys by working on the nerves of the visiting team with whammy words, catcalls, wisecracks, the kind of sustained jockeying that exhausted the rival pitchers and sometimes drove them out of the game. Now the old faithful were spouting steam—the Hungarian cook outcrowed a flock of healthy roosters, Gloria, the vestibule lady, acquired a better type customer, and Sadie Sutter gave up Dave Olson and now beat her hectic gong for the man of the hour. "Oh, you Roy," she screeched in her yolky cackle, "embracez moy," and the stands went wild with laughter. Victory was sweet, except for Otto Zipp, who no longer attended the games. Someone who met him waddling out of a subway station in Canarsie asked how come, but the dwarf only waved a pudgy palm in disgust. Nobody could guess what he meant by that and his honker lay dusty and silent on a shelf in the attic.

Even the weather was better, more temperate after the insulting early heat, with just enough rain to keep the grass a bright green and yet not pile up future double headers. Pop soon got into the spirit of winning, lowered the boom on his dismal thoughts, and showed he had a lighter side. He unwound the oily rags on his fingers and flushed them down the bowl. His hands healed and so did his heart, for even during the tensest struggle he looked a picture of contentment. And he was patient now, extraordinarily so, giving people the impression he had never been otherwise. Let a man bobble a hot one, opening the gate for a worrisome run, and he no longer jumped down his throat but wagged his head in silent sympathy. And sometimes he patted the offender on the surprised back. Formerly his strident yell was everywhere, on the field, in the dugout, clubhouse, players' duffel bags, also in their dreams, but now you never heard it because he no longer raised his voice, not even to Dizzy's cat when it wet on his shoes. Nobody teased him or played jokes on him any more and every tactic he ordered on the field was acted on, usually successfully. He was in the driver's seat. His muscles eased, the apoplexy went out of his system, and for his star fielder a love-light shone in his eyes.

As Roy's fame grew, Bump was gradually forgotten. The fans no longer confused talent with genius. When they cheered, they cheered for Roy Hobbs alone. People wondered about him, wanted news of his life and career. Reporters kept after him for information and Max Mercy, who for some reason felt he ought to know a lot more about Roy than he did, worked a sharp pickax over his shadow but gathered no usable nugget. All that was known was that Roy had first played ball on an orphan asylum team, that his father was a restless itinerant worker and his mother rumored to have been a burlesque actress. Stingy with facts, Roy wouldn't confirm a thing. Mercy sent a questionnaire to one thousand country papers in the West but there were no towns or cities that claimed the hero as their own.

It came about that Roy discovered Memo at one of the home games, though not, as formerly, sitting in the wives' box. Happening to meet her later in the hotel elevator, where they were pressed close together because of the crowd, he got off at her floor. Taking her arm he said, "Memo, I don't know what more I can do to show you how sorry I am about that time and tell you how I feel in my heart for you now."

But Memo stared at him through a veil of tears and said, "I'm strictly a dead man's girl."

He figured she had to be made to forget. If she would go out with him he would give her a good time at the night clubs and musical shows. But to do that and buy her some decent presents a guy needed cash, and on the meager three thousand he got he had beans—barely enough to pay his hotel bill. He considered selling his name for endorsements and approached a sporting goods concern but they paid him only fifty dollars. Elsewhere he got a suit and a pair of shoes but no cash. An agent he consulted advised him that the companies were suspicious he might be a flash in the pan. "Lay

low now," he advised. "By the end of the season, if you keep
on like you're going, they'll be ready to talk turkey, then we'll
put the heat on."

The newspaper boys supplied him with the cue for what to
do next. They pointed out how he filled up Knights Field; and
on the road, as soon as the Knights blew into town the game
was a sellout and the customers weren't exactly coming to see
a strip-tease. One of the columnists (not Mercy) wrote an open
letter to the Judge, saying it was a crying shame that a man as
good as Roy should get a rock-bottom salary when he was
playing better ball than some of the so-called stars who drew
up to a hundred grand. Roy was being gypped, the columnist
wrote, and he called on the Judge to burn up his old contract
and write a decent one instead. Why, even Bump had earned
thirty-five thousand. That decided Roy. He figured for himself a flat forty-five thousand for the rest of the season, plus a
guarantee of a percentage of the gate. He thought that if he
got this sort of arrangement and really piled in the dough, it
would do him no harm with Memo.

So one day after a long double header, both ends of which
the Knights finally took, Roy climbed the slippery stairs up
the tower to the Judge's office. The Judge's male secretary said
he was busy but Roy sat down to wait so they soon let him in.
The huge office was half dark, though lit on the double-
windowed street side (the Judge counted the customers going in and from the opposite window he counted them in the
stands) by the greenish evening sky. The Judge, a massive
rumpled figure in a large chair before an empty mahogany
desk, was wearing a black fedora with a round pot crown and
smoking, under grizzled eyebrows, a fat, black King Oscar I.
This always looked to be the same size in the rare newspaper
photographs of the Judge, and many people maintained it
was the same picture of him all the time, because it was a
known fact that the Judge never left the tower and no photographer ever got in. Roy noted a shellacked half of stuffed
shark, mounted on pine board on the faded green wall, and
a framed motto piece that read:

"Be it ever so humble, there is no place like home"
"Nihil nisi bonum"
"All is not gold that glitters"
"The dog is turned to his vomit again"

The floor of the office was, of course, slanted—because of the way the tower, an addition to the stadium structure, had settled—and to level it the Judge had a rug made a quarter of an inch thick on one side and a good inch on the other, but the few visitors to the place noticed they were not standing strictly on keel so they quickly sat down, which was what Roy did too. He had heard that the door on the opposite side of the room led up to the Judge's apartment. Pop said that though the Judge was a sluggish man with a buck it was a lavish place, and the bathroom had a television set and a sunken bathtub inlaid with mother of pearl. It was also rumored that he kept in there two enormous medicine cabinets loaded with laxatives and cathartics.

The Judge looked Roy over, struck a match under the top of his desk and drew a flame into his dead King Oscar. He blew out a smelly cloud of yellow smoke that hid his face a full minute.

"Nice of you to come," he rumbled. "To what good cause may I attribute this pleasant surprise?"

"I guess you know, Judge," said Roy, trying to make himself comfortable.

The Judge rumbled in his belly.

"I'm reminded of a case that came before me once. 'What do you plead?' I asked the defendant. 'I leave it to you, Judge, take your choice,' he responded. I did and sent him to the penitentiary for twenty years."

The Judge coughed and cackled over that. Roy regarded him closely. Everybody had warned him he was a slick trader, especially Pop who had poured out a hot earful about his partner. "He will peel the skin off of your behind without you knowing it if you don't watch out." That was what had happened to him, he said, and he went on to tell Roy that not long after the Judge had bought into the club—after working up Charlie Gulch, Pop's old-time partner, against him and getting him to sell out—he had taken advantage of some financial troubles Pop was having with his two brothers who owned a paint factory, and also because of his own sickness that kept him in a hospital under expensive medical care all winter long, and the Judge put the squeeze on him to get ten per cent of his stock for a pittance, which had then looked like a life saver because Pop was overdrawn at the bank and they wouldn't lend him another cent on his share of the Knights. Later, when he realized how much of a say in things he had lost to the Judge he kicked himself all over the lot, for the Judge, as Red Blow had told Roy, drummed up all sorts of player deals to turn a buck, and though Pop fought him on these, he showed on paper that they were losing money at the gate and this was the only way to cover their losses and keep the team going, so Pop had to give in on most of them although he had fought the Judge to a standstill when he wanted to sell Bump and would do the same if he tried it with Roy. It beat Pop where Goodie Banner, as he called him, had got the money to operate with in the first place. He had known him years ago as an impoverished shyster but once he got on the bench his fortunes improved. Yet his salary was only twelve thousand a year for the three years he had served so he must have had backing to buy into the club and later—the dratted nerve of the worm—to offer to buy Pop out altogether. He said he wouldn't exactly call the Judge a thief but he wouldn't exactly call him honest either. For instance, the Judge had once casually asked Pop if he wanted to go in for any sideline activities over what they had already contracted for, meaning concessions and the like. Pop said no, he was only interested in the game end of it, so the Judge drew up an agreement offering Pop five per cent of all receipts from enterprises initiated by himself, and he began to rent the place to miniature auto races, meetings, conventions, and dog races, making all sorts of money for himself, while things necessary to the team were being neglected. "When triple talk is invented," Pop said bitterly, "he will own the copyright."

It was dark in the office but the Judge made no attempt to

switch on the lights. He sat there motionless, a lumpy figure aglow around the edges against the darkening sky.

Roy thought he better get down to brass tacks. "Well, Judge," he said, shifting in his chair, "I thought you might be expecting me to drop in and see you. You know what I am doing to the ball both here and on the road. The papers have been writing that you might be considering a new contract for me."

The Judge blew at the ash of his cigar.

Roy grew restless. "I figure forty-five thousand is a fair price for my work. That's only ten grand more than Bump was getting—and you can subtract off the three thousand in my contract now." This last was an afterthought and he had decided to leave out the percentage of the gate till next year.

The Judge rumbled, Roy couldn't tell if it was in his throat or belly.

"I was thinking of Olaf Jespersen." The Judge's eyes took on a faraway, slightly glazed look. "He was a farmer I knew in my youth—terrible life. Yet as farmers often do, he managed to live comfortably because he owned a plot of ground with a house on it and had come into possession of an extraordinary cow, Sieglinde. She was a splendid animal with soft and silky front and well-shaped hooves. Her milk yield was some nine gallons per diem, altogether exceptional. In a word she was a superior creature and had the nicest ways with children—her own of course; but Olaf was deeply disturbed by an ugly skin discoloration that ran across her rump. For a long while he had been eyeing Gussie, an albino cow of his neighbor down the road. One day he approached the man and asked if Gussie was for sale. The neighbor said yes, frankly admitting she gave very little milk although she consumed more than her share of fodder. Olaf said he was willing to trade Sieglinde for her and the neighbor readily agreed. Olaf went back for the cow but on the way to the neighbor's she stepped into a rut in the road and keeled over as if struck dead. Olaf suffered a heart attack. Thus they were found but Sieglinde recovered and became, before very long, her splendid nine-gallon self, whereas Olaf was incapacitated for the remainder of his days.

I often drove past his place and saw him sitting on the moldy front porch, a doddering cripple starving to death with his tubercular albino cow."

Roy worked the fable around in his mind and got the point. It was not an impressive argument: be satisfied with what you have, and he said so to the Judge.

" 'The love of money is the root of all evil,' " intoned the Judge.

"I do not love it, Judge. I have not been near enough to it to build up any affection to speak of."

"Think, on the one hand, of the almost indigent Abraham Lincoln, and on the other of Judas Iscariot. What I am saying is that emphasis upon money will pervert your values. One cannot begin to imagine how ones' life may alter for the worse under the impetus of wealth-seeking."

Roy saw how the land lay. "I will drop it to thirty-five thousand, the same as Bump, but not a cent less."

The Judge struck a match, throwing shadows on the wall. It was now night. He sucked a flame into his cigar. It went in like a slug, out like a moth—in and out, then forever in and the match was out. The cigar glowed, the Judge blew out a black fog of smoke, then they were once more in the dark.

Lights on, you stingy bastard, Roy thought.

"Pardon the absence of light," the Judge said, almost making him jump. "As a youngster I was frightened of the dark—used to wake up sobbing in it, as if it were water and I were drowning—but you will observe that I have disciplined myself so thoroughly against that fear, that I much prefer a dark to a lit room, and water is my favorite beverage. Will you have some?"

"No."

"There is in the darkness a unity, if you will, that cannot be achieved in any other environment, a blending of self with what the self perceives, an exquisite mystical experience. I intend some day to write a disquisition, 'On the Harmony of Darkness; Can Evil Exist in Harmony?' It may profit you to ponder the question."

"All I know about the dark is that you can't see in it."

"A pure canard. You know you can."

"Not good enough."

"You see me, don't you?"

"Maybe I do and maybe I don't."

"What do you mean?"

"I see somebody but I am not sure if it is you or a guy who sneaked in and took your chair."

The cigar glowed just enough to light up the Judge's rubbery lips. It was him all right.

"Twenty-five thousand," Roy said in a low voice. "Ten less than Bump."

The cigar lit for a long pull then went out. Its smell was giving Roy a headache. The Judge was silent so long Roy wasn't sure he would ever hear from him again. He wasn't even sure he was there any more but then he thought yes he is, I can smell him. He is here in the dark and if I come back tomorrow he will still be here and also the year after that.

" 'He that maketh haste to be rich shall not be innocent,' " spoke the Judge.

"Judge," said Roy, "I am thirty-four, going on thirty-five. That's not haste, that's downright slow."

"I hear that you bet money on horse races?"

"In moderation, not more than a deuce on the daily double."

"Avoid gambling like a plague. It will cause your downfall. And stay away from loose ladies. 'Put a knife to thy throat if thou be a man given to appetite.' "

Roy could hear him open a drawer and take something out. Handing it to him, he lit a match over it and Roy read: "The Curse of Venereal Disease."

He tossed the pamphlet on the desk.

"Yes or no?" he said.

"Yes or no what?" The Judge's voice was edged with anger.

"Fifteen thousand."

The Judge rose. "I shall have to ask you to fulfill the obligations of your contract."

Roy got up. "I wouldn't exactly say you were building up my good will for next year."

"I have learned to let the future take care of itself."

The Judge took some other papers out of the drawer. "I presume these are your signatures?" He scratched up another match.

"That's right."

"The first acknowledging the receipt of two uniforms and sundry articles?"

"Right."

"And the second indicating the receipt of a third uniform?"

"That's what it says."

"You were entitled to only two. I understand that some of the other clubs issue four, but that is an extravagance. Here, therefore, is a bill to the amount of fifty-one dollars for property destroyed. Will you remit or shall I deduct the sum from your next check?"

"I didn't destroy them, Bump did."

"They were your responsibility."

Roy picked up the receipts and bill and tore them to pieces. He did the same with the VD pamphlet, then blew the whole business over the judge's head. The scraps of paper fluttered down like snow on his round hat.

"The interview is ended," snapped the Judge. He scratched up a match and with it led Roy to the stairs. He stood on the landing, his oily shadow ripping down the steps as Roy descended.

"Mr. Hobbs."

Roy stopped.

"Resist all evil—"

The match sputtered and went out. Roy went the rest of the way down in the pitch black.

"How'd you make out, kid?"

It was Max Mercy lurking under a foggy street lamp at the corner. He had tailed Roy from the dressing room and had spent a frustrated hour thinking I know the guy but who is he? It was on the tip of his tongue but he couldn't spit it out. He saw the face as he thought he had seen it before somewhere, but what team, where, in what league, and doing what that caused him to be remembered? The mystery was like an itch. The more he scratched the more he drew his own blood. At times the situation infuriated him. Once he dreamed he had the big s.o.b. by the throat and was forcing him to talk. Then he told the world Mercy knew.

The sight of the columnist did not calm Roy as he came out of the tower. Why does he haunt me? He thought he knew what Max sensed and he knew that he didn't want him to know. I don't want his dirty eyes peeking into my past. What luck for me that I had Sam's wallet in my pocket that night, and they wrote down his name. This creep will never find that out, or anything else about me unless I tell him, and the only time I'll do that is when I am dead.

"Listen, El Smearo," he said, "why don't you stay home in bed?"

Max laughed hollowly.

"Who has ever seen the like of it?" he said, trying to put some warmth into his voice. "Here's the public following everything a man does with their tongue hanging out and all he gives out with is little balls of nothing. What are you hiding? If it was something serious you woulda been caught long ago—your picture has been in the papers every day for weeks."

"I ain't hiding a thing."

"Who says you are? But what's all the mystery about? Where were you born? Why'd you stay out of the game so long? What was your life like before this? My paper will guarantee you five grand in cash for five three-thousand word articles on your past life. I'll help you write them. What do you say?"

"I say no. My life is my own business."

"Think of your public."

"All they're entitled to is to pay a buck and watch me play."

"Answer me this—is it true you once tried out with another major league team?"

"I got nothing to say."

"Then you don't deny it?"

"I got nothing to say."

"Were you once an acrobat or something in a circus?"

"Same answer as before."

Max scratched in his mustache. "Hobbs, the man nobody knows. Say, kid, you're not doing it on purpose, are you?"

"What do you mean?"

"To raise speculation and get publicity?"

"Nuts I am."

"I don't catch. You're a public figure. You got to give the fans something once in a while to keep up their good will to you."

Roy thought a second. "Okay, tell them my cheapskate of a boss has turned me down flat on a raise and I am still his slave for a lousy three thousand bucks."

Max wrote a hasty note in his black book.

"Listen, Roy, let's you and I have a little chin-chin. You'll like me better once you get to know me. Have you had your supper yet?"

"No."

"Then have a steak with me at the Pot of Fire. Know the place?"

"I have never been there."

"It's a night club with a nice girlie show. All the hot-shot celebrities like yourself hang out there. They have a good kitchen and a first class bar."

"Okay with me." He was in a mood for something for nothing.

In the cab Max said, "You know, I sometimes get the funny feeling that I have met you some place before. Is that right?"

Roy thrust his head forward. "Where?"

Max contemplated his eyes and solid chin.

"It musta been somebody else."

At the entrance to the Pot of Fire a beggar accosted them.

"Jesus," Max said, "can't I ever get rid of you?"

"All I ask is a buck."

"Go to hell."

The beggar was hurt. "You'll get yours," he said.

"You'll get yours," said Max. "I'll call a cop."

"You'll get yours," the beggar said. "You too," he said to Roy and spat on the sidewalk.

"Friend of yours?" Roy asked as they went down the stairs into the nightspot.

Max's face was inflamed. "I can't get rid of that scurvy bastard. Picks this place to hang around and they can't flush him outa here."

Inside the club the audience was in an uproar. The show was on and some screaming, half-naked girls were being chased by masked devils with tin pitchforks. Then the lights went out and the devils ran around poking at the customers. Roy was jabbed in the rear end. He grabbed at the devil but missed, then he heard a giggle and realized it was a girl. He grabbed for her again but the devil jabbed him and ran. When the lights went on all the girls and devils were gone. The customers guffawed and applauded.

"Come on," Max said.

The captain had recognized him and was beckoning them to a ringside table. Roy sat down. Max looked around and bounced up.

"See a party I know. Be right back."

The band struck up a number and the chorus wriggled out amid weaving spotlights for the finale. They were wearing red spangled briefs and brassieres and looked so pretty that Roy felt lonely.

Max was back.

"We're changing tables. Gus Sands wants us with him."

"Who's he?"

Max looked to see if Roy was kidding.

"You don't know Gus Sands?"

"Never heard of him."

"What d'ye read, the Podunk Pipsqueak? They call him the Supreme Bookie, he nets at least ten million a year. Awfully nice guy and he will give you the silk shirt off his back. Also somebody you know is with him."

"Who's that?"

"Memo Paris."

Roy got up. What's she doing here? He followed Max across the floor to Gus Sands's table. Memo was sitting there alone in a black strapless gown and wearing her hair up. The sight of her, so beautiful, hit him hard. He had been picturing her alone in her room nights. She said hello evasively. At first he thought she was still sore at him, but then he heard voices coming from the floor at the other side of the table and understood that was where she was looking.

A surprising semi-bald dome rose up above the table and Roy found himself staring into a pair of strange eyes, a mournful blue one and the other glowing weirdly golden. His scalp prickled as the bookie, a long stretch of bone, rose to his full height. The angle at which the spotlight had caught his glass eye, lighting it like a Christmas tree, changed, and the eye became just a ball of ice.

"S'matter, Gus?" Mercy said.

"Memo lost two bits." His voice was sugar soft. "Find it yet?" he asked the waiter, still down on all fours.

"Not yet, sir." He got up. "No, sir."

"Forget it." Sands flicked a deft fiver into the man's loose fist.

He shook hands with Roy. "Glad to meet you, slugger. Whyn't you sit down?"

"Tough luck, babyface," he said, giving Memo a smile. Roy sat down facing her but she barely glanced at him. Though dressed up, she was not entirely herself. The blue eye shadow she had on could not hide the dark circles around her eyes and she looked tired. Her chair was close to Gus's. Once he chucked her under the chin and she giggled. It sickened Roy because it didn't make sense.

The busboy cleaned up the remains of two lobsters. Gus slipped him a fiver.

"Nice kid," he said softly. Reaching for the menu, he handed it to Roy.

Roy read it and although he was hungry couldn't concentrate on food. What did this glass-eye bookie, a good fifty years if not more, mean to a lively girl like Memo, a girl who was, after all, just out of mourning for a young fellow like Bump? Over the top of the menu he noticed Gus's soft-boned hands and the thick, yellow-nailed fingers. He had pouches under both the good and fake eyes, and though he smiled a lot, his expression was melancholy. Roy disliked him right off. There was something wormy about him. He belonged in the dark with the Judge. Let them both haunt themselves there.

"Order, guys," Gus said.

Roy did just to have something to do.

The captain came over and asked was everything all right.

"Check and double check." Gus pressed two folded fives into his palm. Roy didn't like the way he threw out the bucks. He thought of the raise he didn't get and felt bad about it.

"Lemme buy you a drink, slugger," Gus said, pointing to his own Scotch.

"No, thanks."

"Clean living, eh?"

"The eyes," Roy said, pointing to his. "Got to keep 'em clear."

Gus smiled. "Nice goin', slugger."

"He needs a drink," Max said. "The Judge gave him nix on a raise."

Roy could have bopped him for telling it in front of Memo.

Gus was interested.

"Y'mean he didn't pull out his pouch and shake you out some rusty two-dollar gold pieces?"

Everybody laughed but Roy.

"I see you met him," Max said.

Gus winked the glass eye. "We had some dealings."

"How'd you make out?"

"No evidence. We were acquitted." He chuckled softly.

Max made a note in his book.

"Don't write that, Max," said Gus.

Max quickly tore out the page. "Whatever you say, Gus."

Gus beamed. He turned to Roy. "How'd it go today, slugger?"

"Fine," Roy said.

"He got five for five in the first, and four hits in the night-cap," Max explained.

"Say, what d'ye know?" Gus whistled softly. "That'll cost me a pretty penny." He focused his good eye on Roy. "I was betting against you today, slugger."

"You mean the Knights?"

"No, just you."

"Didn't know you bet on any special player."

"On anybody or anything. We bet on strikes, balls, hits, runs, innings, and full games. If a good team plays a lousy team we will bet on the spread of runs. We cover anything anyone wants to bet on. Once in a Series game I bet a hundred grand on three pitched balls."

"How'd you make out on that?"

"Guess."

"I guess you didn't."

"Right, I didn't." Gus chuckled. "But it don't matter. The next week I ruined the guy in a different deal. Sometimes we win, sometimes we don't but the percentage is for us. Today we lost on you, some other time we will clean up double."

"How'll you do that?"

"When you are not hitting so good."

"How'll you know when to bet on that?"

Gus pointed to his glass eye. "The Magic Eye," he said. "It sees everything and tells me."

The steaks came and Roy cut into his.

"Wanna see how it works, slugger? Let's you and I bet on something."

"I got nothing I want to bet on," Roy said, his mouth full of meat and potatoes.

"Bet on any old thing and I will come up with the opposite even though your luck is running high now."

"It's a helluva lot more than luck."

"I will bet anyway."

Memo looked interested. Roy decided to take a chance.

"How about that I will get four hits in tomorrow's game?"

Gus paused. "Don't bet on baseball now," he said. "Bet on something we can settle here."

"Well, you pick it and I'll bet against you."

"Done," said Gus. "Tell you what, see the bar over by the entrance?"

Roy nodded.

"We will bet on the next order. You see Harry there, don't you? He's just resting now. In a minute somebody's gonna order drinks and Harry will make them. We'll wait till a waiter goes over and gives him an order—any one of them in the joint any time you say, so nobody thinks it's rigged. Then I will name you one of the drinks that will go on the waiter's tray, before Harry makes them. If there is only one drink there I will have to name it exactly—for a grand."

Roy hesitated. "Make it a hundred."

Max tittered.

"A 'C' it is," Gus said. "Say when."

"Now."

Gus shut his eyes and rubbed his brow with his left hand. "One of the drinks on the tray will be a Pink Lady."

The way they were seated everybody but Mercy could see the bar, so he turned his chair around to watch.

"Your steak might get cold, Max."

"This I got to see."

Memo looked on, amused.

They waited a minute, then a waiter went over to the bar and said something to the bartender. Harry nodded and turned around for a bottle, but they couldn't see what he was mixing because a customer was standing in front of him. When he left, Roy saw a tall pink drink standing on the counter. He felt sick but then he thought maybe it's a sloe gin fizz. Harry poured a Scotch and soda for the same tray and the waiter came for it.

As he passed by, Gus called him over to the table.

"What is that red drink that you have got there?"

"This one?" said the waiter. "A Pink Lady, Mr. Sands."

Gus slipped him a fiver.

Everybody laughed.

"Nothing to it," said Gus.

"It never fails." Max had turned his chair and was eating. "Nice work, Gus."

Gus beamed. Memo patted his hand. Roy felt annoyed.

"That's a hundred," he said.

"It was a freak win," Gus said, "so we will write it off."

"No, I owe it to you but give me a chance to win it back."

He thought Memo was mocking him and it made him stubborn.

"Anything you say," Gus shrugged.

"You can say it," said Roy. "I'll cover you for two hundred."

Gus concentrated a minute. Everybody watched him, Roy tensely. It wasn't the money he was afraid of. He wanted to win in front of Memo.

"Let's play on some kind of a number," Gus said.

"What kind?"

"Of the amount of bills you are carrying on you."

A slow flush crept up Roy's cheeks.

"I will bet I can guess by one buck either way how much you have got on you now," Gus said.

"You're on." Roy's voice was husky.

Gus covered his good eye and pretended he was a mind reader trying to fathom the number. His glass eye stared unblinking.

"Ten bucks," he announced.

Roy's throat went dry. He drew his wallet out of his pants pocket. Max took it from him and loudly counted up a five and four single dollar bills. "Nine." He slapped the table and guffawed.

"Wonderful," Memo murmured.

"Three hundred I owe to you."

"Don't mention it."

"It was a bet. Will you take my IOU?"

"Wanna try again?"

"Sure."

"You'll lose your panties," Max warned.

"On what?" Gus asked.

Roy thought. "What about another number?"

"Righto. What kind?"

"I'll pick out a number from one to ten. You tell me what it is."

Gus considered. "For the three hundred?"

"Yes."

"Okay."

"Do you want me to write the number?"

"Keep it in your head."

"Go ahead."

"Got the number?"

"I have it."

Again Gus eclipsed his good eye and took a slow breath. He made it seem like a kind of magic he was doing. Memo was fascinated.

"Deuce," Gus quickly announced.

Roy felt as if he had been struck on the conk. He considered lying but knew they could tell if he did.

"That's right, how'd you do it?" He felt foolish.

Gus winked.

Max was all but coming apart with laughter. Memo looked away.

Gus swallowed his Scotch. "Two is a magic number," he crooned at Memo. "Two makes the world go around." She smiled slightly, watching Roy.

He tried to eat but felt numbed.

Max just couldn't stop cackling. Roy felt like busting him one in the snoot.

Gus put his long arm around Memo's bare shoulders. "I have lots of luck, don't I, babyface?"

She nodded and sipped her drink.

The lights went on. The m.c. bobbed up from a table he had been sitting at and went into his routine.

"Six hundred I owe to you," Roy said, throwing Max into another whoop of laughter.

"Forget it, slugger. Maybe some day you might be able to do me a favor."

They were all suddenly silent.

"What kind of favor?" Roy asked.

"When I am down and out you can buy me a cup o' coffee."

They laughed, except Roy.

"I'll pay you now." He left the table and disappeared.

In a few minutes he returned with a white tablecloth over his arm.

Roy flapped out the cloth and one of the spotlights happened to catch it in the air. It turned red, then gold.

"What's going on?" Max said.

Roy whisked the cloth over Gus's head.

"The first installment."

He grabbed the bookie's nose and yanked. A stream of silver dollars clattered into his plate.

Gus stared at the money. Memo looked at Roy in intense surprise.

People at the nearby tables turned to see what was going on. Those in the rear craned and got up. The m.c. gave up his jokes and waved both spots to Roy.

"For Pete's sake, sit down," Max hissed.

Roy rippled the green cloth in front of Max's face and dragged out of his astonished mouth a dead herring.

Everybody in the place applauded.

From Memo's bosom, he plucked a duck egg.

Gus got red in the face. Roy grabbed his beak again and twisted—it shed more cartwheels.

"Second installment."

"What the hell is this?" Gus sputtered.

The color wheels spun. Roy turned purple, red, and yellow. From the glum Mercy's pocket he extracted a long salami. Gus's ears ran a third installment of silver. A whirl of the cloth and a white bunny hopped out of Memo's purse. From Max's size sixteen shirt collar, he teased out a pig's tail.

As the customers howled, Max pulled out his black book and furiously scribbled in it. Gus's blue, depressed eye hunted around for a way out but his glass one gleamed like a lamp in a graveyard. And Memo laughed and laughed till the tears streamed down her cheeks.

Maybe I might break my back
while I am at it," Roy spoke into the microphone at home
plate before a hushed sellout crowd jampacked into Knights
Field, "but I will do my best—the best I am able—to be the
greatest there ever was in the game.

"I thank you." He finished with a gulp that echoed like an
electric hiccup through the loudspeakers and sat down, not
quite happy with himself despite the celebration, because
when called on to speak he had meant to begin with a joke,
then thank them for their favor and say what a good team the
Knights were and how he enjoyed working for Pop Fisher,
but it had come out this other way. On the other hand, so
what the hell if they knew what was on his mind?

It was "Roy Hobbs Day," that had been in the making
since two weeks ago, when Max Mercy printed in his column:
"Roy Hobbs, El Swatto, has been ixnayed on a pay raise.
Trying to kill the bird that lays the golden baseball, Judge?"
A grass roots movement developed among the loyal fans to
put the Judge to shame (if possible) and they had quickly
arranged a Day for Roy, which was held after the Knights
had bounced into third place, following a night game win
over the Phils, who now led them by only four games, themselves two behind the first-place Pirates.

The whole thing was kept a surprise, and after batting
practice was over on this particular Saturday afternoon in
early August, the right field gate had swung open and a
whole caravan of cars, led by a limousine full of officials and
American Legionnaires, and followed by a gorgeous, under-
slung white Mercedes-Benz and a lumbering warehouse van
loaded with stuff, drove in and slowly circled the field to the
music of a band playing "Yankee Doodle," while the crowd
cheered shrilly. Someone then tapped Roy and said it was
all for him.

"Who, me?" he said, rising . . .

When he had made his speech and retired to the dugout,
after a quick, unbelieving glance at the mountain of gifts they

were unpacking for him, the fans sat back in frozen silence, some quickly crossing their fingers, some spitting over their left shoulders, onto the steps so they wouldn't get anyone wet, almost all hoping he had not jinxed himself forever by saying what he had said. "The best there ever was in the game" might tempt the wrath of some mighty powerful ghosts. But they quickly recovered from the shock of his audacity and clapped up a thick thunder of applause.

It was everyman's party and they were determined to enjoy it. No one knew exactly who had supplied the big dough, but the loyal everyday fans had contributed all sorts of small change and single bucks to buy enough merchandise to furnish a fair-sized general store. When everything was unloaded from the van, Roy posed in front of it, fiddling with a gadget or two for the benefit of the photographers, though he later tipped off Dizzy to sell whatever he could to whoever had the cash. Mercy himself counted two television sets, a baby tractor, five hundred feet of pink plastic garden hose, a nanny goat, lifetime pass to the Paramount, one dozen hand-painted neckties offering different views of the Grand Canyon, six aluminum traveling cases, and a credit for seventy-five taxi rides in Philadelphia. Also three hundred pounds of a New Jersey brand Swiss cheese, a set of andirons and tongs, forty gallons of pistachio ice cream, six crates of lemons, a frozen side of hog, hunting knife, bearskin rug, snowshoes, four burner electric range, deed to a lot in Florida, twelve pairs of monogrammed blue shorts, movie camera and projector, a Chris-Craft motor boat—and, because everybody thought the Judge (unashamedly looking on from his window in the tower) was too cheap to live—a certified check for thirty-six hundred dollars. Although the committee had tried to keep out all oddball contributions, a few slipped in, including a smelly package of Limburger cheese, one human skull, bundle of comic books, can of rat exterminator, and a package of dull razor blades, this last with a card attached in the crabbed handwriting of Otto Zipp: "Here, cut your throat," but Roy did not take it to heart.

When he was told, to his amazement, that the Mercedes-

Benz was his too, he could only say, "This is the happiest day of my life." Getting in, he drove around the park to the frenzied waving and whistling of the fans and whirring of movie cameras. The gleaming white job was light to the touch of hand and foot and he felt he could float off in it over the stadium wall. But he stopped before Memo's box and asked if she would go with him for a jaunt after the game, to which she, lowering her eyes, replied she was agreeable.

Memo said she longed to see the ocean so they drove over the bridge and down into Long Island toward Jones Beach, stopping when she was hungry, for charcoal-broiled steaks at a roadside tavern. Afterwards it was night, lit up by a full moon swimming in lemon juice, but at intervals eclipsed by rain clouds that gathered in dark blots and shuttered the yellow light off the fields and tree tops.

She spoke little, once remarking it looked like rain.

He didn't answer. Though he had started off riding high (he had paid back the patrons of his Day by walloping a homer that drove in the winning run) he now felt somewhat heavy hearted. For the past two weeks he had been seeing Memo most every day but had made little headway. There were times when he thought yes, I am on my way up in her affections, but no sooner did he think that when something she did or said, or didn't do or didn't say, made him think no, I am not. It was a confusing proposition to want a girl you'd already had and couldn't get because you had; a situation common in his life, of having first and then wanting what he had had, as if he hadn't had it but just heard about it, and it had, in the hearing, aroused his appetite. He even wished he had not had her that night, and wondered—say he hadn't—whether he would be in the least interested in her today.

In another sense it wasn't a bad evening. He was with her, at least, and they were traveling together, relaxed, to the ocean. He didn't exactly know where it was and though he liked the water, tonight he did not much care if they never

came to it. He felt contentment in moving. It rested him by
cutting down the inside motion—that which got him nowhere,
which was where he was and she was not, or where his ambitions were and he was chasing after. Sometimes he wished he
had no ambitions—often wondered where they had come
from in his life, because he remembered how satisfied he had
been as a youngster, and that with the little he had had—a
dog, a stick, an aloneness he loved (which did not bleed him
like his later loneliness), and he wished he could have lived
longer in his boyhood. This was an old thought with him.

Hoping for a better fate in the future he stepped on the
gas and was at once seized by an uneasy fear they were being
followed. Since the mirror showed nobody behind them, he
wondered at his suspicions and then recalled a black sedan
that had been on their tail, he thought, all the way down
from the city, only they had lost it a while back in turning
off the highway. Yet he continued to watch in the mirror,
though it showed only the lifeless moonlit road.

Memo said Jones Beach was too far and told him to stop
the next time they came to a brook or pond where she could
take off her shoes and go wading in the water. When he spied
a small stream running along the edge of a wooded section
between two towns, he slowed down. They parked across the
shoulder of the asphalt and got out but as they crossed this
wooden bridge to the grassy side of the stream, they were
confronted by a sign: DANGER. POLLUTED WATER. NO
SWIMMING. Roy was all for getting into the car to find another place, but Memo said no, they could watch the water
from the bridge. She lit a cigarette, all in light, her hair and
green summer dress, and her naked legs and even the slave
bracelet around her left ankle gleaming in the light of the
moon. Smoking, she watched the water flowing under the
bridge, its movement reflected on her face.

After a while, seeing how silent she was, Roy said, "I bet
I got enough today to furnish a house."

Memo said, "Bump was coming up for a Day just before he
died."

He felt anger rise in his heart and asked coldly, "Well, Memo, what did he have that I haven't got?" He stood to his full height, strong and handsome.

Without looking at him she spoke Bump's name thoughtfully, then shook her head to snap out of it, as if it didn't pay to be thoughtful about Bump. "Oh," she answered, "he was carefree and full of life. He did the craziest things and always kept everybody in stitches. Even when he played ball, there was something carefree and playful about it. Maybe he went all the way after a fly ball or maybe he didn't, but once he made up his mind to catch it, it was exciting how he ran and exciting how he caught it. He made you think you had been wishing for a thing to happen for a long time and then he made it happen. And the same with his hitting. When you catch one, Roy, or go up to hit, everybody knows beforehand that it will land up in your glove, or be a hit. You work at it so—sometimes you even look desperate—but to him it was a playful game and so was his life. Nobody could ever tell what would happen next with Bump, and that was the wonderful thing of it."

Roy thought this is how she sees him now that he is dead. She forgets how hopping sore she was at him after that time in bed with me.

But Bump was dead, he thought, dead and buried in his new box, an inescapable six feet under, so he subtly changed the subject to Gus.

"Gus?" Memo said. At first her face was expressionless. "Oh, he's just like a daddy to me."

He asked her in what way but she laughed and said, "That was a funny business you did with him in the Pot of Fire. How did you do all those tricks?"

"Easy. They had a magic act all laid out to go on. I walked into the guy's dressing room and when they saw who I was they let me use his stuff just for the laughs."

"Who showed you how to use it?"

"Nobody. I have done some different things in my time, Memo."

"Such as what other ones?"

"You name it, I did it."

"What you did to Max was a scream."

A black cloud rolled like a slow wave across the moon.

"It's so strange," she murmured, looking at the moving water.

"What is?"

For a time she didn't speak, then she sighed and said she meant her life. "It's been strange ever since I can remember except for a year or two—mostly the part with Bump. That was the good part only it didn't last very long, not much of the good part ever did. When I was little my daddy walked out on us and I don't ever remember being happy again till the time I got to go to Hollywood when I was nineteen."

He waited.

"I won a beauty contest where they picked a winner from each state and she was sent to Hollywood to be a starlet. For a few weeks I felt like the Queen of the May, then they took a screen test and though I had the looks and figure my test did not come out so good in acting and they practically told me to go home. I couldn't stand the thought of that so I stayed there for three more years, doing night club work and going to an acting school besides, hoping that I would some day be a good enough actress but it didn't take. I knew what I was supposed to do but I couldn't make myself, in my thoughts, into somebody else. You're supposed to forget who you are but I couldn't. Then I came east and had some more bad times after my mother died, till I met Bump."

He thought she would cry but she didn't.

Memo watched the pebbles in the flowing water. "After Bump I realized I could never be happy any more."

"How do you know that?" Roy asked slowly.

"Oh, I know. I can tell from the way I feel. Sometimes in the morning I never want to wake up."

He felt a dreary emptiness at her words.

"What about yourself?" she asked, wanting to change the subject.

"What about me?" he said gloomily.

"Max says you are sort of a mystery."

"Max is a jerk. My past life is nobody's business."

"What was it like?"

"Like yours, for years I took it on the chin." He sounded as if he had caught a cold, took out his handkerchief and blew his nose.

"What happened?"

He wanted to tell her everything, match her story and go her a couple better but couldn't bring himself to. It wasn't, he thought, that he was afraid to tell her what had happened to him that first time (though the thought of doing that raised a hot blush on his pan, for he had never told anybody about it yet), but about the miserable years after that, when everything, everything he tried somehow went to pot as if that was its destiny in the first place, a thing he couldn't understand.

"What happened?" she asked again.

"The hell with it," he said.

"I told you about myself."

He watched the water.

"I have knocked around a lot and been hard hurt in plenty of ways," he said huskily. "There were times I thought I would never get anywhere and it made me eat my guts, but all that is gone now. I know I have the stuff and will get there."

"Get where?"

"Where I am going. Where I will be the champ and have what goes with it."

She drew back but he had caught her arm and tugged her to him.

"Don't."

"You got to live, Memo."

He trapped her lips, tasting of lemon drops, kissing hard. Happening to open his eyes, he saw her staring at him in the middle of the kiss. Shutting them, he dived deep down again. Then she caught his passion, opened her mouth for his tongue and went limp around the knees.

They swayed together and he turned his hand and slipped

it through the top of her dress into her loose brassiere, cupping her warm small breast in his palm.

Her legs stiffened. She pushed at him, sobbing, "Don't touch it."

He was slow to react.

She wailed, "Don't, please don't."

He pulled his hand out, angrily disappointed.

She was crying now, rubbing her hand across her bosom. "Did I hurt you?"

"Yes."

"How the hell did I do that? I was nice with it."

"It's sick," she wept.

He felt like he had had an icy shave and haircut. "Who says so?"

"It hurts. I know."

She could be lying, only her eyes were crisscrossed with fear and her arms goosefleshed.

"Did you go to a doctor?"

"I don't like them."

"You ought to go."

Memo ran off the bridge. He followed her to the car. She sat at the wheel and started the motor. Figuring she would calm down quicker this way he let her.

She backed the car onto the road and drove off. The moon sank into an enormous cloud-sea. Memo sped along the asphalt and turned at a fork down a hard dirt road.

"Put on the lights."

"I like it dark." Her white arms were stiff on the wheel.

He knew she didn't but figured she was still nervous.

Dripping dark cloud spray, the moon bobbed up and flooded the road ahead with bright light. Memo pressed her foot on the gas.

A thundering wind beat across his skull. Let her, he thought. Whatever she has got on her mind, let her get it off, especially if it is still Bump.

He thought about what she had said on the bridge about never being happy again and wondered what it meant. In a

way he was tired of her—she was too complicated—but in a
different way he desired her more than ever. He could not
decide what to say or do next. Maybe wait, but he didn't
want to any more. Yet what else was there to do?

The white moonlight shot through a stretch of woods
ahead. He found himself wishing he could go back somewhere, go home, wherever that was. As he was thinking this,
he looked up and saw in the moonlight a boy coming out of
the woods, followed by his dog. Squinting through the wind-
shield, he was unable to tell if the kid was an illusion thrown
forth by the trees or someone really alive. After fifteen seconds he was still there. Roy yelled to Memo to slow down in
case he wanted to cross the road. Instead, the car shot forward so fast the woods blurred, the trees racing along like
shadows in weak light, then skipping into black and white,
finally all black and the moon was gone.

"Lights!"

She sat there stiffly so he reached over and switched them
on.

As the road flared up, Memo screamed and tugged at the
wheel. He felt a thud and his heart sickened. It was a full
minute before he realized they hadn't stopped.

"For Christ sake, stop—we hit somebody."

"No." Her face was bloodless.

He reached for the brake.

"Don't, it was just something on the road."

"I heard somebody groan."

"That was yourself."

He couldn't remember that he had.

"I want to go back and see."

"If you do, the cops will get us."

"What cops?"

"They have been after us since we started. I've been doing
ninety."

He looked back and saw a black car with dimmed head-
lights speeding after them.

"Turn at the next bend," he ordered her, "and I will take
over."

They were nearer to the Sound than he had suspected, and when a white pea-souper crawled in off the water Roy headed into it. Though the Mercedes showed no lights the whiteness of it was enough to keep it in the sedan's eye, so he welcomed the fog and within it easily ditched those who chased them.

On the way back he attempted to find the road along the woods to see if they had hit somebody. Memo had little patience with him. She was sure, despite Roy's insistence of an outside groan, that they had hit a rock or log in the road. If they went back the cops might be laying for them and they'd be arrested, which would cause no end of trouble.

He said he was going back anyway.

Roy had the feeling that the sedan was still at his shoulder —he could see it wasn't—as he tried to locate the bridge and then the road along the woods. He wasn't convinced they had not hit somebody and if he could do anything for the kid, even this late, he wanted to. So he turned the lights on bright, illuminating the swirling fog, and as they went by the fog-shrouded woods—he couldn't be sure it was the right woods —he searched the road intently for signs of a body or its blood but found nothing. Memo dozed off but was awakened when Roy, paying no heed to what lay ahead, ran off a low embankment, crashing the car into a tree. Though shaken up, neither of them was much hurt. Roy had a black eye and Memo bruised her sick breast. The car was a wreck.

Helping Memo out of a cab that same morning before dawn, Roy glanced into the hotel lobby just as Pop Fisher bounced up out of a couch and came charging at them like a run-away trolley. Memo said to run, so they raced down the street and ducked into the hotel by the side entrance, but they were barely to the stairs when Pop, who had doubled back on his tracks, came at them smoking with anger.

Memo sobbed she had taken all she could tonight and ran up the stairs. Roy had hoped to have another chance at a kiss but when Pop flew at him like a batty, loose-feathered fowl, killing the stillness of the place with his shrill crowing, he figured it best to keep him away from Memo.

He turned to Pop, who then got a closeup of Roy's rainbow eye and all but blew apart. He called him everything from a dadblamed sonovagun to a blankety-blank Judas traitor for breaking training, hurting his eye, and blowing in at almost 5 A.M. on the day of an important twin bill with the Phils.

"You damn near drove me wild," he shouted. "I just about had heart failure when Red told me you weren't in your room at midnight."

He then and there fined Roy two hundred and fifty dollars, but reduced it to an even hundred when Roy sarcastically mentioned how much the Knights were paying him.

"And nothing is wrong with my eye," he said. "It don't hurt but a little and I can see out of it as clear as day, but if you want me to get some sleep before the game don't stand there jawing my head off."

Pop was quickly pacified. "I admit you are entitled to a good time on your Day but you have no idea of all that I have suffered in those hours I was waiting up for you. All kinds of terrible things ran through my mind. I don't hafta tell you it don't take much to kill off a man nowadays."

Roy laughed. "Nothing is going to kill me before my time. I am the type that will die a natural death."

Seeing the affectionate smile this raised up on Pop's puss, he felt sorry for the old man and said, "Even with one eye I will wow them for you today."

"I know you will, son," Pop almost purred. "You're the one I'm depending on to get us up there. We're hot now and I figure, barring any serious accidents, that we will catch up with the Pirates in less than two weeks. Then once we are first we should stay there till we take the flag. My God, when I think of that my legs get dizzy. I guess you know what that would mean to me after all of these years. Sometimes I feel I have been waiting for it my whole life. So take care of yourself. When all is said and done, you ain't a kid any more. At your age the body will often act up, so be wise and avoid any trouble."

"I am young in my mind and healthy in my body," Roy said. "You don't have to worry about me."

"Only be careful," Pop said.

Roy said good night but couldn't move because Pop had gripped his elbow. Leading him to the corner, he whispered to Roy not to have too much to do with Memo.

Roy stiffened.

"Don't get me wrong, son, she's not a bad girl—"

Roy glared.

Pop gulped. "I am the one who is really bad. It was me who introduced her to Bump." He looked sick. "I hoped she would straighten him out and sorta hold him in the team—but—well, you know how these things are. Bump was not the marrying kind and she sorta—well, you know what I mean."

"So what?" said Roy.

"Nothing," he answered brokenly. "Only I was wrong for encouraging them to get together with maybe in the back of my mind the idea of how they would do so—without getting married, that is—and I have suffered from it since."

Roy said nothing and Pop wouldn't look him in the eye. "What I started to say," he went on, "is that although she is not really a bad person, yet she is unlucky and always has been and I think that there is some kind of whammy in her that carries her luck to other people. That's why I would like you to watch out and not get too tied up with her."

"You're a lousy uncle."

"I am considering you."

"I will consider myself."

"Don't mistake me, son. She was my sister's girl and I do love her, but she is always dissatisfied and will snarl you up in her trouble in a way that will weaken your strength if you don't watch out."

"You might as well know that I love her."

Pop listened gloomily. "Does she feel the same to you?"

"Not yet but I think she will."

"Well, you are on your own." He looked so forlorn that

Roy said, "Don't worry yourself about her. I will change her luck too."

"You might at that." Pop took out his billfold and extracted a pink paper that he handed to Roy.

Roy inspected it through his good eye. It was a check for two thousand dollars, made out to him. "What's it for?"

"The balance of your salary for the time you missed before you got here. I figure that you are entitled to at least the minimum pay for the year."

"Did the Judge send it?"

"That worm? He wouldn't send you his bad breath. It's my personal check." Pop was blushing.

Roy handed it back. "I am making out okay. If the Judge wants to raise my pay, all right, but I don't want your personal money."

"My boy, if you knew what you mean to me—"

"Don't say it." Roy's throat was thick with sentiment. "Wait till I get you the pennant."

He turned to go and bumped into Max Mercy at his elbow. Max's sleepy popeyes goggled when he saw Roy's shiner. He sped back into the lobby.

"That slob is up to no good," Roy said.

"He was sleeping on the couch next to where I was waiting for you to come home. He heard Red tell me you hadn't showed up. Kept a camera with him back there."

"He better not take a picture of my eye," Roy said.

He beat it up the back stairs with Max on his tail. Though the columnist carried a camera and a pocketful of flashbulbs he ran faster than Roy had expected, so to ditch him he shot through the second-floor door and sped down the corridor. Seeing over his shoulder that Max was still after him he ducked through a pair of open glass doors into an enormous black ballroom, strewn with chairs, potted palms, and music stands from a dance last night. The lingering odor of perfume mixed with cigarette smoke reminded him of the smell of Memo's hair and haunted him even now. He thought of hiding behind something but that would make him a ridiculous

sitting duck for a chance shot of Max's, so since his good eye
had become accustomed to the dark he nimbly picked his
way among the obstacles, hoping the four-eyed monstrosity
behind him would break his camera or maybe a leg. But Max
seemed to smell his way around in the dark and hung tight.
Reaching the glass doors at the other end of the ballroom,
Roy sidestepped out just as a bulb lit in a wavering flash that
would leave Max with a snapshot of nothing but a deserted
ballroom. The columnist stuck like glue to Roy's shadow,
spiraling after him up the stairs and through the long empty
ninth-floor corridor (broad and soft-carpeted so that their
footsteps were silent) which stretched ahead, it seemed to
Roy, like an endless highway.

He felt he had been running for ages, then this blurred
black forest slid past him, and as he slowed down, each black
tree followed a white, and then all the trees were lit in somber
light till the moon burst forth through the leaves and the
woods glowed. Out of it appeared this boy and his dog, and
Roy in his heart whispered him a confidential message: watch
out when you cross the road, kid, but he had spoken too late,
for the boy lay brokenboned and bleeding in a puddle of
light, with no one to care for him or whisper a benediction
upon his lost youth. A groan rose in Roy's throat (he holding
a flashlight over the remains) for not having forced Memo to
stop and go back to undo some of the harm. A sudden dark
glare flashed over his head, eerily catapulting his shadow forward, and erasing in its incandescence the boy in the road.
Roy felt a burning pain in his gut, yet simultaneously remembered there had been no sign of blood on the bumper or
fender, and Memo said she had screamed because she saw
in the mirror that they were being chased by cops. The black
sedan that trailed them had not stopped either, which it
would have done if there were cops in it and somebody was
dying in the road. So Memo must've been right—either it was
a rock, or maybe the kid's hound, probably not even that,
for it did not appear there ever was any kid in those woods,
except in his mind.

Ahead was his door. Max was panting after him. As Roy

shoved the key into the lock, poking his eye close to do the job quick, Max from fifteen feet away aimed the camera and snapped the shutter. The flashbulb burst in the reflector. The door slammed. Max swore blue bloody murder as Roy, inside, howled with laughing.

He had a whopping good time at the ball game. Doc Casey had squeezed the swelling of his eye down and painted out the black with a flesh-tone color, and Roy led the attack against the Phils that sank them twice that afternoon, sweeping the series for the Knights and raising them into second place, only three games behind the Pirates. Pop was hilarious. The fans went wild. The newspapers called the Knights "the wonder team of the age" and said they were headed for the pennant.

On his way to Memo's after the game, Roy met her, wearing her summer furpiece, coming along the fourth-floor hall.

"I thought I would drop around and see how you are, Memo."

She continued her slightly swaying walk to the elevator.

"I am all right," she said.

He paused. "See the doctor yet?"

Memo blushed and said quickly, "He says it's neuritis—nothing serious."

She pressed the elevator button.

"Nothing serious?"

"That's what he said." She was looking up the elevator shaft and he sensed she had not been to the doctor. He guessed her breast was not sick. He guessed she had said that to get him to slow down. Though he did not care for her technique, he controlled his anger and asked her to go to the movies.

"Sorry. Gus is picking me up."

Back in his room he felt restless. He thought he'd be better off without her but the thought only made him bitter. Red Blow called him to go to the pictures but Roy said he had a headache. Later he went out by himself. That night he dreamed of her all night long. The sick breast had turned green yet he was anxious to have a feel of it.

The next day, against the Braves, Roy got exactly no hits. The Knights won, but against the Dodgers in Brooklyn on Tuesday he went hitless once more and they lost. Since he had never before gone without a hit more than six times in a row there was talk now of a slump. That made him uneasy but he tried not to think of it, concerning himself with Memo and continuing his search through the papers for news of a hit-and-run accident on Long Island. Finding no mention of one he blamed the whole thing on his imagination and thought he'd better forget it. And he told himself not to worry about the slump—it happened to the very best—but after a third day without even a bingle he couldn't help but worry.

As his hitlessness persisted everyone was astonished. It didn't seem possible this could happen to a miracle man like Roy. Enemy pitchers were the last to believe the news. They pitched him warily, fearing an eruption of his wrath, but before long they saw the worry in his eyes and would no longer yield those free and easy walks of yore. They straightened out their curves and whizzed them over the gut of the plate, counting on him either to top a slow roller to the infield or strike himself out. True, he was the same majestic-looking figure up there, well back in the box, legs spread wide, and with Wonderboy gleaming in the sun, raised over his shoulder (he had lowered it from his head). He swung with such power you could see a circle of dust lift off the ground as the bat passed over it, yet all it amounted to was breeze. It made many a pitcher feel like a pretty tough hombre to see Roy drag himself away from the plate and with lowered head enter the dugout.

"What's the matter with me?" he thought with irritation. He didn't feel himself (wondered if he could possibly be sick). He felt blunt and dull—all thumbs, muscles, and joints, Charley horse all over. He missed the sensation of the sock— the moment the stomach galloped just before the wood hit the ball, and the satisfying sting that sped through his arms and shoulders as he belted one. Though there was plenty of fielding to do—the Knights' pitchers were getting to be loose with the hits—he missed the special exercise of running the bases, whirling round them with the speed of a race horse as nine frantic men tried to cut him down. Most of all he missed the gloating that blew up his lungs when he crossed the plate and they ran up another tally opposite his name in the record book. A whole apparatus of physical and mental pleasures was on the kibosh and without them he felt like the Hobbs he thought he had left behind dead and buried.

"What am I doing that's wrong?" he asked himself. No one on the bench or in the clubhouse had offered any advice or information on the subject or even so much as mentioned slump. Not even Pop, also worried, but hoping it would fade as suddenly as it had appeared. Roy realized that he was overanxious and pressing—either hitting impatiently in front of the ball or swinging too late—so that Wonderboy only got little bites of it or went hungry. Thinking he was maybe overstriding and getting his feet too far apart so that he could not pivot freely, he shifted his stride but that didn't help. He tried a new stance and attempted, by counting to himself, to alter his timing. It did no good. To save his eyesight he cut out all reading and going to the pictures. At bat his expression was so dark and foreboding it gave the opposing pitchers the shakes, but still they had his number.

He spent hours fretting whether to ask for help or wait it out. Some day the slump was bound to go, but when? Not that he was ashamed to ask for help but once you had come this far you felt you had learned the game and could afford to give out with the advice instead of being forced to ask for it. He was, as they say, established and it was like breaking up the establishment to go around panhandling an earful. Like making a new beginning and he was sick up to here of new beginnings. But as he continued to whiff he felt a little panicky. In the end he sought out Red Blow, drew him out to center field and asked in an embarrassed voice, "Red, what is the matter with me that I am not hitting them?" He gazed over the right field wall as he asked the question.

Red squirted tobacco juice into the grass.

"Well," he said, rubbing his freckled nose, "what's worrying your mind?"

Roy was slow to reply. "I am worrying that I am missing so many and can't get back in the groove."

"I mean besides that. You haven't knocked up a dame maybe?"

"No."

"Any financial worries about money?"

"Not right now."

"Are you doing something you don't like to do?"

"Such as what?"

"Once we had a guy here whose wife made him empty the garbage pail in the barrel every night and believe it or not it began to depress him. After that he fanned the breeze a whole month until one night he told her to take the damn garbage out herself, and the next day he hit again."

"No, nothing like that."

Red smiled. "Thought I'd get a laugh out of you, Roy. A good belly laugh has more than once broke up a slump."

"I would be glad to laugh but I don't feel much like it. I hate to say it but I feel more like crying."

Red was sympathetic. "I have seen lots of slumps in my time, Roy, and if I could tell you why they come I could make a fortune, buy a saloon and retire. All I know about them is you have to relax to beat 'em. I know how you feel now and I realize that every game we lose hurts us, but if you can take it easy and get rid of the nervousness that is for some reason in your system, you will soon snap into your form. From there on in you will hit like a house on fire."

"I might be dead by then," Roy said gloomily.

Red removed his cap and with the hand that held it scratched his head.

"All I can say is that you have got to figure this out for yourself, Roy."

Pop's advice was more practical. Roy visited the manager in his office after the next (fruitless) game. Pop was sitting at his roll-top desk, compiling player averages in a looseleaf note-book. On the desk were a pair of sneakers, a picture of Ma Fisher, and an old clipping from the *Sporting News* saying how sensational the Knights were going. Pop closed the average book but not before Roy had seen a large red zero for the day's work opposite his name. The Knights had dropped back to third place, only a game higher than the Cardinals, and Pop's athlete's foot on his hands was acting up.

"What do I have to do to get out of this?" Roy asked moodily.

Pop looked at him over his half-moon specs.

"Nobody can tell you exactly, son, but I'd say right off stop climbing up after those bad balls."

Roy shook his head. "I don't think that's it. I can tell when they're bad but the reason I reach for them sometimes is that the pitchers don't throw me any good ones, which hasn't been so lately. Lately, they're almost all good but not for me."

"Danged if I know just what to tell you," Pop said, scratch-ing at his reddened fingers. He too felt a little frightened. But he recommended bunting and trying to beat them out. He said Roy had a fast pair of legs and getting on base, in whichever way, might act to restore his confidence.

But Roy, who was not much of a bunter—never had his

heart in letting the ball hit the bat and roll, when he could just as well lash out and send the same pitch over the fence— could not master the art of it overnight. He looked foolish trying to bunt, and soon gave it up.

Pop then recommended hitting at fast straight ones thrown by different pitchers for thirty minutes every morning, and to do this till he had got his timing back, because it was timing that was lost in a slump. Roy practiced diligently and got so he could connect, yet he couldn't seem to touch the same pitches during the game.

Then Pop advised him to drop all batting practice and to bat cold. That didn't help either.

"How is your eye that got hurt?" Pop asked.

"Doc tested it, he says I see perfect."

Pop looked grimly at Wonderboy. "Don't you think you ought to try another stick for a change? Sometimes that will end up a slump."

Roy wouldn't hear of it. "Wonderboy made all of my records with me and I am staying with him. Whatever is wrong is wrong with me and not my bat."

Pop looked miserable but didn't argue.

Only rarely he saw Memo. She was not around much, never at the games, though she had begun to come quite often a while back. Roy had the morbid feeling she couldn't stand him while he was in this slump. He knew that other people's worries bothered her and that she liked to be where everybody was merry. Maybe she thought the slump proved he was not as good a player as Bump. Whatever it was, she found excuses not to see him and he got only an occasional glimpse of her here and there in the building. One morning when he ran into her in the hotel grill room, Memo reddened and said she was sorry to read he was having a tough time.

Roy just nodded but she went on to say that Bump used to ease his nerves when he wasn't hitting by consulting a fortune-teller named Lola who lived in Jersey City.

"What for?" Roy asked.

"She used to tell him things that gave him a lift, like the time she said he was going to be left money by someone, and he felt so good it raised him clean out of his slump."

"Did he get the dough that she said?"

"Yes. Around Christmas his father died and left him a garage and a new Pontiac. Bump cleared nine thousand cash when he sold the property."

Roy thought it over afterwards. He had little faith that any fortuneteller could help him out of his trouble but the failure of each remedy he tried sank him deeper into the dumps and he was now clutching for any straw. Borrowing a car, he hunted up Lola in Jersey City, locating her in a two-story shack near the river. She was a fat woman of fifty, and wore black felt slippers broken at the seams, and a kitchen towel wrapped around her head.

"Step right inside the parlor," she said, holding aside the beaded curtain leading into a dark and smelly room, "and I will be with you in a jiffy, just as soon as I get rid of this loud mouth on the back porch."

Feeling ill at ease and foolish, Roy waited for her.

Lola finally came in with a Spanish shawl twisted around her. She lit up the crystal ball, passed her gnarled hands over it and peered nearsightedly into the glass. After watching for a minute she told Roy he would soon meet and fall in love with a darkhaired lady.

"Anything else?" he said impatiently.

Lola looked. A blank expression came over her face and she slowly shook her head. "Funny," she said, "there ain't a thing more."

"Nothing about me getting out of a slump in baseball?"

"Nothing. The future has closed down on me."

Roy stood up. "The trouble with what you said is that I am already in love with a swell-looking redhead."

Because of the shortness of the sitting Lola charged him a buck instead of the usual two.

After his visit to her, though Roy was as a rule not superstitious, he tried one or two things he had heard about to see how they would work. He put his socks on inside out, ran a red thread through his underpants, spat between two fingers when he met a black cat, and daily searched the stands for some crosseyed whammy who might be hexing him. He also ate less meat, though he was always hungry, and he arranged for a physical check-up. The doctor told him he was in good shape except for some high blood pressure that was caused by worrying and would diminish as soon as he relaxed. He practiced different grips on Wonderboy before his bureau mirror and sewed miraculous medals and evil-eye amulets of fish, goats, clenched fists, open scissors, and hunchbacks all over the inside of his clothes.

Little of this escaped the other Knights. While the going was good they had abandoned this sort of thing, but now that they were on the skids they felt the need of some extra assistance. So Dave Olson renewed his feud with the lady in the brown-feathered hat, Emil Lajong spun his protective backflips, and Flores revived the business with the birds. Clothes were put on from down up, gloves were arranged to point south when the players left the field to go to bat, and everybody, including Dizzy, owned at least one rabbit's foot. Despite these precautions the boys were once more afflicted by bonehead plays—failing to step on base on a simple force, walking off the field with two out as the winning run scored from first, attempting to stretch singles into triples, and fearing to leave first when the ball was good for at least two. And they were not ashamed to blame it all on Roy.

It didn't take the fans very long to grow disgusted with their antics. Some of them agreed it was Roy's fault, for jinxing himself and the team on his Day by promising the impossible out of his big mouth. Others, including a group of sportswriters, claimed the big boy had all the while been living on borrowed time, a large bag of wind burst by the law of averages. Sadie, dabbing at her eyes with the edge of her petticoat, kept her gong in storage, and Gloria disgustedly swore off men. And Otto Zipp had reappeared like a bad dream with his loud voice and pesky tooter venomously hooting Roy into oblivion. A few of the fans were ashamed that Otto was picking on somebody obviously down, but the majority approved his sentiments. The old-timers began once again to heave vegetables and oddments around, and following the dwarf's lead they heckled the players, especially Roy, calling him everything from a coward to a son of a bitch. Since Roy had always had rabbit ears, every taunt and barb hit its mark. He changed color and muttered at his tormentors. Once in a spasm of weakness he went slowly after a fly ball (lately he had to push himself to catch shots he had palmed with ease before), compelling Flores to rush into his territory to take it. The meatheads rose to a man and hissed. Roy shook his fist at their stupid faces. They booed. He thumbed his nose. "You'll get yours," they howled in chorus.

He had, a vile powerlessness seized him.

Seeing all this, Pop was darkly furious. He all but ripped the recently restored bandages off his pusing fingers. His temper flared wild and red, his voice tore, he ladled out fines like soup to breadline beggars, and he was vicious to Roy.

"It's that goshdamn bat," he roared one forenoon in the clubhouse. "When will you get rid of that danged Wonderboy and try some other stick?"

"Never," said Roy.

"Then rest your ass on the bench."

So Roy sat out the game on the far corner of the bench, from where he could watch Memo, lovelier than ever in a box up front, in the company of two undertakers, the smiling one-eye, Gus, and Mercy, catlike contented, whose lead that night would read: "Hobbs is benched. The All-American Out has sunk the Knights into second division."

He woke in the locker room, stretched out on a bench. He remembered lying down to dry out before dressing but he was still wet with sweat, and a lit match over his wristwatch told him it was past midnight. He sat up stiffly, groaned and rubbed his hard palms over his bearded face. The thinking started up and stunned him. He sat there paralyzed though his innards were in flight—the double-winged lungs, followed by the boat-shaped heart, trailing a long string of guts. He longed for a friend, a father, a home to return to—saw himself packing his duds in a suitcase, buying a ticket, and running for a train. Beyond the first station he'd fling Wonderboy out the window. (Years later, an old man returning to the city for a visit, he would scan the flats to see if it was there, glowing in the mud.) The train sped through the night across the country. In it he felt safe. He tittered.

The mousy laughter irritated him. "Am I outa my mind?" He fell to brooding and mumbled, "What am I doing that's wrong?" Now he shouted the question and it boomed back at him off the walls. Lighting matches, he hurriedly dressed. Before leaving, he remembered to wrap Wonderboy in flannel. In the street he breathed easier momentarily, till he suspected someone was following him. Stopping suddenly, he wheeled about. A woman, walking alone in the glare of the street lamp, noticed him. She went faster, her heels clicking down the street. He hugged the stadium wall, occasionally casting stealthy glances behind. In the tower burned a dark light, the Judge counting his shekels. He cursed him and dragged his carcass on.

A cabbie with a broken nose and cauliflower ear stared but did not recognize him. The hotel lobby was deserted. An old elevator man mumbled to himself. The ninth-floor hall was long and empty. Silent. He felt a driblet of fear . . . like a glug of water backing up the momentarily opened drain and polluting the bath with a dead spider, three lice, a rat turd, and things he couldn't stand to name or look at. For the first time in years he felt afraid to enter his room. The telephone rang. It rang and rang. He waited for it to stop. Finally it did. He warned himself he was acting like a crazy fool. Twisting the key in the lock, he pushed open the door. In the far corner of the room, something moved. His blood changed to falling snow.

Bracing himself to fight without strength he snapped on the light. A white shadow flew into the bathroom. Rushing in, he kicked the door open. An ancient hoary face stared at him. "Bump!" He groaned and shuddered. An age passed . . . His own face gazed back at him from the bathroom mirror, his past, his youth, the fleeting years. He all but blacked out in relief. His head, a jagged rock on aching shoulders, throbbed from its rocky interior. An oppressive sadness weighed like a live pain on his heart. Gasping for air, he stood at the open window and looked down at the dreary city till his legs and arms were drugged with heaviness. He shut the hall door and flopped into bed. In the dark he was lost in an overwhelming weakness . . . I am finished, he muttered. The pages of the record book fell apart and fluttered away in the wind. He slept and woke, finished. All night long he waited for the bloody silver bullet.

On the road Pop was in a foul mood. He cracked down on team privileges: no more traveling wives, no signing of food checks—Red dispensed the cash for meals every morning before breakfast—curfew at eleven and bed check every night. But Roy had discovered that the old boy had invited Memo to come along with them anyway. He went on the theory that Roy had taken to heart his advice to stay away from her and it was making a wreck out of him. Memo had declined the invitation and Pop guiltily kicked himself for asking her.

Roy was thinking about her the morning they came into Chicago and were on their way to the hotel in a cab—Pop, Red, and him. For a time he had succeeded in keeping her out of his thoughts but now, because of the renewed disappointment, she was back in again. He wondered whether Pop was right and she had maybe jinxed him into a slump. If so, would he do better out here, so far away from her?

The taxi turned up Michigan Avenue, where they had a clear view of the lake. Roy was silent. Red happened to glance out the back window. He stared at something and then said, "Have either of you guys noticed the black Cadillac that is following us around? I've seen that damn auto most everywhere we go."

Roy turned to see. His heart jumped. It looked like the car that had chased them halfway across Long Island.

"Drat 'em," Pop said. "I fired those guys a week ago. Guess they didn't get my postcard."

Red asked who they were.

"A private eye and his partner," Pop explained. "I hired them about a month back to watch the Great Man here and keep him outa trouble but it's a waste of good money now." He gazed back and fumed. "Those goshdarn saps."

Roy didn't say anything but he threw Pop a hard look and the manager was embarrassed.

As the cab pulled up before the hotel, a wild-eyed man in shirtsleeves, hairy-looking and frantic, rushed up to them.

"Any of you guys Roy Hobbs?"

"That's him," Pop said grimly, heading into the hotel with Red. He pointed back to where Roy was getting out of the cab.

"No autographs," Roy ducked past the man.

"Jesus God, Roy," he cried in a broken voice. He caught Roy's arm and held on to it. "Don't pass me by, for the love of God."

"What d'you want?" Roy stared, suspicious.

"Roy, you don't know me," the man sobbed. "My name's Mike Barney and I drive a truck for Cudahy's. I don't want a thing for myself, only a favor for my boy Pete. He was hurt in an accident, playin' in the street. They operated him for a broken skull a coupla days ago and he ain't doin' so good. The doctor says he ain't fightin' much."

Mike Barney's mouth twisted and he wept.

"What has that got to do with me?" Roy asked, white-faced.

The truck driver wiped his eyes on his sleeve. "Pete's a fan of yours, Roy. He got a scrapbook that thick fulla pictures of you. Yesterday they lemme go in and see him and I said to Pete you told me you'd sock a homer for him in the game tonight. After that he sorta smiled and looked better. They gonna let him listen a little tonight, and I know if you will hit one it will save him."

"Why did you say that for?" Roy said bitterly. "The way I am now I couldn't hit the side of a barn."

Holding to Roy's sleeve, Mike Barney fell to his knees. "Please, you gotta do it."

"Get up," Roy said. He pitied the guy and wanted to help

him yet was afraid what would happen if he couldn't. He didn't want that responsibility.

Mike Barney stayed on his knees, sobbing. A crowd had collected and was watching them.

"I will do the best I can if I get the chance." Roy wrenched his sleeve free and hurried into the lobby.

"A father's blessing on you," the truck driver called after him in a cracked voice.

Dressing in the visitors' clubhouse for the game that night, Roy thought about the kid in the hospital. He had been thinking of him on and off and was anxious to do something for him. He could see himself walking up to the plate and clobbering a long one into the stands and then he imagined the boy, healed and whole, thanking him for saving his life. The picture was unusually vivid, and as he polished Wonderboy, his fingers itched to carry it into the batter's box and let go at a fat one.

But Pop had other plans. "You are still on the bench, Roy, unless you put that Wonderboy away and use a different stick."

Roy shook his head and Pop gave the line-up card to the ump without his name on it. When Mike Barney, sitting a few rows behind a box above third base, heard the announcement of the Knights' line-up without Roy in it, his face broke out in a sickish sweat.

The game began, Roy taking his non-playing position on the far corner of the bench and holding Wonderboy between his knees. It was a clear, warm night and the stands were just about full. The floods on the roof lit up the stadium brighter than day. Above the globe of light lay the dark night, and high in the sky the stars glittered. Though unhappy not to be playing, Roy, for no reason he could think of, felt better in his body than he had in a week. He had a hunch things could go well for him tonight, which was why he especially regretted not being in the game. Furthermore, Mike Barney was directly in his line of vision and sometimes stared at him. Roy's gaze went past him, farther down the stands, to where a young blackhaired woman, wearing a red dress, was sitting at an aisle seat in short left. He could clearly see the white flower she wore pinned on her bosom and that she seemed to spend more time craning to get a look into the Knight's dugout—at him, he could swear—than in watching the game. She interested him, in that red dress, and he would have liked a close gander at her but he couldn't get out there without arousing attention.

Pop was pitching Fowler, who had kept going pretty well during the two dismal weeks of Roy's slump, only he was very crabby at everybody—especially Roy—for not getting him any runs, and causing him to lose two well-pitched games. As a result Pop had to keep after him in the late innings, because when Fowler felt disgusted he wouldn't bear down on the opposing batters.

Up through the fifth he had kept the Cubs bottled up but he eased off the next inning and they reached him for two runs with only one out. Pop gave him a fierce glaring at and Fowler then tightened and finished off the side with a pop fly and strikeout. In the Knights' half of the seventh, Cal Baker came through with a stinging triple, scoring Stubbs, and was himself driven in by Flores' single. That tied the score but it became untied when, in their part of the inning, the Cubs placed two doubles back to back, to produce another run.

As the game went on Roy grew tense. He considered telling Pop about the kid and asking for a chance to hit. But Pop was a stubborn cuss and Roy knew he'd continue to insist on him laying Wonderboy aside. This he was afraid to do. Much as he wanted to help the boy—and it really troubled him now—he felt he didn't stand a Chinaman's chance at a hit without his own club. And if he once abandoned Wonderboy there was no telling what would happen to him. Probably it would finish his career for keeps, because never since he had made the bat had he swung at a ball with any other.

In the eighth on a double and sacrifice, Pop worked a runner around to third. The squeeze failed so he looked around anxiously for a pinch hitter. Catching Roy's eye, he said, as Roy had thought he would, "Take a decent stick and go on up there."

Roy didn't move. He was sweating heavily and it cost him a great effort to stay put. He could see the truck driver suffering in his seat, wiping his face, cracking his knuckles, and sighing. Roy averted his glance.

There was a commotion in the lower left field stands. This lady in the red dress, whoever she was, had risen, and standing in a sea of gaping faces, seemed to be searching for someone. Then she looked toward the Knights' dugout and sort of half bowed her head. A murmur went up from the crowd. Some of them explained it that she had got mixed up about the seventh inning stretch and others answered how could she when the scoreboard showed the seventh inning was over? As she stood there, so cleanly etched in light, as if trying to communicate something she couldn't express, some of the fans were embarrassed. And the stranger sitting next to her felt a strong sexual urge which he concealed behind an impatient cigarette. Roy scarcely noticed her because he was lost in worry, seriously considering whether he ought to give up on Wonderboy.

Pop of course had no idea what was going on in Roy's head, so he gave the nod to Ed Simmons, a substitute infielder. Ed picked a bat out of the rack and as he approached the plate the standing lady slowly sat down. Everyone seemed to forget her then. Ed flied out. Pop looked scornfully at Roy and shot a stream of snuff into the dust.

Fowler had a little more trouble in the Cubs half of the eighth but a double play saved him, and the score was still 3-2. The ninth opened. Pop appeared worn out. Roy had his eyes shut. It was Fowler's turn to bat. The second guessers were certain Pop would yank him for a pinch hitter but Fowler was a pretty fair hitter for a pitcher, and if the Knights could tie the score, his pitching tonight was too good to waste. He swung at the first ball, connecting for a line drive single, to Pop's satisfaction. Allie Stubbs tried to lay one away but his hard-hit fly ball to center was caught. To everybody's surprise Fowler went down the white line on the next pitch and dove safe into second under a cloud of dust. A long

125 :: *The Natural | Batter Up!*

single could tie the score, but Cal Baker, to his disgust, struck out and flung his bat away. Pop again searched the bench for a pinch hitter. He fastened his gaze on Roy but Roy was unapproachable. Pop turned bitterly away.

Mike Barney, a picture of despair, was doing exercises of grief. He stretched forth his long hairy arms, his knobby hands clasped, pleading. Roy felt as though they were reaching right into the dugout to throttle him.

He couldn't stand it any longer. "I give up." Placing Wonderboy on the bench he rose and stood abjectly in front of Pop.

Pop looked up at him sadly. "You win," he said. "Go on in."

Roy gulped. "With my own bat?"

Pop nodded and gazed away.

Roy got Wonderboy and walked out into the light. A roar of recognition drowned the announcement of his name but not the loud beating of his heart. Though he'd been at bat only three days ago, it felt like years—an ageless time. He almost wept at how long it had been.

Lon Toomey, the hulking Cub hurler, who had twice in the last two weeks handed Roy his lumps, smiled behind his glove. He shot a quick glance at Fowler on second, fingered the ball, reared and threw. Roy, at the plate, watched it streak by.

"Stuh-rike."

He toed in, his fears returning. What if the slump did not give way? How much longer could it go on without destroying him?

Toomey lifted his right leg high and threw. Roy swung from his heels at a bad ball and the umpire sneezed in the breeze.

"Strike two!"

Wonderboy resembled a sagging baloney. Pop cursed the bat and some of the Knights' rooters among the fans booed. Mike Barney's harrowed puss looked yellow.

Roy felt sick with remorse that he hadn't laid aside Wonderboy in the beginning and gone into the game with four licks at bat instead of only three miserable strikes, two of which he already used up. How could he explain to Barney that he had traded his kid's life away out of loyalty to a hunk of wood?

The lady in the stands hesitantly rose for the second time. A photographer who had stationed himself nearby snapped a clear shot of her. She was an attractive woman, around thirty, maybe more, and built solid but not too big. Her bosom was neat, and her dark hair, parted on the side, hung loose and soft. A reporter approached her and asked her name but she wouldn't give it to him, nor would she, blushing, say why she was standing now. The fans behind her hooted, "Down in front," but though her eyes showed she was troubled she remained standing.

Noticing Toomey watching her, Roy stole a quick look. He caught the red dress and a white rose, turned away, then came quickly back for another take, drawn by the feeling that her smile was for him. Now why would she do that for? She seemed to be wanting to say something, and then it flashed on him the reason she was standing was to show her confidence in him. He felt surprised that anybody would want to do that for him. At the same time he became aware that the night had spread out in all directions and was filled with an unbelievable fragrance.

A pitch streaked toward him. Toomey had pulled a fast one. With a sob Roy fell back and swung.

Part of the crowd broke for the exits. Mike Barney wept freely now, and the lady who had stood up for Roy absently pulled on her white gloves and left.

The ball shot through Toomey's astounded legs and began to climb. The second baseman, laying back on the grass on a hunch, stabbed high for it but it leaped over his straining fingers, sailed through the light and up into the dark, like a white star seeking an old constellation.

Toomey, shrunk to a pygmy, stared into the vast sky.

Roy circled the bases like a Mississippi steamboat, lights lit, flags fluttering, whistle banging, coming round the bend. The Knights poured out of their dugout to pound his back, and hundreds of their rooters hopped about in the field. He stood on the home base, lifting his cap to the lady's empty seat.

And though Fowler goose-egged the Cubs in the last of the ninth and got credit for the win, everybody knew it was **Roy** alone who had saved the boy's life.

It seemed perfectly natural to Iris to be waiting for him, with her shoes off to ease her feet, here on the park grass. He had been in her mind so often in the past month she could not conceive of him as a stranger, though he certainly was. She remembered having fallen asleep thinking of him last night. She had been gazing at the stars through her window, unaware just when they dissolved into summer rain, although she remembered opening a brown eye in time to see the two-pronged lightning plunge through a cloud and spread its running fire in all directions. And though she was sometimes afraid she would be hurt by it (this was her particular fear) she did not get up to shut the window but watched the writhing flame roll across the sky, until it disappeared over the horizon. The night was drenched and fragrant. Without the others knowing, she had slipped on a dress and gone across the road to walk in a field of daisies whose white stars lit up her bare feet as she thought of tomorrow in much the way she had at sixteen.

Tonight was a high, free evening, still green and gold above the white fortress of buildings on Michigan Avenue, yet fading over the lake, from violet to the first blue of night. A breeze with a breath of autumn in it, despite that afternoon's heat in the city, blew at intervals through the trees. From time to time she caught herself glancing, sometimes frowning, at her wristwatch although it was her own fault she had come so early. Her arms showed gooseflesh and she wondered if she had been rash to wear a thin dress at night but that was silly because the night was warm. It did not take her long to comprehend that the gooseflesh was not for now but another time, long ago, a time she was, however, no longer afraid to remember.

Half her life ago, just out of childhood it seemed, but that couldn't be because she was too strangely ready for the irrevocable change that followed, she had one night alone in the movies met a man twice her age, with whom she had gone walking in the park. Sensing at once what he so unyieldingly desired, she felt instead of fright, amazement at her willingness to respond, considering she was not, like some she later met, starved of affection. But a mother's love was one thing, and his, when he embraced her under the thick-leaved tree that covered them, was something else again. She had all she could do to tear herself away from him, and rushed through the branches, scratching her face and arms in the bargain. But he would not let her go, leading her always into dark places, hidden from all but the light of the stars, and taught her with his kisses that she could race without running. All but bursting with motion she cried don't look, and when he restlessly turned away, undressed the bottom half of her. She offered herself in a white dress and bare feet and was considerably surprised when he pounced like a tiger.

A horn hooted.

It was Roy driving a hired car. He looked around for a parking place but she had slipped on her shoes and waved she was coming.

He had come across her picture in one of the morning papers the day after he had knocked out the homer for the kid. Slicing it out carefully with his knife, he folded it with-

out creasing the face and kept it in his wallet. Whenever he
had a minute to himself (he was a smashing success at bat—
five for five, three home runs—and was lionized by all) he
took the picture out and studied it, trying to figure out why
she had done that for him; nobody else ever had. Usually
when he was down he was down alone, without flowers or
mourners. He suspected she might be batty or a grownup
bobby soxer gone nuts over him for having his name and
picture in the papers. But from the intelligent look of her it
didn't seem likely. There were some players the ladies might
fall for through seeing their pictures but not him—not that he
was bad-looking or anything, just that he was no dream boy
—nor was she the type to do it. In her wide eyes he saw
something which caused him to believe she knew what life
was like, though you really couldn't be sure.

He made up his mind and telephoned the photographer
who had taken this shot of her, for any information he might
have as to where she lived, but at his office they said he was
covering a forest fire in Minnesota. During the game that
afternoon Roy scanned the stands around him and in the
fifth frame located her practically at his elbow in deep left.
He got one of the ushers to take her a note saying could she
meet him tonight? She wrote back not tonight but enclosed
her phone number. After a shot of Scotch he called her. Her
voice was interesting but she said frankly she wondered if
their acquaintance ought to end now, because these things
could be disillusioning when they dragged past their time.
He said he didn't think she would disappoint him. After
some coaxing she yielded, chiefly because Roy insisted he
wanted to thank her in person for her support of him.

He held the door open and she stepped in.

"I'm Iris Lemon," she said with a blush.

"Roy Hobbs." He felt foolish for of course she knew his
name. Despite his good intentions he was disappointed right
off, because she was heavier than he had thought—the picture didn't show that so much or if it did he hadn't noticed—
and she had lost something, in this soft brown dress, that
she'd had in the red. He didn't like them hefty, yet on second

thought it couldn't be said she really was. Big, yes, but shapely too. Her face and hair were pretty and her body—she knew what to wear on her feet—was well proportioned. He admitted she was attractive although as a rule he never thought so unless they were slim like Memo.

So he asked her right out was she married.

She seemed startled, then smiled and said, "No, are you?"

"Nope."

"How is it the girls missed you?"

Though tempted to go into a long explanation about that, he let it pass with a shrug. Neither of them was looking at the other. They both stared at the road ahead. The car hadn't moved.

Iris felt she had been mistaken to come. He seemed so big and bulky next to her, and close up looked disappointingly different from what she had expected. In street clothes he gained little and lost more, a warrior's quality he showed in his uniform. Now he looked like any big-muscled mechanic or bartender on his night off. Whatever difference could it have made to her that this particular one had slumped? She was amazed at her sentimentality.

Roy was thinking about Memo. If not for her he wouldn't be here trying to make himself at ease with this one. She hadn't treated him right. For a while things had looked good between them but no sooner had he gone into a slump when she began again to avoid him. Had she been nice to him instead, he'd have got out of his trouble sooner. However, he wasn't bitter, because Memo was remote, even unreal. Strange how quick he forgot what she was like, though he couldn't what she looked like. Yet with that thought even her image went up in smoke. Iris, a stranger, had done for him what the other wouldn't, in public view what's more. He felt for her a gratitude it was hard to hold in.

"When you get to know me better you will like me more." He surprised himself with that—the hoarse remark echoed within him—and she, sure she had misjudged him, felt a catch in her throat as she replied, "I like you now."

He stepped on the starter and they drove off in the lilac

dusk. Where to? he had asked and she had said it made no difference, she liked to ride. He felt, once they started, as if he had been sprung from the coop, and only now, as the white moon popped into the sky, did he begin to appreciate how bad it had been with him during the time of his slump.

They drove so they could almost always see the lake. The new moon climbed higher in the blue night, shedding light like rain. They drove along the lit highway to where the lake turned up into Indiana and they could see the lumpy yellow dunes along the shore. Elsewhere the land was shadowless and flat except for a few trees here and there. Roy turned into a winding dirt road and before long they came to this deserted beach, enclosed in a broken arc of white birches. The wind here was balmy and the water lit on its surface.

He shut off the motor. In the silence—everything but the lapping of the lake water—they too were silent. He hesitated at what next move to make and she prayed it would be the right one although she was not quite sure what she meant.

Roy asked did she want to get out. She understood he wanted her to so she said yes. But she surprised him by saying she had been here before.

"How's the water?" he asked.

"Cold. The whole lake is, but you get used to it soon."

They walked along the shore and then to a cluster of birches. Iris sat on the ground under one of the trees and slipped off her shoes. Her movements were graceful, she made her big feet seem small.

He sat nearby, his eyes on her. She sensed he wanted to talk but now felt curiously unconcerned with his problems. She had not expected the night to be this beautiful. Since it was, she asked no more than to be allowed to enjoy it.

But Roy impatiently asked her why she had stood up for him the other night.

She did not immediately reply.

After a minute he asked again.

"I don't know," Iris sighed.

That was not the answer he had expected.

"How come?"

"I've been trying to explain it to myself." She lit a cigarette.

He was now a little in awe of her, something he had not foreseen, though he pretended not to be.

"You're a Knights fan, ain't you?"

"No."

"Then how come—I don't get it."

"I'm not a baseball fan but I like to read about the different players. That's how I became interested in you—your career."

"You read about my slump?" His throat tightened at the word.

"Yes, and before that of your triumphs."

"Ever see me play—before the other night?"

She shook her head. "Once then and again yesterday."

"Why'd you come—the first time?"

She rubbed her cigarette into the dirt. "Because I hate to see a hero fail. There are so few of them."

She said it seriously and he felt she meant it.

"Without heroes we're all plain people and don't know how far we can go."

"You mean the big guys set the records and the little buggers try and bust them?"

"Yes, it's their function to be the best and for the rest of us to understand what they represent and guide ourselves accordingly."

He hadn't thought of it that way but it sounded all right.

"There are so many young boys you influence."

"That's right," said Roy.

"You've got to give them your best."

"I try to do that."

"I mean as a man too."

He nodded.

"I felt that if you knew people believed in you, you'd regain your power. That's why I stood up in the grandstand. I hadn't meant to before I came. It happened naturally. Of course I was embarrassed but I don't think you can do anything for anyone without giving up something of your own. What I gave up was my privacy among all those people. I hope you weren't ashamed of me?"

He said this was the shame in his life, that his fate, some-how, had always been the same (on the train going nowhere) —defeat in sight of his goal.

"Always?"

"Always the same."

"Always with a woman?"

He laughed harshly. "I sure met some honeys in my time. They burned me good."

"Why do you pick that type?"

"It's like I say—they picked me. It's the breaks."

"You could say no, couldn't you?"

"Not to that type dame I always fell for—they weren't like you."

She smiled.

"I mean you are a different kind."

"Does that finish me?"

"No," he said seriously.

"I won't ever hurt you, Roy."

"No.'

"Don't ever hurt me."

"No."

"What beats me," he said with a trembling voice, "is why did it always have to happen to me? What did I do to deserve it?"

"Being stopped before you started?"

He nodded.

"Perhaps it was because you were a good person?"

"How's that?"

"Experience makes good people better."

She was staring at the lake.

"How does it do that?"

"Through their suffering."

"I had enough of that," he said in disgust.

"We have two lives, Roy, the life we learn with and the life we live with after that. Suffering is what brings us toward happiness."

"I had it up to here." He ran a finger across his windpipe.

"Had what?"

"What I suffered—and I don't want any more."

"It teaches us to want the right things."

"All it taught me is to stay away from it. I am sick of all I have suffered."

She shrank away a little.

He shut his eyes.

Afterwards, sighing, she began to rub his brow, and then his lips.

"And is that the mystery about you, Roy?"

"What mystery?"

"I don't know. Everyone seems to think there is one."

"I told you everything."

"Then there really isn't?"

"Nope."

Her cool fingers touched his eyelids. It was unaccountably sweet to him.

"You broke my jinx," he muttered.

"I'm thirty-three," she said, looking at the moonlit water.

He whistled but said, "I am no spring chicken either, honey."

"Iris."

"Iris, honey."

"That won't come between us?"

"What?"

"My age?"

"No."

"Nothing?"

"If you are not married?"

"No."

"Divorced?"

"No."

"A widow?"

"No," said Iris.

He opened his eyes. "How come with all your sex appeal that you never got hitched?"

She gazed away.

Roy suddenly sat up and bounced to his feet. "Jesus, will

you look at that water. What are we waiting for?" He tore at
his tie.

Iris was saying that she had, however, brought a child into
the world, a girl now grown, but Roy seemed not to hear, he
was so busy getting out of his clothes. In no time to speak
of he stood before her stripped to his shorts.

"Get undressed."

The thought of standing naked before him frightened her.
She told herself not to be—she was no longer a child about
the naked body. But she couldn't bring herself to remove her
clothes in front of him so she went back to the car and undressed there. He waited impatiently, then before he expected her, she stepped out without a thing on and ran in the
moonlight straight into the water, through the shallow part,
and dived where it was deep.

Hopping high through the cold water, Roy plunged in
after her. He dived neatly, kicked hard underwater and came
up almost under her. Iris fell back out of his reach and swam
away. He pursued her with less skill than she had but more
strength. At first he damn near froze but as he swam his
blood warmed. She would not stop and before long the white
birches near the beach looked to be the size of match sticks.

Though they were only a dozen strokes apart she wouldn't
let him gain, and after another fifty tiring yards he wondered
how long this would go on. He called to her but she didn't
answer and wouldn't stop. He was beginning to be winded
and considered quitting, only he didn't want to give up. Then
just about when his lungs were frying in live coals, she
stopped swimming. As she trod water, the light on the surface
hid all but her head from him.

He caught up with her at last and attempted to get his
arms around her waist. "Give us a kiss, honey."

She was repelled and shoved him away.

He saw she meant it, realized he had made a mistake, and
felt terrible.

Roy turned tail, kicking himself down into the dark water.
As he sank lower it got darker and colder but he kept going

down. Before long the water turned murky yet there was no bottom he could feel with his hands. Though his legs and arms were numb he continued to work his way down, filled with icy apprehensions and weird thoughts.

Iris couldn't believe it when he did not quickly rise. Before long she felt frightened. She looked everywhere but he was still under water. A sense of abandonment gripped her. She remembered standing up in the crowd that night, and said to herself that she had really stood up because he was a man whose life she wanted to share . . . a man who had suffered. She thought distractedly of a home, children, and him coming home every night to supper. But he had already left her . . .

. . . At last in the murk he touched the liquid mud at the bottom. He dimly thought he ought to feel proud to have done that but his mind was crammed with old memories flitting back and forth like ghostly sardines, and there wasn't a one of them that roused his pride or gave him any comfort.

So he forced himself, though sleepily, to somersault up and begin the slow task of climbing through all the iron bars of the currents . . . too slow, too tasteless, and he wondered was it worth it.

Opening his bloodshot eyes he was surprised how far down the moonlight had filtered. It dripped down like oil in the black water, and then, unexpectedly, there came into his sight this pair of golden arms searching, and a golden head with a frantic face. Even her hair sought him.

He felt relieved no end.

I am a lucky bastard.

He was climbing a long, slow ladder, broad at the base and narrowing on top, and she, trailing clusters of white bubbles, was weaving her way to him. She had golden breasts and when he looked to see, the hair between her legs was golden too.

With a watery howl bubbling from his blistered lungs he shot past her inverted eyes and bobbed up on the surface, inhaling the soothing coolness of the whole sky.

She rose beside him, gasping, her hair plastered to her naked skull, and kissed him full on the lips. He tore off his shorts and held her tight. She stayed in his arms.

"Why did you do it?" she wept.

"To see if I could touch the bottom."

They swam in together, taking their time. As they dragged themselves out of the water, she said, "Go make a fire, otherwise we will have nothing to dry ourselves with."

He covered her shoulders with his shirt and went hunting for wood. Under the trees he collected an armload of branches. Near the dunes he located some heavy boxwood. Then he came back to where she was sitting and began to build a fire. He set an even row of birch sticks down flat and with his knife shaved up a thick branch till he had a pile of dry shavings. These he lit with the only match he had. When they were burning he added some dry birch pieces he had cut up. He split the boxwood against a rock and when the fire was crackling added that, hunk by hunk, to the flames. Before long he had a roaring blaze going. The fire reddened the water and the lacy birches.

It reddened her naked body. Her thighs and rump were broad but her waist was narrow and virginal. Her breasts were hard, shapely. From above her hips she looked like a girl but the lower half of her looked like a woman.

Watching her, he thought he would wait for the fire to die down, when she was warm and dry and felt not rushed.

She was sitting close to the fire with her hair pulled over her head so the inside would dry first. She was thinking why did he go down? Did he touch the bottom of the lake out of pride, because he wants to make records, or did he do it in disappointment, because I wouldn't let him kiss me?

Roy was rubbing his hands before the fire. She looked up and said in a tremulous voice, "Roy, I have a confession to make. I was never married, but I am the mother of a grown girl."

He said he had heard her the first time.

She brushed her hair back with her fingers. "I don't often

talk about it, but I want to tell you I made a mistake long ago and had a hard time afterwards. Anyway, the child meant everything to me and made me happy. I gave her a good up-bringing and now she is grown and on her own, and I am free to think of myself and young enough to want to."

That was the end of it because Roy asked no questions.

He watched the fire. The flames sank low. When they had just about been sucked into the ashes he crept toward her and took her in his arms. Her breasts beat like hearts against him.

"You are really the first," she whispered.

He smiled, never so relaxed in sex.

But while he was in the middle of loving her she spoke: "I forgot to tell you I am a grandmother."

He stopped. Holy Jesus.

Then she remembered something else and tried, in fright, to raise herself.

"Roy, are you—"

But he shoved her back and went on from where he had left off.

After a hilarious celebration in the dining car (which they roused to uproar by tossing baked potatoes and ketchup bottles around) and later in the Pullman, where a wild bunch led by Roy stripped the pa-jamas off players already sound asleep in their berths, peeled

Red Blow out of his long underwear, and totally demolished the pants of a new summer suit of Pop's, who was anyway not sold on premature celebrations, Roy slept restlessly. In his sleep he knew he was restless and blamed it (in his sleep) on all he had eaten. The Knights had come out of Sportsman's Park after trouncing the Cards in a double header and making it an even dozen in a row without a loss, and the whole club had gone gay on the train, including, mildly, Pop himself, considerably thawed out now that the team had leapfrogged over the backs of the Dodgers and Cards into third place. They were again hot on the heels of the Phils and not too distant from the Pirates, with a whole month to go before the end of the season, and about sixty per cent of their remaining games on home grounds. Roy was of course in fine fettle, the acknowledged King of Klouters, whose sensational hitting, pulverizing every kind of pitching, more than made up for his slump. Yet no matter how many bangs he collected, he was ravenously hungry for more and all he could eat besides. The Knights had boarded the train at dinner time but he had stopped off at the station to devour half a dozen franks smothered in sauerkraut and he guzzled down six bottles of pop before his meal on the train, which consisted of two oversize sirloins, at least a dozen rolls, four orders of mashed, and three (some said five) slabs of apple pie. Still that didn't do the trick, for while they were all at cards that evening, he sneaked off the train as it was being hosed and oiled and hustled up another three wieners, and later secretly arranged with the steward for a midnight snack of a long T-bone with trimmings, although that did not keep him from waking several times during the night with pangs of hunger.

When the diner opened in the morning he put away an enormous breakfast and afterwards escaped those who were up, and found himself some privacy in a half-empty coach near the engine, where nobody bothered him because he was not too recognizable in gabardine, behind dark glasses. For a while he stared at the scattered outskirts of the city they were passing through, but in reality he was wondering whether to read the fat letter from Iris Lemon he had been carrying around in his suit pocket. Roy recalled the night on the lake shore, the long swim, the fire and after. The memory of all was not unpleasant, but what for the love of mud had made her take him for a sucker who would be interested in a grandmother? He found that still terrifying to think of, and although she was a nice enough girl, it had changed her in his mind from Iris more to lemon. To do her justice he concentrated on her good looks and the pleasures of her body but when her kid's kid came to mind, despite grandma's age of only thirty-three, that was asking too much and spoiled the appetizing part of her. It was simple enough to him: if he got serious with her it could only lead to one thing—him being a grandfather. God save him from that for he personally felt as young and frisky as a colt. That was what he told himself as the train sped east, and though he had a slight bellyache he fell into a sound sleep and dreamed how on frosty mornings when he was a kid the white grass stood up prickly stiff and the frozen air deep-cleaned his insides.

He awoke with Memo on his mind. To his wonder she turned up in his room in Boston the next night. It was after supper and he was sitting in a rocker near the window reading about himself in the paper when she knocked. He opened the door and she could have thrown him with a breath, so great was his surprise (and sadness) at seeing her. Memo laughingly said she had been visiting a girl friend's summer place on the Cape, and on her way back to New York had heard the boys were in town so she stopped off to say hello, and here she was. Her face and arms were tanned and she looked better than she had in a long while. He felt too that she had changed somehow in the weeks he hadn't seen her. That made him uneasy, as if any change in her would automatically be to his hurt. He searched her face but could not uncover anything new so explained it as the five pounds she said she had put on since he had seen her last.

He felt he still held it against her for giving him very little support at a time when he could use a lot, and also for turning Pop down when he had invited her to join them on the Western trip. Yet here, alone with her in his room, she so close and inevitably desirable—this struck him with the force of an unforgettable truth: the one he had had and always wanted —he thought it wouldn't do to put on a sourpuss and make complaints. True, there was something about her, like all the food he had lately been eating, that left him, after the having of it, unsatisfied, sometimes even with a greater hunger than before. Yet she was a truly beautiful doll with a form like Miss America, and despite the bumps and bruises he had taken, he was sure that once he got an armlock on her things would go better.

His face must have shown more than he intended, because she turned moodily to the window and said, "Roy, don't bawl me out for not seeing you for a while. There are some things I just can't take and one of them is being with people who are blue. I had too much of that in my life with my mother and it really makes me desperate." More tenderly she said, "That's why I had to stand off to the side, though I didn't like to, and wait till you had worked out of it, which I knew you would do. Now here I am the first chance I got and that is the way it used to be between Bump and me."

Roy said soberly, "When are you going to find out that I ain't Bump, Memo?"

"Don't be mad," she said, lifting her face to him. "All I meant to say is that I treat all my friends the same." She was close and warm-breathed. He caught her in his arms and she snuggled tight, and let him feel the "sick" breast without complaining. But when he tried to edge her to the bed, she broke for air and said no.

"Why not?" he demanded.

"I'm not well," said Memo.

He was suspicious. "What's wrong?"

Memo laughed. "Sometimes you are very innocent, Roy. When a girl says she is not well, does she have to draw you a map?"

Then he understood and was embarrassed for being so dimwitted. He did not insist on any more necking and thought it a good sign that she had talked to him so intimately.

The Knights took their three in Boston and the next day won a twi-night double header in Ebbets Field, making it seventeen straight wins on the comeback climb. Before Roy ended his slump they had fallen into fifth place, twelve games behind, then they slowly rose to third, and after this twin bill with Brooklyn, were within two of the Phils, who had been nip and tucking it all season with the Cards and Dodgers. The Pirates, though beaten three in a row by the Knights on their Western swing (the first Knight wins over them this season) were still in first place, two games ahead of the Phils in a tight National League race.

When the Knights returned to their home grounds for a three-game set with the cellar-dwelling Reds, the city awakened in a stampede. The fans, recovered from their stunned surprise at the brilliant progress of the team, turned out in droves. They piled into the stands with foolish smiles, for most of them had sworn off the Knights during the time of Roy's slump. Now for blocks around the field, the neighborhood was in an uproar as hordes fought their way out of subways, trolleys and buses, and along the packed streets to ticket windows that had been boarded up (to Judge Banner's heartfelt regret) from early that morning, while grunting lines of red-faced cops, reinforced by sweating mounties, tried to shove everybody back where they had come from. After many amused years at the expense of the laughingstock Knights, a scorching pennant fever blew through the city. Everywhere people were bent close to their radios or stretching their necks in bars to have a look at the miracle boys (so named by sportswriters from all over the U.S. who now crammed into the once deserted press boxes) whose every move aroused their fanatic supporters to a frenzy of excitement which whirled out of them in concentric rings around the figure of Roy Hobbs, hero and undeniable man of des-

tiny. He, it was said by everyone, would lead the Knights
to it.

The fans dearly loved Roy but Roy did not love the fans.
He hadn't forgotten the dirty treatment they had dished out
during the time of his trouble. Often he felt he would like to
ram their cheers down their throats. Instead he took it out on
the ball, pounding it to a pulp, as if the best way to get even
with the fans, the pitchers who had mocked him, and the
statisticians who had recorded (forever) the kind and quantity of his failures, was to smash every conceivable record. He
was like a hunter stalking a bear, a whale, or maybe the
sight of a single fleeing star the way he went after that ball.
He gave it no rest (Wonderboy, after its long famine, chopping, chewing, devouring) and was not satisfied unless he
lifted it (one eye cocked as he swung) over the roof and
spinning toward the horizon. Often, for no accountable reason, he hated the pill, which represented more of himself than
he was willing to give away for nothing to whoever found it
one dull day in a dirty lot. Sometimes as he watched the ball
soar, it seemed to him all circles, and he was mystified at his
devotion to hacking at it, for he had never really liked the
sight of a circle. They got you nowhere but back to the place
you were to begin with, yet here he stood banging them like
smoke rings out of Wonderboy and everybody cheered like
crazy. The more they cheered the colder he got to them. He
couldn't stop hitting and every hit made him hungry for the
next (a doctor said he had no tapeworm but ate like that
because he worked so hard), yet he craved no cheers from
the slobs in the stands. Only once he momentarily forgave
them—when reaching for a fly, he almost cracked into the
wall and they gasped their fright and shrieked warnings.
After he caught the ball he doffed his cap and they rocked
the rafters with their thunder.

The press, generally snotty to him during his slump, also
changed its tune. To a man (except one) they showered him
with praise, whooped him on, and in their columns unoffi-
cially accoladed him Rookie of the Year (although they

agreed he resembled nothing so much as an old hand, a toughened veteran of baseball wars) and Most Valuable Player, and years before it was time talked of nominating him for a permanent niche in the Cooperstown Hall of Fame. He belonged, they wrote, with the other immortals, a giant in performance, who resembled the burly boys of the eighties and nineties more than the streamlined kids of today. He was a throwback to a time of true heroes, not of the brittle, razzle-dazzle boys that had sprung up around the jack rabbit ball—a natural not seen in a dog's age, and weren't they the lucky ones he had appeared here and now to work his wonders before them? More than one writer held his aching head when he speculated on all Roy might have accomplished had he come into the game at twenty.

The exception was of course Mercy, who continued to concern himself with Roy's past rather than his accomplishments. He spent hours in the morgue, trying to dredge up possible clues to possible crimes (What's he hiding from me?), wrote for information to prison wardens, sheriffs, county truant officers, heads of orphan asylums, and semipro managers in many cities in the West and Northwest, and by offering rewards, spurred all sorts of research on Roy by small-town sportswriters. His efforts proved fruitless until one day, to his surprise, he got a letter from a man who block printed on a sheet of notebook paper that for two hundred bucks he might be tempted to tell a thing or two about the new champ. Max hastily promised the dough and got his first break. Here was an old sideshow freak who swore that Roy had worked as a clown in a small traveling carnival. For proof he sent a poster showing the clown's face—in his white and red warpaint—bursting through a paper hoop. Roy was recognizable as the snubnose Bobo, who despite the painted laugh on his pan, seemed sadeyed and unhappy. Certain the picture would create a sensation, Max had it printed on the first page above the legend, "Roy Hobbs, Clown Prince of Baseball," but most of those who bought the paper refused to believe it was Roy and those who did, didn't give a hoot.

Roy was burned about the picture and vowed to kick the blabbermouth in the teeth. But he didn't exactly do that, for when they met the next evening, in the Midtown lobby, Max made a handsome apology. He said he had to hand it to Roy for beating everybody else in the game ten different ways, and he was sorry about the picture. Roy nodded but didn't show up on time at the chophouse down the block, where he was awaited by Pop, Red, and Max—to Pop's uneasiness, because Roy was prompt for his meals these days.

The waiter, a heavyset German with a schmaltzy accent and handlebar mustaches, approached for their orders. He started the meal by spilling soup on Max's back, then serving him a steak that looked like the charcoal it had been broiled on. When Max loudly complained he brought him, after fifteen minutes, another, a bleeding beauty, but this the waiter snatched from under the columnist's knife because he had already collected Pop's and Red's finished plates and wanted the third. Max let out a yawp, the frightened waiter dropped the dishes on his lap, and while stooping to collect the pieces, lurched against the table and spilled Max's beer all over his pants.

Pop sprang up and took an angry swipe at the man but Red hauled him down. Meanwhile the waiter was trying to wipe Max's pants with a wet towel and Max was swearing bloody murder at him. This got the waiter sore. Seizing the columnist by his coat collar he shook him and said he would teach him to talk like a "shentleman und nod a slob." He laid Max across his knee, and as the customers in the chophouse looked on in disbelief, smacked his rear with a heavy hand. Max managed to twist himself free. Slapping frantically at the German's face, he knocked off his mustache. In a minute everybody in the place was shrieking with laughter, and even Pop had to smile though he said to Red he was not at all surprised it had turned out to be Roy.

Roy had a Saturday date with Memo coming up but he was lonely for her that night so he went up to the fourth floor and

rang her buzzer. She opened the door, dressed in black loung-
ing pajamas with a black ribbon tied around her horsetail of
red hair, which had a stunning effect on him.

Memo's face lit in a slow blush. "Why, Roy," she said, and
seemed not to know what else to say.

"Shut the door," came a man's annoyed voice from inside,
"or I might catch a cold."

"Gus is here," Memo quickly explained. "Come on in."

Roy entered, greatly disappointed.

Memo lived in a large and airy one-room apartment with
a kitchenette, and a Murphy bed out of sight. Gus Sands,
smoking a Between-the-Acts little cigar, was sitting at a table
near the curtained window, examining a hand of double solitaire he and Memo had been playing. His coat was hanging
on the chair and a hand-painted tie that Roy didn't like,
showing a naked lady dancing with a red nose, hung like a
tongue out of his unbuttoned vest, over a heavy gold watch
chain.

Seeing who it was, Gus said, "Welcome home, slugger. I
see you have climbed out of the hole that you were in."

"I suppose it cost you a couple of bucks," said Roy.

Gus was forced to laugh. He had extended his hand but
Roy didn't shake. Memo glanced at Roy as if to say be nice
to Gus.

Roy couldn't get rid of his irritation that he had found
Gus here, and he felt doubly annoyed that she was still seeing
him. He had heard nothing from her about Gus and had
hoped the bookie was out of the picture, but here he was as
shifty-eyed as ever. What she saw in this half-bald apology
for a cigar store Indian had him beat, yet he was conscious of
a fear in his chest that maybe Gus meant more to her than
he had guessed. The thought of them sitting peacefully together playing cards gave him the uneasy feeling they might
even be married or something. But that couldn't be because
it didn't make sense. In the first place why would she marry
a freak like Gus? Sure he had the bucks but Memo was a hot
kid and she couldn't take them to bed with her. And how
could she stand what he looked like in the morning without

the glass eye in the slot? In the second place Gus wouldn't let *his* wife walk around without a potato-sized diamond, and the only piece of jewelry Memo wore was a ring with a small jade stone. Besides, what would they be doing here in this one-room box when Gus owned a penthouse apartment on Central Park West?

No. He blamed these fantastic thoughts on the fact that he was still not sure of her. And he kept wishing he could have her to himself tonight. Memo caught on because, when he looked at her, she shrugged.

Gus got suspicious. He stared at them with the baleful eye, the glass one frosty.

They were sitting around uncomfortably until Memo suggested they play cards. Gus cheered up at once.

"What'll it be, slugger?" he said, collecting the cards.

"Pinochle is the game for three."

"I hate pinochle," Memo said. "Lets play poker but not the open kind."

"Poker is not wise now," Gus said. "The one in the middle gets squeezed. Anybody like to shoot crap?"

He brought forth a pair of green dominoes. Roy said he was agreeable and Memo nodded. Gus wanted to roll on the table but Roy said the rug was better, with the dice bouncing against the wall.

They moved the table and squatted on the floor. Memo, kneeling, rolled first. Gus told her to fade high and in a few minutes she picked up two hundred dollars. Roy hit snake eyes right off, then sevened out after that. Gus shot, teasing Roy to cover the three one hundred dollar bills he had put down. Memo took twenty-five of it and Roy had the rest. Gus made his point and on the next roll took another two hundred from Roy. That was more than he was carrying in cash but Gus said he could play the rest of the game on credit. The bookie continued to roll passes. In no time he was twelve hundred in on Roy, not counting the cash he had lost. Roy was irritated because he didn't like to lose to Gus in front of Memo. He watched Gus's hands to make sure he wasn't palming another pair of dice. What made him suspicious was that

Gus seemed to be uncomfortable. His glass eye was fastened on the dice but the good one roamed restlessly about. And he was now fading three hundred a throw and sidebetting high. Since Memo was taking only a ten spot here and there, Roy was covering the rest. By the end of Gus's second streak Roy was thirty-five hundred behind and his underwear was sweating. Gus finally went out, Memo quickly lost, then Roy, to his surprise, started off on a string of passes. Now he was hot and rolled the cubes for a long haul, growing merrier by the minute as Gus grew glummer. Before Roy was through, Gus had returned the cash he had taken from him and owed him eleven hundred besides. When Roy finally hit seven, Memo got up and said she had to make coffee. Gus and Roy played on but Roy was still the lucky one. Gus said that dice ought never to be played with less than four and gave up in disgust. He dusted off his knees.

"You sure had luck in your pants tonight, slugger."

"Some call it that."

Memo added the figures. She owed Roy two ten but Gus owed him twenty-one hundred. Roy laughed out loud.

Gus wrote out a check, his eye still restless.

Memo said she would write one too.

"Forget it," Roy said.

"I have covered hers in mine," said Gus, circling his pen around before signing.

Memo flushed. "I like to pay my own way."

Gus tore up the check and wrote another. Seeing how she felt about it, Roy took Memo's, figuring he would return it in the form of some present or other.

Gus handed him a check for the twenty-one hundred. "Chicken feed," he said.

Roy gave the paper a loud smack with his lips. "I love it."

Gus dropped his guard and pinned his restless eye on Roy. "Say the word, slugger, and you can make yourself a nice pile of dough quick."

Roy wasn't sure he had heard right. Gus repeated the offer.

This time Roy was sure. "Say it again and I will spit in your good eye."

Gus's grayish complexion turned blue.

"Boys," Memo said uneasily.

Gus stalked into the bathroom.

Memo's face was pale. "Help me with the sandwiches, Roy."

"Did you hear what that bastard said to me?"

"Sometimes he talks through his hat."

"Why do you invite him here?"

She turned away. "He invited himself."

As she was slicing meat for the sandwiches Roy felt tender toward her. He slipped his arm around her waist. She looked up a little unhappily but when he kissed her she kissed back. They broke apart as Gus unlocked the bathroom door and came out glaring at them.

While they were all drinking coffee Roy was in good spirits and no longer minded that Gus was around. Memo kidded him about the way he wolfed the sandwiches, but she showed her affection by also serving him half a cold chicken which he picked to the bone. He demolished a large slab of chocolate cake and made a mental note for a hamburger or two before he went to bed. Though Gus had only had a cup of coffee he was thoughtfully picking his teeth. After a while he looked at his gold watch, buttoned his vest, and said he was going. Roy glanced at Memo but she yawned and said she had to get up very early in the morning.

To everybody's disgust the Reds, as if contemptuous of the bums who had so long lived in the basement below them, snapped the Knights' streak at seventeen and the next day again beat them over a barrel. A great groan went up from the faithful. Stand back everybody, here they go again. Timber! As if by magic, attendance for a single game with the Phils sank to a handful. The Phils gave them another spanking. The press tipped their hats and turned their respectful attention to the Pirates, pointing out again how superb they were. It was beyond everybody how the half-baked Knights could ever hope to win the N.L. pennant. With twenty-one games left to play they were six behind the

Pirates and four in back of the Phils. And to make matters worse, they'd fallen into a third-place tie with the Cards. Pop's boys still retained a mathematical chance all right but they were at best a first-rate third-place team, one writer put it, and ended his piece, "Wait till next year."

Pop held his suffering head. The players stole guilty looks at one another. Even the Great Man himself was in a rut, though not exactly a slump. Still, he was held by inferior pitching to three constipated singles in three days. Everyone on the team was conscious something drastic had to be done but none could say what. Time was after them with a bludgeon. Any game they lost was the last to lose. It was autumn almost. They saw leaves falling and shivered at the thought of the barren winds of winter.

The Pirates blew into town for their last games of the year with the Knights, a series of four. Thus far during the season they had trounced the Knights a fantastic 15-3 and despite the loss of their last three to the Knights (fool's luck) were prepared to blast them out of their field. Watching the way the Pirates cut up the pea patch with their merciless hitting and precision fielding, the New Yorkers grew more dejected. Here was a team that was really a team, not a Rube Goldberg contraption. Every man jack was a fine player and no one guy outstanding. The Knights' fans were embarrassed . . . Yet their boys managed to tease the first away from the Pirates. No one quite knew how, here a lucky bingle, there a lucky error. Opposite the first-place slickers they looked like hayseeds yet the harvest was theirs. But tomorrow was another day. Wait'll the boys from the smoky city had got the stiffness of the train ride out of their legs. Yet the Knights won again in the same inept way. Their own rooters, seeping back into the stands, whistled and cheered. By some freak of nature they took the third too. The last game was sold out before 10 A.M. Again the cops had trouble with the ticketless hordes that descended on them.

Walt Wickitt, the peerless Pirate manager, pitched his ace hurler, Dutch Vogelman, in that last game. Vogelman was a terrific pitcher, a twenty-three game winner, the only speci-

men in either league that season. He was poison to the
Knights who had beat him only once in the past two years.
Facing Roy in some six games, he had held him to a single
in four, and crippled him altogether in the last two, during
Roy's slump. Most everyone kissed this game goodbye, although Roy started with a homer his first time up. Schultz
then gave up two runs to the Pirates. Roy hit another round
tripper. Schultz made it three for the Pirates. Roy ended by
slamming two more homers and that did it, 4-3. High and
mighty to begin with, Vogelman looked like a drowned dog
at the end, and the Pirates hurriedly packed their duffel bags
and slunk out of the stadium. The Phils were now in first
place by a game, the Pirates second, and the Knights were
one behind them and coming up like a rocket. Again pennant
fever raged through the city and there was cheering in the
streets.

Now all that was left for the Knights in this nerve-racking
race were four games in Brooklyn, including a Sunday double
header, four with Boston and two more with the Reds, these
at home. Then three away with the Phils, one of which was
the playoff of the washed-out game in June when Roy had
knocked the cover off the ball. Their schedule called for the
wind-up in the last week of September, against the Reds in
another three-game tilt at home, a soft finish, considering the
fact that the Pirates and Phils had each other to contend
with. If, God willing, the Knights made it (and were still
functioning), the World Series was scheduled to begin on
Tuesday, October first, at the Yankee Stadium, for the Yanks
had already cinched the American League pennant.

The race went touch and go. To begin with the Knights
dropped a squeaker (Roy went absolutely hitless) to the
Dodgers as the Pirates won and the Phils lost—both now running neck and neck for first, the Knights two behind. Just
as the boys were again despairing of themselves, Roy got
after the ball again. He did not let on to anyone, but he had
undergone a terrible day after his slaughter of the Pirates, a
day of great physical weakness, a strange draining of strength
from his arms and legs, followed by a splitting headache that

whooshed in his ears. However, in the second game at Ebbets Field, he took hold of himself, gripped Wonderboy, and bashed the first pitch into the clock on the right field wall. The clock spattered minutes all over the place, and after that the Dodgers never knew what time it was. All they knew was that Roy Hobbs collected a phenomenal fourteen straight hits that shot them dead three times. Carried on by the momentum, the Knights ripped the Braves and brutally trounced the Reds, taking revenge on them for having ended their recent streak of seventeen.

With only six games to play, a triple first-place tie resulted. The Knights' fans beat themselves delirious, and it became almost unbearable when the Phils lost a heartbreaker to the Cards and dropped into second place, leaving the Pirates and Knights in the tie. Before the Phils could recover, the Knights descended upon Shibe Park, followed by wild trainloads of fans who had to be there to see. They saw their loveboys take the crucial playoff (Roy was terrific), squeak through the second game (he had a poor day), and thoroughly wipe the stunned Phils off the map in the last (again stupendous). At this point of highest tension the Pirate mechanism burst. To the insane cheering of the population of the City of New York, the Cubs pounded them twice, and the Reds came in with a surprise haymaker. A pall of silence descended upon Pennsylvania. Then a roar rose in Manhattan and leaped across the country. When the shouting stopped the Knights were undeniably on top by three over the Pirates, the Phils third by one more, and therefore mathematically out of the race. With three last ones to play against the lowly Reds, the Knights looked *in.* The worst that could possibly happen to them was a first-place tie with the Pirates—if the Pirates won their three from the Phils as the Knights lost theirs to the Reds—a fantastic impossibility the way Roy was mauling them.

The ride home from Philadelphia usually took a little more than an hour but it was a bughouse nightmare because of the way the fans on the train pummeled the players. Hearing that a mob had gathered at Penn Station to welcome the team, Pop ordered everyone off at Newark and into cabs. But as they approached the tunnel they were greeted by a deafening roar as every craft in the Hudson, and all the way down the bay, opened up with whistles and foghorns . . .

In their locker room after the last game at Philly, some of the boys had started chucking wet towels around but Pop, who had privately wept tears of joy, put the squelch on that.

"Cut out all that danged foolishness when we still need one more to win," he had sternly yelled.

When they protested that it looked at last that they were in, he turned lobster red and bellowed did they want to jinx themselves and cook their own gooses? As a result, despite all the attention they were receiving, the boys were a glum bunch going home. Some had secretly talked of celebrating once they had ditched the old fusspot but they were afraid to. Even Roy had fallen into low spirits, only he was thinking of Memo.

His heart ached the way he yearned for her (sometimes seeing her in a house they had bought, with a redheaded baby on her lap, and himself going fishing in a way that made it satisfying to fish, knowing that everything was all right behind him, and the home-cooked meal would be hot and plentiful, and the kid would carry the name of Roy Hobbs into generations his old man would never know. With this in mind he fished the stream in peace and later, sitting around the supper table, they ate the fish he had caught), yearning so deep that the depth ran through ever since he could remember, remembering the countless things he had wanted and missed out on, wondering, now that he was famous, if the intensity of his desires would ever go down. The only way that could happen (he relived that time in bed with her) was to have her always. That would end the dissatisfactions that ate him, no matter how great were his triumphs, and made his life still wanting and not having.

It later struck him that the picture he had drawn of Memo sitting domestically home wasn't exactly the girl she was. The kind he had in mind, though it bothered him to admit it, was more like Iris seemed to be, only she didn't suit him. Yet he could not help but wonder what was in her letter and he made up his mind he would read it once he got back in his room. Not that he would bother to answer, but he ought at least to know what she said.

He felt better, at the hotel, to find a note from Memo in his mailbox, saying to come up and celebrate with a drink. She greeted him at the door with a fresh kiss, her face flushed with how glad she was, saying, "Well, Roy, you've really done it. Everybody is talking about what a wonderful marvel you are."

"We still got this last one to take," he said modestly, though tickled at her praise. "I am not counting my onions till that."

"Oh, the Knights are sure to win. All the papers are saying it all depends what you do. You're the big boy, Roy."

He grabbed both her palms. "Bigger than Bump?"

Her eyelids fluttered but she said yes.

He pulled her close. She kissed for kiss with her warm wet mouth. Now is the time, he thought. Backing her against the wall, he slowly rubbed his hand up between her thighs.

She broke away, breathing heavily. He caught her and pressed his lips against her nippled blouse.

There were tears in her eyes.

He groaned, "Honey, we are the ones that are alive, not him."

"Don't say his name."

"You will forget him when I love you."

"Please let's not talk."

He lifted her in his arms and laid her down on the couch. She sat bolt upright.

"For Christ sakes, Memo, I am a grown guy and not a kid. When are you gonna be nice to me?"

"I am, Roy."

"Not the way I want it."

"I will." She was breathing quietly now.

"When?" he demanded.

She thought, distracted, then said, "Tomorrow—tomorrow night."

"That's too long."

"Later." She sighed, "Tonight."

"You are my sugar honey." He kissed her.

Her mood quickly changed. "Come on, let's celebrate."

"Celebrate what?"

"About the team."

Surprised she wanted to do that now, he said he was shaved and ready to go.

"I don't mean to go out." What she meant, she explained, was that she had prepared a snack in one of the party rooms upstairs. "They're bringing it all up from the kitchen—a buffet with cold meats and lots of other things. I thought it'd be fun to get some girls together with the boys and all enjoy ourselves."

Though he had on his mind what he was going to do to her later, and anything in between was a waste of time, still she had gone to all the trouble, and he wanted to please her. Nor was the mention of food exactly distasteful to him. He had made a double steak disappear on the train, but that was hours ago.

Memo served him a drink and finished telephoning the men she couldn't reach before. Though on the whole the players said they wanted to come, some, still remembering Pop, were doubtful they ought to, but Memo convinced them by saying that Roy and others were coming. She didn't ask the married players to bring their wives and they didn't mention the oversight to her.

At ten o'clock Memo went into the bathroom and put on a flaming yellow strapless gown. Roy got the idea that she was wearing nothing underneath and it gave him a tense pleasure. They rode up to the eighteenth floor. The party was already on. There were about a dozen men around but only four or five girls. Memo said more were coming later. Most of the players did not exactly look happy. A few were self-consciously talking to the girls, and the others were sitting on chairs gabbing among themselves. Flores stood in a corner with a melancholy expression on his phiz. Al Fowler, one of those having himself a fine time, called to him when was the wake.

Someone was pounding the keys of the upright piano against the wall. On the other side of the room, a brisk, pint-size chef with a tall puffed cap on, half again as big as him, stood behind a long, cloth-covered table, dishing out the delicatessen.

"Sure is some snack," Roy marveled. "You must've hocked your fur coat."

"Gus chipped in," Memo said absently.

He was immediately annoyed. "Is that ape coming up here?"

She looked hurt. "Don't call him dirty names. He is a fine, generous guy."

"Two bits he had the grub poisoned."

"That's not funny." Memo walked away but Roy went after her and apologized, though her concern for the bookie—even on the night they were going to sleep together—unsettled and irritated him. Furthermore, he was now worried how Pop would take it if he found out about the players at this shindig despite his warning against celebrating too soon.

He asked Memo if the manager knew what was going on.

She was sweet again. "Don't worry about him, Roy. I'd've invited him but he wouldn't fit in at all here because we are all young people. Don't get anxious about the party, because Gus said not to serve any hard liquor."

"Nice kid, Gus. Must be laying his paper on us for a change."

Memo made no reply.

Everybody was there by then. Dave Olson had a cheerful blonde on his arm. Allie, Lajong, Hinkle, and Hill were harmonizing "Down by the Old Mill Stream." Fowler was showing some of the boys how to do a buck and wing. The cigar smoke was thick. To Roy things still did not sit just right. Everybody was watching everybody else, as if they were all waiting for a signal to get up and leave, and some of the players looked up nervously every time the door opened, as if they were expecting Doc Knobb, who used to hypnotize them before the games. Flores, from across the room, stared at Roy with black, mournful eyes, but Roy turned away. He couldn't walk out on Memo.

"Some blowout," Fowler said to him.

"Watch yourself, kid," Roy warned him in an undertone.

"Watch yourself yourself."

Roy threw him a hard look but Memo said, "Just let Roy head over to the table. He is dying for a bite."

It was true. Though the thought of having her tonight was on the top of his mind, he could not entirely forget the appetizing food. She led him to the table and he was surprised and slightly trembly at all there was of it—different kinds of delicatessen meat, appetizing fish, shrimp, crab and lobster, also caviar, salads, cheeses of all sorts, bread, rolls, and three flavors of ice cream. It made his belly ache, as if it had an existence apart from himself.

"What'll it be?" said the little chef. He had a large fork and plate poised but Roy took them from him, to his annoyance, and said he would fix what he wanted himself.

Memo helped. "Don't be stingy, Roy."

"Pile it on, honey."

"You sure are a scream the way you eat."

"I am a picnic." He kidded to ease the embarrassment his appetite caused him.

"Bump liked to shovel it down—" She caught herself.

After his plate was loaded, Memo placed a slice of ham and a roll on her own and they sat at a table in the far corner of the room—away from where Flores was standing—so Roy could concentrate on the food without having to bother with anybody.

Memo watched him, fascinated. She shredded the ham on her plate and nibbled on a roll.

"That all you're eating?" he asked.

"I guess I haven't got much appetite."

He was gobbling it down and it gave him a feeling of both having something and wanting it the same minute he was having it. And every mouthful seemed to have the effect of increasing his desire for her. He thought how satisfying it would be to lift that yellow dress over her bare thighs.

Roy didn't realize it till she mentioned it that his plate was empty. "Let me get you some more, hon."

"I will get it myself."

"Food is a woman's work." She took his plate to the table and the busy little chef heaped it high with corned beef, pastrami, turkey, potato salad, cheese, and pickles.

"You sure are nice to me," he said.

"You are a nice guy."

"Why did you get so much of it?"

"It's good for you, silly."

Roy laughed. "You sound like my grandma."

Memo was interested. "Weren't you brought up in an orphan's home, Roy?"

"I went there after grandma died."

"Didn't you ever live with your mother?"

He was suddenly thoughtful. "Seven years."

"What was she like? Do you remember?"

"A whore. She spoiled my old man's life. He was a good guy but died young."

A group of girls flocked through the door and Memo hastily excused himself. They were her showgirl friends from a Broadway musical that had just let out. She welcomed them and introduced them around. Dancing started and the party got livelier.

Roy polished his plate with a crust of bread. He felt as if he had hardly eaten anything—it was sliced so thin you could hardly chew your teeth into it.

Memo returned. "How about having something different now?" But Roy said no and got up. "Lemmee say hello to some of the gals that came in."

"You are all alike." He thought she sounded jealous and it was all right if she was. The girls she brought him around to were tickled to meet him. They felt his muscles and wanted to know how he belted the ball so hard.

"Clean living," Roy told them.

The girls laughed out loud. He looked them over. The best of the bunch was a slightly chubby one with an appealing face, but in her body she did not compare to Memo.

When he told Memo she had more of what it took than the rest of them put together, she giggled nervously. He looked at her and felt she was different tonight in a way he could not figure out. He worried about Gus, but then he thought that after tonight he would be getting it steady, and then he would tell her he did not want that glass-eye monkey tailing her around.

Memo led him back to the table. She pointed out what she wanted for Roy and the chef ladled it into the plate. Her own came back with a slice of ham and a roll on it. He followed her to the corner table. He wondered if Flores was still standing in the opposite corner, watching, but he didn't look.

Gazing at the mountain of stuff Memo handed him, he said, "I am getting tired of eating."

Memo had returned to the subject of his mother. "But didn't you love her, Roy?"

He stared at her through one eye. "Who wants to know?"

"Just me."

"I don't remember." He helped himself to a forkful of food. "No.'

"Didn't she love you?"

"She didn't love anybody."

Memo said, "Let's try some new combinations with the buffet. Sometimes when you eat things that you didn't know could mix together but they do, you satisfy your appetite all at once. Now let's mix this lobster meat with hidden treats of anchovies, and here we will lay it on this tasty pumpernickel and spread Greek salad over it, then smear this other slice of bread with nice sharp cheese and put it on top of the rest."

"All it needs now is a shovel of manure and a forest will grow out of it."

"Now don't be dirty, Roy."

"It looks like it could blow a man apart."

"All the food is very fresh."

After making the sandwich she went to the ladies' room. He felt depressed. Now why the hell did she have to go and ask him questions about his old lady? Thinking about her, he chewed on the sandwich. With the help of three bottles of lemon pop he downed it but had to guzzle three more of lime to get rid of the artificial lemon taste. He felt a little drunk and snickered because it was a food and pop drunk. He had the odd feeling he was down on his hands and knees searching for something that he couldn't find.

Flores stood at the table.

"If you tell them to go home," he hissed, "they weel."

Roy stared. "Tell who?"

"The players. They are afraid to stay here but they don't go because you stay."

"Go ahead and tell them to go."

"You tell them," Flores urged. "They weel leesten to your word."

"Right," said Roy.

Memo returned and Flores left him. Roy struggled to his feet, broke into a sweat, and sat down again. Fowler grabbed Memo and they whirled around. Roy didn't like them pressed so close together.

His face was damp. He reached into his pocket for a handkerchief and felt Iris' letter. For a second he thought he had found what he was looking for. More clearly than ever he remembered her pretty face and the brown eyes you could look into and see yourself as something more satisfying than you were, and he remembered telling her everything, the first time he had ever told anybody about it, and the relieved feeling he had afterward, and the long swim and Iris swimming down in the moonlit water searching for him, and the fire on the beach, she naked, and finally him banging her. For some reason this was the only thing he was ashamed of, though it couldn't be said she hadn't asked for it.

Fat girls write fat letters, he thought, and then he saw the little chef looking at him and was astonished at how hungry he felt.

Roy pushed himself up and headed for the table. The chef shined up a fast plate and with delight lifted the serving fork.

"I've had a snootful," Roy said.

The chef tittered. "It's all fresh food."

Roy looked into his button eyes. They were small pig's eyes. "Who says so?"

"It's the best there is."

"It stinks." He turned and walked stiffly to the door. Memo saw him. She waved gaily and kept on dancing.

He dragged his belly through the hall. When the elevator came it dropped him down in the lobby. He went along the corridor into the grill room. Carefully sitting down at the table, he ordered six hamburgers and two tall glasses of milk —clean food to kill the pangs of hunger.

The waiter told the cook the order, who got six red meat patties out of the refrigerator and pressed them on the grill. They softly sputtered. He thought he oughtn't to eat any more, but then he thought I am hungry. No, I am not hungry, I am hungry, whatever that means . . . What must I do not to be hungry? He considered fasting but he hadn't fasted since he was a kid. Besides, it made him hungry. He tried hard to recapture how it felt when he was hungry after a day of fishing and was sizzling lake bass over an open fire and boiling coffee in a tin can. All around his head were the sharp-pointed stars.

He was about to lift himself out of the chair but remembered his date with Memo and stayed put. There was time to kill before that so he might as well have a bite.

A hand whacked him across the shoulders.

It was Red Blow . . . Roy slowly sat down.

"Looked for a minute like you were gonna murder me," said Red.

"I thought it was somebody else."

"Who, for instance?"

Roy thought. "I am not sure. Maybe the Mex."

"Flores?"

"Sometimes he gets on my nerves."

"He is really a nice guy."

"I guess so."

Red sat down. "Don't eat too much crap. We have a big day comin' up."

"I am just taking a bite."

"Better get to bed and have plenty of sleep."

"Yes."

Red looked glum. "Can't sleep myself. Don't know what's the matter with me." He yawned and twitched his shoulders. "You all right?"

"Fine and dandy. Have a hamburger."

"Not for me, thanks. Guess I will go for a little walk. Best thing when you can't sleep."

Roy nodded.

"Take care of yourself, feller. Tomorrow's our day. Pop'll dance a jig after tomorrow. You'll be his hero."

Roy didn't answer.

Red smiled a little sadly. "I'm gonna be sorry when it's over."

The waiter brought the six hamburgers. Red looked at them absently. "It's all up to you." He got up and left.

Through the window Roy watched him go down the street.

"I'll be the hero."

The hamburgers looked like six dead birds. He took up the first one and gobbled it down. It was warm but dry. No more dead birds, he thought . . . not without ketchup. He poured a blop on three of the birds. Then he shuffled them up with the other two so as not to know which three had the ketchup and which two hadn't. Eating them, he could not tell the difference except that they all tasted like dead birds. They were not satisfying but the milk was. He made a mental note to drink more milk.

He paid and left. The elevator went up like a greased shot. As it stopped he felt a ripping pain on the floor of the stomach. The wax-faced elevator man watched him with big eyes. He stared at the old scarecrow, then stumbled out. He stood alone in the hall, trying to figure it out. Something was happening that he didn't understand. He roused himself to do battle, wishing for Wonderboy, but no enemy was visible. He rested and the pain left him.

The party was quiet. Flores had disappeared. The lights were dimmed and there was some preliminary sex work going on. Olson had his blonde backed into a corner. A group near the piano were passing a secret bottle around. In the center of the darkened room one of the girls held her dress over her pink panties and was doing bumps and grinds. A silent circle watched her.

Roy buttonholed Fowler. "Stay off the rotgut, kid."

"Stay away from the stuffin's, big shot."

Roy swiped at him but Fowler was gone. He wiped his sweaty face with his sleeve and searched for Memo to tell her it was time. He couldn't find her in the fog that had blown up, so he left the party and reeled down the stairs to the fourth floor. Feeling for her buzzer, he found the key left in the lock and softly turned it.

She was lying naked in bed, chewing a turkey drumstick as she looked at the pictures in a large scrapbook. Not till he was quite close did she see him. She let out a scream.

"You frightened me, Roy." Memo shut the scrapbook.

He had caught a glimpse of Bump's face. I'll take care of that bastard. He unzipped his fly.

Her green eyes closely watched him, her belly heaving above the red flame.

Undressing caused him great distress. Inside him they were tearing up a street. The sweat dripped from his face . . . Yet there was music, the sweetest piping he had ever heard. Dropping his pants he approached for the piping fulfillment.

She drew her legs back. Her expression puzzled him. It was not—the lights were wavering, blinking on and off. A thundering locomotive roared through the mountain. As it burst out of the rock with a whistle howl he felt on the verge of an extraordinary insight, but a bolt of shuddering lightning came at him from some unknown place. He threw up his arms for protection and it socked him, yowling, in the shattered gut. He lived a pain he could not believe existed. Agonized at the extent of it, Roy thudded to his knees as a picture he had long carried in his mind broke into pieces. He keeled over.

The raft with the singing green-eyed siren guarding the forbidden flame gave off into the rotting flood a scuttering one-eyed rat. In the distance though quite near, a toilet flushed, and though the hero braced himself against it, a rush of dirty water got a good grip and sucked him under.

Judge Banner had a money-saving contract with a small maternity hospital near Knights Field (it was there Bump had died) to treat all player emergencies, so that was where they had rushed Roy. The flustered obstetrician on duty decided to deliver the hero of his appendix. However, he fought them deliriously and his strength was too much for the surgeon, anesthetist, attendant, and two mild maternity nurses. They subdued him with a hypo only to uncover a scar snaking down his belly. Investigation showed he had no appendix—it had long ago been removed along with some other stuff. (All were surprised at his scarred and battered body.) The doctors considered cutting out the gall bladder or maybe part of the stomach but nobody wanted to be responsible for the effect of the operation upon the Knights and the general public. (The city was aghast. Crowds gathered outside the hospital, waiting for bulletins. The Japanese government issued an Edict of Sorrow.) So they used the stomach pump instead and dredged up unbelievable quantities of bilge. The patient moaned along with the ladies in labor on the floor, but the doctors adopted a policy of watchful waiting and held off anything drastic.

His belly racked his mind. Icy streams coursed through the fiery desert. He chattered and steamed, rarely conscious, tormented by his dreams. In them he waxed to gigantic heights then abruptly fell miles to be a little Roy dwarf (Hey, mister, you're stepping on my feet). He was caught in roaring gales amid loose, glaring lights, so bright they smothered the eyeballs. Iris' sad head topped Memo's dancing body, with Memo's vice versa upon the shimmying rest of Iris, a confused fusion that dizzied him. He hungered in nightmare for quantities of exotic food—wondrous fowl stuffed with fruit, and the multitudinous roe of tropical fish. When he bent his toothy head to devour, every last morsel vanished. So they served him a prime hunk of beef and he found it enormously delicious only to discover it was himself he was chewing. His thunderous roars sent nurses running from all directions. They were powerless before his flailing fists.

In delirium he hopped out of bed and hunted through the corridors in a nightgown—frightening the newly delivered mothers—for a mop or broom that he snatched back to his aseptic chamber and practiced vicious cuts with before the dresser mirror . . . They found him on the floor . . . At dawn he warily rose and ferreted a plumber's plunger out of the utility closet but this time he was caught by three attendants and dragged back to bed. They strapped him down and there he lay a prisoner, as the frightened Knights dropped the third of three hot potatoes to the scarred and embittered last-place Reds. Since the resurgent Pirates had scattered the brains of the Phils, three in a bloody row, the season ended in a dead heat. A single playoff game in Knights Field was arranged for Monday next, the day before the World Series.

Late that afternoon the fever abated. He returned, unstrapped, to consciousness and recognized a harried Memo at his bedside. From her he learned what had happened to the team, and groaned in anguish. When she left, with a hankie pressed to her reddened nostrils, he discovered his troubles had only just begun. The specialist in the case, a tall stoop-shouldered man with a white mustache and sad eyes, who absently hefted a heavy gold watch as he spoke, gave Roy a bill of particulars. He began almost merrily by telling him there wasn't much doubt he would participate in the Monday playoff (Roy just about leaped out of the bed but the doctor held him back with a gesture). He could play, yes, though he'd not feel at his best, nor would he be able to extend himself so far as he would like, but he would certainly be present and in the game, which, as the doctor understood it, was the big thing for both Roy and his public. (Interest in the matter was so great, he said, that he had permitted release of this news to the press.) Public clamor had compelled his reluctant yielding, though it was his considered opinion that, ideally, Roy ought to rest a good deal longer before getting back to his— ah—normal activities. But someone had explained to him that baseball players were in a way like soldiers, and since he knew that the body's response to duty sometimes achieved many of the good results of prolonged care and medication, he had agreed to let him play.

However, all good news has its counterpart of bad, he almost sadly said, and to prove the point let it come out that it would be best for Roy to say goodbye forever to baseball— if he hoped to stay alive. His blood pressure—at times amazingly high—complicated by an athlete's heart—could conceivably cause his sudden death if he were to attempt to play next season, whereas if he worked at something light and relaxing, one might say he could go one for years, as many had. The doctor slipped the gold watch into his vest pocket, and nodding to the patient, departed. Roy felt that this giant hand holding a club had broken through the clouds and with a single blow crushed his skull.

The hours that followed were the most terrifying of his life (more so than fifteen years ago). He lived in the thought of death, would not move, speak, take food or receive visitors. Yet all the while he fanatically fought the doctor's revelation, wrestled it every waking second, though something in him said the old boy with the white mustache was right. He felt he had for years suspected something wrong, and this was it. Too much pressure in the pipes—blew your conk off. (He saw it blown sky high.) He was through—finished. Only he couldn't—just couldn't believe it. Me. I. Roy Hobbs forever out of the game? Inconceivable. He thought of the fantastic hundreds of records he had broken in so short a time, which had made him a hero to the people, and he thought of the thousands—tens of thousands—that he had pledged himself to break. A moan escaped him.

Still a doubt existed. Maybe white mustache was wrong? They could misjudge them too. Maybe there was a mite less wind behind the ball than he thought, and it would hit the ground at his feet rather than land in the glove. Mistakes could happen in everything. Wouldn't be the first time a saw-bones was wrong. *Maybe he was a hundred per cent dead wrong.*

The next evening, amid a procession of fathers leaving the hospital at baby-feeding time, he sneaked out of the building. A cab got him to Knights Field, and Happy Pellers, the astonished groundskeeper, let him in. A phone call brought Dizzy to the scene. Roy changed into uniform (he almost wept to behold Wonderboy so forlorn in the locker) and Happy donned catcher's gear. Dizzy prepared to pitch. It was just to practice, Roy said, so he would have his eye and timing alert for the playoff Monday. Happy switched on the night floods to make things clearer. Dizzy practiced a few pitches and then with Roy standing at the plate, served one over the middle. As he swung, Roy felt a jet of steam blow through the center of his skull. They gathered him up, bundled him into a cab, and got him back to the hospital, where nobody had missed him.

It was a storm on and Roy out in it. Not exactly true, it was Sam Simpson who was lost and Roy out searching him. He tracked up and down the hills, leaving his white tracks, till he come to this shack with the white on the roof.

Anybody in here? he calls.

Nope.

You don't know my friend Sam?

Nope.

He wept and try to go away.

Come on in, kiddo, I was only foolin'.

Roy dry his eyes and went in. Sam was settin' at the table under the open bulb, his collar and tie off, playing solitaire with all spades.

Roy sit by the fire till Sam finish. Sam looked up wearing his half-moon specs, glinting moonlight.

Well, son, said Sam, lightin' up on his cigar.

I swear I didn't do it, Sam.

Didn't do what?

Didn't do nothin'.

Who said you did?

Roy wouldn't answer, shut tight as a clam.

Sam stayed awhile, then he say to Roy, Take my advice, kiddo.

Yes, Sam.

Don't do it.

No, said Roy, I won't. He rose and stood headbent before Sam's chair.

Let's go back home, Sam, let's now.

Sam peered out the window.

I would like to, kiddo, honest, but we can't go out there now. Heck, it's snowin' baseballs.

When he came to, Roy made the specialist promise to tell no one about his condition just in case he had the slightest chance of improving enough to play for maybe another season. The specialist frankly said he didn't see that chance, but he was willing to keep mum because he believed in the principle of freedom of action. So he told no one and neither did Roy— not even Memo. (No one had even mentioned the subject of his playing in the Series but Roy had already privately decided to take his chances in that.)

But mostly his thoughts were dismal. That frightened feel-

ing: bust before beginning. On the merry-go-round again
about his failure to complete his mission in the game. About
this he suffered most. He lay for hours staring at the window.
Often the glass looked wet though it wasn't raining. A man
who had been walking in bright sunshine limped away into
a mist. This broke the heart . . . When the feeling passed,
if it ever did, there was the necessity of making new choices.
Since it was already the end of the season, he had about four
months in which to cash in on testimonials, endorsements,
ghost-written articles, personal appearances, and such like. But
what after that, when spring training time came and he disappeared into the backwoods? He recalled a sickening procession of jobs—as cook, well-driller, mechanic, logger, bean-
picker, and for whatever odd change, semipro ballplayer. He
dared not think further.

And the loneliness too, from job to job, never some place
in particular for any decent length of time because of the dissatisfaction that grew, after a short while, out of anything he
did . . . But supposing he could collect around twenty-five
G's—could that amount, to begin with, satisfy a girl like Memo
if she married him? He tried to think of ways of investing
twenty-five thousand—maybe in a restaurant or tavern—to
build it up to fifty, and then somehow to double that. His
mind skipped from money to Memo, the only one who came
to see him every day. He remembered the excitement he felt
for her in that strapless yellow dress the night of the party.
And bad as he felt now he couldn't help but think how desirable she had looked, waiting for him naked in bed.

Such thoughts occupied him much of the time as he sat in the
armchair, thumbing through old magazines, or resting in bed.
He sometimes considered suicide but the thought was too
oppressive to stay in his mind. He dozed a good deal and
usually woke feeling lonely. (Except for Red, once, nobody
from the team had come to see him, though small knots of
fans still gathered in the street and argued whether he would
really be in Monday's game.) Saturday night he awoke from
an after supper nap more gloomy than ever, so he reached
under his pillow for Iris' letter. But just then Memo came

into the room with an armful of flowers so he gladly let it lay where it was.

Despite how attractive she usually managed to keep herself (he could appreciate that in spite of a momentary return of the nausea) she appeared worn out now, with bluish shadows under her eyes. And he noticed, as she stuffed the flowers and red autumn leaves into the vase, that she was wearing the same black dress she had worn all week, a thing she never did before, and that her hair was lusterless and not well kept. She had days ago sorrowed it was her fault that this had happened to the team. How stupid not to have waited just a day or two more. (Pop, she wept, had called her filthy names.) She had despaired every minute—really despaired—up to the time she heard he was going to be in the playoff. At least she did not have it on her conscience that he would be out of that, so she felt better now. Not better enough, he worried, or she wouldn't be so lost and lonely-looking.

After she had arranged the flowers, Memo stood mutely at the open window, gazing down into the darkening street. When he least expected it, she sobbed out in a voice full of misery, "Oh, Roy, I can't stand it any longer, I can't."

He sat up. "What's wrong?"

Her voice was choked. "I can't go on with my life as it is." Memo dropped into the armchair and began to weep. In a minute everything around her was wet.

Tossing aside the blanket he swung his legs out of bed. She looked up, attempting to smile. "Don't get up, hon. I'll be all right."

Roy sat uneasily at the edge of the bed. He never knew what to do when they cried.

"It's just that I'm fed up," she wept. "Fed up. Pop is terrible to me and I don't want to go on living off him, even if he is my uncle. I have to get a job or something, or go somewhere."

"What did that bastard shrimp say to you?"

She found a handkerchief in her purse and blew her nose.

"It isn't his words," she said sadly. "Words can't kill. It's that I'm sick of this kind of life. I want to get away."

Then she let go again and looked like a little lost bird beating around in a cage. He was moved, and hovered over her like an old maid aunt trying to stop a leak.

"Don't cry, Memo. Just say the word and I will take care of you." In a cracked voice he said, "Just marry me."

She sobbed for the longest time. So long he grew jumpy with doubts about their future relations, but then she stopped crying and said in a damp voice, "Would you have me, Roy?"

He swayed with emotion as he got out thickly, "Would I?" To keep from hitting the ground he hopped into bed and sprawled out.

She came to him, her white hands clasped, her wet eyelids like sparkling flowers. "There's one thing you have to understand, Roy, and then maybe you won't want me. That is that I am afraid to be poor." She said it with intensity, her face turning dark at her words. "Maybe I am weak or spoiled, but I am the type who has to have somebody who can support her in a decent way. I'm sick of living like a slave. I got to have a house of my own, a maid to help me with the hard work, a decent car to shop with and a fur coat for winter time when it's cold. I don't want to have to worry every time a can of beans jumps a nickel. I suppose it's wrong to want all of that but I can't help it. I've been around too long and seen too much. I saw how my mother lived and I know it killed her. I made up my mind to have certain things. You understand that, don't you, Roy?"

He nodded.

"We have to face it," she said. "You're thirty-five now and that don't give you much time left as a ball player."

"What d'ye mean?" he asked, deadpan.

But it wasn't his blood pressure she was referring to. For a minute he was afraid she had found out.

"I'm sorry to say this, Roy, but I have to be practical. Suppose the next one is your last season, or that you will have one more after that? Sure, you'll probably get a good contract till then but it costs money to live, and then what'll we do for the rest of our lives?"

It was dark in the room now. He could scarcely see her.

"Turn on the lights."

She smeared powder over her nose and under her eyes, then pressed the button.

He stared at her.

She grew restless. "Roy—"

"I was just thinking, even if I had to quit right now I could still scrounge up about twenty-five grand in the next few months. That's a lotta dough."

She seemed doubtful. "What would you do with it?"

"We'd get hitched and I would invest in a business. Everybody does that. My name is famous already. We will make out okay. You will have what you want."

"What kind of business?" Memo asked.

"I can't say for sure—maybe a restaurant."

She made a face.

"What do you have in mind?" Roy asked.

"Oh, something big, Roy. I would like you to buy into a company where you could have an executive job and won't have to go poking your nose into the stew in a smelly restaurant."

A jet of nausea shot up from his gizzard. He admitted to himself he wanted nothing to do with restaurants.

"How much dough do we need to get in on one of those big companies?"

"I should think more than twenty-five thousand."

He gulped. "Around thirty-five?"

"More like fifty."

Roy frowned. Talk of that kind of dough gave him a belly-ache. But Memo was right. It had to be something big or it wouldn't pay back enough. And if it was a big company he could take it a little easy, to protect his health, without anybody kicking. He pondered where to get another twenty-five thousand, and it had to be before the start of the next baseball season because as soon as everybody saw he wasn't playing, it wouldn't be easy to cash in on his name. People had no use for a has-been. He had to be married and have the dough, both before next spring—in case he never did get to play. He thought of other means to earn some money fast—selling the story of his life to the papers, barnstorming a bit this fall and winter, not too strenuously. But neither of these things added up to much—not twenty-five grand. Roy lay back with his eyes shut.

Memo whispered something. His lids flew open. What was she doing with an old black dress on, her hair uncombed, looking like Lola, the Jersey City fortuneteller? Yet her voice was calm . . .

"Who sent you," he spoke harshly, "—that bastard Gus?"

She turned flame-faced but answered quietly, "The Judge."

"Banner?" Somebody inside of him—this nervous character lately hanging around—crashed a glass to the floor. Roy's pulses banged.

"He said he'd pay you fifteen thousand now and more next season. He says it would depend on you."

"I thought I smelled skunk."

"He asked me to deliver the message. I have nothing to do with it."

"Who else is in on this?"

"I don't know."

"Pop?"

"No."

He lay motionless for an age. She said no more, did not plead or prod. It grew late. An announcemnt was made for visitors to leave. She rose and tiredly put on her coat.

"I was thinking of all the years you would be out of the game."

"What does he want me to do?"

"It's something about the playoff—I don't know."

"They want me to drop it?"

She didn't answer.

"No," he said out loud.

She shrugged. "I told them you wouldn't."

She was thin and haggard-looking. Her shoulders drooped, her hands were bloodless. To refuse her just about broke his heart.

·   ·   ·

He fell into a deep slumber but had not slept very long before this rat-eyed vulture, black against the ceiling, began to flap around the room and dripping deep fat spiraled down toward his face. Wrestling together, they knocked over the tables and chairs, when the lights went on and waked him. Roy grabbed under the pillow for a gun he thought was there, only it wasn't. Awake, he saw through the glare that Judge Goodwill Banner, in dark glasses and hairy black fedora, was staring at him from the foot of the bed.

"What the hell do you want here?"

"Don't be alarmed," the Judge rumbled. "Miss Paris informed me you were not asleep, and the authorities granted me a few minutes to visit with you."

"I got nothing to say to you." The nightmare had weakened him. Not wanting the Judge to see that, he pulled himself into a sitting position.

The Judge, yellow-skinned in the electric light, and rumpled-looking, sat in the armchair with his potlike hat on. He sucked an unwilling flame into his King Oscar and tossed the burnt-out match on the floor.

"How is your health, young man?"

"Skip it. I am all right now."

The Judge scrutinized him.

"Wanna bet?" Roy said.

The Judge's rubbery lips tightened around his cigar. After a minute he removed it from his mouth and said cautiously, "I assume that Miss Paris has acquainted you with the terms of a certain proposal?"

"Leave her name out of it."

"An admirable suggestion—a proposal, you understand, made by persons unknown."

"Don't make me laugh. I got a good mind to sick the FBI on you."

The Judge examined his cigar. "I rely on your honor. You might consider, however, that there is no witness other than Miss Paris, and I assume you would be solicitious of her?"

"I said to leave her name out."

"Quite so. I believe she erred concerning the emolument offered—fifteen thousand, was it? My understanding is that twenty thousand, payable in cash in one sum, is closer to the correct amount. I'm sure you know the prevailing rate for this sort of thing is ten thousand dollars. We offer twice that. Any larger sum is unqualifiedly out of the question because it will impair the profitableness of the venture. I urge you to consider carefully. You know as well as I that you are in no condition to play."

"Then what are you offering me twenty thousand smackers for—to show your gratitude for how I have built up your bank account?"

"I see no reason for sarcasm. You were paid for your services as contracted. As for this offer, I frankly confess it is insurance. There is the possibility that you may get into the game and unexpectedly wreck it with a single blow. I personally doubt this will occur, but we prefer to take no chances."

"Don't kid yourself that I am too weak to play. You know that the doctor himself said I'll be in there Monday."

The Judge hesitated. "Twenty-five thousand," he finally said. "Absolutely my last offer."

"I hear the bookies collect ten million a day on baseball bets."

"Ridiculous."

"That's what I hear."

"It makes no difference, I am not a bookie. What is your answer?"

"I say no."

The Judge bit his lip.

Roy said, "Ain't you ashamed that you are selling a club down the river that hasn't won a pennant in twenty-five years and now they have a chance to?"

"We'll have substantially the same team next year," the Judge answered, "and I have no doubt that we will make a better job of the entire season, supported as we shall be by new players and possibly another manager. If we take on the Yankees now—that is, if we are foolish enough to win the playoff match—they will beat us a merciless four in a row, despite your presence. You are not strong enough to withstand the strain of a World Series, and you know it. We'd be ground to pulp, made the laughingstock of organized baseball, and your foolish friend, Pop Fisher, would this time destroy himself in his humiliation."

"What about all the jack you'd miss out on, even if we only played four Series games and lost every one?"

"I have calculated the amount and am certain I can do better, on the whole, in the way I suggest. I have reason to believe that, although we are considered to be the underdogs, certain gambling interests have been betting heavily on the Knights to win. Now it is my purpose, via the uncontested— so to speak—game, to teach these parasites a lesson they will never forget. After that they will not dare to infest our stands again."

"Pardon me while I throw up."

The Judge looked hurt.

"The odds favor us," Roy said. "I saw it in tonight's paper."

"In one only. The others quote odds against us."

Roy laughed out loud.

The Judge flushed through his yellow skin. "Honi soit qui mal y pense."

"Double to you," Roy said.

"Twenty-five thousand," said the Judge with an angry gesture. "The rest is silence."

Though Roy had a splitting headache he tried to think the situation out. The way he now felt, he wouldn't be able to stand at the plate with a feather duster on his shoulder, let alone a bat. Maybe the Judge's hunch was right, and he might not be able to do a single thing to help the Knight's win their game. On the other hand—maybe he'd be himself, his real self. If he helped them win the playoff—no matter if they later dropped the Series four in a row—there would still be all sorts of endorsement offers and maybe even a contract to do a baseball movie. Then he'd have the dough to take care of Memo in proper style. Yet suppose he played and because of his

weakness flopped as miserably as he had during his slump?
That might sour the endorsements and everything else, and
he'd end up with nothing—or very little. His mind went
around in drunken circles.

All this time the Judge's voice was droning on. "I have observed," he was saying, "how one moral condition may lead
to or become its opposite. I recall an occasion on the bench
when out of the goodness of my heart and a warm belief in
humanity, I resolved to save a boy from serving a prison sentence. Though his guilt was clear, because of his age I sus-
pended sentence and paroled him for a period of five years.
That afternoon as I walked down the courthouse steps, I felt
I could surely face my maker without a blush. However, not
one week later the boy stood before me, arraigned as a most
wicked parricide. I asked myself can any action—no matter
what its origin or motive—which ends so evilly—can such an
action possibly be designated as good?"

He took out a clotted handkerchief, spat into it, folded it
and thrust it into his pocket. "Contrarily," he went on, "a deed
of apparently evil significance may come to pure and beautiful
flower. I have in mind a later case tried before me in which
a physician swindled his patient, a paralytic, out of almost a
quarter of a million dollars. So well did he contrive to hide
the loot that it has till this day not been recovered. Nevertheless, the documentary evidence was strong enough to convict
the embezzler and I sentenced him to a term of from forty to
fifty years in prison, thus insuring he would not emerge from
the penitentiary to enjoy his ill-gotten gains before he is
eighty-three years of age. Yet, while testifying from his wheel
chair at the trial, the paralytic astonished himself and all present by rising in righteous wrath against the malcontent and,
indeed, tottered across the floor to wreak upon him his venge-
ance. Naturally the bailiff restrained him, but would you
have guessed that he was, from that day on, sound in wind and
limb, and as active as you or I? He wrote me afterwards that
the return of his power of locomotion more than compensated
him for the loss of his fortune."

Roy frowned. "Come out of the bushes."

The Judge paused. "I was trying to help you assess this action in terms of the future."

"You mean if I sell out?"

"Put it that way if you like."

"And that maybe some good might come out of it?"

"That is my assumption."

"For me, you mean?"

"For others too. It is impossible to predict who will be benefited."

"I thought you said you were doing this to get rid of the gamblers—that's good right off, ain't it?"

The Judge cleared his throat. "Indeed it is. However, one might consider, despite the difficulty of the personal situation —that is to say, within the context of one's own compunctions —that it is impossible to predict what further good may accrue to one, and others, in the future, as a result of an initially difficult decision."

Roy laughed. "You should be selling snake oil."

He had thought there might be something to the argument. He was now sure there wasn't, for as the Judge had talked he recalled an experience he had had when he was a kid. He and his dog were following an old skid road into the heart of a spooky forest when the hound suddenly let out a yelp, ran on ahead, and got lost. It was late in the afternoon and he couldn't stand the thought of leaving the dog there alone all night, so he went into the wood after it. At first he could see daylight between the trees—to this minute he remembered how still the trunks were, as the tree tops circled around in the breeze—and in sight of daylight it wasn't so bad, nor a little deeper in, despite the green gloom, but just at about the time the darkness got so thick he was conscious of having to shove against it as he hallooed for the dog, he got this scared and lonely feeling that he was impossibly lost. With his heart whamming against his ribs he looked around but could recognize no direction in the darkness, let alone discover the right one. It was cold and he shivered. Only, the payoff of it was that the mutt found him and led him out of the woods. That was good out of good.

Roy pulled the covers over his head. "Go home."

The Judge didn't move. "There is also the matter of next season's contract."

Roy listened. Would there ever be a next season? He uncovered his head. "How much?"

"I shall offer—provided we agree on the other matter—a substantial raise."

"Talk figures."

"Forty-five thousand for the season. We might also work out some small percentage on the gate."

"Twenty-five thousand for dropping the game is not enough," said Roy. As he spoke an icicle of fright punctured his spine.

The Judge scowled and drew on his half-gone cigar. "Thirty," he said, "and no more."

"Thirty-five," Roy got out. "Don't forget I stand to lose a couple of thousand on the pay I could get in the Series."

"Utterly outrageous," snapped the Judge.

"Don't slam the door on your way out."

The Judge rose, brushed his wrinkled pants and left.

Roy stared at the ceiling—relieved.

The Judge returned. He removed his hat and wiped his perspiring face with his dirty handkerchief. His head was covered with a thick black wig. You never got to the bottom of that creep.

"You are impossible to deal with—but I accept." His voice was flat. He covered his head with his hat.

But Roy said he had changed his mind when the Judge was out of the room. He had thought it over and decided the boys wanted to win that game and he wanted to help them. That was good. He couldn't betray his own team and manager. That was bad.

The Judge then hissed, "You may lose Miss Paris to someone else if you are not careful."

Roy bolted up. "To who for instance?"

"A better provider."

"You mean Gus Sands?"

The Judge did not directly reply. "A word to the wise—"

"That's none of your business," said Roy. He lay back. Then he asked, "What if I couldn't lose the game by myself? The Pirates ain't exactly world beaters. We roasted them the last seven times. The boys might do it again even if I didn't hit a thing."

The Judge rubbed his scaly hands. "The Knights are demoralized. Without you, I doubt they can win over a sandlot team, contrary opinion notwithstanding. As for the contingency of the flat failure of the opposing team, we have made the necessary arrangements to take care of that."

Roy was up again. "You mean there's somebody else in on this deal?"

The Judge smiled around his cigar.

"Somebody on our team?"

"A key man."

"In that case—" Roy said slowly.

"The thirty-five thousand is final. There'll be no changing that."

"With forty-five for the contract—"

"Agreed. You understand you are not under any circumstances to hit the ball safely?"

After a minute Roy said slowly, "I will take the pitch."

"I beg your pardon?"

"The fix is on."

The Judge caught on and said with a laugh, "I see you share my philological interests." He lit his dead King Oscar.

Through the nausea Roy remembered an old saying. He quoted, "Woe unto him who calls evil good and good evil."

The Judge glared at him.

Memo returned and covered his face with wet kisses. She tweaked his nose, mussed his hair, and called him wonderful. After she left he couldn't sleep so he reached under his pillow and got out Iris' letter.

". . . After my baby was born, the women of the home

where my father had brought me to save himself further shame were after me to give it up. They said it would be bad for her to be brought up by an unmarried mother, and that I would have no time to myself or opportunity to take up my normal life. I tried, as they said, to be sensible and offer her for adoption, but I had been nursing her—although warned against it, nursing shrinks the breasts you know, and they were afraid for my figure—and the thought of tearing myself away from her forever was too much for me. Since Papa wouldn't have her in his house I decided to find a job and bring her up myself. That turned out to be a lot harder than I had expected, because I earned not very much and had to pay for baby's care all day, her things, the rent of course, and the clothes I had to have for work. At night I had supper to think of, bathing her, laundry, house cleaning, and preparing for the next day, which never changed from any other.

"Except for my baby I was nearly always alone, reading, mostly, to improve myself, although sometimes it was unbearable, especially before I was twenty and just after. It also took quite a while until I got rid of my guilt, or could look upon her as innocent of it, but eventually I did, and soon her loveliness and gaiety and all the tender feelings I had in my heart for her made up for a lot I had suffered. Yet I was tied to time—not so much to the past—nor to the expectations of the future, which was really too far away—only to here and now, day after day, until suddenly the years unrolled and a change came—more a reward of standing it so long than any sudden magic—and more quickly than I could believe, she had grown into a young woman, and almost as if I had wished it on her, fell in love with a wonderful boy and married him. Like me she was a mother before she was seventeen. Suddenly everywhere I looked seemed to be tomorrow, and I was at last free to take up my life where I had left it off one summer night when I went for a walk in the park with a stranger . . ."

He read down to the last page, where she once more mentioned herself as a grandmother. Roy crumpled the letter and pitched it against the wall.

On the morning of the game fist fights broke out all over the stands in Knights Field. Hats, bottles, apple cores, bananas, and the mushy contents of sack lunches were thrown around. A fan in one of the boxes had a rock bounced off his skull, opening a bleeding gash. Two special cops rushed up the steps and got hold of an innocent-looking guy with glasses, whose pockets were stuffed with odd-shaped rocks. They dragged him forth, although he was hollering he had collected them for his rock garden, and flung him headlong out of the park. He was from Pittsburgh and cursed the Knights into the ground. A disappointed truck driver who couldn't get in to see the game tackled him from behind, knocking the rock collector's head against the sidewalk and smashing his glasses. He spat out two bloody teeth and sat there sobbing till the ambulance came.

The sun hid behind the clouds for the most part. The day was chilly, football weather, but the stands were decorated with colored bunting, the flags on the grandstand roof rode high in the breeze and the crowd was raucous. The PA man tried to calm them but they were packed together too tight to be peaceful, for the Judge had sold hundreds of extra tickets and the standees raced for any seat that was vacant for a second. Besides, the Knights' fans were jumpy, their nerves ragged from following the ups and downs of the team. Some glum-faced gents bitterly cursed Roy out, calling him welsher, fool, pig-horse for eating himself into that colossal bellyache. But he had his defenders, who claimed the Big Man's body burned food so fast he needed every bit he ate. They blamed the damage on ptomaine. The accusers wanted to know why no one else at the party had come down sick. They were answered where would the Knights be without Roy—at the bottom of the heap. The one who spoke got a rap on the ear for his trouble. The rapper was grabbed by a cop, run down the catwalk, and pitched into the rotunda. Yet though the fans were out of sorts and crabbing at each other, they presented a solid front when it came to laying bets. Many pessimistically shook their heads, but they counted up the seven straight wins over the Pirates, figured in that Hobbs was back, and reached into their pockets. Although there were not too many Pirate rooters around, the bets were quickly covered for every hard-earned buck.

Otto Zipp was above all this. He sat like a small mountain behind the rail in short left, reading the sports page of his newspaper. He looked neither right nor left, and if somebody tried to talk to him Otto gave him short shrift. Then when they least expected it, he would honk his horn and cry out in shrill tones, "Throw him to the hawks." After that he went back to the sports page.

When the players began drifting into the clubhouse they were surprised to see Roy there. He was wearing his uniform and slowly polishing Wonderboy. The boys said hello and not much more. Flores looked at his feet. Some of them were embarrassed that they hadn't gone to see him in the hospital. Secretly they were pleased he was here. Allie Stubbs even began to kid around with Olson. Roy thought they would not act so chipper if they knew he felt weak as piss and was dreading the game. The Judge was absolutely crazy to pay him thirty-five grand not to hit when he didn't feel able to even lift a stick. He hoped Pop would guess how shaky he was and bench him. What a laugh that would be on the Judge—serve the bastard right. But when Pop came in, he didn't so much as glance in Roy's direction. He walked straight into his office and slammed the door, which suited Roy fine.

Pop had ordered everybody kept out of the clubhouse until after the game but Mercy weaseled in. All smiles, he approached Roy, asking for the true story of what went on at the party that night, but Red Blow saw him and told him to stay outside. Max had tried the same act in the hospital last week. The floor nurse caught him sneaking toward Roy's room and had him dropped out on the front steps. After leaving the clubhouse Max sent in a note, inviting Roy to come out and make a statement. People were calling him a filthy coward and what did he intend to say to that? Roy gave out a one-word unprintable reply. Mercy shot in a second note. "You'll get yours—M.M." Roy tore it up and told the usher to take no more slop from him.

Pop poked his baldy out of his door and called for Roy. The players looked around uneasily. Roy got up and finally went into the office. For an insufferable time Pop failed to speak. He was unshaven, his face exuding gray stubble that made him look eighty years old. His thin frame seemed shrunken and his left eye was a little crossed with fatigue. Pop leaned back in his creaking swivel chair, staring with tears in his eyes over his half moons at the picture of Ma on his desk. Roy examined his fingernails.

Pop sighed, "Roy, it's my own fault."

It made Roy edgy. "What is?"

"This mess that we are now in. I am not forgetting I kept you on the bench for three solid weeks in June. If I hadn't done that foolish thing we'da finished the season at least half a dozen games out in front."

Roy offered no reply.

"But your own mistake was a bad one too."

Roy nodded.

"A bad one, with the team right on top of hooking the pennant." Pop shook his head. Yet he said he wouldn't blame Roy too much because it wasn't entirely of his own doing. He then apologized for not coming to see him in the hospital. He had twice set out to but felt too grumpy to be fit company for a sick man, so he hadn't come. "It's not you that I am mad at, Roy—it's that blasted Memo. I shoulda pitched her out on her ass the first day she showed up at my door."

Roy got up.

"Sit down." Pop bent forward. "We can win today." His cold breath smelled bad. Roy drew his head back.

"Well, we can, can't we?"

He nodded.

"What's the matter with you?"

"I feel weak," Roy said, "and I am not betting how I will hit today."

Pops voice got kindly again. "I say we can win it whichever

way you feel. Once you begin to play you will feel stronger. And if the rest of those birds see you hustling they will break their backs to win. All they got to feel is there is somebody on this team who thinks they can."

Pop then related a story about a rookie third baseman he once knew, a lad named Mulligan. He was a fine hitter and thrower but full of hard luck all his life. Once he was beaned at the plate and had his skull cracked. He returned for spring practice the following year and the first day out he crashed into another fielder and broke his arm. On the return from that he was on first running to second on a hit and run play and the batter smacked the ball straight at him, breaking two ribs and dislocating a disc in his spine. After that he quit baseball, to everybody's relief.

"He was just unlucky," Pop said, "and there wasn't a thing anybody could do to take the whammy off of him and change his hard luck. You know, Roy, I been lately thinking that a whole lot of people are like him, and for one reason or the other their lives will go the same way all the time, without them getting what they want, no matter what. I for one."

Then to Roy's surprise he said he never hoped to have a World Series flag. Pop swiveled his chair closer. "It ain't in the cards for me—that's all. I am wise to admit it to myself. It took a long time but I finally saw which way the arrow has been pointing." He sighed deeply. "But that don't hold true about our league pennant, Roy. That's the next best thing and I feel I am entitled to it. I feel if I win it just this once—I will be satisfied. I will be satisfied, and win or lose in the Series, I will quit baseball forever." He lowered his voice. "You see what it means to me, son?"

"I see."

"Roy, I would give my whole life to win this game and take the pennant. Promise me that you will go in there and do your damndest."

"I will go in," Roy sighed.

After the practice bell had rung, when he reluctantly climbed up out of the dugout and shoved himself toward the batting

cage with his bat in his hand, as soon as the crowd got a look
at him the boo birds opened up, alternating with shrill whistles
and brassy catcalls. Roy hardened his jaws, but then a rumble
erupted that sounded like bubbling tubfuls of people laughing
and sobbing. The noise grew to a roar, boiled over, and to his
astonishment, drowned out the disapprovers in an ovation of
cheering. Men flung their hats into the air, scaling straws and
limp felts, pounded each other's skulls, and cried themselves
hoarse. Women screeched and ended up weeping. The shouting grew, piling reverberation upon reverberation, till it
reached blast proportions. When it momentarily wore thin,
Sadie Sutter's solemn gong could be heard, but as the roar
rose again, the gonging grew faint and died in the distance.
Roy felt feverish. The applause was about over when he removed his cap to clean the sweat off his brow, and once more
thunder rolled across the field, continuing in waves as he
entered the cage. With teeth clenched to stop the chattering,
he took three swipes at the ball, driving each a decent distance. At Pop's urging he also went out onto the field to shag
some flies. Again the cheers resounded, although he wished
they wouldn't. He speared a few flies in his tracks, dropped
his glove and walked to the dugout. The cheers trailed him in
a foaming billow, but above the surflike roar and the renewed
tolling of Sadie's gong, he could hear Otto Zipp's shrill curses.
The dwarf drew down on his head a chorus of hisses but
thumbed his cherry nose as Roy passed by. Roy paid him no
heed whatsoever, infuriating Otto.

The Pirates flipped through their practice and the game
began. Pop had picked Fowler to start for the Knights. Roy
figured then that he knew who was in this deal with him.
Leave it to the Judge to tie the bag in the most economical
way—with the best hitter and pitcher. He had probably asked
Pop who he was intending to pitch and then went out and
bought him, though no doubt paying a good deal less than
the price Roy was getting. What surprised and shocked him
was that Fowler could be so corrupt though so young and in
the best of health. If he only had half the promise of the future
Fowler had, he would never have dirtied his paws in this busi-

ness. However, as he watched Fowler pitch during the first
inning he wasn't certain he was the one. His fast ball hopped
today and he got rid of the first two Pirates with ease. Maybe
he was playing it cagey first off, time would tell. Roy's
thoughts were broken up by the sound, and echo behind him,
of the crack of a bat. The third man up had taken hold of one
and it was arching into deep left. Already Flores was hot
footing it in from center. It occurred to Roy that although he
had promised the Judge he wouldn't hit, he had made no com-
mitments as to catching them. Waving Flores aside, he ran
several shaky steps and made a throbbing stab at the ball,
spearing it on the half run for the third out. As he did so he
noticed a movement up in the tower window and saw the
Judge's stout figure pressed against the window. He then
recollected he hadn't seen Memo since Saturday.

To nobody's surprise, Dutch Vogelman went to the mound
for the Pirates. In a few minutes it was clear to all he was
working with championship stuff, because he knocked the first
three Knights off without half trying, including Flores, who
was no easy victim. Roy had no chance to bat, for which he
felt relieved. But after Fowler had also rubbed out the oppo-
sition, he was first up in the second inning. As he dragged
Wonderboy up to the plate, the stands, after a short outburst,
were hushed. Everybody remembered the four homers he had
got off Vogelman the last time he had faced him. In the dugout Pop and the boys were peppering it up for him to give
the ball a big ride, and so were Red Blow and Earl Wilson,
on the baselines. What they didn't know was that Roy had
been struck giddy with weakness. His heart whammed like a
wheezing steam engine, his head felt nailed to a pole, his ear-
drums throbbed as if he were listening to the bottom of the
sea, and his arms hung like dead weights. It was with the
greatest effort that he raised Wonderboy. As he was slowly
getting set, he sneaked a cautious glance up at the tower, and
it did not exactly surprise him that Memo, still in black, was
standing at the window next to the Judge, blankly gazing
down at him. Anyway, he knew where she was now.

Vogelman had been taking his time. For a pitcher he was a

comparatively short duck, with a long beak, powerful arms and legs, red sleeves leaking out of a battered jersey, and a nervous delivery. Despite the fact that he had ended the regular season as a twenty-five game winner, he worried to bursting beads of sweat at the thought of pitching to Roy. Every time he recalled those four gopher balls, one after the other landing in the stands, he cringed with embarrassment. And he knew, although there was nobody on base at the moment, that if he served one of them up now, it could conceivably ice the game for the Knights and louse up the very peak of his year of triumph. So Vogelman delayed by wiping the shine off the ball, inspecting the stitches, fumbling for the resin bag, scuffing his cleats in the dirt, and removing his cap to rub away the sweat he had worked up. When the boos of the crowd got good and loud, Stuffy Briggs bellowed for him to throw and Vogelman reluctantly let go with a pitch.

The ball was a whizzer but dripping lard. Weak as he felt, Roy had to smile at what he could really do to that baby if he had his heart set on it, but he swung the slightest bit too late, grunting as the ball shot past Wonderboy—which almost broke his wrists to get at it—and plunked in the pocket of the catcher's glove.

. . . Where had she been since Saturday? Sunday was the first day she hadn't come to the hospital, the day she knew he was getting out of the joint. He had left alone, followed by some reporters he wouldn't talk to, and had taken a cab to the hotel. Once in his room he got into pajamas, and wondering why she hadn't at least called him, fell asleep. He had then had this dream of her—seeing her in some city, it looked like Boston—and she didn't recognize him when they passed but walked on fast in her swaying walk. He chased after her and she was (he remembered) swallowed up in the crowd. But he saw the red hair and followed after that, only it turned out to be a dyed redhead with a mean mouth and dirty eyes. Where's Memo? he called, and woke thinking she was here in the room, but she wasn't, and he hadn't seen her till he located her up there in the tower.

Roy gazed at the empty bases. Striking out with nobody on

was the least harm he could do the team, yet his fingers itched to sock it a little. He couldn't trust himself to because—who could tell?—it might go over the fence, the way Wonderboy was tugging at his muscles. Vogelman then tried a low-breaking curve that Roy had to "take" for ball one. The pitcher came back with a foolish floater that he pretended to almost break his back reaching after.

Strike two. There were only three.

. . . He was remembering the time his old lady drowned the black tomcat in the tub. It had gotten into the bathroom with her and bit at her bare ankles. She once and for all grabbed the cursed thing and dropped it into the hot tub. The cat fought to get out, but she shrilly beat it back and though it yowled mournfully, gave it no mercy. Yet it managed in its hysterical cat-way to stay afloat in the scalding water that she bathed in to cut her weight down, until she shoved its dirty biting head under, from which her hand bled all over. But when the water was drained, and the cat, all glossy wet, with its pink tongue caught between its teeth, lay there dead, the whole thing got to be too much for her and she couldn't lift it out of the tub.

He closed his eyes before the next pitch in the hope it would be quickly called against him, but it curved out for a ripe ball two. Opening his lids, he saw Mercy in a nearby seat, gazing at him with a malevolent sneer. You too, Max, Roy thought, tightening his hold on the bat. Vogelman was beginning to act more confident. You too, Vogelman, and he shut his eyes again, thinking how, after that time with Iris on the beach, when they were driving home, she rested her head against his arm. She was frightened, wanted him to comfort her but he wouldn't. "When will you grow up, Roy?" she said.

Vogelman blistered across a hot, somewhat high one, not too bad to miss, and that made it three and out. Otto Zipp held his nose and pulled the chain, and Roy, quivering, remained for a few seconds with the stick raised over his head, shriveling the dwarf into the silence and immobility that prevailed elsewhere. He threw Wonderboy aside—some in the front boxes let out a gasp—and returned empty-handed to the bench. The Judge and Memo had gone from the tower window.

As the Pirates came to bat for their half of the third (there were no Knight hits after Roy struck out) a breeze blew dust all over the place. Some of the fans with nothing better to do were shoveling the rotten fruit and slices of buttered sandwich bread into paper sacks, or kicking it under their seats. Nobody seemed to be hungry and the Stevens boys, despite all their barking, sold only a few hot coffees. Nor was there much talk of the past half inning. A few complained that Roy had never looked so bad—like a sloppy walrus. Others reminded them the game was young yet.

Neither team scored in either the third or fourth. The way the Knights fanned made Roy wonder if they had all been bought off by the Judge. Yet it didn't seem likely. He was too stingy. In the fifth came his next turn, again first up, a small break.

The stands awoke and began a rhythmic clapping. "Lift 'at pill, Roy. Bust its guts. Make it bleed. You can do it, kid."

"You can do it," Pop hollered from the dugout steps.

With a heavy heart Roy pulled himself up to the plate. He had shooting pains in back muscles that had never bothered him before and a crick in his neck. He couldn't comfortably straighten up and the weight of Wonderboy crouched him further. But Vogelman, despite Roy's strikeout, was burdened with worry over what he still *might* do. He wiped his face with his red sleeve but failed to calm down. By wide margins his first two throws were balls. To help him out, Roy swung under the third pitch. Otto Zipp then let out a string of boos, bahs, and bums, Roy thought he better foul the next one for strike two but Vogelman wouldn't let him, throwing almost over his head. Remembering he could walk if he wanted to, Roy waited. There was no harm to anybody in that and it would look better for him. The next pitch came in too close, and that was how he got to first and the Judge again to the window. But it made no difference one way or the other, for though Lajong sacrificed him to second, Gabby slashed a high one across the diamond which the second baseman jumped for, and he tagged Roy for an unassisted double play. Nobody could blame *him* for that, Roy thought, as he headed out to the field. He stole a look back at Pop and the manager was muttering to himself out of loose lips in a bony face. It seemed to Roy he had known the old man all his life long.

He found himself thinking of maybe quitting the deal with the Judge. He could send a note up there saying the fix was off. But he couldn't think what to write Memo. He tried to imagine what it would be like living without her and couldn't stand the thought of the loneliness.

Dave Olson opened the sixth with the Knights' first hit, a thumping double. The stands sounded like a gigantic drawerful of voices that had suddenly been pulled open. But Benz went down swinging, then Fowler bunted into another quick d.p. and the drawerful of voices was shut. Roy wondered about that bunt. He had a notion Fowler would commit himself soon because time was on the go. But Fowler didn't, making it another sweep of three Pirates. He had thus far given up only two safeties. In the seventh, the Knights, sensing Vogelman was tiring, found their way to him. Allie Stubbs chopped a grass cutter through a hole in the infield for a single. Baker, attempting to lay down a bunt, was overanxious and struck out. Then Flores lifted one just above the first base-man's frantic fingers, and Stubbs, running with his head down, sprang safely into third. Roy was on deck but with two on base his heart misgave him. The crowd jumped to its feet, roaring for him to come through.

As he approached the plate, the sun, that had been plumb-ing the clouds since the game began, at last broke through and bathed the stadium in a golden glow that caused the crowd to murmur. As the warmth fell upon him, Roy felt a sob break in his throat. The weakness left his legs, his heart beat steadily, his giddy gut tightened, and he stood firm and strong upon the earth. Though it startled him to find it so, he had regained a sense of his own well-being. A thousand springlike thoughts crowded through his mind, blotting out the dark diagnosis of the white-mustached specialist. He felt almost happy, and that he could do anything he wanted, if he wanted. His eyes scanned the forward rows in left field but stopped at Zipp's surly face. He felt suddenly anguished at what he had promised the Judge.

On his first swing—at a bad pitch—Otto let out a stream of jeers, oaths, and horn hoots that burned Roy to his bones. I will get that little ass-faced bastard. On the next pitch he shortened his hold on Wonderboy, stepped in front of the ball, and pulled it sharply foul. The ball whizzed past Otto's nose and boomed down an entrance way. The dwarf turned into flour, then as the blood rushed back to his face, grew furious. He jumped up and down on his seat, shook his fist, and screeched curses.

"Carrion, offal, turd—flush the bowl."

Roy tried to send the next ball through his teeth. It hit the rail with a bong and bounced into the air. A man behind Otto caught it in his straw hat. Though the crowd laughed, the boos at Roy grew louder. Red Blow held up two warning fingers. Roy chopped a third foul at the dwarf. With a shriek he covered his face with his arms and ducked.

Several rows up from Otto, a dark-haired woman in a white dress had risen and was standing alone amid the crowd. Christ, another one, Roy thought. At the last split second he had tried to hold his swing but couldn't. The ball spun like a shot at Otto, struck his hard skull with a thud, and was deflected upward. It caught the lady in the face, and to the crowd's horror, she went soundlessly down.

A commotion rose in the stands. Fans by the hundreds piled out of their seats to get at her but the cops and ushers blocked their way, warning them not to crush her to death. Stuffy Briggs called time. Roy dropped his bat, hopped into the boxes and ran up the stairs—his clacking cleats shooting sparks—and along the aisle to where she lay. Many of the fans were standing on their seats to see and there was a crowd pressed around her. Murmuring lynch threats, they let Roy through. A doctor was attending her but she was stretched out unconscious.

Roy already knew who it was. "Iris," he groaned.

Iris woke, opened her good eye and sighed, "Roy."

Lifting her in his arms, he carried her to the clubhouse. Doc Casey and Dizzy kept everybody out. Max Mercy, hot for news, jammed his foot in the door but Dizzy crushed it hard, and Max danced as he cursed.

Roy gently laid her on the trainer's table. The left side of her face was hurt, bruised and rainbow-colored. Her eye was black and the lid thick. But the right side was still calm and lovely.

What have I done, he thought, and why did I do it? And he thought of all the wrong things he had done in his life and tried to undo them but who could?

The doctor went out to call an ambulance. Roy closed the door after him.

"Oh, Roy," sighed Iris.

"Iris, I am sorry."

"Roy, you must win—"

He groaned. "Why didn't you come here before?"

"My letter—you never answered."

He bowed his head.

The doctor entered. "Contusions and lacerations. Not much to worry about, but to be on the safe side she ought to be X-rayed."

"Don't spare any expenses," Roy said.

"She'll be fine. You can go back to the game now."

"You must win, Roy," said Iris.

Seeing there was more to this than he had thought, the doctor left.

Roy turned to her trying to keep in mind that she was a grandmother but when he scanned the fine shape of her body, he couldn't. Instead there rose in him an odd disgust for Memo. It came quickly, nauseating him.

"Darling," whispered Iris, "win for our boy."

He stared at her. "What boy?"

"I am pregnant." There were tears in her eyes.

Her belly was slender . . . then the impact hit him.

"Holy Jesus."

Iris smiled with quivering lips.

Bending over, he kissed her mouth and tasted blood. He kissed her breasts, they smelled of roses. He kissed her hard belly, wild with love for her and the child.

"Win for us, you were meant to."

She took his head in her hands and drew it to her bosom. How like the one who jumped me in the park that night he looks, she thought, and to drive the thought away pressed his head deeper into her breasts, thinking, this will be different. Oh, Roy, be my love and protect me. But by then the ambulance had come so they took her away.

In the dugout Pop confronted him with withering curses. "Get in there and attend to business. No more monkey shines or I will pitch you out on your banana."

Roy nodded. Climbing out of the dugout, to his dismay he found Wonderboy lying near the water fountain, in the mud. He tenderly wiped it dry. Stuffy called time in and the Pirates, furious at the long delay (Wickitt had demanded the forfeit of the game, but Pop had scared Stuffy into waiting for Roy by threatening to go to court), returned to ther positions, Allie and Flores to third and first, and Roy stepped into the batter's box to face a storm of Bronx cheers. They came in wind-driven sheets until Vogelman reared and threw, then they stopped.

It was 0 and 2 on him because, except for the one he had purposely missed, Roy had turned each pitch into a foul. He watched Vogelman with burning eyes. Vogelman was almost hypnotized. He saw a different man and didn't like what he saw. His next throw was wide of the plate. Ball one. Then a quick ball two, and the pitcher was nervous again. He took a very long time with the next throw but to his horror the pellet slipped away from him and hit the dirt just short of the plate. Allie broke for home but the catcher quickly trapped it and threw to third. Flopping back, Allie made it with his fingers. Flores, in the meantime, had taken second.

And that was ball three. Roy now prayed for a decent throw.

Vogelman glanced at Allie edging into a lead again, kicked, and threw almost in desperation. Roy swung from his cleats.

Thunder crashed. The pitcher stuffed his maimed fingers into his ears. His eyes were blinded. Pop rose and crowed himself hoarse. Otto Zipp, carrying a dark lump on his noodle, cowered beneath the ledge. Some of the fans had seen lightning, thought it was going to rain, and raised their coat collars. Most of them were on their feet, raving at the flight of the ball. Allie had raced in to score, so had Flores, and Roy was heading into second, when the umpire waved them all back. The ball had landed clearly foul. The fans groaned in shuddering tones.

Wonderboy lay on the ground split lengthwise, one half pointing to first, the other to third.

The Knights' bat boy nervously collected both the pieces and thrust a Louisville Slugger into Roy's limp hand. The crowd sat in raw silence as the nerveless Vogelman delivered his next pitch. It floated in, perfect for pickling, but Roy failed to lift the bat.

Lajong, who followed, also struck out.

With the Knights back in the field, Fowler quickly gave up a whacking triple to the first Pirate hitter. This was followed by a hard double, and almost before any of the stunned fans could realize it, the first run of the game was in. Pop bounced off the bench as if electrocuted and signaled the bullpen into hot activity. Red Blow sauntered out to the mound to quiet Fowler down but Fowler said he was all right so Red left.

The next Pirate laced a long hopper to left. The shouting of the crowd woke Roy out of his grief for Wonderboy. He tore in for the ball, made a running jab for it and held it. With an effort he heaved to third, holding both runners to one bag. He knew now he was right about Fowler. The pitcher had pulled the plug. Roy signaled time and drifted in to talk to him. Both Red and Dave Olson also walked forward for a mound conference but Roy waved them back. As he approached the dark-faced Fowler, he saw the Judge up at the window, puffing his cigar.

Roy spoke in a low voice. "Watch out, kid, we don't want to lose the game."

Fowler studied him craftily. "Cut the crap, big shot. A lotta winning you been doing."

"Throw the ball good," Roy advised him.

"I will, when you start hitting it."

"Listen," Roy said patiently. "This might be my last season in the game for I am already thirty-five. You want it to be yours?"

Fowler paled. "You wouldn't dare open your trap."

"Try something funny again and you will see."

Fowler turned angrily away. The fans began to whistle and stamp. "Set 'em up," called Stuffy Briggs. Roy returned to left but after that, Fowler somehow managed to keep the next two men from connecting, and everybody said too bad that Roy hadn't given him that pep talk after the first hit. Some of the fans remarked had anybody noticed that Roy had thumbed his nose up to the tower at the end of the inning?

Every time Vogelman put Roy away, he felt infinitely better, consequently his pitching improved as the game progressed. Though he was suprised in the eighth to have Gabby Laslow touch him for a sharp single, he forced Olson to pop to short, Benz to line to him, and Fowler obliged by biting at three gamey ones for the last out. Counting up who he would have to throw to in the ninth, Vogelman discovered that if he got Stubbs, Baker, and the more difficult Flores out, there would be no Roy Hobbs to pitch to. The idea so excited him he determined to beat his brains out trying. Fowler, on the other hand, despite Roy's good advice to him, got sloppier in his throwing, although subtly, so that nobody could be sure why, only his support was a whole lot better than he had hoped for, and neither of the first two Pirates up in the ninth, though they had walloped the ball hard, could land on base. Flores, the Mexican jumping bean, had nailed both shots. The third Pirate then caught a juicy pitch and poled out a high looping beauty to left, but Roy, running back—back—back, speared it against the wall. Though he was winded and cursed Fowler through his teeth, he couldn't help but smile, picturing the pitcher's disgust. And he felt confident that the boys would hold him a turn at bat and he would destroy Vogelman and save the game, the most important thing he ever had to do in his life.

Pop, on the other hand, was losing hope. His hands trembled and his false teeth felt like rocks in his mouth, so he plucked them out and dropped them into his shirt pocket. Instead of Allie, he called Ed Simmons to pinch hit, but Vogelman, working with renewed speed and canniness, got Ed to hit a soft one to center field. Pop swayed on the bench, drooling a little out of the corners of his puckered mouth. Red was a ghost, even his freckles were pale. The stands were shrouded in darkening silence. Baker spat and approached the plate. Remembering he hadn't once hit safely today, Pop called him back and substituted Hank Kelly, another pinch hitter.

Vogelman struck him out. He dried his mouth on his sleeve, smiling faintly to himself for the first time since the game began. One more—the Mex. To finish him meant slamming the door on Hobbs, a clean shut-out, and tomorrow the World Series. The sun fell back in the sky and a hush hung like a smell in the air. Flores, with a crazed look in his eye, faced the pitcher. Fouling the first throw, he took for a ball, and swung savagely at the third pitch. He missed. Two strikes, there were only three . . . Roy felt himself slowly dying. You died alone. At least if he were up there batting . . . The Mexican's face was lit in anguish. With bulging eyes he rushed at the next throw, and cursing in Spanish, swung. The ball wobbled crazily in the air, took off, and leaped for the right field wall. Running as though death dogged him, Flores made it, sliding headlong into third. Vogelman, drained of his heart's blood, stared at him through glazed eyes.

The silence shattered into insane, raucous noise.

Roy rose from the bench. When he saw Pop searching among the other faces, his heart flopped and froze. He would gladly get down on his knees and kiss the old man's skinny, crooked feet, do anything to get up there this last time. Pop's haunted gleam settled on him, wavered, traveled down the line of grim faces . . . and came back to Roy. He called his name.

Up close he had black rings around his eyes, and when he spoke his voice broke.

"See what we have come to, Roy."

Roy stared at the dugout floor. "Let me go in."

"What would you expect to do?"

"Murder it."

"Murder which?"

"The ball—I swear."

Pop's eyes wavered to the men on the bench. Reluctantly his gaze returned to Roy. "If you weren't so damn busy gunning fouls into the stands that last time, you woulda straightened out that big one, and with three scoring, that woulda been the game."

"Now I understand why they call them fouls."

"Go on in," Pop said. He added in afterthought, "Keep us alive."

Roy selected out of the rack a bat that looked something like Wonderboy. He swung it once and advanced to the plate. Flores was dancing on the bag, beating his body as if it were burning, and jabbering in Spanish that if by the mercy of St. Christopher he was allowed to make the voyage home from third, he would forever after light candles before the saint.

The blank-faced crowd was almost hidden by the darkness crouching in the stands. Home plate lay under a deepening dusty shadow but Roy saw things with more light than he ever had before. A hit, tying up the game, would cure what ailed him. Only a homer, with himself scoring the winning run, would truly redeem him.

Vogelman was contemplating how close he had come to paradise. If the Mex had missed that pitch, the game would now be over. All night long he'd've felt eight foot tall, and when he got into bed with his wife, she'd've given it to him the way they do to heroes.

The sight of his nemesis crouched low in the brooding darkness around the plate filled him with fear.

Sighing, he brought himself, without conviction, to throw. "Bo-ool one."

The staring faces in the stands broke into a cry that stayed till the end of the game.

Vogelman was drenched in sweat. He could have thrown a

spitter without half trying but didn't know how and was afraid
to monkey with them.

The next went in cap high.

"Eee bo-ool."

Wickitt, the Pirate manager, ambled out to the mound.

"S'matter, Dutch?"

"Take me outa here," Vogelman moaned.

"What the hell for? You got that bastard three times so
far and you can do it again."

"He gives me the shits, Walt. Look at him standing there
like a goddamn gorilla. Look at his burning eyes. He ain't
human."

Wickitt talked low as he studied Roy. "That ain't what I
see. He looks old and beat up. Last week he had a mile-high
bellyache in a ladies' hospital. They say he could drop dead
any minute. Bear up and curve 'em low. I don't think he
can bend to his knees. Get one strike on him and he will be
your nookie."

He left the mound.

Vogelman threw the next ball with his flesh screaming.

"Bo-ool three."

He sought for Wickett but the manager kept his face hidden.
In that case, the pitcher thought, I will walk him. They
could yank him after that—he was a sick man.

Roy was also considering a walk. It would relieve him of
responsibility but not make up for all the harm he had done.
He discarded the idea. Vogelman made a bony steeple with
his arms. Gazing at the plate, he found his eyes were misty
and he couldn't read the catcher's sign. He looked again and
saw Roy, in full armor, mounted on a black charger. Vogelman stared hard, his arms held high so as not to balk. Yes,
there he was coming at him with a long lance as thick as a
young tree. He rubbed his arm across his eyes and keeled over
in a dead faint.

A roar ascended skywards.

The sun slid behind the clouds. It got cold again. Wickitt,
leaning darkly out of the dugout, raised his arm aloft to the

center field bullpen. The boy who had been pitching flipped the ball to the bullpen catcher, straightened his cap, and began the long trek in. He was twenty, a scrawny youth with light eyes.

"Herman Youngberry, number sixty-six, pitching for the Pirates."

Few in the stands had heard of him, but before his long trek to the mound was finished his life was common knowledge. He was a six-footer but weighed a skinny one fifty-eight. One day about two years ago a Pirate scout watching him pitching for his home town team had written on a card, "This boy has a fluid delivery of a blinding fast ball and an exploding curve." Though he offered him a contract then and there, Youngberry refused to sign because it was his lifelong ambition to be a farmer. Everybody, including the girl he was engaged to, argued him into signing. He didn't say so but he had it in mind to earn enough money to buy a three hundred acre farm and then quit baseball forever. Sometimes when he pitched, he saw fields of golden wheat gleaming in the sun.

He had come to the Pirates on the first of September from one of their class A clubs, to help in the pennant drive. Since then he'd worked up a three won, two lost record. He'd seen what Roy had done to Vogelman the day he hit the four homers, and just now, and wasn't anxious to face him. After throwing his warm-ups he stepped off the mound and looked away as Roy got back into the box.

Despite the rest he had had, Roy's armpits were creepy with sweat. He felt a bulk of heaviness around his middle and that the individual hairs on his legs and chest were bristling.

Youngberry gazed around to see how they were playing Roy. It was straightaway and deep, with the infield pulled back too. Flores, though hopping about, was on the bag. The pitcher took a full wind-up and became aware the Knights were yelling dirty names to rattle him.

Roy had considered and decided against a surprise bunt. As things were, it was best to take three good swings.

He felt the shadow of the Judge and Memo fouling the air

around him and turned to shake his fist at them but they had left the window.

The ball lit its own path.

The speed of the pitch surprised Stuffy Briggs and it was a little time before he could work his tongue free.

"Stuh-rike."

Roy's nose was full of the dust he had raised.

"Throw him to the pigs," shrilled Otto Zipp.

If he bunted, the surprise could get him to first, and Flores home for the tying run. The only trouble was he had not much confidence in his ability to bunt. Roy stared at the kid, trying to hook his eye, but Youngberry wouldn't look at him. As Roy stared a fog blew up around the young pitcher, full of old ghosts and snowy scenes. The fog shot forth a snaky finger and Roy carefully searched under it for the ball but it was already in the catcher's mitt.

"Strike two."

"Off with his head," Otto shrieked.

It felt like winter. He wished for fire to warm his frozen fingers. Too late for the bunt now. He wished he had tried it. It would have caught them flatfooted.

Pop ran out with a rabbit's foot but Roy wouldn't take it. He would never give up, he swore. Flores had fallen to his knees on third and was imploring the sky.

Roy caught the pitcher's eye. His own had blood in them. Youngberry shuddered. He threw—a bad ball—but the batter leaped at it.

He struck out with a roar.

Bump Baily's form glowed red on the wall. There was a wail in the wind. He feared the mob would swarm all over him, tear him apart, and strew his polluted remains over the field, but they had vanished. Only O. Zipp climbed down out of his seat. He waddled to the plate, picked up the bat and took a vicious cut at something. He must've connected, because his dumpy bow legs went like pistons around the bases. Thundering down from third he slid into the plate and called himself safe.

Otto dusted himself off, lit a cigar and went home.

When it was night he dragged the two halves of the bat into left field, and with his jackknife cut a long rectangular slash into the turf and dug out the earth. With his hands he deepened the grave in the dry earth and packed the sides tight. He then placed the broken bat in it. He couldn't stand seeing it in two pieces so he removed them and tried squeezing them together in the hope they would stick but the split was smooth, as if the bat had willed its own brokenness, and the two parts would not stay together. Roy undid his shoelaces and wound one around the slender handle of the bat, and the other he tied around the hitting part of the wood, so that except for the knotted laces and the split he knew was there it looked like a whole bat. And this was the way he buried it, wishing it would take root and become a tree. He poured back the earth, carefully pressing it down, and replaced the grass. He trod on it in his stocking feet, and after a last long look around, walked off the field. At the fountain he considered whether to carry out a few handfuls of water to wet the earth above Wonderboy but they would only leak through his fingers before he got there, and since he doubted he could find the exact spot in the dark he went down the dugout steps and into the tunnel.

He felt afraid to go in the clubhouse and so was glad the lights were left on with nobody there. From the looks of things everybody had got their clothes on and torn out. All was silence except the drip drop of the shower and he did not want to go in there. He got rid of his uniform in the soiled clothes can, then dressed in street clothes. He felt something thick against his chest and brought out a sealed envelope. Tearing it open, he discovered a package of thousand dollar bills. He had never seen one before and here were thirty-five. In with the bills was a typewritten note: "The contract will have to wait. There are grave doubts that your cooperation was wholehearted." Roy burned the paper with a match. He considered burning the bills but didn't. He tried to stuff them into his wallet. The wad was too thick so he put them back in the envelope and slipped it into his pocket.

The street was chill and its swaying lights, dark. He shivered as he went to the corner. At the tower he pulled himself up the unlit stairs.

The Judge's secretary was gone but his private door was unlocked so Roy let himself in. The office was pitch black. He located the apartment door and stumbled up the narrow stairs. When he came into the Judge's overstuffed apartment, they were all sitting around a table, the redheaded Memo, the Judge with a green eyeshade over his black wig, and the Supreme Bookie, enjoying a little cigar. They were counting piles of betting slips and a mass of bills. Memo was adding the figures with an adding machine.

Gus got up quickly when he saw Roy. "Nice goin', slugger," he said softly. Smiling, he advanced with his arm extended. "That was some fine show you put on today."

Roy slugged the slug and he went down in open-mouthed wonder. His head hit the floor and the glass eye dropped out and rolled into a mousehole.

Memo was furious. "Don't touch him, you big bastard. He's worth a million of your kind."

Roy said, "You act all right, Memo, but only like a whore."

"Tut," said the Judge.

She ran to him and tried to scratch his eyes but he pushed her aside and she fell over Gus. With a cry she lifted the bookie's head on her lap and made mothering noises over him.

Roy took the envelope out of his pocket. He slapped the Judge's wig and eyeshade off and showered the thousand dollar bills on his wormy head.

The Judge raised a revolver.

"That will do, Hobbs. Another move and I shall be forced to defend myself."

Roy snatched the gun and dropped it in the wastebasket. He twisted the Judge's nose till he screamed. Then he lifted him onto the table and pounded his back with his fists. The

Judge made groans and pig squeals. With his foot Roy shoved the carcass off the table. He hit the floor with a crash and had a bowel movement in his pants. He lay moaning amid the betting slips and bills.

Memo had let Gus's head fall and ran around the table to the basket. Raising the pistol, she shot at Roy's back. The bullet grazed his shoulder and broke the Judge's bathroom mirror. The glass clattered to the floor.

Roy turned to her.

"Don't come any nearer or I'll shoot."

He slowly moved forward.

"You filthy scum, I hate your guts and always have since the day you murdered Bump."

Her finger tightened on the trigger but when he came very close she sobbed aloud and thrust the muzzle into her mouth. He gently took the gun from her, opened the cylinder, and shook the cartridges into his palm. He pocketed them and again dumped the gun into the basket.

She was sobbing hysterically as he left.

Going down the tower stairs he fought his overwhelming self-hatred. In each stinking wave of it he remembered some disgusting happening of his life.

He thought, I never did learn anything out of my past life, now I have to suffer again.

When he hit the street he was exhausted. He had not shaved, and a black beard gripped his face. He felt old and grimy.

He stared into faces of people he passed along the street but nobody recognized him.

"He coulda been a king," a woman remarked to a man.

At the corner near some stores he watched the comings and goings of the night traffic. He felt the insides of him beginning to take off (chug chug choo choo . . .). Pretty soon they were in fast flight. A boy thrust a newspaper at him. He wanted to say no but had no voice. The headline screamed, "Suspicion of Hobbs's Sellout—Max Mercy." Under this was a photo Mercy had triumphantly discovered, showing Roy on his back, an obscene bullet imbedded in his gut. Around him danced a naked lady: "Hobbs at nineteen."

And there was also a statement by the baseball commissioner. "If this alleged report is true, that is the last of Roy Hobbs in organized baseball. He will be excluded from the game and all his records forever destroyed."

Roy handed the paper back to the kid.

"Say it ain't true, Roy."

When Roy looked into the boy's eyes he wanted to say it wasn't but couldn't, and he lifted his hands to his face and wept many bitter tears.

The Assistant

For Ann with love

The early November street was dark though night had ended, but the wind, to the grocer's surprise, already clawed. It flung his apron into his face as he bent for the two milk cases at the curb. Morris Bober dragged the heavy boxes to the door, panting. A large brown bag of hard rolls stood in the doorway along with the sour-faced, gray-haired Poilisheh huddled there, who wanted one.

"What's the matter so late?"

"Ten after six," said the grocer.

"Is cold," she complained.

Turning the key in the lock he let her in. Usually he lugged in the milk and lit the gas radiators, but the Polish woman was impatient. Morris poured the bag of rolls into a wire basket on the counter and found an unseeded one for her. Slicing it in halves, he wrapped it in white store paper. She tucked the roll into her cord market bag and left three pennies on the counter. He rang up the sale on an old noisy cash register, smoothed and put away the bag the rolls had come in, finished pulling in the milk, and stored the bottles at the bottom of the refrigerator. He lit the gas radiator at the front of the store and went into the back to light the one there.

He boiled up coffee in a blackened enamel pot and sipped it, chewing on a roll, not tasting what he was eating. After he had cleaned up he waited; he waited for Nick Fuso, the upstairs tenant, a young mechanic who worked in a garage in the neighborhood. Nick came in every morning around seven for twenty cents' worth of ham and a loaf of bread.

But the front door opened and a girl of ten entered, her face pinched and eyes excited. His heart held no welcome for her.

"My mother says," she said quickly, "can you trust her till tomorrow for a pound of butter, loaf of rye bread and a small bottle of cider vinegar?"

He knew the mother. "No more trust."

The girl burst into tears.

Morris gave her a quarter-pound of butter, the bread and vinegar. He found a penciled spot on the worn counter, near the cash register, and wrote a sum under "Drunk Woman." The total now came to $2.03, which he never hoped to see. But Ida would nag if she noticed a new figure, so he reduced the amount to $1.61. His peace—the little he lived with—was worth forty-two cents.

He sat in a chair at the round wooden table in the rear of the store and scanned, with raised brows, yesterday's Jewish paper that he had already thoroughly read. From time to time he looked absently through the square windowless window cut through the wall, to see if anybody had by chance come into the store. Sometimes when he looked up from his newspaper, he was startled to see a customer standing silently at the counter.

Now the store looked like a long dark tunnel.

The grocer sighed and waited. Waiting he thought he did poorly. When times were bad time was bad. It died as he waited, stinking in his nose.

A workman came in for a fifteen-cent can of King Oscar Norwegian sardines.

Morris went back to waiting. In twenty-one years the store had changed little. Twice he had painted all over, once added new shelving. The old-fashioned double windows at the front a carpenter had made into a large single one. Ten years ago the sign hanging outside fell to the ground but he had never replaced it. Once, when business hit a long good spell, he had had the wooden icebox ripped out and a new white refrigerated showcase put in. The showcase stood at the front in line with the old counter and he often leaned against it as he stared out of the window. Otherwise the store was the same. Years ago it was more a delicatessen; now, though he still sold a little delicatessen, it was more a poor grocery.

A half-hour passed. When Nick Fuso failed to appear, Morris got up and stationed himself at the front window, behind a large cardboard display sign the beer people had rigged up in an otherwise empty window. After a while the hall door opened, and Nick came out in a thick, hand-knitted green sweater. He trotted around the corner and soon returned carrying a bag of groceries. Morris was now visible at the window. Nick saw the look on his face but didn't look long. He ran into the house, trying to make it seem it was the wind that was chasing him. The door slammed behind him, a loud door.

The grocer gazed into the street. He wished fleetingly that he could once more be out in the open, as when he was a boy —never in the houses, but the sound of the blustery wind frightened him. He thought again of selling the store but who would buy? Ida still hoped to sell. Every day she hoped. The thought caused him grimly to smile, although he did not feel like smiling. It was an impossible idea so he tried to put it out of his mind. Still, there were times when he went into the back, poured himself a spout of coffee and pleasantly thought of selling. Yet if he miraculously did, where would he go, where? He had a moment of uneasiness as he pictured himself without a roof over his head. There he stood in all kinds of weather, drenched in rain, and the snow froze on his head. No, not for an age had he lived a whole day in the open. As a boy, always running in the muddy, rutted streets of the village, or across the fields, or bathing with the other boys in the river; but as a man, in America, he rarely saw the sky. In the early days when he drove a horse and wagon, yes, but not since his first store. In a store you were entombed.

The milkman drove up to the door in his truck and hurried in, a bull, for his empties. He lugged out a caseful and returned with two half-pints of light cream. Then Otto Vogel, the meat provisions man, entered, a bushy-mustached German carrying a smoked liverwurst and string of wieners in his oily meat basket. Morris paid cash for the liverwurst; from a German he wanted no favors. Otto left with the wieners. The bread driver, new on the route, exchanged three fresh loaves for three stale and walked out without a word. Leo, the cake man, glanced hastily at the package cake on top of the refrigerator and called, "See you Monday, Morris."

Morris didn't answer.

Leo hesitated. "Bad all over, Morris."

"Here is the worst."

"See you Monday."

A young housewife from close by bought sixty-three cents worth; another came in for forty-one cents'. He had earned his first cash dollar for the day.

Breitbart, the bulb peddler, laid down his two enormous cartons of light bulbs and diffidently entered the back.

"Go in," Morris urged. He boiled up some tea and served it in a thick glass, with a slice of lemon. The peddler eased himself into a chair, derby hat and coat on, and gulped the hot tea, his Adam's apple bobbing.

"So how goes now?" asked the grocer.

"Slow," shrugged Breitbart.

Morris sighed. "How is your boy?"

Breitbart nodded absently, then picked up the Jewish paper and read. After ten minutes he got up, scratched all over,

lifted across his thin shoulders the two large cartons tied together with clothesline and left.

Morris watched him go.

The world suffers. *He* felt every schmerz.

At lunchtime Ida came down. She had cleaned the whole
house.

Morris was standing before the faded couch, looking out of
the rear window at the back yards. He had been thinking of
Ephraim.

His wife saw his wet eyes.

"So stop sometime, please." Her own grew wet.

He went to the sink, caught cold water in his cupped palms
and dipped his face into it.

"The Italyener," he said, drying himself, "bought this morning across the street."

She was irritated. "Give him for twenty-nine dollars five
rooms so he should spit in your face."

"A cold water flat," he reminded her.

"You put in gas radiators."

"Who says he spits? This I didn't say."

"You said something to him not nice?"

"Me?"

"Then why he went across the street?"

"Why? Go ask him," he said angrily.

"How much you took in till now?"

"Dirt."

She turned away.

He absent-mindedly scratched a match and lit a cigarette.

"Stop with the smoking," she nagged.

He took a quick drag, clipped the butt with his thumb nail
and quickly thrust it under his apron into his pants pocket.
The smoke made him cough. He coughed harshly, his face lit
like a tomato. Ida held her hands over her ears. Finally he
brought up a gob of phlegm and wiped his mouth with his
handkerchief, then his eyes.

"Cigarettes," she said bitterly. "Why don't you listen what
the doctor tells you?"

"Doctors," he remarked.

Afterward he noticed the dress she was wearing. "What is the picnic?"

Ida said, embarrassed, "I thought to myself maybe will come today the buyer."

She was fifty-one, nine years younger than he, her thick hair still almost all black. But her face was lined, and her legs hurt when she stood too long on them, although she now wore shoes with arch supports. She had waked that morning resenting the grocer for having dragged her, so many years ago, out of a Jewish neighborhood into this. She missed to this day their old friends and landsleit—lost for parnusseh unrealized. That was bad enough, but on top of their isolation, the endless worry about money embittered her. She shared unwillingly the grocer's fate though she did not show it and her dissatisfaction went no farther than nagging—her guilt that she had talked him into a grocery store when he was in the first year of evening high school, preparing, he had said, for pharmacy. He was, through the years, a hard man to move. In the past she could sometimes resist him, but the weight of his endurance was too much for her now.

"A buyer," Morris grunted, "will come next Purim."

"Don't be so smart. Karp telephoned him."

"Karp," he said in disgust. "Where he telephoned—the cheapskate?"

"Here."

"When?"

"Yesterday. You were sleeping."

"What did he told him?"

"For sale a store—yours, cheap."

"What do you mean cheap?"

"The key is worth now nothing. For the stock and the fixtures that they are worth also nothing, maybe three thousand, maybe less."

"I paid four."

"Twenty-one years ago," she said irritably. "So don't sell, go in auction."

"He wants the house too?"

"Karp don't know. Maybe."

"Big mouth. Imagine a man that they held him up four times in the last three years and he still don't take in a telephone. What he says ain't worth a cent. He promised me he wouldn't put in a grocery around the corner, but what did he put?—a grocery. Why does he bring me buyers? Why didn't he keep out the German around the corner?"

She sighed. "He tries to help you now because he feels sorry for you."

"Who needs his sorrow?" Morris said. "Who needs him?"

"So why *you* didn't have the sense to make out of your grocery a wine and liquor store when came out the licenses?"

"Who had cash for stock?"

"So if you don't have, don't talk."

"A business for drunken bums."

"A business is a business. What Julius Karp takes in next door in a day we don't take in in two weeks."

But Ida saw he was annoyed and changed the subject.

"I told you to oil the floor."

"I forgot."

"I asked you special. By now would be dry."

"I will do later."

"Later the customers will walk in the oil and make everything dirty."

"What customers?" he shouted. "Who customers? Who comes in here?"

"Go, she said quietly. "Go upstairs and sleep. I will oil myself."

But he got out the oil can and mop and oiled the floor until the wood shone darkly. No one had come in.

She had prepared his soup. "Helen left this morning without breakfast."

"She wasn't hungry."

"Something worries her."

He said with sarcasm, "What worries her?" Meaning: the store, his health, that most of her meager wages went to keep up payments on the house; that she had wanted a college education but had got instead a job she disliked. Her father's daughter, no wonder she didn't feel like eating.

"If she will only get married," Ida murmured.

"She will get."

"Soon." She was on the verge of tears.

He grunted.

"I don't understand why she don't see Nat Pearl anymore. All summer they went together like lovers."

"A showoff."

"He'll be someday a rich lawyer."

"I don't like him."

"Louis Karp also likes her. I wish she will give him a chance."

"A stupe," Morris said, "like the father."

"Everybody is a stupe but not Morris Bober."

He was staring out at the back yards.

"Eat already and go to sleep," she said impatiently.

He finished the soup and went upstairs. The going up was easier than coming down. In the bedroom, sighing, he drew down the black window shades. He was half asleep, so pleasant was the anticipation. Sleep was his one true refreshment; it excited him to go to sleep. Morris took off his apron, tie and trousers, and laid them on a chair. Sitting at the edge of the sagging wide bed, he unlaced his misshapen shoes and slid under the cold covers in shirt, long underwear and white socks. He nudged his eye into the pillow and waited to grow warm. He crawled toward sleep. But upstairs Tessie Fuso was running the vacuum cleaner, and though the grocer tried to blot the incident out of his mind, he remembered Nick's visit to the German and on the verge of sleep felt bad.

He recalled the bad times he had lived through, but now times were worse than in the past; now they were impossible. This store was always a marginal one, up today, down tomorrow—as the wind blew. Overnight business could go down enough to hurt; yet as a rule it slowly recovered—sometimes it seemed to take forever—went up, not high enough to be really *up*, only not down. When he had first bought the grocery it was all right for the neighborhood; it had got worse as the neighborhood had. Yet even a year ago, staying open seven days a week, sixteen hours a day, he could still eke out a living.

What kind of living?—a living; you lived. Now, though he toiled the same hard hours, he was close to bankruptcy, his patience torn. In the past when bad times came he had somehow lived through them, and when good times returned, they more or less returned to him. But now, since the appearance of H. Schmitz across the street ten months ago, all times were bad.

Last year a broken tailor, a poor man with a sick wife, had locked up his shop and gone away, and from the minute of the store's emptiness Morris had felt a gnawing anxiety. He went with hesitation to Karp, who owned the building, and asked him to please keep out another grocery. In this kind of neighborhood one was more than enough. If another squeezed in they would both starve. Karp answered that the neighborhood was better than Morris gave it credit (for schnapps, thought the grocer), but he promised he would look for another tailor or maybe a shoemaker, to rent to. He said so but the grocer didn't believe him. Yet weeks went by and the store stayed empty. Though Ida pooh-poohed his worries, Morris could not overcome his underlying dread. Then one day, as he daily expected, there appeared a sign in the empty store window, announcing the coming of a new fancy delicatessen and grocery.

Morris ran to Karp. "What did you do to me?"

The liquor dealer said with a one-shouldered shrug, "You saw how long stayed empty the store. Who will pay my taxes? But don't worry," he added, "he'll sell more delicatessen but you'll sell more groceries. Wait, you'll see he'll bring you in customers."

Morris groaned; he knew his fate.

Yet as the days went by, the store still sitting empty— emptier, he found himself thinking maybe the new business would never materialize. Maybe the man had changed his mind. It was possible he had seen how poor the neighborhood was and would not attempt to open the new place. Morris wanted to ask Karp if he had guessed right but could not bear to humiliate himself further.

Often after he had locked his grocery at night, he would go

secretly around the corner and cross the quiet street. The empty store, dark and deserted, was one door to the left of the corner drugstore; and if no one was looking the grocer would peer through its dusty window, trying to see through shadows whether the emptiness had changed. For two months it stayed the same, and every night he went away reprieved. Then one time—after he saw that Karp was, for once, avoiding him—he spied a web of shelves sprouting from the rear wall, and that shattered the hope he had climbed into.

In a few days the shelves stretched many arms along the other walls, and soon the whole tiered and layered place glowed with new paint. Morris told himself to stay away but he could not help coming nightly to inspect, appraise, then guess the damage, in dollars, to himself. Each night as he looked, in his mind he destroyed what had been built, tried to make of it nothing, but the growth was too quick. Every day the place flowered with new fixtures—streamlined counters, the latest refrigerator, fluorescent lights, a fruit stall, a chromium cash register; then from the wholesalers arrived a mountain of cartons and wooden boxes of all sizes, and one night there appeared in the white light a stranger, a gaunt German with a German pompadour, who spent the silent night hours, a dead cigar stuck in his teeth, packing out symmetrical rows of brightly labeled cans, jars, gleaming bottles. Though Morris hated the new store, in a curious way he loved it too, so that sometimes as he entered his own old-fashioned place of business, he could not stand the sight of it; and now he understood why Nick Fuso had that morning run around the corner and crossed the street—to taste the newness of the place and be waited on by Heinrich Schmitz, an energetic German dressed like a doctor, in a white duck jacket. And that was where many of his other customers had gone, and stayed, so that his own poor living was cut in impossible half.

Morris tried hard to sleep but couldn't and grew restless in bed. After another quarter of an hour he decided to dress and go downstairs, but there drifted into his mind, with ease and no sorrow, the form and image of his boy Ephraim, gone so long from him, and he fell deeply and calmly asleep.

.   .   .

Helen Bober squeezed into a subway seat between two women and was on the last page of a chapter when a man dissolved in front of her and another appeared; she knew without looking that Nat Pearl was standing there. She thought she would go on reading, but couldn't, and shut her book.

"Hello, Helen." Nat touched a gloved hand to a new hat. He was cordial but as usual held back something—his future. He carried a fat law book, so she was glad to be protected with a book of her own. But not enough protected, for her hat and coat felt suddenly shabby, a trick of the mind, because on her they would still do.

"*Don Quixote?*"

She nodded.

He seemed respectful, then said in an undertone, "I haven't seen you a long time. Where've you been keeping yourself?"

She blushed under her clothes.

"Did I offend you in some way or other?"

Both of the women beside her seemed stolidly deaf. One held a rosary in her heavy hand.

"No." The offense was hers against herself.

"So what's the score?" Nat's voice was low, his gray eyes annoyed.

"No score," she murmured.

"How so?"

"You're you, I'm me."

This he considered a minute, then remarked, "I haven't much of a head for oracles."

But she felt she had said enough.

He tried another way. "Betty asks for you."

"Give her my best." She had not meant it but this sounded funny because they all lived on the same block, separated by one house.

Tight-jawed, he opened his book. She returned to hers, hiding her thoughts behind the antics of a madman until memory overthrew him and she found herself ensnared in scenes of summer that she would gladly undo, although she loved the season; but how could you undo what you had done again in the fall, unwillingly willing? Virginity she thought she had parted with without sorrow, yet was surprised by torments of conscience, or was it disappointment at being valued under her expectations? Nat Pearl, handsome, cleft-chinned, gifted, ambitious, had wanted without too much trouble a lay and she, half in love, had obliged and regretted. Not the loving, but that it had taken her so long to realize how little he wanted. Not her, Helen Bober.

Why should he?—magna cum laude, Columbia, now in his second year at law school, she only a high school graduate with a year's evening college credit mostly in lit; he with first-rate prospects, also rich friends he had never bothered to introduce her to; she as poor as her name sounded, with little promise of a better future. She had more than once asked herself if she had meant by her favors to work up a claim on him. Always she denied it. She had wanted, admittedly, satisfaction, but more than that—respect for the giver of what she had to give, had hoped desire would become more than just that. She wanted, simply, a future in love. Enjoyment she had somehow had, felt very moving the freedom of fundamental intimacy with a man. Though she wished for more of the same, she wanted it without aftermath of conscience, or pride, or sense of waste. So she promised herself next time it would go the other way; first mutual love, then loving, harder maybe on the nerves, but easier in memory. Thus she had reasoned, until one night in September, when coming up to see his sister Betty, she had found herself alone in the house with Nat and had done again what she had promised herself she wouldn't. Afterward she fought self-hatred. Since then, to this day, without telling him why, she had avoided Nat Pearl.

Two stations before their stop, Helen shut her book, got up in silence and left the train. On the platform, as the train moved away, she caught a glimpse of Nat standing before her empty seat, calmly reading. She walked on, lacking, wanting, not wanting, not happy.

Coming up the subway steps, she went into the park by a side entrance, and despite the sharp wind and her threadbare coat, took the long way home. The leafless trees left her with unearned sadness. She mourned the long age before spring and feared loneliness in winter. Wishing she hadn't come, she left the park, searching the faces of strangers although she couldn't stand their stares. She went quickly along the Parkway, glancing with envy into the lighted depths of private houses that were, for no reason she could give, except experience, not for her. She promised herself she would save every cent possible and register next fall for a full program at NYU, night.

When she reached her block, a row of faded yellow brick houses, two stories squatting on ancient stores, Sam Pearl, stifling a yawn, was reaching into his corner candy store window to put on the lamp. He snapped the string and the dull glow from the fly-specked globe fell upon her. Helen quickened her step. Sam, always sociable, a former cabbie, bulky, wearing bifocals and chewing gum, beamed at her but she pretended no see. Most of the day he sat hunched over dope sheets spread out on the soda fountain counter, smoking as he chewed gum, making smeary marks with a pencil stub under horses' names. He neglected the store; his wife Goldie was the broad-backed one, yet she did not much complain, because Sam's luck with the nags was exceptional and he had nicely supported Nat in college until the scholarships started rolling in.

Around the corner, through the many-bottled window that blinked in neon "KARP wines and liquors," she glimpsed paunchy Julius Karp, with bushy eyebrows and an ambitious mouth, blowing imaginary dust off a bottle as he slipped a deft fifth of something into a paper bag, while Louis, slightly popeyed son and heir, looking up from clipping to the quick his poor fingernails, smiled amiably upon a sale. The Karps, Pearls and Bobers, representing attached houses and stores, but otherwise detachment, made up the small Jewish segment of this gentile community. They had somehow, her father first, then Karp, later Pearl, drifted together here where no other Jews dwelt, except on the far fringes of the neighborhood. None of them did well and were too poor to move elsewhere until Karp, who with a shoe store that barely made him a living, got the brilliant idea after Prohibition gurgled down

the drain and liquor licenses were offered to the public, to borrow cash from a white-bearded rich uncle and put in for one.
To everybody's surprise he got the license, though Karp, when
asked how, winked a heavy-lidded eye and answered nothing.
Within a short time after cheap shoes had become expensive
bottles, in spite of the poor neighborhood—or maybe because
of it, Helen supposed—he became astonishingly successful and
retired his overweight wife from the meager railroad flat above
the store to a big house on the Parkway—from which she
hardly ever stepped forth—the house complete with two-car
garage and Mercury; and at the same time as Karp changed
his luck—to hear her father tell it—he became wise without
brains.

The grocer, on the other hand, had never altered his fortune, unless degrees of poverty meant alteration, for luck and
he were, if not natural enemies, not good friends. He labored
long hours, was the soul of honesty—he could not escape his
honesty, it was bedrock; to cheat would cause an explosion in
him, yet he trusted cheaters—coveted nobody's nothing and
always got poorer. The harder he worked—his toil was a form
of time devouring time—the less he seemed to have. He was
Morris Bober and could be nobody more fortunate. With that
name you had no sure sense of property, as if it were in your
blood and history not to possess, or if by some miracle to own
something, to do so on the verge of loss. At the end you were
sixty and had less than at thirty. It was, she thought, surely
a talent.

Helen removed her hat as she entered the grocery. "Me,"
she called, as she had from childhood. It meant that whoever
was sitting in the back should sit and not suddenly think he
was going to get rich.

Morris awoke, soured by the long afternoon sleep. He dressed,
combed his hair with a broken comb and trudged downstairs;
a heavy-bodied man with sloping shoulders and bushy gray
hair in need of a haircut. He came down with his apron on.
Although he felt chilly he poured out a cup of cold coffee, and

backed against the radiator, slowly sipped it. Ida sat at the table, reading.

"Why you let me sleep so long?" the grocer complained.

She didn't answer.

"Yesterday or today's paper?"

"Yesterday."

He rinsed the cup and set it on the top of the gas range. In the store he rang up "no sale" and took a nickel out of the drawer. Morris lifted the lid of the cash register, struck a match on the underside of the counter, and holding the flame cupped in his palm, peered at the figure of his earnings. Ida had taken in three dollars. Who could afford a paper?

Nevertheless he went for one, doubting the small pleasure he would get from it. What was so worth reading about the world? Through Karp's window, as he passed, he saw Louis waiting on a customer while four others crowded the counter. Der oilem iz a goilem. Morris took the *Forward* from the newsstand and dropped a nickel into the cigar box. Sam Pearl, working over a green racing sheet, gave him a wave of his hammy hand. They never bothered to talk. What did he know about race horses? What did the other know of the tragic quality of life? Wisdom flew over his hard head.

The grocer returned to the rear of his store and sat on the couch, letting the diminishing light in the yard fall upon the paper. He read nearsightedly, with eyes stretched wide, but his thoughts would not let him read long. He put down the newspaper.

"So where is your buyer?" he asked Ida.

Looking absently into the store she did not reply.

"You should sell long ago the store," she remarked after a minute.

"When the store was good, who wanted to sell? After came bad times, who wanted to buy?"

"Everything we did too late. The store we didn't sell in time. I said, 'Morris, sell now the store.' You said, 'Wait.' What for? The house we bought too late, so we have still a big mortgage that it's hard to pay every month. 'Don't buy,' I said, 'times are bad.' 'Buy,' you said, 'will get better. We will save rent.' "

He answered nothing. If you had failed to do the right thing, talk was useless.

When Helen entered, she asked if the buyer had come. She had forgotten about him but remembered when she saw her mother's dress.

Opening her purse, she took out her pay check and handed it to her father. The grocer, without a word, slipped it under his apron into his pants pocket.

"Not yet," Ida answered, also embarrassed. "Maybe later."

"Nobody goes in the night to buy a store," Morris said. "The time to go is in the day to see how many customers. If this man comes here he will see with one eye the store is dead, then he will run home."

"Did you eat lunch?" Ida asked Helen.

"Yes."

"What did you eat?"

"I don't save menus, Mama."

"Your supper is ready." Ida lit the flame under the pot on the gas range.

"What makes you think he'll come today?" Helen asked her.

"Karp told me yesterday. He knows a refugee that he looks to buy a grocery. He works in the Bronx, so he will be here late."

Morris shook his head.

"He's a young man," Ida went on, "maybe thirty—thirty-two. Karp says he saved a little cash. He can make alterations, buy new goods, fix up modern, advertise a little and make here a nice business."

"Karp should live so long," the grocer said.

"Let's eat." Helen sat at the table.

Ida said she would eat later.

"What about you, Papa?"

"I am not hungry." He picked up his paper.

She ate alone. It would be wonderful to sell out and move but the possibility struck her as remote. If you had lived so long in one place, all but two years of your life, you didn't move out overnight.

Afterward she got up to help with the dishes but Ida wouldn't let her. "Go rest," she said.

Helen took her things and went upstairs.

She hated the drab five-room flat; a gray kitchen she used for breakfast so she could quickly get out to work in the morning. The living room was colorless and cramped; for all its overstuffed furniture of twenty years ago it seemed barren because it was lived in so little, her parents being seven days out of seven in the store; even their rare visitors, when invited upstairs, preferred to remain in the back. Sometimes Helen asked a friend up, but she went to other people's houses if she had a choice. Her bedroom was another impossibility, tiny, dark, despite the two by three foot opening in the wall, through which she could see the living room windows; and at night Morris and Ida had to pass through her room to get to theirs, and from their bedroom back to the bathroom. They had several times talked of giving her the big room, the only comfortable one in the house, but there was no place else that would hold their double bed. The fifth room was a small ice-box off the second floor stairs, in which Ida stored a few odds and ends of clothes and furniture. Such was home. Helen had once in anger remarked that the place was awful to live in, and it had made her feel bad that her father had felt so bad.

She heard Morris's slow footsteps on the stairs. He came aimlessly into the living room and tried to relax in a stiff arm-chair. He sat with sad eyes, saying nothing, which was how he began when he wanted to say something.

When she and her brother were kids, at least on Jewish holidays Morris would close the store and venture forth to Second Avenue to see a Yiddish play, or take the family visiting; but after Ephraim died he rarely went beyond the corner. Thinking about his life always left her with a sense of the waste of her own.

She looks like a little bird, Morris thought. Why should she be lonely? Look how pretty she looks. Whoever saw such blue eyes?

He reached into his pants pocket and took out a five-dollar bill.

"Take," he said, rising and embarrassedly handing her the money. "You will need for shoes."

"You just gave me five dollars downstairs."

"Here is five more."

"Wednesday was the first of the month, Pa."

"I can't take away from you all your pay."

"You're not taking, I'm giving."

She made him put the five away. He did, with renewed shame. "What did I ever give you? Even your college education I took away."

"It was my own decision not to go, yet maybe I will yet. You can never tell."

"How can you go? You are twenty-three years old."

"Aren't you always saying a person's never too old to go to school?"

"My child," he sighed, "for myself I don't care, for you I want the best but what did I give you?"

"I'll give myself," she smiled. "There's hope."

With this he had to be satisfied. He still conceded her a future.

But before he went down, he said gently, "What's the matter you stay home so much lately? You had a fight with Nat?"

"No." Blushing, she answered, "I don't think we see things in the same way."

He hadn't the heart to ask more.

Going down, he met Ida on the stairs and knew she would cover the same ground.

In the evening there was a flurry of business. Morris's mood quickened and he exchanged pleasantries with the customers. Carl Johnsen, the Swedish painter, whom he hadn't seen in weeks, came in with a wet smile and bought two dollars' worth of beer, cold cuts and sliced Swiss cheese. The grocer was at first worried he would ask to charge—he had never paid what he owed on the books before Morris had stopped giving trust —but the painter had the cash. Mrs. Anderson, an old loyal customer, bought for a dollar. A stranger then came in and left eighty-eight cents. After him two more customers appeared. Morris felt a little surge of hope. Maybe things were picking up. But after half-past eight his hands grew heavy with nothing to do. For years he had been the only one for miles around who stayed open at night and had just about made a living from it, but now Schmitz matched him hour for hour. Morris sneaked a little smoke, then began to cough. Ida pounded on the floor upstairs, so he clipped the butt and put it away. He felt restless and stood at the front window, watching the street. He watched a trolley go by. Mr. Lawler, formerly a customer, good for at least a fiver on Friday nights, passed the store. Morris hadn't seen him for months but knew where he was going. Mr. Lawler averted his gaze and hurried along. Morris watched him disappear around the corner. He lit a match and again checked the register—nine and a half dollars, not even expenses.

Julius Karp opened the front door and poked his foolish head in.

"Podolsky came?"

"Who Podolsky?"

"The refugee."

Morris said in annoyance, "What refugee?"

With a grunt Karp shut the door behind him. He was short, pompous, a natty dresser in his advanced age. In the past, like Morris, he had toiled long hours in his shoe store, now he stayed all day in silk pajamas until it came time to relieve Louis before supper. Though the little man was insensitive and a blunderer, Morris had got along fairly well with him, but since Karp had rented the tailor shop to another grocer, sometimes they did not speak. Years ago Karp had spent much time in the back of the grocery, complaining of his poverty as if it were a new invention and he its first victim. Since his success with wines and liquors he came in less often, but he still visited Morris more than his welcome entitled him to, usually to run down the grocery and spout unwanted advice. His ticket of admission was his luck, which he gathered wherever he reached, at a loss, Morris thought, to somebody else.

Once a drunk had heaved a rock at Karp's window, but it had shattered his. Another time, Sam Pearl gave the liquor dealer a tip on a horse, then forgot to place a bet himself. Karp collected five hundred for his ten-dollar bill. For years the grocer had escaped resenting the man's good luck, but lately he had caught himself wishing on him some small misfortune.

"Podolsky is the one I called up to take a look at your gesheft," Karp answered.

"Who is this refugee, tell me, an enemy yours?"

Karp stared at him unpleasantly.

"Does a man," Morris insisted, "send a friend he should buy such a store that you yourself took away from it the best business?"

"Podolsky ain't you," the liquor dealer replied. "I told him about this place. I said, 'The neighborhood is improving. You can buy cheap and build up this store. It's run down for years, nobody changed anything there for twenty years.'"

"You should live so long how much I changed—" Morris began but he didn't finish, for Karp was at the window, peering nervously into the dark street.

"You saw that gray car that just passed," the liquor dealer said. "This is the third time I saw it in the last twenty minutes." His eyes were restless.

Morris knew what worried him. "Put in a telephone in your store," he advised, "so you will feel better."

Karp watched the street for another minute and worriedly replied, "Not for a liquor store in this neighborhood. If I had a telephone, every drunken bum would call me to make deliveries, and when you go there they don't have a cent."

He opened the door but shut it in afterthought. "Listen, Morris," he said, lowering his voice, "if they come back again, I will lock my front door and put out my lights. Then I will call you from the back window so you can telephone the police."

"This will cost you five cents," Morris said grimly.

"My credit is class A."

Karp left the grocery, disturbed.

God bless Julius Karp, the grocer thought. Without him I

would have my life too easy. God made Karp so a poor grocery man will not forget his life is hard. For Karp, he thought, it was miraculously not so hard, but what was there to envy? He would allow the liquor dealer his bottles and gelt just not to be him. Life was bad enough.

At nine-thirty a stranger came in for a box of matches. Fifteen minutes later Morris put out the lights in his window. The street was deserted except for an automobile parked in front of the laundry across the car tracks. Morris peered at it sharply but could see nobody in it. He considered locking up and going to bed, then decided to stay open the last few minutes. Sometimes a person came in at a minute to ten. A dime was a dime.

A noise at the side door which led into the hall frightened him.

"Ida?"

The door opened slowly. Tessie Fuso came in in her housecoat, a homely Italian girl with a big face.

"Are you closed, Mr. Bober?" she asked embarrassedly.

"Come in," said Morris.

"I'm sorry I came through the back way but I was undressed and didn't want to go out in the street."

"Don't worry."

"Please give me twenty cents' ham for Nick's lunch tomorrow."

He understood. She was making amends for Nick's trip around the corner that morning. He cut her an extra slice of ham.

Tessie bought also a quart of milk, package of paper napkins and loaf of bread. When she had gone he lifted the register lid. Ten dollars. He thought he had long ago touched bottom but now knew there was none.

I slaved my whole life for nothing, he thought.

Then he heard Karp calling him from the rear. The grocer went inside, worn out.

Raising the window he called harshly, "What's the matter there?"

"Telephone the police," cried Karp. "The car is parked across the street."

"What car?"

"The holdupniks."

"There is nobody in this car, I saw myself."

"For God's sake, I tell you call the police. I will pay for the telephone."

Morris shut the window. He looked up the phone number and was about to dial the police when the store door opened and he hurried inside.

Two men were standing at the other side of the counter, with handkerchiefs over their faces. One wore a dirty yellow clotted one, the other's was white. The one with the white one began pulling out the store lights. It took the grocer a half-minute to comprehend that he, not Karp, was their victim.

Morris sat at the table, the dark light of the dusty bulb falling on his head, gazing dully at the few crumpled bills before him, including Helen's check, and the small pile of silver. The gunman with the dirty handkerchief, fleshy, wearing a fuzzy black hat, waved a pistol at the grocer's head. His pimply brow was thick with sweat; from time to time with furtive eyes he glanced into the darkened store. The other, a taller man in an old cap and torn sneakers, to control his trembling leaned against the sink, cleaning his fingernails with a matchstick. A cracked mirror hung behind him on the wall above the sink and every so often he turned to stare into it.

"I know damn well this ain't everything you took in," said the heavy one to Morris, in a hoarse, unnatural voice. "Where've you got the rest hid?"

Morris, sick to his stomach, couldn't speak.

"Tell the goddam truth." He aimed the gun at the grocer's mouth.

"Times are bad," Morris muttered.

"You're a Jew liar."

The man at the sink fluttered his hand, catching the other's attention. They met in the center of the room, the other with the cap hunched awkwardly over the one in the fuzzy hat, whispering into his ear.

"No," snapped the heavy one sullenly.

His partner bent lower, whispering earnestly through his handkerchief.

"I say he hid it," the heavy one snarled, "and I'm gonna get it if I have to crack his goddam head."

At the table he whacked the grocer across the face.

Morris moaned.

The one at the sink hastily rinsed a cup and filled it with water. He brought it to the grocer, spilling some on his apron as he raised the cup to his lips.

Morris tried to swallow but managed only a dry sip. His frightened eyes sought the man's but he was looking elsewhere.

"Please," murmured the grocer.

"Hurry up," warned the one with the gun.

The tall one straightened up and gulped down the water. He rinsed the cup and placed it on the cupboard shelf.

He then began to hunt among the cups and dishes there and pulled out the pots on the bottom. Next, he went hurriedly through the drawers of an old bureau in the room, and on hands and knees searched under the couch. He ducked into the store, removed the empty cash drawer from the register and thrust his hand into the slot, but came up with nothing.

Returning to the kitchen he took the other by the arm and whispered to him urgently.

The heavy one elbowed him aside.

"We better scram out of here."

"Are you gonna go chicken on me?"

"That's all the dough he has, let's beat it."

"Business is bad," Morris muttered.

"Your Jew ass is bad, you understand?"

"Don't hurt me."

"I will give you your last chance. Where have you got it hid?"

"I am a poor man." He spoke through cracked lips.

The one in the dirty handkerchief raised his gun. The

other, staring into the mirror, waved frantically, his black eyes bulging, but Morris saw the blow descend and felt sick of himself, of soured expectations, endless frustration, the years gone up in smoke, he could not begin to count how many. He had hoped for much in America and got little. And because of him Helen and Ida had less. He had defrauded them, he and the bloodsucking store.

He fell without a cry. The end fitted the day. It was his luck, others had better.

During the week that Morris lay in bed with a thickly bandaged head, Ida tended the store fitfully. She went up and down twenty times a day until her bones ached and her head hurt with all her worries. Helen stayed home Saturday, a half-day in her place, and Monday, to help her mother, but she could not risk longer than that, so Ida, who ate in snatches and had worked up a massive nervousness, had to shut the store for a full day, although Morris angrily protested. He needed no attention, he insisted, and urged her to keep open at least half the day or he would lose his remaining few customers; but Ida, short of breath, said she hadn't the strength, her legs hurt. The grocer attempted to get up and pull on his pants but was struck by a violent headache and had to drag himself back to bed.

On the Tuesday the store was closed a man appeared in the neighborhood, a stranger who spent much of his time standing on Sam Pearl's corner with a toothpick in his teeth, intently observing the people who passed by; or he would drift down the long block of stores, some empty, from Pearl's to the bar at the far end of the street. Beyond that was a freight yard, and in the distance, a bulky warehouse. After an occasional slow beer in the tavern, the stranger turned the corner and wandered past the high-fenced coal yard; he would go around the block until he got back to Sam's candy store. Once in a while the man would walk over to Morris's closed grocery, and with both hands shading his brow, stare through the window; sighing, he went back to Sam's. When he had as much as he could take on the corner he walked around the block again, or elsewhere in the neighborhood.

Helen had pasted a paper on the window of the front door, that said her father wasn't well but the store would open on Wednesday. The man spent a good deal of time studying this paper. He was young, dark-bearded, wore an old brown rain-stained hat, cracked patent leather shoes and a long black overcoat that looked as if it had been lived in. He was tall and not bad looking, except for a nose that had been broken and badly set, unbalancing his face. His eyes were melancholy. Sometimes he sat at the fountain with Sam Pearl, lost in his thoughts, smoking from a crumpled pack of cigarettes he had bought with pennies. Sam, who was used to all kinds of people, and had in his time seen many strangers appear in the neighborhood and as quickly disappear, showed no special concern for the man, though Goldie, after a full day of his presence, complained that too much was too much; he didn't pay rent. Sam did notice that the stranger sometimes seemed to be under stress, sighed much and muttered inaudibly to himself. However, he paid the man scant attention—everybody to their own troubles. Other times the stranger, as if he had somehow squared himself with himself, seemed relaxed, even satisfied with his existence. He read through Sam's magazines, strolled around in the neighborhood and when he returned, lit a fresh cigarette as he opened a paper-bound book from the rack in the store. Sam served him coffee when he asked for it, and the stranger, squinting from the smoke of the butt in his mouth, carefully counted out five pennies to pay. Though nobody had asked him he said his name was Frank Alpine and he had lately come from the West, looking for a better opportunity. Sam advised if he could qualify for a chauffeur's license, to try for work as a hack driver. It wasn't a bad life. The man agreed but stayed around as if he was expecting something else to open up. Sam put him down as a moody gink.

The day Ida reopened the grocery the stranger disappeared but he returned to the candy store the next morning, and seating himself at the fountain, asked for coffee. He looked bleary, unhappy, his beard hard, dark, contrasting with the pallor of his face; his nostrils were inflamed and his voice was husky. He looks half in his grave, Sam thought. God knows what hole he slept in last night.

As Frank Alpine was stirring his coffee, with his free hand he opened a magazine lying on the counter, and his eye was caught by a picture in color of a monk. He lifted the coffee cup to drink but had to put it down, and he stared at the picture for five minutes.

Sam, out of curiosity, went behind him with a broom, to see what he was looking at. The picture was of a thin-faced, dark-bearded monk in a coarse brown garment, standing barefooted on a sunny country road. His skinny, hairy arms were raised to a flock of birds that dipped over his head. In the background was a grove of leafy trees; and in the far distance a church in sunlight.

"He looks like some kind of a priest," Sam said cautiously.

"No, it's St. Francis of Assisi. You can tell from that brown robe he's wearing and all those birds in the air. That's the time he was preaching to them. When I was a kid, an old priest used to come to the orphans' home where I was raised, and every time he came he read us a different story about St. Francis. They are clear in my mind to this day."

"Stories are stories," Sam said.

"Don't ask me why I never forgot them."

Sam took a closer squint at the picture. "Talking to the birds? What was he—crazy? I don't say this out of any harm."

The stranger smiled at the Jew. "He was a great man. The way I look at it, it takes a certain kind of a nerve to preach to birds."

"That makes him great, because he talked to birds?"

"Also for other things. For instance, he gave everything away that he owned, every cent, all his clothes off his back. He enjoyed to be poor. He said poverty was a queen and he loved her like she was a beautiful woman."

Sam shook his head. "It ain't beautiful, kiddo. To be poor is dirty work."

"He took a fresh view of things."

The candy store owner glanced again at St. Francis, then poked his broom into a dirty corner. Frank, as he drank his coffee, continued to study the picture. He said to Sam, "Every time I read about somebody like him I get a feeling inside of me I have to fight to keep from crying. He was born good, which is a talent if you have it."

He spoke with embarrassment, embarrassing Sam.

Frank drained his cup and left.

That night as he was wandering past Morris's store he glanced through the door and saw Helen inside, relieving her mother. She looked up and noticed him staring at her through the plate glass. His appearance startled her; his eyes were haunted, hungry, sad; she got the impression he would come in and ask for a handout and had made up her mind to give him a dime, but instead he disappeared.

On Friday Morris weakly descended the stairs at six A.M., and Ida, nagging, came after him. She had been opening at eight o'clock and had begged him to stay in bed until then, but he refused, saying he had to give the Poilisheh her roll.

"Why does three cents for a lousy roll mean more to you than another hour sleep?" Ida complained.

"Who can sleep?"

"You need rest, the doctor said."

"Rest I will take in my grave."

She shuddered. Morris said, "For fifteen years she gets here her roll, so let her get."

"All right, but let me open up. I will give her and you go back to bed."

"I stayed in bed too long. Makes me feel weak."

But the woman wasn't there and Morris feared he had lost her to the German. Ida insisted on dragging in the milk boxes, threatening to shout if he made a move for them. She packed the bottles into the refrigerator. After Nick Fuso they waited hours for another customer. Morris sat at the table, reading the paper, occasionally raising his hand gently to feel the bandage around his head. When he shut his eyes he still experienced moments of weakness. By noon he was glad to go upstairs and crawl into bed and he didn't get up until Helen came home.

The next morning he insisted on opening alone. The Poilisheh was there. He did not know her name. She worked somewhere in a laundry and had a little dog called Polaschaya. When she came home at night she took the little Polish dog for a walk around the block. He liked to run loose in the coal yard. She lived in one of the stucco houses nearby. Ida called her *die antisemitke*, but that part of her didn't bother Morris. She had come with it from the old country, a different kind of anti-Semitism from in America. Sometimes he suspected she needled him a little by asking for a "Jewish roll," and once or twice, with an odd smile, she wanted a "Jewish pickle." Generally she said nothing at all. This morning Morris handed her her roll and she said nothing. She didn't ask him about his bandaged head though her quick beady eyes stared at it, nor why he had not been there for a week; but she put six pennies on the counter instead of three. He figured she had taken a roll from the bag one of the days the store hadn't opened on time. He rang up the six-cent sale.

Morris went outside to pull in the two milk cases. He gripped the boxes but they were like rocks, so he let one go and tugged at the other. A storm cloud formed in his head and blew up to the size of a house. Morris reeled and almost fell into the gutter, but he was caught by Frank Alpine, in his long coat, steadied and led back into the store. Frank then hauled in the milk cases and refrigerated the bottles. He quickly swept up behind the counter and went into the back. Morris, recovered, warmly thanked him.

Frank said huskily, his eyes on his scarred and heavy hands, that he was new to the neighborhood but living here now with a married sister. He had lately come from the West and was looking for a better job.

The grocer offered him a cup of coffee, which he at once accepted. As he sat down Frank placed his hat on the floor at his feet, and he drank the coffee with three heaping spoonfuls of sugar, to get warm quick, he said. When Morris offered him a seeded hard roll, he bit into it hungrily. "Jesus, this is good bread." After he had finished he wiped his mouth with his handkerchief, then swept the crumbs off the table with one hand into the other, and though Morris protested, he rinsed the cup and saucer at the sink, dried them and set them on top of the gas range, where the grocer had got them.

"Much obliged for everything." He had picked up his hat but made no move to leave.

"Once in San Francisco I worked in a grocery for a couple of months," he remarked after a minute, "only it was one of those supermarket chain store deals."

"The chain store kills the small man."

"Personally I like a small store myself. I might someday have one."

"A store is a prison. Look for something better."

"At least you're your own boss."

"To be a boss of nothing is nothing."

"Still and all, the idea of it appeals to me. The only thing is I would need experience on what goods to order. I mean about brand names, and et cetera. I guess I ought to look for a job in a store and get more experience."

"Try the A&P," advised the grocer.

"I might."

Morris dropped the subject. The man put on his hat.

"What's the matter," he said, staring at the grocer's bandage, "did you have some kind of accident to your head?"

Morris nodded. He didn't care to talk about it, so the stranger, somehow disappointed, left.

He happened to be in the street very early on Monday when Morris was again struggling with the milk cases. The stranger tipped his hat and said he was off to the city to find a job but he had time to help him pull in the milk. This he did and quickly left. However, the grocer thought he saw him pass by in the other direction about an hour later. That afternoon when he went for his *Forward* he noticed him sitting at the fountain with Sam Pearl. The next morning, just after six, Frank was there to help him haul in the milk bottles and he willingly accepted when Morris, who knew a poor man when he saw one, invited him for coffee.

"How is going now the job?" Morris asked as they were eating.

"So-so," said Frank, his eyes shifting. He seemed preoccupied, nervous. Every few minutes he would set down his cup and uneasily look around. His lips parted as if to speak, his eyes took on a tormented expression, but then he shut his jaw as if he had decided it was better never to say what he intended. He seemed to need to talk, broke into sweat—his brow gleamed with it—his pupils widening as he struggled. He looked to Morris like someone who had to retch—no matter where; but after a brutal interval his eyes grew dull. He sighed heavily and gulped down the last of his coffee. After, he brought up a belch. This for a moment satisfied him.

Whatever he wants to say, Morris thought, let him say it to somebody else. I am only a grocer. He shifted in his chair, fearing to catch some illness.

Again the tall man leaned forward, drew a breath and once more was at the point of speaking, but now a shudder passed through him, followed by a fit of shivering.

The grocer hastened to the stove and poured out a cup of steaming coffee. Frank swallowed it in two terrible gulps. He soon stopped shaking, but looked defeated, humiliated, like somebody, the grocer felt, who had lost out on something he had wanted badly.

"You caught a cold?" he asked sympathetically.

The stranger nodded, scratched up a match on the sole of his cracked shoe, lit a cigarette and sat there, listless.

"I had a rough life," he muttered, and lapsed into silence.

Neither of them spoke. Then the grocer, to ease the other's mood, casually inquired, "Where in the neighborhood lives your sister? Maybe I know her."

Frank answered in a monotone. "I forget the exact address. Near the park somewheres."

"What is her name?"

"Mrs. Garibaldi."

"What kind name is this?"

"What do you mean?" Frank stared at him.

"I mean the nationality?"

"Italian. I am of Italian extraction. My name is Frank Alpine—Alpino in Italian."

The smell of Frank Alpine's cigarette compelled Morris to light his butt. He thought he could control his cough and tried but couldn't. He coughed till he feared his head would pop off. Frank watched with interest. Ida banged on the floor upstairs, and the grocer ashamedly pinched his cigarette and dropped it into the garbage pail.

"She don't like me to smoke," he explained between coughs. "My lungs ain't so healthy."

"Who don't?"

"My wife. It's a catarrh some kind. My mother had it all her life and lived till eighty-four. But they took a picture of my chest last year and found two dried spots. This frightened my wife."

Frank slowly put out his cigarette. "What I started out to say before about my life," he said heavily, "is that I have had a funny one, only I don't mean funny. I mean I've been through a lot. I've been close to some wonderful things—jobs, for instance, education, women, but close is as far as I go." His hands were tightly clasped between his knees. "Don't ask me why, but sooner or later everything I think is worth hav-

ing gets away from me in some way or other. I work like a
mule for what I want, and just when it looks like I am going
to get it I make some kind of a stupid move, and everything
that is just about nailed down tight blows up in my face."

"Don't throw away your chance for education," Morris advised. "It's the best thing for a young man."

"I could've been a college graduate by now, but when the
time came to start going, I missed out because something else
turned up that I took instead. With me one wrong thing leads
to another and it ends in a trap. I want the moon so all I get
is cheese."

"You are young yet."

"Twenty-five," he said bitterly.

"You look older."

"I feel old—damn old."

Morris shook his head.

"Sometimes I think your life keeps going the way it starts
out on you," Frank went on. "The week after I was born my
mother was dead and buried. I never saw her face, not even
a picture. When I was five years old, one day my old man
leaves this furnished room where we were staying, to get a
pack of butts. He takes off and that was the last I ever saw
of him. They traced him years later but by then he was
dead. I was raised in an orphans' home and when I was eight
they farmed me out to a tough family. I ran away ten times,
also from the next people I lived with. I think about my life
a lot. I say to myself, 'What do you expect to happen after
all of that?' Of course, every now and again, you understand, I hit some nice good spots in between, but they are few
and far, and usually I end up like I started out, with nothing."

The grocer was moved. Poor boy.

"I've often tried to change the way things work out for
me but I don't know how, even when I think I do. I have it
in my heart to do more than I can remember." He paused,
cleared his throat and said, "That makes me sound stupid
but it's not as easy as that. What I mean to say is that when I
need it most something is missing in me, in me or on ac-

count of me. I always have this dream where I want to tell somebody something on the telephone so bad it hurts, but then when I am in the booth, instead of a phone being there, a bunch of bananas is hanging on a hook."

He gazed at the grocer then at the floor. "All my life I wanted to accomplish something worthwhile—a thing people will say took a little doing, but I don't. I am too restless—six months in any one place is too much for me. Also I grab at everything too quick—too impatient. I don't do what I have to —that's what I mean. The result is I move into a place with nothing, and I move out with nothing. You understand me?"

"Yes," said Morris.

Frank fell into silence. After a while he said, "I don't understand myself. I don't really know what I'm saying to you or why I am saying it."

"Rest yourself," said Morris.

"What kind of a life is that for a man my age?"

He waited for the grocer to reply—to tell him how to live his life, but Morris was thinking, I am sixty and he talks like me.

"Take some more coffee," he said.

"No, thanks." Frank lit another cigarette and smoked it to the tip. He seemed eased yet not eased, as though he had accomplished something (What? wondered the grocer) yet had not. His face was relaxed, almost sleepy, but he cracked the knuckles of both hands and silently sighed.

Why don't he go home? the grocer thought. I am a working man.

"I'm going." Frank got up but stayed.

"What happened to your head?" he asked again.

Morris felt the bandage. "This Friday before last I had here a holdup."

"You mean they slugged you?"

The grocer nodded.

"Bastards like that ought to die." Frank spoke vehemently. Morris stared at him.

Frank brushed his sleeve. "You people are Jews, aren't you?"

"Yes," said the grocer, still watching him.

"I always liked Jews." His eyes were downcast.

Morris did not speak.

"I suppose you have some kids?" Frank asked.

"Me?"

"Excuse me for being curious."

"A girl." Morris sighed. "I had once a wonderful boy but he died from an ear sickness that they had in those days."

"Too bad." Frank blew his nose.

A gentleman, Morris thought with a watery eye.

"Is the girl the one that was here behind the counter a couple of nights last week?"

"Yes," the grocer replied, a little uneasily.

"Well, thanks for all the coffee."

"Let me make you a sandwich. Maybe you'll be hungry later."

"No thanks."

The Jew insisted, but Frank felt he had all he wanted from him at the moment.

Left alone, Morris began to worry about his health. He felt dizzy at times, often headachy. Murderers, he thought. Standing before the cracked and faded mirror at the sink he unwound the bandage from his head. He wanted to leave it off but the scar was still ugly, not nice for the customers, so he tied a fresh bandage around his skull. As he did this he thought of that night with bitterness, recalling the buyer who hadn't come, nor had since then, nor ever would. Since his recovery, Morris had not spoken to Karp. Against words the liquor dealer had other words, but silence silenced him.

Afterward the grocer looked up from his paper and was startled to see somebody out front washing his window with a brush on a stick. He ran out with a roar to drive the intruder away, for there were nervy window cleaners who did the job without asking permission, then held out their palms to collect. But when Morris came out of the store he saw the window washer was Frank Alpine.

"Just to show my thanks and appreciation." Frank explained he had borrowed the pail from Sam Pearl and the brush and squeegee from the butcher next door.

Ida then entered the store by the inside door, and seeing the window being washed, hurried outside.

"You got rich all of a sudden?" she asked Morris, her face inflamed.

"He does me a favor," the grocer replied.

"That's right," said Frank, bearing down on the squeegee.

"Come inside, it's cold." In the store Ida asked, "Who is this goy?"

"A poor boy, an Italyener he looks for a job. He gives me a help in the morning with the cases milk."

"If you sold containers like I told you a thousand times, you wouldn't need help."

"Containers leak. I like bottles."

"Talk to the wind," Ida said.

Frank came in blowing his breath on water-reddened fists. "How's it look now, folks, though you can't really tell till I do the inside."

Ida remarked under her breath, "Pay now for your favor."

"Fine," Morris said to Frank. He went to the register and rang up "no sale."

"No, thanks," Frank said, holding up his hand. "For services already rendered."

Ida reddened.

"Another cup coffee?" Morris asked.

"Thanks. Not as of now."

"Let me make you a sandwich?"

"I just ate."

He walked out, threw the dirty water into the gutter, returned the pail and brush, then came back to the grocery. He went behind the counter and into the rear, pausing to rap on the doorjamb.

"How do you like the clean window?" he asked Ida.

"Clean is clean." She was cool.

"I don't want to intrude here but your husband was nice to me, so I just thought maybe I could ask for one more small favor. I am looking for work and I want to try some kind of a grocery job just for size. Maybe I might like it, who knows? It happens I forgot some of the things about cutting and weighing and such, so I am wondering if you would mind me working around here for a couple-three weeks without wages just so I could learn again? It won't cost you a red cent. I know I am a stranger but I am an honest guy. Whoever keeps an eye on me will find that out in no time. That's fair enough, isn't it?"

Ida said, "Mister, isn't here a school."

"What do you say, pop?" Frank asked Morris.

"Because somebody is a stranger don't mean they ain't honest," answered the grocer. "This subject don't interest me. Interests me what you can learn here. Only one thing"—he pressed his hand to his chest—"a heartache."

"You got nothing to lose on my proposition, has he now, Mrs?" Frank said. "I understand he don't feel so hot yet, and if I helped him out a short week or two it would be good for his health, wouldn't it?"

Ida didn't answer.

But Morris said flatly, "No. It's a small, poor store. Three people would be too much."

Frank flipped an apron off a hook behind the door and before either of them could say a word, removed his hat and dropped the loop over his head. He tied the apron strings around him.

"How's that for fit?"

Ida flushed, and Morris ordered him to take it off and put it back on the hook.

"No bad feelings, I hope," Frank said on his way out.

Helen Bober and Louis Karp walked, no hands touching, in the windy dark on the Coney Island boardwalk.

Louis had, on his way home for supper that evening, stopped her in front of the liquor store, on her way in from work.

"How's about a ride in the Mercury, Helen? I never see

you much anymore. Things were better in the bygone days in high school."

Helen smiled. "Honestly, Louis, that's so far away." A sense of mourning at once oppressed her, which she fought to a practiced draw.

"Near or far, it's all the same for me." He was built with broad back and narrow head, and despite prominent eyes was presentable. In high school, before he quit, he had worn his wet hair slicked straight back. One day, after studying a picture of a movie actor in the *Daily News*, he had run a part across his head. This was as much change as she had known in him. If Nat Pearl was ambitious, Louis made a relaxed living letting the fruit of his father's investment fall into his lap.

"Anyway," he said, "why not a ride for old-times' sake?"

She thought a minute, a gloved finger pressed into her cheek; but it was a fake gesture because she was lonely.

"For old-times' sake, where?"

"Name your scenery—continuous performance."

"The Island?"

He raised his coat collar. "Brr, it's a cold, windy night. You wanna freeze?"

Seeing her hesitation, he said, "But I'll die game. When'll I pick you up?"

"Ring my bell after eight and I'll come down."

"Check," Louis said. "Eight bells."

They walked to Seagate, where the boardwalk ended. She gazed with envy through a wire fence at the large lit houses fronting the ocean. The Island was deserted, except here and there an open hamburger joint or pinball machine concession. Gone from the sky was the umbrella of rosy light that glowed over the place in summertime. A few cold stars gleamed down. In the distance a dark Ferris wheel looked like a stopped clock. They stood at the rail of the boardwalk, watching the black, restless sea.

All during their walk she had been thinking about her life, the difference between her aloneness now and the fun when she was young and spending every day of summer in a lively crowd of kids on the beach. But as her high school friends had got married, she had one by one given them up; and as others of them graduated from college, envious, ashamed of how little she was accomplishing, she stopped seeing them too. At first it hurt to drop people but after a time it became a not too difficult habit. Now she saw almost no one, occasionally Betty Pearl, who understood, but not enough to make much difference.

Louis, his face reddened by the wind, sensed her mood.

"What's got in you, Helen?" he said, putting his arm around her.

"I can't really explain it. All night I've been thinking of the swell times we had on this beach when we were kids. And do you remember the parties? I suppose I'm blue that I'm no longer seventeen."

"What's so wrong about twenty-three?"

"It's old, Louis. Our lives change so quickly. You know what youth means?"

"Sure I know. You don't catch me giving away nothing for nothing. I got my youth yet."

"When a person is young he's privileged," Helen said, "with all kinds of possibilities. Wonderful things might happen, and when you get up in the morning you feel they will. That's what youth means, and that's what I've lost. Nowadays I feel that every day is like the day before, and what's worse, like the day after."

"So now you're a grandmother?"

"The world has shrunk for me."

"What do you wanna be—Miss Rheingold?"

"I want a larger and better life. I want the return of my possibilities."

"Such as which ones?"

She clutched the rail, cold through her gloves. "Education," she said, "prospects. Things I've wanted but never had."

"Also a man?"

"Also a man."

His arm tightened around her waist. "Talk is too cold, baby, how's about a kiss?"

She brushed his cold lips, then averted her head. He did not press her.

"Louis," she said, watching a far-off light on the water, "what do you want out of your life?"

He kept his arm around her. "The same thing I got— plus."

"Plus what?"

"Plus more, so my wife and family can have also."

"What if she wanted something different than you do?"

"Whatever she wanted I would gladly give her."

"But what if she wanted to make herself a better person, have bigger ideas, live a more worthwhile life? We die so quickly, so helplessly. Life *has* to have some meaning."

"I ain't gonna stop anybody from being better," Louis said, "That's up to them."

"I suppose," she said.

"Say, baby, let's drop this deep philosophy and go trap a hamburger. My stomach complains."

"Just a little longer. It's been ages since I came here this late in the year."

He pumped his arms. "Jesus, this wind, it flies up my pants. At least gimme another kiss." He unbuttoned his overcoat.

She let him kiss her. He felt her breast. Helen stepped back out of his embrace. "Don't, Louis."

"Why not?" He stood there awkwardly, annoyed.

"It gives me no pleasure."

"I suppose I'm the first guy that ever gave it a nip?"

"Are you collecting statistics?"

"Okay," he said, "I'm sorry. You know I ain't a bad guy, Helen."

"I know you're not, but please don't do what I don't like."

"There was a time you treated me a whole lot better."

"That was the past, we were kids."

It's funny, she remembered, how necking made glorious dreams.

"We were older than that, up till the time Nat Pearl started in college, then you got interested in him. I suppose you got him in mind for the future?"

"If I do, I don't know it."

"But he's the one you want, ain't he? I like to know what that stuck up has got beside a college education? I work for my living."

"No, I don't want him, Louis." But she thought, Suppose Nat said I love you? For magic words a girl might do magic tricks.

"So if that's so, what's wrong with me?"

"Nothing. We're friends."

"Friends I got all I need."

"What do you need, Louis?"

"Cut out the wisecracks, Helen. Would it interest you that I would honestly like to marry you?" He paled at his nerve.

She was surprised, touched.

"Thank you," she murmured.

"Thank you ain't good enough. Give me yes or no."

"No, Louis."

"That's what I thought." He gazed blankly at the ocean.

"I never guessed you were at all remotely interested. You go with girls who are so different from me."

"Please, when I go with them you can't see my thoughts."

"No," she admitted.

"I can give you a whole lot better than you got."

"I know you can, but I want a different life from mine now, or yours. I don't want a storekeeper for a husband."

"Wines and liquors ain't exactly pisher groceries."

"I know."

"It ain't because your old man don't like mine?"

"No."

She listened to the wind-driven, sobbing surf. Louis said, "Let's go get the hamburgers."

"Gladly." She took his arm but could tell from the stiff way he walked that he was hurt.

As they drove home on the Parkway, Louis said, "If you can't have everything you want, at least take something. Don't be so goddam proud."

Touché. "What shall I take, Louis?"

He paused. "Take less."

"Less I'll never take."

"People got to compromise."

"I won't with my ideals."

"So what'll you be then, a dried-up prune of an old maid? What's the percentage of that?"

"None."

"So what'll you do?"

"I'll wait. I'll dream. Something will happen."

"Nuts," he said.

He let her off in front of the grocery.

"Thanks for everything."

"You'll make me laugh." Louis drove off.

The store was closed, upstairs dark. She pictured her father asleep after his long day, dreaming of Ephraim. What am I saving myself for? she asked herself. What unhappy Bober fate?

It snowed lightly the next day—too early in the year, complained Ida, and when the snow had melted it snowed again. The grocer remarked, as he was dressing in the dark, that he would shovel after he had opened the store. He enjoyed shoveling snow. It reminded him that he had practically lived in it in his boyhood; but Ida forbade him to exert himself because he still complained of dizziness. Later, when he tried to lug the milk cases through the snow, he found it all but impossible. And there was no Frank Alpine to help him, for he had disappeared after washing the window.

Ida came down shortly after her husband, in a heavy cloth coat, a woolen scarf pinned around her head and wearing galoshes. She shoveled a path through the snow and together they pulled in the milk. Only then did Morris notice that a quart bottle was missing from one of the cases.

"Who took it?" Ida cried.

"How do I know?"

"Did you count yet the rolls?"

"No."

"I told you always to count right away."

"The baker will steal from me? I know him twenty years."

"Count what everybody delivers, I told you a thousand times."

He dumped the rolls out of the basket and counted them. Three were missing and he had sold only one to the Poil-isheh. To appease Ida he said they were all there.

The next morning another quart of milk and two rolls were gone. He was worried but didn't tell Ida the truth when she asked him if anything else was missing. He often hid unpleasant news from her because she made it worse. He mentioned the missing bottles to the milkman, who answered, "Morris, I swear I left every bottle in that case. Am I re-sponsible for this lousy neighborhood?"

He promised to cart the milk cases into the vestibule for a few days. Maybe whoever was stealing the bottles would be afraid to go in there. Morris considered asking the milk company for a storage box. Years ago he had had one at the curb, a large wooden box in which the milk was padlocked; but he had given it up after developing a hernia lifting the heavy cases out, so he decided against a box.

On the third day, when a quart of milk and two rolls had again been taken, the grocer, much disturbed, considered calling the police. It wasn't the first time he had lost milk and rolls in this neighborhood. That had happened more than once—usually some poor person stealing a breakfast. For this reason Morris preferred not to call the police but to get rid of the thief by himself. To do it, he would usually wake up very early and wait at his bedroom window in the dark. Then when the man—sometimes it was a woman—showed up and was helping himself to the milk, Morris would quickly raise the window and shout down, "Get outa here, you thief you." The thief, startled—sometimes it was a customer who could afford to buy the milk he was stealing—would drop the bottle and run. Usually he never appeared again—a lost cus-tomer cut another way—and the next goniff was somebody else.

So this morning Morris arose at four-thirty, a little before

the milk was delivered, and sat in the cold in his long underwear, to wait. The street was heavy with darkness as he
peered down. Soon the milk truck came, and the milkman,
his breath foggy, lugged the two cases of milk into the vestibule. Then the street was silent again, the night dark, the
snow white. One or two people trudged by. An hour later,
Witzig, the baker, delivered the rolls, but no one else stopped
at the door. Just before six Morris dressed hastily and went
downstairs. A bottle of milk was gone, and when he counted
the rolls, so were two of them.

He still kept the truth from Ida. The next night she awoke
and found him at the window in the dark.

"What's the matter?" she asked, sitting up in bed.

"I can't sleep."

"So don't sit in your underwear in the cold. Come back to
bed."

He did as she said. Later, the milk and rolls were missing.

In the store he asked the Poilisheh whether she had seen
anyone sneak into the vestibule and steal a quart of milk.
She stared at him with small eyes, grabbed the sliced roll and
slammed the door.

Morris had a theory that the thief lived on the block. Nick
Fuso wouldn't do such a thing; if he did Morris would have
heard him going down the stairs, then coming up again. The
thief was somebody from outside. He sneaked along the
street close to the houses, where Morris couldn't see him because of the cornice that hung over the store; then he softly
opened the hall door, took the milk, two rolls from the bag,
and stole away, hugging the house fronts.

The grocer suspected Mike Papadopolous, the Greek boy
who lived on the floor above Karp's store. He had served a
reformatory sentence at eighteen. A year later he had in the
dead of night climbed down the fire escape overhanging
Karp's back yard, boosted himself up on the fence and forced
a window into the grocery. There he stole three cartons of
cigarettes, and a roll of dimes that Morris had left in the cash
register. In the morning, as the grocer was opening the store,
Mike's mother, a thin, old-looking woman, returned the ciga-

rettes and dimes to him. She had caught her son coming in with them and had walloped his head with a shoe. She clawed his face, making him confess what he had done. Returning the cigarettes and dimes, she had begged Morris not to have the boy arrested and he had assured her he wouldn't do such a thing.

On this day that he had guessed it might be Mike taking the milk and rolls, shortly after eight A.M., Morris went up the stairs and knocked reluctantly on Mrs. Papadopolous' door.

"Excuse me that I bother you," he said, and told her what had been happening to his milk and rolls.

"Mike work all nights in restaurants," she said. "No come home till nine o'clock in mornings. Sleep all days." Her eyes smoldered. The grocer left.

Now he was greatly troubled. Should he tell Ida and let her call the police? They were bothering him at least once a week with questions about the holdup but had produced nobody. Still, maybe it would be best to call them, for this stealing had gone on for almost a week. Who could afford it? Yet he waited, and that night as he was leaving the store by the side door, which he always padlocked after shutting the front door from inside, he flicked on the cellar light and as he peered down the stairs, his nightly habit, his heart tightened with foreboding that somebody was down there. Morris unlocked the lock, went back into the store and got a hatchet. Forcing his courage, he slowly descended the wooden steps. The cellar was empty. He searched in the dusty storage bins, poked around all over, but there was no sign of anybody.

In the morning he told Ida what was going on and she, calling him big fool, telephoned the police. A stocky, red-faced detective came, Mr. Minogue, from a nearby precinct, who was in charge of investigating Morris's holdup. He was a soft-spoken, unsmiling man, bald, a widower who had once lived in this neighborhood. He had a son Ward, who had gone to Helen's junior high school, a wild boy, always in trouble for manhandling girls. When he saw one he knew playing in front of her house, or on the stoop, he would come swooping down and chase her into the hall. There, no matter how desperately the girl struggled, or tenderly begged him to stop, Ward forced his hand down her dress and squeezed her breast till she screamed. Then by the time her mother came running down the stairs he had ducked out of the hall, leaving the girl sobbing. The detective, when he heard of these happenings, regularly beat up his son, but it didn't do much good. Then one day, about eight years ago, Ward was canned from his job for stealing from the company. His father beat him sick and bloody with his billy and drove him out of the neighborhood. After that, Ward disappeared and nobody knew where he had gone. People felt sorry for the detective, for he was a strict man and they knew what it meant to him to have such a son.

Mr. Minogue seated himself at the table in the rear and listened to Ida's complaint. He slipped on his glasses and wrote in a little black notebook. The detective said he would have a cop watch the store mornings after the milk was delivered, and if there was any more trouble to let him know.

As he was leaving, he said, "Morris, would you recognize Ward Minogue if you happened to see him again? I hear he's been seen around but whereabouts I don't know."

"I don't know," said Morris. "Maybe yes or maybe no. I didn't see him for years."

"If I ever meet up with him," said the detective, "I might bring him in to you for identification."

"What for?"

"I don't know myself—just for possible identification."

Ida said afterward that if Morris had called the police in the first place, he might have saved himself a few bottles of milk that they could hardly afford to lose.

That night, on an impulse, the grocer closed the store an hour later than usual. He snapped on the cellar light and cautiously descended the stairs, gripping his hatchet. Near the bottom he uttered a cry and the hatchet fell from his hands. A man's drawn and haggard face stared up at him in dismay. It was Frank Alpine, gray and unshaven. He had been asleep with his hat and coat on, sitting on a box against the wall. The light had awakened him.

"What do you want here?" Morris cried out.

"Nothing," Frank said dully. "I have just been sleeping in the cellar. No harm done."

"Did you steal from me my milk and rolls?"

"Yes," he confessed. "On account of I was hungry."

"Why didn't you ask me?"

Frank got up. "Nobody has any responsibility to take care of me but myself. I couldn't find any job. I used up every last cent I had. My coat is too thin for this cold and lousy climate. The snow and the rain get in my shoes so I am always shivering. Also, I had no place to sleep. That's why I came down here."

"Don't you stay any more with your sister?"

"I have no sister. That was a lie I told you. I am alone by myself."

"Why you told me you had a sister?"

"I didn't want you to think I was a bum."

Morris regarded the man silently. "Were you ever in prison sometimes?"

"Never, I swear to Christ."

"How you came to me in my cellar?"

"By accident. One night I was walking around in the snow, so I tried the cellar door and found out you left it unlocked, then I started coming down at night about an hour after you closed the store. In the morning, when they delivered the milk and rolls, I sneaked up through the hall, opened the door and took what I needed for breakfast. That's practically all I ate all day. After you came down and got busy with some customer or a salesman, I left by the hallway with the empty milk bottle under my coat. Later I threw it away in a lot. That's all there is to it. Tonight I took a chance and came in while you were still in the back of the store, because I have a cold and don't feel too good."

"How can you sleep in such a cold and drafty cellar?"

"I slept in worse."

"Are you hungry now?"

"I'm always hungry."

"Come upstairs."

Morris picked up his hatchet, and Frank, blowing his nose in his damp handkerchief, followed him up the stairs.

Morris lit a light in the store and made two fat liverwurst sandwiches with mustard, and in the back heated up a can of bean soup. Frank sat at the table in his coat, his hat lying at his feet. He ate with great hunger, his hand trembling as he brought the spoon to his mouth. The grocer had to look away.

As the man was finishing his meal, with coffee and cup cakes, Ida came down in felt slippers and bathrobe.

"What happened?" she asked in fright, when she saw Frank Alpine.

"He's hungry," Morris said.

She guessed at once. "He stole the milk!"

"He was hungry," explained Morris. "He slept in the cellar."

"I was practically starving," said Frank.

"Why didn't you look for a job?" Ida asked.

"I looked all over."

After, Ida said to Frank, "When you finish, please go someplace else." She turned to her husband. "Morris, tell him to go someplace else. We are poor people."

"This he knows."

"I'll go away," Frank said, "as the lady wishes."

"Tonight is already too late," Morris said. "Who wants he should walk all night in the streets?"

"I don't want him here." She was tense.

"Where you want him to go?"

Frank set his coffee cup on the saucer and listened with interest.

"This ain't my business," Ida answered.

"Don't anybody worry," said Frank. "I'll leave in ten minutes' time. You got a cigarette, Morris?"

The grocer went to the bureau and took out of the drawer a crumpled pack of cigarettes.

"It's stale," he apologized.

"Don't make any difference." Frank lit a stale cigarette, inhaling with pleasure.

"I'll go after a short while," he said to Ida.

"I don't like trouble," she explained.

"I won't make any. I might look like a bum in these clothes, but I am not. All my life I lived with good people."

"Let him stay here tonight on the couch," Morris said to Ida.

"No. Give him better a dollar he should go someplace else."

"The cellar would be fine," Frank remarked.

"It's too damp. Also rats."

"If you let me stay there one more night I promise I will get out the first thing in the morning. You don't have to be afraid to trust me. I am an honest man."

"You can sleep here," Morris said.

"Morris, you crazy," shouted Ida.

"I'll work it off for you," Frank said. "Whatever I cost you I'll pay you back. Anything you want me to do, I'll do it."

"We will see," Morris said.

"No," insisted Ida.

But Morris won out, and they went up, leaving Frank in the back, the gas radiator left lit.

"He will clean out the store," Ida said wrathfully.

"Where is his truck?" Morris asked, smiling. Seriously he said, "He's a poor boy. I feel sorry for him."

They went to bed. Ida slept badly. Sometimes she was racked by awful dreams. Then she awoke and sat up in bed, straining to hear noises in the store—of Frank packing huge bags of groceries to steal. But there was no sound. She dreamed she came down in the morning and all the stock was gone, the shelves as barren as the picked bones of dead birds. She dreamed, too, that the Italyener had sneaked up into the house and was peeking through the keyhole of Helen's door. Only when Morris got up to open the store did Ida fall fitfully asleep.

The grocer trudged down the stairs with a dull pain in his head. His legs felt weak. His sleep had not been refreshing.

The snow was gone from the streets and the milk boxes were again lying on the sidewalk near the curb. None of the bottles were missing. The grocer was about to drag in the milk cases when the Poilisheh came by. She went inside and placed three pennies on the counter. He entered with the brown bag of rolls, cut up one and wrapped it. She took it wordlessly and left.

Morris looked through the window in the wall. Frank was asleep on the couch in his clothes, his coat covering him. His beard was black, his mouth loosely open.

The grocer went out into the street, grabbed both milk boxes and yanked. The shape of a black hat blew up in his head, flared into hissing light, and exploded. He thought he was rising but felt himself fall.

Frank dragged him in and laid him on the couch. He ran upstairs and banged on the door. Helen, holding a housecoat over her nightdress, opened it. She suppressed a cry.

"Tell your mother your father just passed out. I called the ambulance."

She screamed. As he ran down the stairs he could hear Ida moaning. Frank hurried into the back of the store. The Jew lay white and motionless on the couch. Frank gently removed his apron. Draping the loop over his own head, he tied the tapes around him.

"I need the experience," he muttered.

Morris had reopened the wound on his head. The ambulance doctor, the same who had treated him after the holdup, said he had got up too soon last time and worn himself out. He again bandaged the grocer's head, saying to Ida, "This time let him lay in bed a good couple of weeks till his strength comes back." "You tell him, doctor," she begged, "he don't listen to me." So the doctor told Morris, and Morris weakly nodded. Ida, in a gray state of collapse, remained with the patient all day. So did Helen, after calling the ladies' underthings concern where she worked. Frank Alpine stayed competently downstairs in the store. At noon Ida remembered him and came down to tell him to leave. Recalling her dreams, she connected him with their new misfortune. She felt that if he had not stayed the night, this might not have happened.

Frank was clean-shaven in the back, having borrowed Morris's safety razor, his thick hair neatly combed, and when she appeared he hopped up to ring open the cash register, showing her a pile of puffy bills.

"Fifteen," he said, "count every one."

She was astonished. "How is so much?"

He explained, "We had a busy morning. A lot of people stopped in to ask about Morris's accident."

Ida had planned to replace him with Helen for the time being, until she herself could take over, but she was now of two minds.

"Maybe you can stay," she faltered, "if you want to, till tomorrow."

"I'll sleep in the cellar, Mrs. You don't have to worry about me. I am as honest as the day."

"Don't sleep in the cellar," she said with a tremble to her voice, "my husband said on the couch. What can anybody steal here? We have nothing."

"How is he now?" Frank asked in a low voice.

She blew her nose.

The next morning Helen went reluctantly to work. Ida came down at ten to see how things were. This time there were only eight dollars in the drawer, but still better than lately. He apologized, "Not so good today, but I wrote down every article I sold so you'll know nothing stuck to my fingers." He produced a list of goods sold, written on wrapping paper. She happened to notice that it began with three cents

for a roll. Glancing around, Ida saw he had packed out the
few cartons delivered yesterday, swept up, washed the window from the inside and had straightened the cans on the
shelves. The place looked a little less dreary.

During the day he also kept himself busy with odd jobs.
He cleaned the trap of the kitchen sink, which swallowed water slowly, and in the store fixed a light whose chain wouldn't
pull, making useless one lamp. Neither of them mentioned
his leaving. Ida, still uneasy, wanted to tell him to go but she
couldn't ask Helen to stay home any more, and the prospect
of two weeks alone in the store, with her feet and a sick man
in the bargain to attend upstairs, was too much for her.
Maybe she would let the Italian stay ten days or so. With
Morris fairly well recovered there would be no reason to keep
him after that. In the meantime he would have three good
meals a day and a bed, for being little more than a watchman.
What business, after all, did they do here? And while Morris
was not around she would change a thing or two she should
have done before. So when the milkman stopped by for yesterday's empties, she ordered containers brought from now
on. Frank Alpine heartily approved. "Why should we bother
with bottles?" he said.

Despite all she had to do upstairs, and her recent good im-
pressions of him, Ida haunted the store, watching his every
move. She was worried because, now, not Morris but she was
responsible for the man's presence in the store. If something
bad happened, it would be her fault. Therefore, though she
climbed the stairs often to tend to her husband's needs, she
hurried back down, arriving pale and breathless to see what
Frank was up to. But anything he happened to be doing was
helpful. Her suspicions died slowly, though they never wholly
died.

She tried not to be too friendly to him, to make him feel
that a distant relationship meant a short one. When they were
in the back or for a few minutes together behind the counter
she discouraged conversation, took up something to do, or
clean, or her paper to read. And in the matter of teaching him
the business there was also little to say. Morris had price

tags displayed under all items on the shelves, and Ida supplied Frank with a list of prices for meats and salads and for the miscellaneous unmarked things like loose coffee, rice or beans. She taught him how to wrap neatly and efficiently, as Morris had long ago taught her, how to read the scale and to set and handle the electric meat slicer. He caught on quickly; she suspected he knew more than he said he did. He added rapidly and accurately, did not overcut meats or overload the scale on bulk items, as she had urged him not to do, and judged well the length of paper needed to wrap with, and what number bag to pack goods into, conserving the larger bags which cost more money. Since he learned so fast, and since she had seen in him not the least evidence of dishonesty (a hungry man who took milk and rolls, though not above suspicion, was not the same as a thief), Ida forced herself to remain upstairs with more calm, in order to give Morris his medicine, bathe her aching feet and keep up the house, which was always dusty from the coal yard. Yet she felt, whenever she thought of it, always a little troubled at the thought of a stranger's presence below, a goy, after all, and she looked forward to the time when he was gone.

Although his hours were long—six to six, at which time she served him his supper—Frank was content. In the store he was quits with the outside world, safe from cold, hunger and a damp bed. He had cigarettes when he wanted them and was comfortable in clean clothes Morris had sent down, even a pair of pants that fitted him after Ida lengthened and pressed the cuffs. The store was fixed, a cave, motionless. He had all his life been on the move, no matter where he was; here he somehow couldn't be. Here he could stand at the window and watch the world go by, content to be here.

It wasn't a bad life. He woke before dawn. The Polish dame was planted at the door like a statue, distrusting him with beady eyes to open the place in time for her to get to work. Her he didn't like; he would gladly have slept longer. To get up in the middle of the night for three lousy cents was a joke but he did it for the Jew. After packing away the milk containers, turning bottomside up the occasional one that leaked, he swept the store and then the sidewalk. In the back he washed, shaved, had coffee and a sandwich, at first made with meat from a ham or roast pork butt, then after a few days, from the best cut. As he smoked after coffee he thought of everything he could do to improve this dump if it were his. When somebody came into the store he was up with a bound, offering service with a smile. Nick Fuso, on Frank's first day, was surprised to see him there, knowing Morris could not afford a clerk. But Frank said that though the pay was scarce there were other advantages. They spoke about this and that, and when the upstairs tenant learned Frank Alpine was a paisan, he told him to come up and meet Tessie. She cordially invited him for macaroni that same night, and he said he would come if they let him bring the macs.

Ida, after the first few days, began to go down at her regular hour, around ten, after she had finished the housework; and she busied herself with writing in a notebook which bills they had got and which paid. She also wrote out, in a halting hand, a few meager special-account checks for bills that could not be paid in cash directly to the drivers, mopped the kitchen floor, emptied the garbage pail into the metal can on the curb outside and prepared salad if it was needed. Frank watched her shred cabbage on the meat slicer for coleslaw, which she made in careful quantity, because if it turned sour it had to be dumped into the garbage. Potato salad was a bigger job, and she cooked up a large pot of new potatoes, which Frank helped her peel hot in their steaming jackets. Every Friday she prepared fish cakes and a panful of homemade baked beans, first soaking the little beans overnight, pouring out the water, then spreading brown sugar on top before baking. Her expression as she dipped in among the soggy beans pieces of ham from a butt she had cut up caught his eye, and he felt for her repugnance for hating to touch the ham, and some for himself because he had never lived this close to Jews before. At lunchtime there was a little "rush," which meant that a few dirty-faced laborers from the coal yard and a couple of store clerks from on the block wanted sandwiches and containers of hot coffee. But the "rush," for which they both went behind the counter, petered out in a matter of minutes and then came the dead hours of the afternoon. Ida said he ought to take some time off, but he answered that he had nowhere special to go and stayed in the back, reading the *Daily News* on the couch, or flipping through some magazines that he had got out of the public library, which he had discovered during one of his solitary walks in the neighborhood.

At three, when Ida departed for an hour or so to see if Morris needed something, and to rest, Frank felt relieved. Alone, he did a lot of casual eating, sometimes with unexpected pleasure. He sampled nuts, raisins, and small boxes of stale dates or dried figs, which he liked anyway; he also opened packages of crackers, macaroons, cupcakes and doughnuts, tearing up their wrappers into small pieces and flushing them down the toilet. Sometimes in the middle of eating sweets he would get very hungry for something more substantial, so he made a thick meat and Swiss cheese sandwich on a seeded hard roll spread with mustard, and swallowed it down with a bottle of ice-cold beer. Satisfied, he stopped roaming in the store.

Now and then there were sudden unlooked-for flurries of customers, mostly women, whom he waited on attentively, talking to them about all kinds of things. The drivers, too, liked his sociability and cheery manner and stayed to chew the fat. Otto Vogel, once when he was weighing a ham, warned him in a low voice, "Don't work for a Yid, kiddo. They will steal your ass while you are sitting on it." Frank, though he said he didn't expect to stay long, felt embarrassed for being there; then, to his surprise, he got another warning, from an apologetic Jew salesman of paper products, Al Marcus, a prosperous, yet very sick and solemn character who wouldn't stop working. "This kind of a store is a death tomb, positive," Al Marcus said. "Run out while you can. Take my word, if you stay six months, you'll stay forever."

"Don't worry about that," answered Frank.

Alone afterward, he stood at the window, thinking thoughts about his past, and wanting a new life. Would he ever get what he wanted? Sometimes he stared out of the back yard window at nothing at all, or at the clothesline above, moving idly in the wind, flying Morris's scarecrow union suits, Ida's hefty bloomers, modestly folded lengthwise, and her house-dresses guarding her daughter's flower-like panties and rest-less brassières.

In the evening, whether he wanted to or not, he was "off." Ida insisted, fair was fair. She fed him a quick supper and al-lowed him, with apologies because she couldn't afford more, fifty cents spending money. He occasionally passed the time upstairs with the Fusos or went with them to a picture at the local movie house. Sometimes he walked, in spite of the cold, and stopped off at a poolroom he knew, about a mile and a half from the grocery store. When he got back, always before closing, for Ida wouldn't let him keep a key to the store in his pocket, she counted up the day's receipts, put most of the cash into a small paper bag and took it with her, leaving Frank five dollars to open up with in the morning. After she had gone, he turned the key in the front door lock, hooked the side door through which she had left, put out the store lights and sat in his undershirt in the rear, reading tomorrow's pink-sheeted paper that he had picked off Sam Pearl's stand on his way home. Then he undressed and went restlessly to bed in a pair of Morris's bulky, rarely used, flannel pajamas.

The old dame, he thought with disgust, always hurried him out of the joint before her daughter came down for sup-per.

The girl was in his mind a lot. He couldn't help it, imagined seeing her in the things that were hanging on the line—he had always had a good imagination. He pictured her as she came down the stairs in the morning; also saw himself stand-ing in the hall after she came home, watching her skirts go fly-ing as she ran up the stairs. He rarely saw her around, had never spoken to her but twice, on the day her father had passed out. She had kept her distance—who could blame her, dressed as he was and what he looked like then? He had the feeling as he spoke to her, a few hurried words, that he knew more about her than anybody would give him credit for. He had got this thought the first time he had ever laid eyes on her, that night he saw her through the grocery window. When she had looked at him he was at once aware of something starved about her, a hunger in her eyes he couldn't forget because it made him remember his own, so he knew how wide open she must be. But he wouldn't try to push anything, for he had heard that these Jewish babes could be troublemakers and he was not looking for any of that now— at least no more than usual; besides, he didn't want to spoil anything before it got started. There were some dames you had to wait for—for them to come to you.

His desire grew to get to know her, he supposed because she had never once come into the store in all the time he was there except after he left at night. There was no way to see and talk to her to her face, and this increased his curiosity. He felt they were both lonely but her old lady kept her away from him as if he had a dirty disease; the result was he grew more impatient to find out what she was like, get to be friends with her for whatever it was worth. So, since she was never around, he listened and watched for her. When he heard her walking down the stairs he went to the front window and stood there waiting for her to come out; he tried to look casual, as if he weren't watching, just in case she happened to glance back and see him; but she never did, as if she liked nothing about the place enough to look back on. She had a pretty face and a good figure, small-breasted, neat, as if she had meant herself to look that way. He liked to watch her brisk, awkward walk till she turned the corner. It was a sexy walk, with a wobble in it, a strange movement, as though she might dart sideways although she was walking forward. Her legs were just a bit bowed, and maybe that was the sexy part of it. She stayed in his mind after she had turned the corner; her legs and small breasts and the pink brassières that covered them. He would be reading something or lying on his back on the couch, smoking, and she would appear in his mind, walking to the corner. He did not have to shut his eyes to see her. Turn around, he said out loud, but in his thoughts she wouldn't.

To see her coming toward him he stood at the lit grocery window at night, but often before he could catch sight of her she was on her way upstairs, or already changing her dress in her room, and his chance was over for the day. She came home about a quarter to six, sometimes a little earlier, so he tried to be at the window around then, which wasn't so easy because that was the time for Morris's few supper customers to come in. So he rarely saw her come home from work, though he always heard her on the stairs. One day things were slower than usual in the store, it was dead at five-thirty, and Frank said to himself, Today I will see her. He combed his hair in the toilet so that Ida wouldn't notice, changed into a clean apron, lit a cigarette, and stood at the window, visible in its light. At twenty to six, just after he had practically shoved a woman out of the joint, a dame who had happened to walk in off the trolley, he saw Helen turn Sam Pearl's corner. Her face was prettier than he had remembered and his throat tightened as she walked to within a couple of feet of him, her eyes blue, her hair, which she wore fairly long, brown, and she had an absent-minded way of smoothing it back off the side of her face. He thought she didn't look Jewish, which was all to the good. But her expression was discontented, and her mouth a little drawn. She seemed to be thinking of something she had no hope of ever getting. This moved him, so that when she glanced up and saw his eyes on her, his face plainly showed his emotion. It must have bothered her because she quickly walked, without noticing him further, to the hall and disappeared inside.

The next morning he didn't see her—as if she had sneaked out on him—and at night he was waiting on somebody when she returned from work; regretfully he heard the door slam behind her. Afterward he felt downhearted; every sight lost to a guy who lived with his eyes was lost for all time. He thought up different ways to meet her and exchange a few words. What he had on his mind to say to her about himself was beginning to weigh on him, though he hadn't clearly figured out the words. Once he thought of coming in on her unexpectedly while she was eating her supper, but then he

would have Ida to deal with. He also had the idea of opening
the door the next time he saw her and calling her into the
store; he could say that some guy had telephoned her, and
after that talk about something else, but nobody did call her.
She was in her way a lone bird, which suited him fine, though
why she should be with her looks he couldn't figure out. He
got the feeling that she wanted something big out of life, and
this scared him. Still, he tried to think of schemes of getting
her inside the store, even planning to ask her something like
did she know where her old man kept his saw; only she
mightn't like that, her mother being around all day to tell him.
He had to watch out not to scare her any farther away than
the old dame had done.

For a couple of nights after work he stood in a hallway next
door to the laundry across the street in the hope that she
would come out to do some errand, then he would cross over,
tip his hat and ask if he could keep her company to where she
was going. But this did not pay off either, because she didn't
leave the house. The second night he waited fruitlessly until
Ida put out the lights in the grocery window.

One evening toward the end of the second week after Morris's accident, Frank's loneliness burdened him to the point of
irritation. He was eating his supper a few minutes after Helen
had returned from work, while Ida happened to be upstairs
with Morris. He had seen Helen come round the corner and
had nodded to her as she approached the house. Caught by
surprise, she half-smiled, then entered the hall. It was then
the lonely feeling gripped him. While he was eating, he felt he
had to get her into the store before her old lady came down
and it was time for him to leave. The only excuse he could
think of was to call Helen to answer the phone and after he
would say that the guy must've hung up. It was a trick but he
had to do it. He warned himself not to, because it would be
starting out the wrong way with her and he might someday
regret it. He tried to think of a better way but time was pressing him and he couldn't.

Frank got up, went over to the bureau, and took the phone
off its cradle. He then walked out into the hall, opened the

vestibule door, and holding his breath, pressed the Bober bell.

Ida looked over the banister. "What's the matter?"

"Telephone for Helen."

He could see her hesitate, so he returned quickly to the store. He sat down, pretending to be eating, his heart whamming so hard it hurt. All he wanted, he told himself, was to talk to her a minute so the next time would be easier.

Helen eagerly entered the kitchen. On the stairs she had noticed the excitement that flowed through her. My God, it's gotten to be that a phone call is an event.

If it's Nat, she thought, I might give him another chance.

Frank half-rose as she entered, then sat down.

"Thanks," she said to him as she picked up the phone.

"Hello." While she waited he could hear the buzz in the receiver.

"There's nobody there," she said, mystified.

He laid down his fork. "This girl called you," he said gently.

But when he saw the disappointment in her eyes, how bad she felt, he felt bad.

"You must've been cut off."

She gave him a long look. She was wearing a white blouse that showed the firmness of her small breasts. He wet his dry lips, trying to figure out some quick way to square himself, but his mind, usually crowded with all sorts of schemes, had gone blank. He felt very bad, as he had known he would, that he had done what he had. If he had it to do over he wouldn't do it this way.

"Did she leave you her name?" Helen asked.

"No."

"It wasn't Betty Pearl?"

"No."

She absently brushed back her hair. "Did she say anything to you?"

"Only to call you." He paused. "Her voice was nice—like yours. Maybe she didn't get me straight when I said you were upstairs but I would ring your doorbell, and that's why she hung up."

"I don't know why anybody would do that."

Neither did he. He wanted to step clear of his mess but saw no way other than to keep on lying. But lying made their talk useless. When he lied he was somebody else lying to somebody else. It wasn't the two of them as they were. He should have kept that in his mind.

She stood at the bureau, holding the telephone in her hand as if still expecting the buzz to become a voice; so he waited for the same thing, a voice to speak and say he had been telling the truth, that he was a man of fine character. Only that didn't happen either.

He gazed at her with dignity as he considered saying the simple truth, starting from there, come what would, but the thought of confessing what he had done almost panicked him.

"I'm sorry," he said brokenly, but by then she was gone, and he was attempting to fix in his memory what she had looked like so close.

Helen too was troubled. Not only could she not explain why she believed yet did not fully believe him, nor why she had lately become so conscious of his presence among them, though he never strayed from the store, but she was also disturbed by her mother's efforts to keep her away from him. "Eat when he leaves," Ida had said. "I am not used to goyim in my house." This annoyed Helen because of the assumption that she would keel over for somebody just because he happened to be a gentile. It meant, obviously, her mother didn't trust her. If she had been casual about him, Helen doubted she would have paid him any attention to speak of. He was interesting looking, true, but what except a poor grocery clerk? Out of nothing Ida was trying to make something.

Though Ida was still concerned at having the young Italian around the place, she observed with pleased surprise how, practically from the day of his appearance, the store had improved. During the first week there were days when they had taken in from five to seven dollars more than they were averaging daily in the months since summer. And the same held for the second week. The store was of course still a poor store, but with this forty to fifty a week more they might at least limp along until a buyer appeared. She could at first not understand why more people were coming in, why more goods were being sold. True, the same thing had happened before. Without warning, after a long season of dearth, three or four customers, lost faces, straggled in one day, as if they had been let out of their poor rooms with a few pennies in their pockets. And others, who had skimped on food, began to buy more. A storekeeper could tell almost at once when times were getting better. People seemed less worried and irritable, less in competition for the little sunlight in the world. Yet the curious thing was that business, according to most of the drivers, had not very much improved anywhere. One of them said that Schmitz around the corner was having his troubles too; furthermore he wasn't feeling so good. So the sudden pickup of business in the store, Ida thought, would not have happened without Frank Alpine. It took her a while to admit this to herself.

The customers seemed to like him. He talked a lot as he waited on them, sometimes saying things that embarrassed Ida but made the customers, the gentile housewives, laugh. He somehow drew in people she had never before seen in the neighborhood, not only women, men too. Frank tried things that Morris and she could never do, such as attempting to sell people more than they asked for, and usually he succeeded. "What can you do with a quarter of a pound?" he would say. "A quarter is for the birds—not even a mouthful. Better make it a half." So they would make it a half. Or he would say, "Here's a new brand of mustard that we just got in today. It weighs two ounces more than the stuff they sell you in the supermarkets for the same price. Why don't you give it a try? If you don't like it, bring it back and I will gargle it." And they laughed and bought it. This made Ida wonder if Morris and she were really suited to the grocery business. They had never been salesmen.

One of the women customers called Frank a supersales-
man, a word that brought a pleased smile to his lips. He was
clever and worked hard. Ida's respect for him reluctantly
grew; gradually she became more relaxed in his presence.
Morris was right in recognizing that he was not a bum but a
boy who had gone through bad times. She pitied him for having lived in an orphan asylum. He did his work quickly, never
complained, kept himself neat and clean now that he had
soap and water around, and answered her politely. The one
or two times, just lately, that he had briefly talked to Helen in
her presence, he had spoken like a gentleman and didn't try
to stretch a word into a mouthful. Ida discussed the situation
with Morris and they raised his "spending money" from fifty
cents a day to five dollars for the week. Despite her good will
to him, this worried Ida, but, after all, he was bringing more
money into the store, the place looked spic and span—let him
keep five dollars of their poor profit. Bad as things still were,
he willingly did so much extra around the store—how could
they not pay him a little something? Besides, she thought, he
would soon be leaving.

Frank accepted the little raise with an embarrassed smile.
"You don't have to pay me anything more, Mrs, I said I
would work for nothing to make up for past favors from your
husband and also to learn the business. Besides that, you give
me my bed and board, so you don't owe me a thing."

"Take," she said, handing him a crumpled five-dollar bill.
He let the money lie on the counter till she urged him to put
it into his pocket. Frank felt troubled about the raise because
he was earning something for his labor that Ida knew nothing
of, for business was a little better than she thought. During
the day, while she was not around, he sold at least a bucks
worth, or a buck and a half, that he made no attempt to ring
up on the register. Ida guessed nothing; the list of sold items
he had supplied her with in the beginning they had discon-
tinued as impractical. It wasn't hard for him to scrape up
here a bit of change, there a bit. At the end of the second
week he had ten dollars in his pocket. With this and the five

she gave him he bought a shaving kit, a pair of cheap brown suede shoes, a couple of shirts and a tie or two; he figured that if he stayed around two more weeks he would own an inexpensive suit. He had nothing to be ashamed of, he thought —it was practically his own dough he was taking. The grocer and his wife wouldn't miss it because they didn't know they had it, and they wouldn't have it if it wasn't for his hard work. If he weren't working there, they would have less than they had with him taking what he took.

Thus he settled it in his mind only to find himself remorseful. He groaned, scratching the backs of his hands with his thick nails. Sometimes he felt short of breath and sweated profusely. He talked aloud to himself when he was alone, usually when he was shaving or in the toilet, exhorted himself to be honest. Yet he felt a curious pleasure in his misery, as he had at times in the past when he was doing something he knew he oughtn't to, so he kept on dropping quarters into his pants pocket.

One night he felt very bad about all the wrong he was doing and vowed to set himself straight. If I could do one right thing, he thought, maybe that would start me off; then he thought if he could get the gun and get rid of it he would at least feel better. He left the grocery after supper and wandered restlessly in the foggy streets, feeling cramped in the chest from his long days in the store and because his life hadn't changed much since he had come here. As he passed by the cemetery, he tried to keep out of his mind the memory of the holdup but it kept coming back in. He saw himself sitting with Ward Minogue in the parked car, waiting for Karp to come out of the grocery, but when he did his store lights went out and he hid in the back among the bottles. Ward said to drive quick around the block so they would flush the Jew out, and he would slug him on the sidewalk and take his fat wallet away; but when they got back, Karp's car was gone with him in it, and Ward cursed him into an early grave. Frank said Karp had beat it, so they ought to scram, but Ward sat there with heartburn, watching, with his small eyes, the grocery store, the one lit place on the block besides the candy store on the corner.

"No," Frank urged, "it's just a little joint, I got my doubts if they took in thirty bucks today."

"Thirty is thirty," Ward said. "I don't care if it's Karp or Bober, a Jew is a Jew."

"Why not the candy store?"

Ward made a face. "I can't stand penny candy."

"How do you know his name?" asked Frank.

"Who?"

"The Jew grocer."

"I used to go to school with his daughter. She has a nice ass."

"Then if that's so, he will recognize you."

"Not with a rag around my snoot, and I will rough up my voice. He ain't seen me for eight or nine years. I was a skinny kid then."

"Have it your way. I will keep the car running."

"Come in with me," Ward said. "The block is dead. Nobody will expect a stickup in this dump."

But Frank hesitated. "I thought you said Karp was the one you were out after?"

"I will take Karp some other time. Come on."

Frank put on his cap and crossed the car tracks with Ward Minogue. "It's your funeral," he said, but it was really his own.

He remembered thinking as they went into the store, a Jew is a Jew, what difference does it make? Now he thought, I held him up because he was a Jew. What the hell are they to me so that I gave them credit for it?

But he didn't know the answer and walked faster, from time to time glancing through the spiked iron fence at the shrouded gravestones. Once he felt he was being followed and his heart picked up a hard beat. He hurried past the cemetery and turned right on the first street after it, hugging the stoops of the stone houses as he went quickly down the dark street. When he reached the poolroom he felt relieved.

Pop's poolroom was a dreary four-table joint, owned by a glum old Italian with a blue-veined bald head and droopy hands, who sat close to his cash register.

"Seen Ward yet?" Frank said.

Pop pointed to the rear where Ward Minogue, in his fuzzy black hat and a bulky overcoat, was practicing shots alone at a table. Frank watched him place a black ball at a corner pocket and aim a white at it. Ward leaned tensely forward, his face strained, a dead butt hanging from his sick mouth. He shot but missed. He banged his cue on the floor.

Frank had drifted past the players at the other tables. When Ward looked up and saw him, his eyes lit with fear. The fear drained after he recognized who it was. But his pimply face was covered with sweat.

He spat his butt to the floor. "What have you got on your feet, you bastard, gumshoes?"

"I didn't want to spoil your shot."

"Anyway you did."

"I've been looking for you about a week."

"I was on my vacation." Ward smiled in the corner of his mouth.

"On a drunk?"

Ward put his hand to his chest and brought up a belch. "I wish to hell it was. Somebody tipped my old man I was around here, so I hid out for a while. I had a rough time. My heartburn is acting up." He hung up his cue, then wiped his face with a dirty handkerchief.

"Why don't you go to a doctor?" Frank said.

"The hell with them."

"Some medicine might help you."

"What will help me is if my goddam father drops dead."

"I want to talk to you, Ward," Frank said in a low voice.

"So talk."

Frank nodded toward the players at the next table.

"Come out in the yard," Ward said. "I got something I want to say to you."

Frank followed him out the rear door into a small enclosed back yard with a wooden bench against the building.

A weak bulb shone down on them from the top of the door-jamb.

Ward sat down on the bench and lit a cigarette. Frank did the same, from his own pack. He puffed but got no pleasure from the butt, so he threw it away.

"Sit down," said Ward.

Frank sat on the bench. Even in the fog he stinks, he thought.

"What do you want me for?" Ward asked, his small eyes restless.

"I want my gun, Ward. Where is it?"

"What for?"

"I want to throw it in the ocean."

Ward snickered. "Cat got your nuts?"

"I don't want some dick coming around and asking me do I own it."

"I thought you said you bought the rod off a fence."

"That's right."

"Then nobody's got a record of it, so what are you scared of?"

"If you lost it," Frank said, "they trace them even without a record."

"I won't lose it," Ward said. After a minute he ground his cigarette into the dirt. "I will give it back to you after we do this job I have on my mind."

Frank looked at him. "What kind of a job?"

"Karp. I want to stick him up."

"Why Karp?—there are bigger liquor stores."

"I hate that Jew son of a bitch and his popeyed Louis. When I was a kid all I had to do was go near banjo eyes and they would complain to my old man and get me beat up."

"They would recognize you if you go in there."

"Bober didn't. I will use a handkerchief and wear some different clothes. Tomorrow I will go out and pick up a car. All you got to do is drive and I will make the heist."

"You better stay away from that block," Frank warned. "Somebody might recognize you."

Ward moodily rubbed his chest. "All right, you sold me. We will go somewhere else."

"Not with me," Frank said.

"Think it over."

"I've had all I want."

Ward showed his disgust. "The minute I saw you I knew you would puke all over."

Frank didn't answer.

"Don't act so innocent," Ward said angrily. "You're hot, the same as me."

"I know," Frank said.

"I slugged him because he was lying where he hid the rest of the dough," Ward argued.

"He didn't hide it. It's a poor, lousy store."

"I guess you know all about that."

"What do you mean?"

"Can the crud. I know you been working there."

Frank drew a breath. "You following me again, Ward?"

Ward smiled. "I followed you one night after you left the poolroom. I found out you were working for a Jew and living on bird crap."

Frank slowly got up. "I felt sorry for him after you slugged him, so I went back to give him a hand while he was in a weak condition. But I won't be staying there long."

"That was real sweet of you. I suppose you gave him back the lousy seven and a half bucks that was your part of the take?"

"I put it back in the cash register. I told the Mrs the business was getting better."

"I never thought I would meet up with a goddam Salvation Army soldier."

"I did it to quiet my conscience," Frank said.

Ward rose. "That ain't your conscience you are worried about."

"No?"

"It's something else. I hear those Jew girls make nice ripe lays."

Frank went back without his gun.

Helen was with her mother as Ida counted the cash.

Frank stood behind the counter, cleaning his fingernails with his jackknife blade, waiting for them to leave so he could close up.

"I think I'll take a hot shower before I go to bed," Helen said to her mother. "I've felt chilled all night."

"Good night," Ida said to Frank. "I left five dollars change for the morning."

"Good night," said Frank.

They left by the rear door and he heard them go up the stairs. Frank closed the store and went into the back. He thumbed through tomorrow's *News*, then got restless.

After a while he went into the store and listened at the side door; he unlatched the lock, snapped on the cellar light, closed the cellar door behind him so no light would leak out into the hall, then quietly descended the stairs.

He found the air shaft where an old unused dumb-waiter stood, pushed the dusty box back and gazed up the vertical shaft. It was pitch-dark. Neither the Bobers' bathroom window nor the Fusos' showed any light.

Frank struggled against himself but not for long. Shoving the dumb-waiter back as far as it would go, he squeezed into the shaft and then boosted himself up on top of the box. His heart shook him with its beating.

When his eyes got used to the dark he saw that her bathroom window was only a couple of feet above his head. He felt along the wall as high as he could reach and touched a narrow ledge around the air shaft. He thought he could anchor himself on it and see into the bathroom.

But if you do it, he told himself, you will suffer.

Though his throat hurt and his clothes were drenched in sweat, the excitement of what he might see forced him to go up.

Crossing himself, Frank grabbed both of the dumb-waiter ropes and slowly pulled himself up, praying the pulley at the skylight wouldn't squeak too much.

A light went on over his head.

Holding his breath, he crouched motionless, clinging to the swaying ropes. Then the bathroom window was shut with a bang. For a while he couldn't move, the strength gone out of him. He thought he might lose his grip and fall, and he thought of her opening the bathroom window and seeing him lying at the bottom of the shaft in a broken, filthy heap.

It was a mistake to do it, he thought.

But she might be in the shower before he could get a look at her, so, trembling, he began again to pull himself up. In a few minutes he was straddling the ledge, holding onto the ropes to steady himself yet keep his full weight off the wood.

Leaning forward, though not too far, he could see through the uncurtained crossed sash window into the old-fashioned bathroom. Helen was there looking with sad eyes at herself in the mirror. He thought she would stand there forever, but at last she unzippered her housecoat, stepping out of it.

He felt a throb of pain at her nakedness, an overwhelming desire to love her, at the same time an awareness of loss, of never having had what he had wanted most, and other such memories he didn't care to recall.

Her body was young, soft, lovely, the breasts like small birds in flight, her ass like a flower. Yet it was a lonely body in spite of its lovely form, lonelier. Bodies are lonely, he thought, but in bed she wouldn't be. She seemed realer to him now than she had been, revealed without clothes, personal, possible. He felt greedy as he gazed, all eyes at a banquet, hungry so long as he must look. But in looking he was forcing her out of reach, making her into a thing only of his seeing, her eyes reflecting his sins, rotten past, spoiled ideals, his passion poisoned by his shame.

Frank's eyes grew moist and he wiped them with one hand. When he gazed up again she seemed, to his horror, to be staring at him through the window, a mocking smile on her lips, her eyes filled with scorn, pitiless. He thought wildly of jumping, bolting, broken-boned, out of the house; but she turned on the shower and stepped into the tub, drawing the flowered plastic curtain around her.

The window was quickly covered with steam. For this he

was relieved, grateful. He let himself down silently. In the cellar, instead of the grinding remorse he had expected to suffer, he felt a moving joy.

On a Saturday morning in December, Morris, after a little more than two impatient weeks upstairs, came down with his head healed. The night before, Ida told Frank he would have to leave in the morning, but when Morris later learned this they had an argument. Although he hadn't said so to Ida, the grocer, after his long layoff, was depressed at the prospect of having to take up his dreary existence in the store. He dreaded the deadweight of hours, mostly sad memories of his lost years of youth. That business was better gave him some comfort but not enough, for he was convinced from all Ida had told him that business was better only because of their assistant, whom he remembered as a stranger with hungry eyes, a man to be pitied. Yet the why of it was simple enough—the store had improved not because this cellar dweller was a magician, but because he was not Jewish. The goyim in the neighborhood were happier with one of their own. A Jew stuck in their throats. Yes, they had, on and off, patronized his store, called him by his first name and asked for credit as if he were obliged to give it, which he had, in the past, often foolishly done; but in their hearts they hated him. If it weren't so, Frank's presence could not have made such a quick difference in income. He was afraid that the extra forty-five dollars weekly would melt away overnight if the Italian left and he vehemently said so to Ida. She, though she feared he was right, still argued that Frank must be let go. How could they, she asked, keep him working seven days a week, twelve hours a day, for a miserable five dollars? It was unjust. The grocer agreed, but why push the boy into the street if he wanted to stay longer? The five dollars, he admitted, was nothing, but what of the bed and board, the free packs of cigarettes, the bottles of beer she said he guzzled in the store? If things went on well, he would offer him more, maybe even a small commission, very small— maybe on all they took in over a hundred and fifty a week, a sum they had not realized since Schmitz had opened up around the corner; meantime he would give him his Sundays off and otherwise reduce his hours. Since Morris was now able to open the store, Frank could stay in bed till nine. This proposition was no great bargain but the grocer insisted that the man have the chance to take or refuse it.

Ida, a red flush spreading on her neck, said, "Are you crazy, Morris? Even with the forty more that comes in, which we give him away five dollars, our little profit, who can afford to keep him here? Look what he eats. It's impossible."

"We can't afford to keep him but we can't afford to lose him, on account he might improve more the business if he stays," Morris answered.

"How can three people work in such a small store?" she cried.

"Rest your sick feet," he answered. "Sleep longer in the morning and stay more upstairs in the house. Who needs you should be so tired every night?"

"Also," Ida argued, "who wants him in the back all night so we can't go inside after the store is closed when we forget something?"

"This I thought about also. I think I will take off from Nick's rent upstairs a couple dollars and tell him he should give Frank the little room to sleep in. They don't use it for nothing, only storage. There, with plenty blankets he will be comfortable, with a door which it goes right in the hall so he can come in and go out with his own key without bothering anybody. He can wash himself here in the store."

"A couple dollars less from the rent comes also from our poor pocket," Ida replied, pressing her clasped hands to her bosom. "But the most important is I don't want him here on account of Helen. I don't like the way he looks on her."

Morris gazed at her. "So you like maybe how Nat looks on her, or Louis Karp? That's the way they look, the boys. Tell me better, how does she look on him?"

She shrugged stiffly.

"This is what I thought. You know yourself Helen wouldn't be interested in such a boy. A grocery clerk don't interest her. Does she go out with the salesmen where she works, that they ask her? No. She wants better—so let her have better."

"Will be trouble," she murmured.

He belittled her fears, and when he came down on Saturday morning, spoke to Frank about staying on for a while. Frank had arisen before six and was sitting dejectedly on the couch when the grocer came in. He agreed at once to continue on in the store under the conditions Morris offered.

More animated now, the clerk said he liked the idea of living upstairs near Nick and Tessie; and Morris that day arranged it, in spite of Ida's misgivings, by promising three dollars off their rent. Tessie lugged out of the room a trunk, garment bags and a few odds and ends of furniture; after, she dusted and vacuumed. Between what she offered, and what Morris got out of his bin in the cellar, they supplied a bed with a fairly good mattress, a usable chest of drawers, chair, small table, electric heater and even an old radio Nick had around. Although the room was cold, because it had no radiator and was locked off from the Fusos' gas-heated bedroom, Frank was satisfied. Tessie worried about what would happen if he had to go to the bathroom at night, and Nick talked the matter over with Frank, saying apologetically that she was ashamed to have him go through their bedroom, but Frank said he never woke up at night. Anyway, Nick had a key made to the front door patent lock. He said if Frank ever had to get up he could walk across the hall and let himself in through the front without waking them. And he could also use their bathtub, just so long as he told them when he would want it.

This arrangement suited Tessie. Everyone was satisfied but Ida, who was unhappy with herself for having kept Frank on. She made the grocer promise he would send the clerk away before the summer. Business was always more active in the summertime, so Morris agreed. She asked him to tell Frank at once that he would be let go then, and when the grocer did, the clerk smiled amiably and said the summer was a long ways off but anyway it was all right with him.

The grocer felt his mood change. It was a better mood than he had expected. A few of his old customers had returned. One woman told him that Schmitz was not giving as good service as he once did; he was having trouble with his health and was thinking of selling the store. Let him sell, thought Morris. He thought, let him die, then severely struck his chest.

Ida stayed upstairs most of the day, reluctantly at first, less so as time went by. She came down to prepare lunch and supper—Frank still ate before Helen—or to make a salad when it was needed. She attended to little else in the store; Frank did the cleaning and mopping. Upstairs, Ida took care of the house, read a bit, listened to the Jewish programs on the radio and knitted. Helen bought some wool and Ida knitted her a sweater. In the night, after Frank had gone, Ida spent her time in the store, added up the accounts in her notebook and left with Morris when he closed up.

The grocer got along well with his assistant. They divided tasks and waited on alternate customers, though the waiting in between was still much too long. Morris went up for naps to forget the store. He too urged Frank to take some time off in the afternoon, to break the monotony of the day. Frank, somewhat restless, finally began to. Sometimes he went up to his room and lay on the bed, listening to the radio. Usually he put his coat on over his apron and visited one of the other stores on the block. He liked Giannola, the Italian barber across the street, an old man who had recently lost his wife and sat in the shop all day, even when it was long past time to go home; the old barber gave a fine haircut. Occasionally Frank dropped in on Louis Karp and gassed with him, but generally Louis bored him. Sometimes he went into the butcher store, next door to Morris, and talked in the back room with Artie, the butcher's son, a blond fellow with a bad complexion who was interested in riding horses. Frank said he might go riding with him sometime but he never did though Artie invited him. Once in a while he drank a beer in the bar on the corner, where he liked Earl, the bartender. Yet when the clerk got back to the grocery he was glad to go in.

When he and Morris were together in the back they spent a lot of time talking. Morris liked Frank's company; he liked to hear about strange places, and Frank told him about some of the cities he had been to, in his long wandering, and some of the different jobs he had worked at. He had passed part of his early life in Oakland, California, but most of it across the bay in a home in San Francisco. He told Morris stories about his hard times as a kid. In this second family the home had sent him to, the man used to work him hard in his machine shop. "I wasn't twelve," Frank said, "and he kept me out of school as long as he could get away with."

After staying with that family for three years, he took off. "Then began my long period of travels." The clerk fell silent, and the ticking clock, on the shelf above the sink, sounded flat and heavy. "I am mostly self-educated," he ended.

Morris told Frank about life in the old country. They were poor and there were pogroms. So when he was about to be conscripted into the czar's army his father said, "Run to America." A landsman, a friend of his father, had sent money for his passage. But he waited for the Russians to call him up, because if you left the district before they had conscripted you, then your father was arrested, fined and imprisoned. If the son got away after induction, then the father could not be blamed; it was the army's responsibility. Morris and his father, a peddler in butter and eggs, planned that he would try to get away on his first day in the barracks.

So on that day, Morris said, he told the sergeant, a peasant with red eyes and a bushy mustache which smelled of tobacco, that he wanted to buy some cigarettes in the town. He felt scared but was doing what his father had advised him to do. The half-drunk sergeant agreed he could go, but since Morris was not yet in uniform he would have to go along with him. It was a September day and had just rained. They walked along a muddy road till they reached the town. There, in an inn, Morris bought cigarettes for himself and the sergeant; then, as he had planned it with his father, he invited the soldier to drink some vodka with him. His stomach became rigid at the chance he was taking. He had never drunk in an inn before, and he had never before tried to deceive anybody to this extent. The sergeant, filling his glass often, told Morris the story of his life, crying when he came to the part where, through forgetfulness, he had not attended his mother's funeral. Then he blew his nose, and wagging a thick finger in Morris's face, warned him if he had any plans to skip, he had better forget them if he expected to live. A dead Jew was of less consequence than a live one. Morris felt a heavy gloom descend on him. In his heart he surrendered his freedom for years to come. Yet once they had left the inn and were trudging in the mud back to the barracks, his hopes rose as the sergeant, in his stupor, kept falling behind. Morris walked slowly on, then the sergeant would cup his hands to his mouth, and cursing, haloo for him to wait. Morris waited. They would go on together, the sergeant muttering to himself, Morris uncertain what would happen next. Then the soldier stopped to urinate into a ditch in the road. Morris pretended to wait but he walked on, every minute expecting a bullet to crash through his shoulders and leave him lying in the dirt, his future with the worms. But then, as if seized by his fate, he began to run. The halooing and cursing grew louder as the red-faced sergeant, waving a revolver, stumbled after him; but when he reached the bend of the tree-lined road where he had last seen Morris, nobody was there but a yellow-bearded peasant driving a nag pulling a load of hay.

Telling this story excited the grocer. He lit a cigarette and smoked without coughing. But when he had finished, when there was no more to say, a sadness settled on him. Sitting in his chair, he seemed a small, lonely man. All the time he had been upstairs his hair had grown bushier and he wore a thick pelt of it at the back of his neck. His face was thinner than before.

Frank thought about the story Morris had just told him. That was the big jig in his life but where had it got him? He had escaped out of the Russian Army to the U.S.A., but once in a store he was like a fish fried in deep fat.

"After I came here I wanted to be a druggist," Morris said. "I went for a year in night school. I took algebra, also German and English. ' "Come," said the wind to the leaves one day, "come over the meadow with me and play." ' This is a poem I learned. But I didn't have the patience to stay in night school, so when I met my wife I gave up my chances." Sighing, he said, "Without education you are lost."

Frank nodded.

"You're still young," Morris said. "A young man without a family is free. Don't do what I did."

"I won't," Frank said.

But the grocer didn't seem to believe him. It made the clerk uncomfortable to see the wet-eyed old bird brooding over him. His pity leaks out of his pants, he thought, but he would get used to it.

When they were behind the counter together, Morris kept an eye on Frank and tried to improve some of the things Ida had taught him. The clerk did very well what he was supposed to. As if ashamed somebody could learn the business so easily, Morris explained to him how different it had been to be a grocer only a few years ago. In those days one was more of a macher, a craftsman. Who was ever called on nowadays to slice up a loaf of bread for a customer, or ladle out a quart of milk?

"Now is everything in containers, jars, or packages. Even hard cheeses that they cut them for hundreds of years by hand come now sliced up in cellophane packages. Nobody has to know anything any more."

"I remember the family milk cans," Frank said, "only my family sent me out to get beer in them."

But Morris said it was a good idea that milk wasn't sold loose any more. "I used to know grocers that they took out a quart or two cream from the top of the can, then they put in water. This water-milk they sold at the regular price."

He told Frank about some other tricks he had seen. "In some stores they bought two kinds loose coffee and two kinds tub butter. One was low grade, the other was medium, but the medium they put half in the medium bin and half in the best. So if you bought the best coffee or the best butter you got medium—nothing else."

Frank laughed. "I'll bet some of the customers came back saying that the best butter tasted better than the medium."

"It's easy to fool people," said Morris.

"Why don't you try a couple of those tricks yourself, Morris? Your amount of profit is small."

Morris looked at him in surprise. "Why should I steal from my customers? Do they steal from me?"

"They would if they could."

"When a man is honest he don't worry when he sleeps. This is more important than to steal a nickel."

Frank nodded.

But he continued to steal. He would stop for a few days then almost with relief go back to it. There were times stealing made him feel good. It felt good to have some change in his pocket, and it felt good to pluck a buck from under the Jew's nose. He would slip it into his pants pocket so deftly that he had to keep himself from laughing. With this money, and what he earned, he bought a suit and hat, and got new tubes for Nick's radio. Now and then, through Sam Pearl, who telephoned it in for him, he laid a two-buck bet on a horse, but as a rule he was careful with the dough. He opened a small savings account in a bank near the library and hid the bankbook under his mattress. The money was for future use.

When he felt pepped up about stealing, it was also because he felt he had brought them luck. If he stopped stealing he bet business would fall off again. He was doing them a favor, at the same time making it a little worth his while to stay on and give them a hand. Taking this small cut was his way of showing himself he had something to give. Besides, he planned to return everything sometime or why would he be marking down the figure of what he took? He kept it on a small card in his shoe. He might someday plunk down a tenner or so on some longshot and then have enough to pay back every lousy cent of what he had taken.

For this reason he could not explain why, from one day to another, he should begin to feel bad about snitching the bucks from Morris, but he did. Sometimes he went around with a quiet grief in him, as if he had just buried a friend and was carrying the fresh grave within himself. This was an old feeling of his. He remembered having had something like it for years back. On days he felt this way he sometimes got headaches and went around muttering to himself. He was afraid to look into the mirror for fear it would split apart and drop into the sink. He was wound up so tight he would spin for a week if the spring snapped. He was full of sudden rages at himself. These were his worst days and he suffered trying to hide his feelings. Yet they had a curious way of ending. The rage he felt disappeared like a windstorm that quietly pooped out, and he felt a sort of gentleness creeping in. He felt gentle to the people who came into the store, especially the kids, whom he gave penny crackers to for nothing. He was gentle to Morris, and the Jew was gentle to him. And he was filled with a quiet gentleness for Helen and no longer climbed the air shaft to spy on her, naked in the bathroom.

And there were days when he was sick to death of everything. He had had it, up to here. Going downstairs in the

morning he thought he would gladly help the store burn if
it caught on fire. Thinking of Morris waiting on the same
lousy customers day after day throughout the years, as they
picked out with dirty fingers the same cheap items they ate
every day of their flea-bitten lives, then when they were gone,
waiting for them to come back again, he felt like leaning over
the banister and throwing up. What kind of a man did you
have to be born to shut yourself up in an overgrown coffin
and never once during the day, so help you, outside of going
for your Yiddish newspaper, poke your beak out of the door
for a snootful of air? The answer wasn't hard to say—you
had to be a Jew. They were born prisoners. That was what
Morris was, with his deadly patience, or endurance, or whatever the hell it was; and it explained Al Marcus, the paper
products salesman, and that skinny rooster Breitbart, who
dragged from store to store his two heavy cartons full of bulbs.

Al Marcus, who had once, with an apologetic smile, warned
the clerk not to trap himself in a grocery, was a well-dressed
man of forty-six, but he looked, whenever you saw him, as
if he had just lapped up cyanide. His face was the whitest
Frank had ever seen, and what anybody saw in his eyes if he
took a good look, would not help his appetite. The truth of it
was, the grocer had confided to Frank, that Al had cancer
and was supposed to be dead in his grave a year ago, but
he fooled the doctors; he stayed alive if you could call it that.
Although he had a comfortable pile, he wouldn't quit working and showed up regularly once a month to take orders for
paper bags, wrapping paper and containers. No matter how
bad business was, Morris tried to have some kind of little
order waiting for him. Al would suck on an unlit cigar, scrib-
ble an item or two on a pink page in his metal-covered sales-
book, then stand around a few minutes, making small talk,
his eyes far away from what he was saying; and after that,
tip his hat and take off for the next place. Everybody knew
how sick he was, and a couple of the storekeepers earnestly
advised him to quit working, but Al, smiling apologetically,
took his cigar out of his mouth and said, "If I stay home,

somebody in a high hat is gonna walk up the stairs and put
a knock on my door. This way let him at least move his bony
ass around and try and find me."

As for Breitbart, according to Morris, nine years ago he
had owned a good business, but his brother ran it into the
ground, gambling, then he took off with what was left of the
bank account, persuading Breitbart's wife to come along and
keep it company. That left him with a drawerful of bills and
no credit; also a not too bright five-year-old boy. Breitbart
went bankrupt; his creditors plucked every feather. For
months he and the boy lived in a small, dirty furnished room,
Breitbart not having the heart to go out to look for work.
Times were bad. He went on relief and later took to peddling.
He was now in his fifties but his hair had turned white and
he acted like an old man. He bought electric bulbs at whole-
sale and carried two cartons of them slung, with clothesline
rope, over his shoulder. Every day, in his crooked shoes, he
walked miles, looking into stores and calling out in a mournful
voice, "Lights for sale." At night he went home and cooked
supper for his Hymie, who played hooky whenever he could
from the vocational school where they were making him into
a shoemaker.

When Breitbart first came to Morris's neighborhood and
dropped into the store, the grocer, seeing his fatigue, offered
him a glass of tea with lemon. The peddler eased the rope
off his shoulder and set his boxes on the floor. In the back
he gulped the hot tea in silence, warming both hands on
the glass. And though he had, besides his other troubles, the
seven-year itch, which kept him awake half the night, he
never complained. After ten minutes he got up, thanked the
grocer, fitted the rope onto his lean and itchy shoulder and
left. One day he told Morris the story of his life and they both
wept.

That's what they live for, Frank thought, to suffer. And
the one that has got the biggest pain in the gut and can
hold onto it the longest without running to the toilet is the
best Jew. No wonder they got on his nerves.

.   .   .

Winter tormented Helen. She ran from it, hid in the house. In the house she revenged herself on December by crossing off the calendar all its days. If Nat would only call, she thought endlessly, but the telephone was deaf and dumb. She dreamed of him nightly, felt deeply in love, famished for him; would gladly have danced into his warm white bed if only he nodded, or she dared ask him to ask her; but Nat never called. She hadn't for a minute glimpsed him since running into him on the subway early in November. He lived around the corner but it might as well be Paradise. So with a sharp-pointed pencil she scratched out each dead day while it still lived.

Though Frank hungered for her company he rarely spoke to her. Now and then he passed her on the street. She murmured hello and walked on with her books, conscious of his eyes following her. Sometimes in the store, as if in defiance of her mother, she stopped to talk for a minute with the clerk. Once he startled her by abruptly mentioning this book he was reading. He longed to ask her to go out with him, but never dared; the old lady's eyes showed distrust of the goings on. So he waited. Mostly he watched for her at the window. He studied her hidden face, sensed her lacks, which deepened his own, but didn't know what to do about it.

December yielded nothing to spring. She awoke to each frozen, lonely day with dulled feeling. Then one Sunday afternoon winter leaned backward for an hour and she went walking. Suddenly she forgave everyone everything. A warmish breath of air was enough to inspire; she was again grateful for living. But the sun soon sank and it snowed pellets. She returned home, leaden. Frank was standing at Sam Pearl's deserted corner but she seemed not to see him though she brushed by. He felt very bad. He wanted her but the facts made a terrible construction. They were Jews and he was not. If he started going out with Helen her mother would throw a double fit and Morris another. And Helen made him feel, from the way she carried herself, even when she seemed most lonely, that she had plans for something big in her life —nobody like F. Alpine. He had nothing, a backbreaking past, had committed a crime against her old man, and in spite of his touchy conscience, was stealing from him too. How complicated could impossible get?

He saw only one way of squeezing through the stone knot; start by shoveling out the load he was carrying around in his mind by admitting to Morris that he was one of the guys that had held him up. It was a funny thing about that; he wasn't really sorry they had stuck up a Jew but he hadn't expected to be sorry that they had picked on this particular one, Bober; yet now he was. He had not minded, if by mind you meant in expectation, but what he hadn't minded no longer seemed to matter. The matter was how he now felt, and he now felt bad he had done it. And when Helen was around he felt worse.

So the confession had to come first—this stuck like a bone through the neck. From the minute he had tailed Ward Minogue into the grocery that night, he had got this sick feeling that he might someday have to vomit up in words, no matter how hard or disgusting it was to do, the thing he was then engaged in doing. He felt he had known this, in some frightful way, a long time before he went into the store, before he had met Minogue, or even come east; that he had really known all his life he would sometime, through throat blistered with shame, his eyes in the dirt, have to tell some poor son of a bitch that he was the one who had hurt or betrayed him. This thought had lived in him with claws; or like a thirst he could never spit out, a repulsive need to get out of his system all that had happened—for whatever had happened had happened wrong; to clean it out of his self and bring in a little peace, a little order; to change the beginning, beginning with the past that always stupendously stank up the now—to change his life before the smell of it suffocated him.

Yet when the chance came to say it, when he was alone with Morris that November morning in the back of the store, as they were drinking the coffee that the Jew had served him, and the impulse came on him to spill everything now, *now*, he had strained to heave it up, but it was like tearing up your whole life, with the broken roots and blood; and a fear burned in his gut that once he had got started saying the wrongs he had done he would never leave off until he had turned black; so instead he had told him a few hurried things about how ass-backward his life had gone, which didn't even begin to say what he wanted. He had worked on Morris's pity and left halfway satisfied, but not for long, because soon the need to say it returned and he heard himself groaning, but groans weren't words.

He argued with himself that he was smart in not revealing to the grocer more than he had. Enough was enough; besides, how much of a confession was the Jew entitled to for the seven and a half bucks he had taken, then put back into his cash register drawer, and for the knock on the head he had got from Ward, whom he himself had come with unwillingly? Maybe willing, but not to do what had finally been done. That deserved some consideration, didn't it? Furthermore, he had begged the creep not to hurt anybody, and had later turned him down when he cooked up another scheme of stickup against Karp, who they were out to get in the first place. That showed his good intentions for the future, didn't it? And who was it, after all was said and done, that had waited around shivering in his pants in the dark cold, to pull in Morris's milk boxes, and had worked his ass to a frazzle twelve hours a day while the Jew lay upstairs resting in his bed? And was even now keeping him from starvation in his little rat hole? All that added up to something too.

That was how he argued with himself, but it didn't help for long, and he was soon again fighting out how to jump free of what he had done. He would someday confess it all— he promised himself. If Morris accepted his explanation and solemn apology, it would clear the rocks out of the road for the next move. As for his present stealing from the cash register, he had decided that once he had told the grocer all there was to say about the holdup, he would at the same time start paying back into the drawer, out of his little salary and the few bucks he had put away in the bank, what he had taken, and that would fix that. It wouldn't necessarily mean

that Helen Bober would then and there fall for him—the opposite could happen—but if she *did*, he wouldn't feel bad
about it.

He knew by heart what he would say to the grocer once
he got to say it. One day while they were talking in the back,
he would begin, as he had once done, about how his life was
mostly made up of lost chances, some so promising he could
still not stand to remember them. Well, after certain bad
breaks through various causes, mostly his own mistakes—he
was piled high with regrets—after many such failures, though
he tried every which way to free himself from them, usually he failed; so after a time he gave up and let himself be a
bum. He lived in gutters, cellars if he was lucky, slept in lots,
ate what the dogs wouldn't, or couldn't, and what he
scrounged out of garbage cans. He wore what he found,
slept where he flopped and guzzled anything.

By rights this should have killed him, but he lived on,
bearded, smelly, dragging himself through the seasons without a hope to go by. How many months he had existed this
way he would never know. Nobody kept the score of it. But
one day while he lay in some hole he had crawled into, he
had this terrific idea that he was really an important guy, and
was torn out of his reverie with the thought that he was living
this kind of life only because he hadn't known he was meant
for something a whole lot better—to do something big, different. He had not till that minute understood this. In the past
he had usually thought of himself as an average guy, but
there in this cellar it came to him he was wrong. That was
why his luck had so often curdled, because he had the wrong
idea of what he really was and had spent all his energy trying to do the wrong things. Then when he had asked himself
what should he be doing, he had another powerful idea, that
he was meant for crime. He had at times teased himself with
this thought, but now it wouldn't let go of him. At crime he
would change his luck, make adventure, live like a prince.
He shivered with pleasure as he conceived robberies, assaults
—murders if it had to be—each violent act helping to satisfy
a craving that somebody suffer as his own fortune im-

proved. He felt infinitely relieved, believing that if a person figured for himself something big, something different in his life, he had a better chance to get it than some poor jerk who couldn't think that high up.

So he gave up his outhouse existence. He began to work again, got himself a room, saved and bought a gun. Then he headed east, where he figured he could live the way he wanted—where there was money, nightclubs, babes. After a week of prowling around in Boston, not sure where he ought to start off, he hopped a freight to Brooklyn and a couple of days after he got there met Ward Minogue. As they were shooting pool one night, Ward cannily detected the gun on him and made him the proposition that they do a holdup together. Frank welcomed the idea of some kind of start but said he wanted to think about it more. He went to Coney Island, and while sitting on the boardwalk, worrying about what he ought to do, got this oppressive feeling he was being watched. When he turned around it was Ward Minogue. Ward sat down and told him that it was a Jew he planned to rob, so Frank agreed to go with him.

But on the night of the holdup he found himself nervous. In the car Ward sensed it and cursed him. Frank felt he had to stick it out, but the minute they were both in the grocery and tying handkerchiefs around their mouths, the whole idea seemed senseless. He could feel it poop out in his mind. His plans of crime lay down and died. He could hardly breathe in his unhappiness, wanted to rush out into the street and be swallowed up out of existence, but he couldn't let Ward stay there alone. In the back, nauseated by the sight of the Jew's bloodied head, he realized he had made the worst mistake yet, the hardest to wipe out. And that ended his short life of violent crime, another pipe dream, and he was trapped tighter in the tangle of his failures. All this he thought he would someday tell Morris. He knew the Jew well enough to feel sure of his mercy.

Yet there were times when he imagined himself, instead, telling it all to Helen. He wanted to do something that would open her eyes to his true self, but who could be a hero in a grocery store? Telling her would take guts and guts was something. He continued to feel he deserved a better fate, and he would find it if he only once—*once*—did the right thing— the thing to do at the right time. Maybe if they were ever together for any decent amount of time, he would ask her to listen. At first she might be embarrassed, but when he started telling her about his life, he knew she would hear him to the end. After that—who knew? With a dame all you needed was a beginning.

But when the clerk caught himself coldly and saw the sentimentality of his thinking—he was a sentimental wop at heart—he knew he was having another of his hopped-up dreams. What kind of a chance did he think he would have with her after he had admitted the stickup of her old man? So he figured the best thing was to keep quiet. At the same time a foreboding crept into him that if he said nothing now, he would someday soon have a dirtier past to reveal.

A few days after Christmas, on the night of a full moon, Frank, dressed in his new clothes, hurried to the library, about a dozen blocks from the grocery. The library was an enlarged store, well lit, with bulging shelves of books that smelled warm on winter nights. In the rear there were a few large reading tables. It was a pleasant place to come to out of the cold. His guess was good, soon Helen arrived. She wore a red woolen scarf on her head, one end thrown over her shoulder. He was at a table reading. She noticed him as she closed the door behind her; he knew it. They had met here, briefly, before. She had wondered what he read at the table, and once in passing, glanced quickly over his shoulder. She had guessed *Popular Mechanics,* but it was the life of somebody or other. Tonight, as usual, she was aware of his eyes on her as she moved about from shelf to shelf. When, after an hour, she left, he caught a tight hidden glance in his direction. Frank got up and checked out a book. She was halfway down the street before he caught up with her.

"Big moon." He reached up to tip his hat and awkwardly discovered he wasn't wearing any.

"It feels like snow," Helen answered.

He glanced at her to see if she was kidding, then at the sky. It was cloudless, flooded with moonlight.

"Maybe." As they approached the street corner, he remarked, "We could take a walk in the park if it's okay with you."

She shivered at the suggestion, yet turned with a nervous laugh at the corner, and walked by his side. She had said almost nothing to him since the night he had called her to answer the empty phone. Who it had been she would never know; the incident still puzzled her.

Helen felt for him, as they walked, an irritation bordering on something worse. She knew what caused it—her mother, in making every gentile, by definition, dangerous; therefore he and she, together, represented some potential evil. She was also annoyed that his eating eyes were always on her, for he saw, she felt, more than his occasionally trapped gaze revealed. She fought her dislike of him, reasoning it wasn't his fault if her mother had made him into an enemy; and if he was always looking at her, it meant at least he saw something attractive or why would he look? Considering her lonely life, for that she owed him gratitude.

The unpleasant feeling passed and she glanced guardedly up at him. He was walking unmarked in moonlight, innocent of her reaction to him. She felt then—this thought had come to her before—that there might be more to him than she had imagined. She felt ashamed she had never thanked him for the help he had given her father.

In the park the moon was smaller, a wanderer in the white sky. He was talking about winter. "It's funny you mentioned snow before," Frank said. "I was reading about the life of St. Francis in the library, and when you mentioned the snow it made me think about this story where he wakes up one winter night, asking himself did he do the right thing to be a monk. My God, he thought, supposing I met some nice young girl and got married to her and by now I had a wife and a family? That made him feel bad so he couldn't sleep. He got out of his straw bed and went outside of the church or monastery or wherever he was staying. The ground was all covered with snow. Out of it he made this snow woman, and he said, 'There, that's my wife.' Then he made two or three kids out of the snow. After, he kissed them all and went inside and laid down in the straw. He felt a whole lot better and fell asleep."

The story surprised and touched her.

"Did you just read that?"

"No. I remember it from the time I was a kid. My head is full of those stories, don't ask me why. A priest used to read them to the orphans in this home I was in, and I guess I never forgot them. They come into my thoughts for no reason at all."

He had had a haircut and in his new clothes was hardly recognizable as her father's baggy-pants assistant who had slept a week in their cellar. Tonight he looked like somebody she had never seen before. His clothes showed taste, and he was, in his way, interesting looking. Without an apron on he seemed younger.

They passed an empty bench. "What do you say if we sit down?" Frank said.

"I'd rather walk."

"Smoke?"

"No."

He lit a cigarette, then caught up with her.

"Sure is some night."

"I want to say thanks for helping my father," Helen said, "You've been very kind. I should have mentioned it before."

"Nobody has to thank me. Your father did me some good favors." He felt uncomfortable.

"Anyway, don't make a career of a grocery," she said. "There's no future in it."

He puffed with a smile on his lips. "Everybody warns me. Don't worry, my imagination is too big for me to get stuck in a grocery. It's only temporary work."

"It isn't what you usually do?"

"No." He set himself to be honest. "I'm just taking a breather, you could call it. I started out wrong and have to change my direction where I am going. The way it happened I landed up in your father's store, but I'm only staying there till I figure out what's my next move."

He remembered the confession he had considered making to her, but the time wasn't ready yet. You could confess as a stranger, and you could confess as a friend.

"I've tried about everything," he said, "now I got to choose one thing and stick with it. I'm tired of being on the move all the time."

"Isn't it a little late for you to be getting started?"

"I'm twenty-five. There are plenty of guys who start that late and some I have read about started later. Age don't mean a thing. It doesn't make you less than anybody else."

"I never said so." At the next empty bench she paused. "We could sit here for a few minutes if you like."

"Sure." Frank wiped the seat with his handkerchief before she sat down. He offered her his cigarettes.

"I said I don't smoke."

"Sorry, I thought you didn't want to smoke while you were walking. Some girls don't like to." He put his pack away.

She noticed the book he was carrying. "What are you reading?"

He showed it to her.

"*The Life of Napoleon*"?

"That's right."

"Why him?"

"Why not—he was great, wasn't he?"

"Others were in better ways."

"I'll read about them too," Frank said.

"Do you read a lot?"

"Sure. I am a curious guy. I like to know why people tick. I like to know the reason they do the things they do, if you know what I mean."

She said she did.

He asked her what book she was reading.

"*The Idiot*. Do you know it?"

"No. What's it about?"

"It's a novel."

"I'd rather read the truth," he said.

"It is the truth."

Helen asked, "Are you a high school graduate?"

He laughed. "Sure I am. Education is free in this country."

She blushed. "It was a silly question."

"I didn't mean any wisecrack," he said quickly.

"I didn't take it as such."

"I went to high school in three different states and finally got finished up at night—in a night school. I planned on going to college but this job came along that I couldn't turn down, so I changed my mind, but it was a mistake."

"I had to help my mother and father out," Helen said, "so I couldn't go either. I've taken courses in NYU at night—mostly lit courses—and I've added up about a year's credit, but it's very hard at night. My work doesn't satisfy me. I would still like to go full time in the day."

He flipped his butt away. "I've been thinking about starting in college lately, even if I am this age. I know a guy who did it."

"Would you go at night?" she asked.

"Maybe, maybe in the day if I could get the right kind of a job—in an all-night cafeteria or something like that, for instance. This guy I just mentioned did that—assistant manager or something. After five or six years he graduated an engineer. Now he's making his pile, working all over the country."

"It's hard doing it that way—very hard."

"The hours are rough but you get used to it. When you got something good to do, sleep is a waste of time."

"It takes years at night."

"Time don't mean anything to me."

"It does to me."

"The way I figure, anything is possible. I always think about the different kinds of chances I have. This has stuck in my mind—don't get yourself trapped in one thing, because maybe you can do something else a whole lot better. That's why I guess I never settled down so far. I've been exploring conditions. I still have some very good ambitions which I would like to see come true. The first step to that, I know for sure now, is to get a good education. I didn't use to think like that, but the more I live the more I do. Now it's always on my mind."

"I've always felt that way," Helen said.

He lit another cigarette, throwing the burnt match away. "What kind of work do you do?"

"I'm a secretary."

"You like it?" He smoked with half-closed eyes. She sensed he knew she didn't care for her job and suspected he had heard her father or mother say so.

After a while, she answered, "No, I don't. The job never changes. And I could live happily without seeing some of those characters I have to deal with all day long, the salesmen, I mean."

"They get fresh?"

"They talk a lot. I'd like to be doing something that feels useful—some kind of social work or maybe teaching. I have no sense of accomplishment in what I'm doing now. Five o'clock comes and at last I go home. That's about all I live for, I guess."

She spoke of her daily routine, but after a minute saw he was only half-listening. He was staring at the moon-drenched trees in the distance, his face drawn, his lit eyes elsewhere.

Helen sneezed, unwound her scarf and wrapped it tightly around her head.

"Shall we go now?"

"Just till I finish my cigarette."

Some fat nerve, she thought.

Yet his face, even with the broken nose, was sensitive in the dark light. What makes me so irritable? She had had the wrong idea of him but it was her own fault, the result of staying so long apart from people.

He drew a long jagged breath.

"Is something the matter?" she asked.

Frank cleared his throat but his voice was hoarse. "No, just something popped into my mind when I was looking at the moon. You know how your thoughts are."

"Nature sets you thinking?"

"I like scenery."

"I walk a lot for that reason."

"I like the sky at night, but you see more of it in the West. Out here the sky is too high, there are too many big buildings."

He squashed his cigarette with his heel and wearily rose, looking now like someone who had parted with his youth.

She got up and walked with him, curious about him. The moon moved above them in the homeless sky.

After a long silence, he said as they were walking, "I'd like to tell you what I was thinking about."

"Please, you don't have to."

"I feel like talking," he said. "I got to thinking about this carnie outfit I worked for one time when I was about twenty-one. Right after I got the job I fell for a girl in an acrobatic act. She was built something like you—on the slim side, I would say. At first I don't think I rated with her. I think she thought I wasn't a serious type of guy. She was kind of a complicated girl, you know, moody, with lots of problems in her mind that she kept to herself. Well, one day we got to talking and she told me she wanted to be a nun. I said, 'I don't think it will suit you.' 'What do you know about me?' she said. I didn't tell her, although I know people pretty well, don't ask me why, I guess you are born with certain things. Anyway, the whole summer long I was nuts about her but she wouldn't give me another look though there was nobody else around that I saw she went with. 'Is it my age?' I asked her. 'No, but you haven't lived,' she answered me. 'If you only could see in my heart all I have lived through,' I said, but I have my doubts if she believed me. All we ever did was talk like that. Once in a while I would ask her for a date, not thinking I would ever get one, and I never did. 'Give up,' I said to myself, 'all she is interested in is herself.'

"Then one morning, when it was getting to be around fall and you could smell the season changing, I said to her I was taking off when the show closed. 'Where are you going?' she asked me. I said I was going to look for a better life. She

didn't answer anything to that. I said, 'Do you still want to be
a nun?' She got red and looked away, then she answered she
wasn't sure about that any more. I could see she had changed
but I wasn't fool enough to think it was account of me. But I
guess it really was, because by accident our hands sort of
touched, and when I saw the way she looked at me, it was
hard to breathe. My God, I thought, we are both in love. I
said to her, 'Honey, meet me here after the show tonight and
let's go where we will be alone.' She said yes. Before she left
she gave me a quick kiss.

"Anyway, that same afternoon she took off in her old man's
jalopy to buy a blouse she had seen in some store window in
the last town, but on the way back it started to rain. Exactly
what happened I don't know. I guess she misjudged a curve
or something and went flying off the road. The jalopy bounced
down the hill, and her neck was broken. . . . That's how it
ended."

They walked in silence. Helen was moved. But why, she
thought, all the sad music?

"I'm awfully sorry."

"It was years ago."

"It was a tragic thing to happen."

"I couldn't expect better," he said.

"Life renews itself."

"My luck stays the same."

"Go on with your plans for an education."

"That's about it," Frank said. "That's what I got to do."

Their eyes met, she felt her scalp prickle.

Then they left the park and went home.

Outside the dark grocery store she quickly said good night.

"I'll stay out a little longer," Frank said. "I like to see the
moon."

She went upstairs.

In bed she thought of their walk, wondering how much to
believe of what he had told her about his ambitions and plans
for college. He could not have said anything to make a better
impression on her. And what was the purpose of the sad tale
of the carnival girl "built something like you"? Who was he

mixing up with his carnival girls? Yet he had told the story simply, without any visible attempt to work on her sympathy. Probably it was a true memory, recalled because he happened to be feeling lonely. She had had her own moonlit memories to contend with. Thinking about Frank, she tried to see him straight but came up with a confusing image: the grocery clerk with the greedy eyes, on top of the ex-carnival hand and future serious college student, a man of possibilities.

On the verge of sleep she sensed a desire on his part to involve her in his life. The aversion she felt for him before returned but she succeeded without too much effort in dispelling it. Thoroughly awake now, she regretted she could not see the sky from her window in the wall, or look down into the street. Who was he making into a wife out of snowy moonlight?

Earnings in the grocery, especially around Christmas and New Year's, continued to rise. For the last two weeks in December Morris averaged an unusual one hundred and ninety. Ida had a new theory to explain the spurt of business: an apartment house had opened for rentals a few blocks away; furthermore, she had heard that Schmitz was not so attentive to his store as he was before. An unmarried storekeeper was sometimes erratic. Morris didn't deny these things but he still attributed their good for-

tune mostly to his clerk. For reasons that were clear to him
the customers liked Frank, so they brought in their friends.
As a result, the grocer could once more meet his running expenses, and with pinching and scrimping, even pay off some
outstanding bills. Grateful to Frank—who seemed to take for
granted the upswing of business—he planned to pay him
more than the measly five dollars they shamefacedly gave
him, but cautiously decided to see if the added income would
continue in January, when business usually slackened off.
Even if he regularly took in two hundred a week, with the
slight profit he made he could hardly afford a clerk. Before
things were easier they had to take in a minimum of two-
fifty or three hundred, an impossibility.

Since, though, the situation was better, Morris told Helen
that he wanted her to keep more of her hard-earned twenty-
five dollars; he said she must now keep fifteen, and if business stayed as it was maybe he would not need her assistance
any more. He hoped so. Helen was overwhelmed at having
fifteen a week to spend on herself. She needed shoes badly
and could use a new coat—hers was little better than a rag—
and a dress or two. And she wanted to put away a few dollars
for future tuition at NYU. She felt like her father about Frank
—he had changed their luck. Remembering what he had
said in the park that night about his ambitions and desire for
education, she felt he someday would get what he wanted
because he was obviously more than just an ordinary person.

He was often at the library. Almost every time Helen went
there she saw him sitting over an open book at one of the
tables; she wondered if all he did in his spare time was come
here and read. She respected him for it. She herself averaged
two weekly visits, each time checking out only a book or two,
because it was one of her few pleasures to return for another.
Even at her loneliest she liked being among books, although
she was sometimes depressed to see how much there was to
read that she hadn't. Meeting Frank so often, she was at first
uneasy: he haunted the place, for what? But, a library was a
library; he came here, as she did, to satisfy certain needs. Like
her he read a lot because he was lonely, Helen thought. She

thought this after he had told her about the carnival girl. Gradually her uneasiness left her.

Although he left, as a rule, when she did, if she wanted to walk home alone, he did not intrude. Sometimes he rode back on the trolley while she walked. Sometimes she was on the trolley and saw him walking. But generally, so long as the weather was not too bad, they went home together, a couple of times turning off into the park. He told her more about himself. He had lived a different life from most people she had known, and she envied him all the places he had been to. Her own life, she thought, was much like her father's, restricted by his store, his habits, hers. Morris hardly ever journeyed past the corner, except on rare occasions, usually to return something a customer had left on the counter. When Ephraim was alive, when they were kids, her father liked to go bathing Sunday afternoons at Coney Island; and on Jewish holidays they would sometimes see a Yiddish play, or ride on the subway to the Bronx to call on landsleit. But after Ephraim died Morris had for years gone nowhere. Neither had she, for other reasons. Where could she go without a cent? She read with eagerness of far-off places but spent her life close to home. She would have given much to visit Charleston, New Orleans, San Francisco, cities she had heard so much about, but she hardly ever got beyond the borough of Manhattan. Hearing Frank talk of Mexico, Texas, California, other such places, she realized anew the meagerness of her movements: every day but Sunday on the BMT to Thirty-fourth Street and back. Add to that a twice-weekly visit to the library at night. In summer, the same as before, except a few times—usually during her vacation—to Manhattan Beach; also, if she were lucky, to a concert or two at Lewisohn Stadium. Once when she was twenty and worn out, her mother had insisted she go for a week to an inexpensive adult camp in New Jersey. Before that, while in high school, she had traveled to Washington, D. C., with her American history class for a week end of visiting government buildings. So far and no further in the open world. To stick so close to where she had lived her whole life was a crime. His stories made her impatient—she wanted to travel, experience, live.

One night as they were sitting on a bench in an enclosed part of the park beyond the tree-lined plaza, Frank said he had definitely made up his mind to start college in the fall. This excited her, and for hours afterward Helen couldn't stop thinking about it. She imagined all the interesting courses he could take, envied him the worthwhile people he'd meet in his classes, the fun he'd have studying. She pictured him in nice clothes, his hair cut shorter, maybe his nose straightened, speaking a more careful English, interested in music and literature, learning about politics, psychology, philosophy; wanting to know more the more he knew, in this way growing in value to himself and others. She imagined herself invited by him to a campus concert or play, where she would meet his college friends, people of promise. Afterward as they crossed the campus in the dark, Frank would point out the buildings his classes met in, classes taught by distinguished professors. And maybe if she closed her eyes she could see a time—miracle of miracles—when Helen Bober was enrolled here, not just a stranger on the run, pecking at a course or two at night, and tomorrow morning back at Levenspiel's Louisville Panties and Bras. At least he made her dream.

To help him prepare for college Helen said he ought to read some good novels, some of the great ones. She wanted Frank to like novels, to enjoy in them what she did. So she checked out *Madame Bovary, Anna Karenina* and *Crime and Punishment,* all by writers he had barely heard of, but they were very satisfying books, she said. He noticed she handled each yellow-paged volume as though she were holding in her respectful hands the works of God Almighty. As if—according to her—you could read in them everything you couldn't afford not to know—the Truth about Life. Frank carried the three books up to his room, and, huddled in a blanket to escape the cold that seeped in through the loose window frames, had rough going. The stories were hard to get into because the people and places were strange to him,

their crazy names difficult to hold in his mind and some of
the sentences were so godawful complicated he forgot the beginning before he got to the end. The opening pages irritated
him as he pushed through forests of odd facts and actions.
Though he stared for hours at the words, starting one book,
then another, then the third—in the end, in exasperation, he
flung them aside.

But because Helen had read and respected these books, it
shamed him that he hadn't, so he picked one up from the
floor and went back to it. As he dragged himself through the
first chapters, gradually the reading became easier and he
got interested in the people—their lives in one way or another
wounded—some to death. Frank read, at the start, in
snatches, then in bursts of strange hunger, and before too
long he had managed to finish the books. He had started
Madame Bovary with some curiosity, but in the end he felt
disgusted, wearied, left cold. He did not know why people
would want to write about that kind of a dame. Yet he felt a
little sorry for her and the way things had happened, till
there was no way out of it but her death. *Anna Karenina* was
better; she was more interesting and better in bed. He didn't
want her to kill herself under the train in the end. Still, although Frank felt he could also take the book or leave it, he
was moved at the deep change that came over Levin in the
woods just after he had thought of hanging himself. At least
he wanted to live. *Crime and Punishment* repelled yet fascinated him, with everybody in the joint confessing to something every time he opened his yap—to some weakness, or
sickness, or crime. Raskolnikov, the student, gave him a pain,
with all his miseries. Frank first had the idea he must be a
Jew and was surprised when he found he wasn't. He felt,
in places in the book, even when it excited him, as if his face
had been shoved into dirty water in the gutter; in other
places, as if he had been on a drunk for a month. He was
glad when he was finished with the book, although he liked
Sonia, the prostitute, and thought of her for days after he had
read it.

Afterward Helen suggested other novels by the same writ-

ers, so he would know them better, but Frank balked, saying
he wasn't sure that he had understood those he had read.
"I'm sure you have," she answered, "if you got to know the
people." "I know them," he muttered. But to please her he
worked through two more thick books, sometimes tasting
nausea on his tongue, his face strained as he read, eyes bright
black, frowning, although he usually felt some relief at the
end of the book. He wondered what Helen found so satisfying in all this goddamned human misery, and suspected her
of knowing he had spied on her in the bathroom and was
using the books to punish him for it. But then he thought it
was an unlikely idea. Anyway, he could not get out of his
thoughts how quick some people's lives went to pot when
they couldn't make up their minds what to do when they had
to do it; and he was troubled by the thought of how easy it
was for a man to wreck his whole life in a single wrong act.
After that the guy suffered forever, no matter what he did to
make up for the wrong. At times, as the clerk had sat in his
room late at night, a book held stiffly in his reddened hands,
his head numb although he wore a hat, he felt a strange
falling away from the printed page and had this crazy sensation that he was reading about himself. At first this picked
him up but then it deeply depressed him.

One rainy night, as Helen was about to go up to Frank's
room to ask him to take back something he had given her
that she didn't want, before she could go the phone rang,
and Ida hastened out into the hall to call her. Frank, lying
on his bed in his room, watching the rainy window, heard
her go downstairs. Morris was in the store waiting on someone as Helen came in, but her mother sat in the back over a
cup of tea.

"It's Nat," Ida whispered, not moving.

She'll tell herself she isn't listening, thought Helen.

Her first feeling was that she didn't want to talk to the
law student, but his voice was warm, which for him meant
extended effort, and a warm voice on a wet night was a
warm voice. She could easily picture what he looked like as

he spoke into the phone. Yet she wished he had called her in December, when she had so desperately wanted him, for now she was again aware of a detachment in herself that she couldn't account for.

"Nobody sees you any more, Helen," Nat began. "Where've you disappeared to?"

"Oh, I've been around," she said, trying to hide a slight tremble in her voice. "And you?"

"Is somebody there where you're talking that you sound so restrained?"

"That's right."

"I thought so. So let me make it quick and clean. Helen, it's been a long time. I want to see you. What do you say if we take in a play this Saturday night? I can stop off for tickets on my way uptown tomorrow."

"Thanks, Nat. I don't think so." She heard her mother sigh.

Nat cleared his throat. "Helen, I honestly want to know how somebody's supposed to defend himself when he hasn't any idea what's in the indictment against him? What kind of a crime have I committed? Yield the details."

"I'm not a lawyer—I don't make indictments."

"So call it a cause—what's the cause? One day we're close to each other, the next I'm alone on an island, holding my hat. What did I do, please tell me?"

"Let's drop this subject."

Here Ida rose and went into the store, softly closing the door behind her. Thanks, thought Helen. She kept her voice low so they wouldn't hear her through the window in the wall.

"You're a funny kid," Nat was saying. "You've got some old-fashioned values about some things. I always told you you punish yourself too much. Why should anybody have such a hot and heavy conscience in these times? People are freer in the twentieth century. Pardon me for saying it but it's true."

She blushed. His insight was to his credit. "My values are my values," she replied.

"What," Nat argued, "would people's lives be like if everybody regretted every beautiful minute of all that happened? Where's the poetry of living?"

"I hope you're alone," she said angrily, "where you're so blithely discussing this subject."

He sounded weary, hurt. "Of course I'm alone. My God, Helen, how low have I fallen in your opinion?"

"I told you what was going on at this end. Up to a minute ago my mother was still in the room."

"I'm sorry. I forgot."

"It's all right now."

"Look, girl," he said affectionately, "the telephone is no place to hash out our personal relations. What do you say if I run upstairs and see you right away? We got to come to some kind of a sensible understanding. I'm not exactly a pig, Helen. What you don't want is your privilege, if I may be so frank. So you don't want, but at least let's be friends and go out once in a while. Let me come up and talk to you."

"Some other time, Nat, I have to do something now."

"For instance?"

"Some other time," she said.

"Why not?" Nat answered amiably.

When he had hung up, Helen stood at the phone, wondering if she had done right. She felt she hadn't.

Ida entered the kitchen. "What did he want—Nat?"

"Just to talk."

"He asked you to go out?"

She admitted it.

"What did you answer him?"

"I said I would some other time."

"What do you mean 'some other time?' " Ida said sharply. "What are you already, Helen, an old lady? What good is it to sit so many nights alone upstairs? Who gets rich from reading? What's the matter with you?"

"Nothing's the matter, Mama." She left the store and went into the hall.

"Don't forget you're twenty-three years old," Ida called after her.

"I won't."

Upstairs her nervousness grew. When she thought what she had to do she didn't want to, yet felt she must.

They had met, she and Frank, last night at the library, the third time in eight days. Helen noticed as they were leaving that he clumsily carried a package she took to contain some shirts or underwear, but on the way home Frank flung away his cigarette, and under a street lamp handed it to her. "Here, this is for you."

"For me? What is it?"

"You'll find out."

She took it half-willingly, and thanked him. Helen carried it awkwardly the rest of the way home, neither of them saying much. She had been caught by surprise. If she had given herself a minute to think, she would have refused it on grounds that it was wise just to stay friends; because, she thought, neither of them really knew the other. But once she had the thing in her hands she hadn't the nerve to ask him to take it back. It was a medium-sized box of some sort with something heavy in it—she guessed a book; yet it seemed too big for a book. As she held it against her breast, she felt a throb of desire for Frank and this disturbed her. About a block from the grocery, nervously saying good night, she went on ahead. This was how they parted when the store window was still lit.

Ida was downstairs with Morris when Helen came into the house, so no questions were asked. She shivered a little as she unwrapped the box on her bed, ready to hide it the minute she heard a footstep on the stairs. Lifting the carton lid, she found two packages in it, each wrapped in white tissue paper and tied with red ribbons with uneven bows, obviously by Frank. When she had untied the first present, Helen gasped at the sight of a long, hand-woven scarf—rich black wool interlaced with gold thread. She was startled to discover that the second present was a red leather copy of Shakespeare's plays. There was no card.

She sat weakly down on the bed. I can't, she told herself. They were expensive things, probably had cost him every penny of the hard-earned money he was saving for college. Even supposing he had enough for that, she still couldn't take his gifts. It wasn't right, and coming from him, it was, somehow, less than not right.

She wanted then and there to go up to his room and leave them at the door with a note, but hadn't the heart to the very night he had given them to her.

The next evening, after a day of worry, she felt she must return them; and now she wished she had done it before Nat had called, then she might have been more relaxed on the phone.

Helen got down on her hands and knees and reached under the bed for the carton with Frank's scarf and book in it. It touched her that he had given her such lovely things—so much nicer than anyone else ever had. Nat, at his best, had produced a half-dozen small pink roses.

For gifts you pay, Helen thought. She drew a deep breath, and taking the box went quietly up the stairs. She tapped hesitantly on Frank's door. He had recognized her step and was waiting behind the door. His fists were clenched, the nails cutting his palms.

When he opened the door and his glance fell on what she was carrying, he frowned as though struck in the face.

Helen stepped awkwardly into the little room, quickly shutting the door behind her. She suppressed a shudder at the smallness and barrenness of the place. On his unmade bed lay a sock he had been trying to mend.

"Are the Fusos home?" she asked in a low voice.

"They went out." He spoke dully, his eyes hopelessly stuck to the things he had given her.

Helen handed him the box with the presents. "Thanks so much, Frank," she said, trying to smile, "but I really don't think I ought to take them. You'll need every cent for your college tuition in the fall."

"That's not the reason you mean," he said.

Her face reddened. She was about to explain that her mother would surely make a scene if she saw his gifts, but instead said, "I can't keep them."

"Why not?"

It wasn't easy to answer and he didn't make it easier, just held the rejected presents in his big hands as if they were living things that had suddenly died.

"I can't," she got out. "You're taste is so nice, I'm sorry."

"Okay," he said wearily. He tossed the box on the bed and the Shakespeare fell to the floor. She stooped quickly to pick it up and was unnerved to see it had opened to "Romeo and Juliet."

"Good night." She left his room and went hastily downstairs. In her room she thought she heard the distant sound of a man crying. She listened tensely, her hand on her throbbing throat, but no longer heard it.

Helen took a shower to relax, then got into a nightgown and housecoat. She picked up a book but couldn't read. She had noticed before signs he might be in love with her, but now she was almost sure of it. Carrying his package as he had walked with her last night, he had been somebody different, though the hat and overcoat were the same. There seemed to be about him a size and potentiality she had not seen before. He did not say love but love was in him. When the insight came to her, at almost the minute he was handing her the package, she had reacted with gooseflesh. That it had gone this far was her own fault. She had warned herself not to get mixed up with him but hadn't obeyed her warning. Out of loneliness she had encouraged him. What else, going so often to the library, knowing he would be there? And she had stopped off with him, on their walks, for pizzas and coffee; had listened to his stories, discussed with him plans for college, talked at length about books he was reading; at the same time she had been concealing these meetings from her father and mother. He knew it, no wonder he had built up hopes.

The strange thing was there were times she felt she liked him very much. He was, in many ways, a worthwhile person, and where a man gave off honest feeling, was she a machine to shut off her own? Yet she knew she mustn't become seri-

ously attracted to him because there would be trouble in
buckets. Trouble, thank you, she had had enough of. She
wanted now a peaceful life without worry—any more worries.
Friends they could be, in a minor key; she might on a moonlit night even hold hands with him, but beyond that nothing.
She should have said something of the sort; he would have
saved his presents for a better prospect and she would not
now be feeling guilt at having hurt him. Yet in a way he had
surprised her by his apparent depth of affection. She had not
expected anything to happen so quickly, because, for her,
things had happened in reverse order. Usually she fell in love
first, then the man, if he wasn't Nat Pearl, responded. So the
other way around was nice for a change, and she wished it
would happen more often, but with the right one. She must
go, she decided, less to the library; he would then understand,
if he didn't already, and give up any idea of having her
love. When he realized what was what he would get over his
pain, if he really felt any. But her thoughts gave her no
peace, and though she tried often, she could still not concentrate on her books. When Morris and Ida trudged through
her room, her light was out and she seemed to be sleeping.

As she left the house for work the next morning, to her
dismay she spied the carton containing his presents on top of
some greasy garbage bags in the stuffed rubbish can at the
curb. The cover of the can apparently had been squeezed
down on the box but had fallen off and now lay on the sidewalk. Lifting the carton cover, Helen saw the two gifts,
loosely covered with the tissue paper. Angered by the waste,
she plucked the scarf and book out of the crushed cardboard
box and went quickly into the hall with them. If she took
them upstairs Ida would want to know what she had, so she
decided to hide them in the cellar. She turned on the light
and went quietly down, trying to keep her high heels from
clicking on the stairs. Then she removed the tissue paper and
hid the presents, neither of which had been harmed, in the
bottom drawer of a broken chiffonier in their bin. The dirty
tissue paper and red ribbons she rolled up in a sheet of old

newspaper, then went upstairs and pressed it into the garbage can. Helen noticed her father at the window, idly watching her. She passed into the store, said good morning, washed her hands and left for work. On the subway she felt despondent.

After supper that night, while Ida was washing dishes, Helen sneaked down into the cellar, got the scarf and book and carried them up to Frank's room. She knocked and nobody answered. She considered leaving them at the door but felt he would throw them away again unless she spoke to him first.

Tessie opened her door. "I heard him go out a while before, Helen." Her eyes were on the things in her hands.

Helen blushed. "Thanks, Tessie."

"Any message?"

"No." She returned to her floor and once more pushed the gifts under her bed. Changing her mind, she put the book and scarf in different bureau drawers, hiding them under her underwear. When her mother came up she was listening to the radio.

"You going someplace tonight, Helen?"

"Maybe, I don't know. Maybe to the library."

"Why so much to the library? You went a couple days ago."

"I go to meet Clark Gable, Mama."

"Helen, don't get fresh."

Sighing, she said she was sorry.

Ida sighed too. "Some people want their children to read more. I want you to read less."

"That won't get me married any faster."

Ida knitted but soon grew restless and went down to the store again. Helen got out Frank's things, packed them in heavy paper she had bought on her way home, tied the bundle with cord, and took the trolley to the library. He wasn't there.

The next night she tried first his room, then when she was able to slip out of the house, again the library, but found him in neither place.

"Does Frank still work here?" she asked Morris in the morning.

"Of course he works."

"I haven't seen him for a while," she said. "I thought he might be gone."

"In the summer he leaves."

"Did he say that?"

"Mama says."

"Does he know?"

"He knows. Why you ask me?"

She said she was just curious.

As Helen came into the hall that evening she heard the clerk descending the stairs and waited for him at the landing. Lifting his hat, he was about to pass when she spoke.

"Frank, why did you throw your two presents into the garbage?"

"What good were they to me?"

"It was a terrible waste. You should have got your money back."

He smiled in the corners of his mouth. "Easy come, easy go."

"Don't joke. I took them out of the rubbish and have them in my room for you. They weren't damaged."

"Thanks."

"Please give them back and get your money. You'll need every penny for the fall."

"Since I was a kid I hate to go back with stuff I bought."

"Then let me have the sales checks and I'll return them during my lunch hour."

"I lost them," he answered.

She said gently, "Frank, sometimes things turn out other than we plan. Don't feel hurt."

"When I don't feel hurt, I hope they bury me."

He left the house, she walked up the stairs.

Over the week end Helen went back to crossing off the days on the calendar. She found she had crossed nothing since New Year's. She fixed that. On Sunday the weather turned fair and she grew restless. She wished again for Nat to call her; instead his sister did and they walked, in the early afternoon, on the Parkway.

Betty was twenty-seven and resembled Sam Pearl. She was large-boned and on the plain side but made good use of reddish hair and a nice nature. She was in her ideas, Helen thought, somewhat dull. They had not too much in common and saw each other infrequently, but liked to talk once in a while, or go to a movie together. Recently Betty had become engaged to a CPA in her office and was with him most of the time. Now she sported a prosperous diamond ring on her stylish finger. Helen, for once, envied her, and Betty, as if she had guessed, wished her the same good luck.

"And it should happen soon," she said.

"Many thanks, Betty."

After they had gone a few blocks, Betty said, "Helen, I don't like to butt in somebody else's private business but for a long time I wanted to ask you what happened between you and my brother Nat. I once asked him and he gave me double talk."

"You know how such things go."

"I thought you liked him?"

"I did."

"Then why don't you see him any more? Did you have some kind of a fight?"

"No fights. We didn't have the same things in mind."

Betty asked no more. Later, she remarked, "Sometime give him another chance, Helen. Nat really has the makings of a good person. Shep, my boy friend, thinks so too. His worst fault is he thinks his brains entitle him to certain privileges. You'll see, in time he'll get over it."

"I may," Helen said. "We'll see sometime."

They returned to the candy store, where Shep Hirsch, Betty's stout, eyeglassed, future husband was waiting to take her for a drive in his Pontiac.

"Come along, Helen," said Betty.

"With pleasure." Shep tipped his hat.

"Go, Helen," advised Goldie Pearl.

"Thanks, all, from the bottom of my heart," said Helen, "but I have some of my underthings to iron."

Upstairs, she stood at the window, looking out at the back yards. The remnants of last week's dirty snow. No single blade of green, or flower to light the eye or lift the heart. She felt as if she were made of knots and in desperation got on her coat, tied a yellow kerchief around her head and left the house again, not knowing which way to go. She wandered toward the leafless park.

At the approach to the park's main entrance there was a small island in the street, a concrete triangle formed by intersecting avenues. Here people sat on benches during the day and tossed peanuts or pieces of bread to the noisy pigeons that haunted the place. Coming up the block, Helen saw a man squatting by one of the benches, feeding the birds. Otherwise, the island was deserted. When the man rose, the pigeons fluttered up with him, a few landing on his arms and shoulders, one perched on his fingers, pecking peanuts from his cupped palm. Another fat bird sat on his hat. The man clapped his hands when the peanuts were gone and the birds, beating their wings, scattered.

When she recognized Frank Alpine, Helen hesitated. She felt in no mood to see him, but remembering the package hidden in her bureau drawer, determined once and for all to get rid of it. Reaching the corner, she crossed over to the island.

Frank saw her coming and wasn't sure he cared one way or the other. The return of his presents had collapsed his hopes. He had thought that if she ever fell for him it would change his life in the way he wanted it to happen, although at times the very thought of another change, even in this sense of it, made him miserable. Yet what was the payoff, for instance, of marrying a dame like her and having to do with Jews the rest of his life? So he told himself he didn't care one way or the other.

"Hi," Helen said.

He touched his hat. His face looked tired but his eyes were clear and his gaze steady, as if he had been through something and had beat it. She felt sorry if she had caused him any trouble.

"I had a cold," Frank remarked.

"You should get more sun."

Helen sat down on the edge of the bench, as if she were afraid, he thought, she would be asked to take a lease on it; and he sat a little apart from her. One of the pigeons began to chase another running in circles and landed on its back. Helen looked away but Frank idly watched the birds until they flew off.

"Frank," she said, "I hate to sound like a pest on this subject, but if there's anything I can't stand it's waste. I know you're not Rockefeller, so would you mind giving me the names of the stores where you bought your kind presents so that I can return them? I think I can without the sales checks."

Her eyes, he noticed, were a hard blue, and though he thought it ridiculous, he was a little scared of her, as if she were far too determined, too dead serious for him. At the same time he felt he still liked her. He had not thought so, but with them sitting together like this he thought again that he did. It was in a way a hopeless feeling, yet it was more than that because he did not exactly feel hopeless. He felt, as he sat next to her and saw her worn, unhappy face, that he still had a chance.

Frank cracked his knuckles one by one. He turned to her. "Look, Helen, maybe I try to work too fast. If so, I am sorry. I am the type of a person, who if he likes somebody, has to show it. I like to give her things, if you understand that, though I do know that not everybody likes to take. That's their business. My nature is to give and I couldn't change it even if I wanted. So okay. I am also sorry I got sore and dumped your presents in the can and you had to take them out. But what I want to say is this. Why don't you just go ahead and keep one of those things that I got for you? Let it be a little memory of a guy you once knew that wants to thank you for the good books you told him to read. You don't have to worry that I expect anything for what I give you."

"Frank . . ." she said, reddening.

"Just let me finish. How's this for a deal? If you keep one of those things, I will take the other back to the store and get what I paid for it. What do you say?"

She was not sure what to say, but since she wanted to be finished with it, nodded at his proposal.

"Fine," Frank said. "Now what do you want the most?"

"Well, the scarf is awfully nice, but I'd rather keep the book."

"So keep the book then," he said. "You can give me the scarf anytime you want and I promise I will bring it back."

He lit a cigarette and inhaled deeply.

She considered whether to say good-by, now that the matter had been settled, and go on with her walk.

"You busy now?" he asked.

She guessed a short stroll. "No."

"How about a movie?"

It took her a minute to reply. Was he starting up once more? She felt she must quickly set limits to keep him from again creeping too close. Yet out of respect for his already hurt feelings, she thought it best that she think out exactly what to say and tactfully say it, later on.

"I'll have to be back early."

"So let's go," he said, getting up.

Helen slowly untied her kerchief, then knotted it, and they went off together.

As they walked she kept wondering if she hadn't made a mistake in accepting the book. In spite of what he had said about expecting nothing she felt a gift was a claim, and she wanted none on her. Yet, when, almost without noticing, she once more asked herself if she liked him at all, she had to admit she did a little. But not enough to get worried about; she liked him but not with an eye to the possibility of any deeper feeling. He was not the kind of man she wanted to be in love with. She made that very clear to herself, for among his other disadvantages there was something about him, evasive, hidden. He sometimes appeared to be more than he was, sometimes less. His aspirations, she

sensed, were somehow apart from the self he presented nor-
mally when he wasn't trying, though he was always more or
less trying; therefore when he was trying less. She could not
quite explain this to herself, for if he could make himself
seem better, broader, wiser when he tried, then he had these
things in him because you couldn't make them out of nothing. There was more to him than his appearance. Still, he
hid what he had and he hid what he hadn't. With one hand
the magician showed his cards, with the other he turned
them into smoke. At the very minute he was revealing himself, saying who he was, he made you wonder if it was true.
You looked into mirrors and saw mirrors and didn't know
what was right or real or important. She had gradually got
the feeling that he only pretended to be frank about himself,
that in telling so much about his experiences, his trick was to
hide his true self. Maybe not purposely—maybe he had no
idea he was doing it. She asked herself whether he might have
been married already. He had once said he never was. And
was there more to the story of the once-kissed, tragic carnival
girl? He had said no. If not, what made her feel he had done
something—committed himself in a way she couldn't guess?

As they were approaching the movie theater, a thought of
her mother crossed her mind and she heard herself say,
"Don't forget I'm Jewish."

"So what?" Frank said.

Inside in the dark, recalling what he had answered her,
he felt this elated feeling, as if he had crashed head on
through a brick wall but hadn't bruised himself.

She had bitten her tongue but made no reply.

Anyway, by summer he'd be gone.

Ida was very unhappy that she had kept Frank on when
she could have got rid of him so easily. She was to blame
and she actively worried. Though she had no evidence, she
suspected Helen was interested in the clerk. *Something* was
going on between them. She did not ask her daughter what,
because a denial would shame her. And though she had tried
she felt she could not really trust Frank. Yes, he had helped
the business, but how much would they have to pay for it?

Sometimes when she came upon him alone in the store, his expression, she told herself, was sneaky. He sighed often, muttered to himself, and if he saw he was observed, pretended he hadn't. Whatever he did there was more in it than he was doing. He was like a man with two minds. With one he was here, with the other someplace else. Even while he read he was doing more than reading. And his silence spoke a language she couldn't understand. Something bothered him and Ida suspected it was her daughter. Only when Helen happened to come into the store or the back while he was there, did he seem to relax, become one person. Ida was troubled, although she could not discover in Helen any response to him. Helen was quiet in his presence, detached, almost cold to the clerk. She gave him for his restless eyes, nothing—her back. Yet for this reason, too, Ida worried.

One night, after Helen had left the house, when her mother heard the clerk's footsteps going down the stairs, she quickly got into a coat, wrapped a shawl around her head and trudged through a sprinkle of snow after him. He walked to the movie house several blocks away, paid his money, and passed in. Ida was almost certain that Helen was inside, waiting for him. She returned home with nails in her heart and found her daughter upstairs, ironing. Another night she followed Helen to the library. Ida waited across the street, shivering for almost an hour in the cold, until Helen emerged, then followed her home. She chided herself for her suspicions but they would not fly from her mind. Once, listening from the back, she heard her daughter and the clerk talking about a book. This annoyed her. And when Helen later happened to mention that Frank had plans to begin college in the autumn, Ida felt he was saying that only to get her interested in him.

She spoke to Morris and cautiously asked if he had noticed anything developing between Helen and the clerk.

"Don't be foolish," the grocer replied. He had thought about the possibility, at times felt concerned, but after pondering how different they were, had put the idea out of his head.

"Morris, I am afraid."

"You are afraid of everything, even which it don't exist."

"Tell him to leave now—business is better."

"So is better," he muttered, "but who knows how will be next week. We decided he will stay till summer."

"Morris, he will make trouble."

"What kind trouble will he make?"

"Wait," she said, clasping her hands, "a tragedy will happen."

Her remark at first annoyed, then worried him.

The next morning the grocer and his clerk were sitting at the table, peeling hot potatoes. The pot had been drained of water and dumped on its side; they sat close to the steaming pile of potatoes, hunched over, ripping off the salt-stained skins with small knives. Frank seemed ill at ease. He hadn't shaved and had dark blobs under his eyes. Morris wondered if he had been drinking but there was never any smell of liquor about him. They worked without speaking, each lost in his thoughts.

After a half-hour, Frank, squirming restlessly in his chair, remarked, "Say, Morris, suppose somebody asked you what do the Jews believe in, what would you tell them?"

The grocer stopped peeling, unable at once to reply.

"What I like to know is what is a Jew anyway?"

Because he was ashamed of his meager education Morris was never comfortable with such questions, yet he felt he must answer.

"My father used to say to be a Jew all you need is a good heart."

"What do you say?"

"The important thing is the Torah. This is the Law—a Jew must believe in the Law."

"Let me ask you this," Frank went on. "Do you consider yourself a real Jew?"

Morris was startled, "What do you mean if I am a real Jew?"

"Don't get sore about this," Frank said, "But I can give you an argument that you aren't. First thing, you don't go to the synagogue—not that I have ever seen. You don't keep your kitchen kosher and you don't eat kosher. You don't even wear one of those little black hats like this tailor I knew in South Chicago. He prayed three times a day. I even hear the Mrs say you kept the store open on Jewish holidays, it makes no difference if she yells her head off."

"Sometimes," Morris answered, flushing, "to have to eat, you must keep open on holidays. On Yom Kippur I don't keep open. But I don't worry about kosher, which is to me old-fashioned. What I worry is to follow the Jewish Law."

"But all those things are the Law, aren't they? And don't the Law say you can't eat any pig, but I have seen you taste ham."

"This is not important to me if I taste pig or if I don't. To some Jews is this important but not to me. Nobody will tell me that I am not Jewish because I put in my mouth once in a while, when my tongue is dry, a piece ham. But they will tell me, and I will believe them, if I forget the Law. This means to do what is right, to be honest, to be good. This means to other people. Our life is hard enough. Why should we hurt somebody else? For everybody should be the best, not only for you or me. We ain't animals. This is why we need the Law. This is what a Jew believes."

"I think other religions have those ideas too," Frank said. "But tell me why it is that the Jews suffer so damn much, Morris? It seems to me that they like to suffer, don't they?"

"Do you like to suffer? They suffer because they are Jews."

"That's what I mean, they suffer more than they have to."

"If you live, you suffer. Some people suffer more, but not because they want. But I think if a Jew don't suffer for the Law, he will suffer for nothing."

"What do you suffer for, Morris?" Frank said.

"I suffer for you," Morris said calmly.

Frank laid his knife down on the table. His mouth ached. "What do you mean?"

"I mean you suffer for me."

The clerk let it go at that.

"If a Jew forgets the Law," Morris ended, "he is not a good Jew, and not a good man."

Frank picked up his knife and began to tear the skins off the potatoes. The grocer peeled his pile in silence. The clerk asked nothing more.

When the potatoes were cooling, Morris, troubled by their talk, asked himself why Frank had brought up this subject. A thought of Helen, for some reason, crossed his mind.

"Tell me the truth," he said, "why did you ask me such questions?"

Frank shifted in his chair. He answered slowly, "To be truthful to you, Morris, once I didn't have much use for the Jews."

Morris looked at him without moving.

"But that was long ago," said Frank, "before I got to know what they were like. I don't think I understood much about them."

His brow was covered with sweat.

"Happens like this many times," Morris said.

But his confession had not made the clerk any happier.

One afternoon, shortly after lunch, happening to glance at himself in the mirror, Morris saw how bushy his hair was and how thick the pelt on his neck; he felt ashamed. So he said to Frank he was going across the street to the barber. The clerk, studying the racing page of the *Mirror,* nodded. Morris hung up his apron and went into the store to get some change from the cash register. After he took a few quarters out of the drawer, he checked the receipts for the day and was pleased. He left the grocery and crossed the car tracks to the barber shop.

The chair was empty and he didn't have to wait. As Mr. Giannola, who smelled of olive oil, worked on him and they talked, Morris, though embarrassed at all the hair that had to be cut by the barber, found himself thinking mostly of his store. If it would only stay like this—no Karp's paradise, but at least livable, not the terrible misery of only a few months ago—he would be satisfied. Ida had again been nagging him to sell, but what was the use of selling until things all over got better and he could find a place he would have confidence in? Al Marcus, Breitbart, all the drivers he talked to, still complained about business. The best thing was not to look for trouble but stay where he was. Maybe in the summer, after Frank left, he would sell out and search for a new place.

As he rested in the barber's chair, the grocer, watching through the window his own store, saw with satisfaction that at least three customers had been in since he had sat down. One man left with a large lumpy bag, in which Morris imagined at least six bottles of beer. Also, two women had come out with heavy packages, one carrying a loaded market bag. Figuring, let's say, at least two dollars apiece for the women, he estimated he had taken in a nice fiver and earned his haircut. When the barber unpinned the sheet around him and Morris returned to the grocery, he struck a match over the cash register and peered with anticipation at the figures. To his great surprise he saw that only a little more than three dollars had been added to the sum he had noted on leaving the store. He was stunned. How could it be only three if the bags had been packed tight with groceries? Could it be they contained maybe a couple of boxes of some large item like cornflakes, that came to nothing? He could hardly believe this and felt upset to the point of illness.

In the back he hung up his overcoat, and with fumbling fingers tied his apron strings.

Frank glanced up from the racing page with a smile. "You look different without all the kelp on you, Morris. You look like a sheep that had the wool clipped off it."

The grocer, ashen, nodded.

"What's the matter your face is so pale?"

"I don't feel so good."

"Whyn't you go up then and take your snooze?"

"After."

He shakily poured himself a coup of coffee.

"How's business?" he asked, his back to the clerk.

"So-so," said Frank.

"How many customers you had since I went to the barber?"

"Two or three."

Unable to meet Frank's eye, Morris went into the store and stood at the window, staring at the barber shop, his thoughts in a turmoil, tormented by anxiety. Was the Italyener stealing from the cash register? The customers had come out with stuffed bags, what was there to show for it? Could he have given things on credit? They had told him never to. So what then?

A man entered and Morris waited on him. The man spent forty-one cents. When Morris rang up the sale, he saw it added correctly to the previous total. So the register was not broken. He was now almost certain that Frank had been stealing, and when he asked himself how long, he was numbed.

Frank went into the store and saw the dazed grocer at the window.

"Don't you feel any better, Morris?"

"It will go away."

"Take care of yourself. You don't want to get sick any more."

Morris wet his lips but made no reply. All day he went around, dragging his heart. He had said nothing to Ida, he didn't dare.

For the next few days he carefully watched the clerk. He had decided to give him the benefit of doubt yet not rest till he knew the truth. Sometimes he sat at the table inside, pretending to be reading, but he was carefully listening to each item the customer ordered. He jotted down the prices and when Frank packed the groceries, quickly calculated the approximate sum. After the customer had gone he went idly to the register and secretly examined the amount the clerk had rung up. Always it was near the figure he had figured, a few pennies more or less. So Morris said he would go upstairs for a few minutes, but instead stationed himself in the hall, behind the back door. Peering through a crack in the wood, he could see into the store. Standing here, he added in his head the prices of the items ordered, and later, about fifteen minutes, casually checked the receipts and found totaled there

the sum he had estimated. He began to doubt his suspicions.
He may have wrongly guessed the contents of the customers'
bags when he was at the barber's. Yet he could still not believe they had spent only three dollars; maybe Frank had
caught on and was being wary.

Morris then thought, yes, the clerk could have been stealing, but if so it was more his fault than Frank's. He was a
grown man with a man's needs and all he was paying him,
including his meager commission, was about six or seven
dollars a week. True, he got his room and meals free, plus
cigarettes, but what was six or seven dollars to anybody in
times like these, when a decent pair of shoes cost eight to
ten? The fault was therefore his for paying slave wages for a
workman's services, including the extra things Frank did,
like last week cleaning out the stopped sewer pipe in the
cellar with a long wire and so saving five or ten dollars that
would surely have gone to the plumber, not to mention how
his presence alone had improved the store.

So although he worked on a slim markup, one late afternoon when he and Frank were packing out some cartons of
goods that had just been delivered, Morris said to his assistant
standing on the stepladder, "Frank, I think from now on till it
comes summer I will raise you your wages to straight fifteen
dollars without any commission. I would like to pay you
more, but you know how much we do here business."

Frank looked down at the grocer. "What for, Morris? The
store can't afford to pay me any more than I am getting. If I
take fifteen your profit will be shot. Let it go the way it is
now. I am satisfied."

"A young man needs more and he spends more."

"I got all I want."

"Let it be like I said."

"I don't want it," said the clerk, annoyed.

"Take," insisted the grocer.

Frank finished his packing then got down, saying he was
going to Sam Pearl's. His eyes were averted as he went past
the grocer.

Morris continued to pack the cans on the shelves. Rather

than admit Frank's raise to Ida and start a fuss, he decided
to withhold from the register the money he would need to
pay him, a little every day so it would not be noticed. He
would privately give it to the clerk sometime on Saturday, before Ida handed him his regular wages.

Helen felt herself, despite the
the strongest doubts, falling in love with Frank. It was a diz-
zying dance, she didn't want to. The month was cold—it
often snowed—she had a rough time, fighting hesitancies,
fears of a disastrous mistake. One night she dreamed their
house had burned down and her poor parents had nowhere
to go. They stood on the sidewalk, wailing in their underwear. Waking, she fought an old distrust of the broken-faced
stranger, without success. The stranger had changed, grown
unstrange. That was the clue to what was happening to her.
One day he seemed unknown, lurking at the far end of an unlit cellar; the next he was standing in sunlight, a smile on his
face, as if all she knew of him and all she didn't, had fused
into a healed and easily remembered whole. If he was hiding anything, she thought, it was his past pain, his orphan-
hood and consequent suffering. His eyes were quieter, wiser.
His crooked nose fitted his face and his face fitted him. It
stayed on straight. He was gentle, waiting for whatever he
awaited with a grace she respected. She felt she had changed

him and this affected her. That she had willed to stay free of him made little difference now. She felt tender to him, wanted him close by. She had, she thought, changed in changing him.

After she had accepted his gift of a book their relationship had subtly altered. What else, if whenever she read in her Shakespeare, she thought of Frank Alpine, even heard his voice in the plays? Whatever she read, he crept into her thoughts; in every book he haunted the words, a character in a plot somebody else had invented, as if all associations had only one end. He was, to begin with, everywhere. So, without speaking of it, they met again in the library. That they were meeting among books relieved her doubt, as if she believed, what possible wrong can I do among books, what possible harm can come to me here?

In the library he too seemed surer of himself—though once they were on their way home he became almost remote, strangely watchful, looking back from time to time as though they were being followed, but who or what would follow them? He never took her as far as the store; as before, by mutual consent, she went on ahead, then he walked around the block and entered the hall from the other way so he wouldn't have to go past the grocery window and possibly be seen coming from the direction she had come from. Helen interpreted his caution to mean he sensed victory and didn't want to endanger it. It meant he valued her more than she was altogether sure she wanted to be.

Then one night they walked across a field in the park and turned to one another. She tried to awaken in herself a feeling of danger, but danger was dulled, beyond her, in his arms. Pressed against him, responsive to his touch, she felt the cold ebb out of the night, and a warmth come over her. Her lips parted—she drew from his impassioned kiss all she had long desired. Yet at the moment of sweetest joy she felt again the presence of doubt, almost a touch of illness. This made her sad. The fault was her. It meant she still could not fully accept him. There were still signals signaling no. She had only to think of them and they would work in her, pinching the nerves. On their way home she could not forget the first happiness of their kiss. But why should a kiss become anxiety? Then she saw that his eyes were sad, and she wept when he wasn't looking. Would it never come spring?

She stalled love with arguments, only to be surprised at their swift dissolution; found it difficult to keep her reasons securely nailed down, as they were before. They flew up in the mind, shifted, changed, as if something had altered familiar weights, values, even experience. He wasn't, for instance, Jewish. Not too long ago this was the greatest barrier, her protection against ever taking him seriously; now it no longer seemed such an urgently important thing—how could it in times like these? How could anything be important but love and fulfillment? It had lately come to her that her worry he was a gentile was less for her own sake than for her mother and father. Although she had only loosely been brought up as Jewish she felt loyal to the Jews, more for what they had gone through than what she knew of their history or theology—loved them as a people, thought with pride of herself as one of them; she had never imagined she would marry anybody but a Jew. But she had recently come to think that in such unhappy times—when the odds were so high against personal happiness—to find love was miraculous, and to fulfill it as best two people could was what really mattered. Was it more important to insist a man's religious beliefs be exactly hers (if it was a question of religion), or that the two of them have in common ideals, a desire to keep love in their lives, and to preserve in every possible way what was best in themselves? The less difference among people, the better; thus she settled it for herself yet was dissatisfied for those for whom she hadn't settled it.

But her logic, if it was logic, wouldn't decide a thing for her unhappy parents once they found out what was going on. With Frank enrolled in college maybe some of Ida's doubts of his worth as a person might wither away, but college was not the synagogue, a B.A. not a bar mitzvah; and her mother and even her father with his liberal ideas would insist that Frank had to be what he wasn't. Helen wasn't at all sure she could handle them if it ever came to a showdown. She dreaded the arguments, their tear-stained pleas and her own misery for taking from the small sum of peace they had in the world, adding to the portion of their unhappiness. God knows they had had enough of that. Still, there was just so much time to live, so little of youth among the years; one had to make certain heartbreaking choices. She foresaw the necessity of upholding her own, enduring pain yet keeping to her decisions. Morris and Ida would be grievously hurt, but before too long their pain would grow less and perhaps leave them; yet she could not help but hope her own children would someday marry Jews.

And if she married Frank, her first job would be to help him realize his wish to be somebody. Nat Pearl wanted to be "somebody," but to him this meant making money to lead the life of some of his well-to-do friends at law school. Frank, on the other hand, was struggling to realize himself as a person, a more worthwhile ambition. Though Nat had an excellent formal education, Frank knew more about life and gave the impression of greater potential depth. She wanted him to become what he might, and conceived a plan to support him through college. Maybe she could even see him through a master's degree, once he knew what he wanted to do. She realized this would mean the end of her own vague plans for going to day college, but that was really lost long ago, and she thought she would at last accept the fact once Frank had got what she hadn't. Maybe after he was working, perhaps as an engineer or chemist, she could take a year of college just to slake her thirst. By then she would be almost thirty, but it would be worth postponing having a family to give him a good start and herself a taste of what she had always wanted. She also hoped they would be able to leave New York. She wanted to see more of the country. And if things eventually worked out, maybe Ida and Morris would someday sell the store and come to live near them. They might all live in California, her parents in a little house of their own where they could take life easy and be near their grandchildren. The future offered more in the way of realizable possibilities, Helen thought, if a person dared take a chance with it. The question was, did she?

She postponed making any important decision. She feared most of all the great compromise—she had seen so many of the people she knew settle for so much less than they had always wanted. She feared to be forced to choose beyond a certain point, to accept less of the good life than she had hungered for, appreciably less—to tie up with a fate far short of her ideals. That she mustn't do, whether it meant taking Frank or letting him go. Her constant fear, underlying all others, was that her life would not turn out as she had hoped, or would turn out vastly different. She was willing to change, make substitutions, but she would not part with the substance of her dreams. Well, she would know by summertime what to do. In the meantime Frank went every third night to the library and there she was. But when the old-maid librarian smiled knowingly upon them, Helen felt embarrassed, so they met elsewhere. They met in cafeterias, movie houses, the pizza place—where it was impossible to say much, or hold him or be held. To talk they walked, to kiss they hid.

Frank said he was getting the college bulletins he had written for, and around May he would have a transcript of his high school record sent to whichever place they picked for him to go. He showed he knew she had plans for him. He didn't say much more, for he was always afraid the old jinx would grab hold of him if he opened his mouth a little too wide.

At first he waited patiently. What else was there to do? He had waited and was still waiting. He had been born waiting. But before long, though he tried not to show it, he was beginning to be fed up with his physical loneliness. He grew tired of the frustrations of kissing in doorways, a cold feel on a bench in the park. He thought of her as he had seen her in the bathroom, and the memory became a burden. He was the victim of the sharp edge of his hunger. So he wanted her to the point where he thought up schemes for getting her into his room and in bed. He wanted satisfaction, relief, a stake in the future. She's not yours till she gives it to you, he thought. That's the way they all are. It wasn't always true, but it was true enough. He wanted an end to the torment of coming to a boil, then thank you, no more. He wanted to take her completely.

They met more often now. At a bench on the Parkway, on street corners—in the wide windy world. When it rained or snowed, they stepped into doorways, or went home.

He complained one night, "What a joke. We leave the same warm house to meet out in the cold here."

She said nothing.

"Forget it," Frank said, looking into her troubled eyes, "we will take it the way it is."

"This is our youth," she said bitterly.

He wanted then to ask her to come to his room but felt she wouldn't, so he didn't ask.

One cold, starry night she led him through the trees in the park near where they usually sat, onto a broad meadow where on summer nights lovers lay in the grass.

"Come on and sit down on the ground for a minute," Frank urged, "there's nobody here now."

But Helen wouldn't.

"Why not?" he asked.

"Not now," she said.

She realized, though he later denied it, that the situation had made him impatient. Sometimes he was moody for hours. She worried, wondering what rusty wound their homelessness had opened in him.

One evening they sat alone on a bench on the Parkway, Frank with his arm around her; but because they were so close to home Helen was jumpy and moved away whenever somebody passed by.

After the third time Frank said, "Listen, Helen, this is no good. Some night we will have to go where we can be inside."

"Where?" she asked.

"Where do you say?"

"I can't say anything, Frank. I don't know."

"How long is this going to keep up like this?"

"As long as we like," she said, smiling faintly, "or as long as we like each other."

"I don't mean it that way. What I am talking about is not having any place private to go to."

She answered nothing.

"Maybe some night we ought to sneak up to my room," he suggested. "We could do it easy enough—I don't mean to-night but maybe Friday, after Nick and Tessie go to the show and your mother is down in the store. I bought a new heater and the room keeps warm. Nobody will know you are there. We would be alone for once. We have never been alone that way."

"I couldn't," Helen said.

"Why?"

"Frank, I can't."

"When will I get a chance to put my arms around you without being an acrobat?"

"Frank," said Helen, "there's one thing I wish to make clear to you. I won't sleep with you now, if that's what you mean. It'll have to wait till I am really sure I love you, maybe till we're married, if we ever are."

"I never asked you to," Frank said. "All I said was for you to come up to my room so we could spend the time more comfortable, not you bucking away from me every time a shadow passes."

He lit a cigarette and smoked in silence.

"I'm sorry." After a minute she said, "I thought I ought to tell you how I feel on this subject. I was going to sometime anyway."

They got up and walked, Frank gnawing his wound.

A cold rain washed the yellow slush out of the gutters. It rained drearily for two days. Helen had promised to see Frank on Friday night but she didn't like the thought of going out in the wet. When she came home from work, and got the chance, she slipped a note under his door, then went down.

The note said that if Nick and Tessie did go to the movies, she would try to come up to his room for a while.

At half past seven Nick knocked on Frank's door and asked him if he wanted to go to the pictures. Frank said no, he thought he had seen the picture that was playing. Nick said good-by and he and Tessie, bundled in raincoats and carrying umbrellas, left the house. Helen waited for her mother to go down to Morris, but Ida complained that her feet hurt, and said she would rest. Helen then went down herself, knowing Frank would hear her on the stairs and figure something had gone wrong. He would understand she could not go up to see him so long as anyone might hear her.

But a few minutes later, Ida came down, saying she felt restless upstairs. Helen then said she intended to drop in on Betty Pearl and might go along with her to the dressmaker who was making her wedding things.

"It's raining," said Ida.

"I know, Mama," Helen answered, hating her deceit.

She went up to her room, got her hat and coat, rubbers and an umbrella; then walked down, letting the door bang, as if she had just left the house. She quietly opened it and went on tiptoe up the stairs.

Frank had guessed what was going on and opened his door to her quick tap. She was pale, obviously troubled, but very lovely. He held her hard and could feel her heartbeat against his chest.

She will let me tonight, he told himself.

Helen was still uneasy. It took her a while to quiet her conscience for having lied to her mother. Frank had put out the light and tuned in the radio to soft dance music; now he lay on the bed, smoking. For a time she sat awkwardly in his chair, watching the glow of his cigarette, and when not that, the drops of lit rain on the window, reflecting the street light. But after he had rubbed his butt into an ash tray on the floor, Helen stepped out of her shoes and lay down beside him on the narrow bed, Frank moving over to the wall.

"This is more like it," he sighed.

She lay with closed eyes in his arms, feeling the warmth of the heater like a hand on her back. For a minute she half-dozed, then woke to his kisses. She lay motionless, a little tense, but when he stopped kissing her, relaxed. She listened to the quiet sound of the rain in the street, making it in her mind into spring rain, though spring was weeks away; and within the rain grew all sorts of flowers; and amid the spring flowers, in this flowering dark—a sweet spring night—she lay with him in the open under new stars and a cry rose to her throat. When he kissed her again, she responded with passion.

"Darling."

"I love you, Helen, you are my girl."

They kissed breathlessly, then he undid the buttons of her blouse. She sat up to unhook her brassière but as she was doing it, felt his fingers under her skirt.

Helen grabbed his hand. "Please, Frank. Let's not get that hot and bothered."

"What are we waiting for, honey?" He tried to move his hand but her legs tightened and she swung her feet off the bed.

He pulled her back, pressing her shoulders down. She felt his body trembling on hers and for a fleeting minute thought he might hurt her; but he didn't.

She lay stiff, unresponsive on the bed. When he kissed her again she didn't move. It took a while before he lay back. She saw by the reflected glow of the heater how unhappy he looked.

Helen sat on the edge of the bed, buttoning her blouse.

His hands covered his face. He said nothing but she could feel his body shivering on the bed.

"Christ," he muttered.

"I'm sorry," she said softly. "I told you I wouldn't."

Five minutes passed. Frank slowly sat up. "Are you a virgin, is that what's eating you?"

"I'm not," she said.

"I thought you were," he said, surprised. "You act like one."

"I said I wasn't."

"Then why do you act like one? Don't you know what it does to people?"

"I'm people."

"Then why do you do it for?"

"Because I believe in what I'm doing."

"I thought you said you weren't a virgin?"

"You don't have to be a virgin to have ideals in sex."

"What I don't understand is if you did it before, what's the difference if we do it now?"

"We can't, just because I did," she said, brushing her hair back. "That's the point. I did it and that's why I can't with you now. I said I wouldn't, that night on the Parkway."

"I don't get it," Frank said.

"Loving should come with love."

"I said I love you, Helen, you heard me say it."

"I mean I have to love you too. I think I do but sometimes I'm not sure."

He fell again into silence. She listened absent-mindedly to the radio but nobody was dancing now.

"Don't be hurt, Frank."

"I'm tired of that," he said harshly.

"Frank," said Helen, "I said I slept with somebody before and the truth of it is, if you want to know, I'm sorry I did. I admit I had some pleasure, but after, I thought it wasn't worth it, only I didn't know at the time I would feel that way, because at the time I didn't know what I wanted. I suppose I felt I wanted to be free, so I settled for sex. But if you're not in love sex isn't being free, so I made a promise to myself that I never would any more unless I really fell in love with somebody. I don't want to dislike myself. I want to be disciplined, and you have to be too if I ask it. I ask it so I might someday love you without reservations."

"Crap," Frank said, but then, to his surprise, the idea seized him. He thought of himself as disciplined, then wished he were. This seemed to him like an old and faraway thought, and he remembered with regret and strange sadness how often he had wished for better control over himself, and how little of it he had achieved.

He said, "I didn't mean to say what I just now did, Helen."

"I know," she answered.

"Helen," he said huskily, "I want you to know I am a very good guy in my heart."

"I don't think otherwise."

"Even when I am bad I am good."

She said she thought she knew what he meant.

They kissed, again and again. He thought there were a whole lot worse things than waiting for something that was going to be good once he got it.

Helen lay back on the bed and dozed, awaking when Nick and Tessie came into their bedroom, talking about the movie they had seen. It was a love story and Tessie had liked it very much. After they undressed and got into bed their double bed creaked. Helen felt bad for Frank but Frank did not seem to feel bad. Nick and Tessie soon fell asleep. Helen, breathing lightly, listened to their heavy breathing, worrying how she was going to get down to her floor, because if Ida was awake she would hear her on the stairs. But Frank said in a low voice that he would carry her to the vestibule, then she could go up after a few minutes, as if she had just come home from some place.

She put on her coat, hat and rubbers, and was careful to remember her umbrella. Frank carried her down the stairs. There were only his slow, heavy steps going down. And not long after they had kissed good night and he had gone for a walk in the rain, Helen opened the hall door and went up.

Then Ida fell asleep.

Thereafter Helen and Frank met outside the house.

It was snowing in the afternoon, when the front door opened and in came Detective Minogue, pushing before him this stocky handcuffed guy, unshaven, and wearing a faded green wind-breaker and denim slacks. He was about twenty-seven, with tired eyes and no hat. In the store he lifted his mana-cled hands to wipe the snow off his wet hair.

"Where's Morris?" the detective asked the clerk.

"In the back."

"Go on in," said Detective Minogue to the handcuffed man.

They went into the back. Morris was sitting on the couch, stealing a smoke. He hurriedly put out the butt and dropped it into the garbage pail.

"Morris," said the detective, "I think I have got the one who hit you on the head."

The grocer's face turned white as flour. He stared at the man but didn't approach him.

After a minute he muttered, "I don't know if it's him. He had his face covered with a handkerchief."

"He's a big son of a bitch," the detective said. "The one that hit you was big, wasn't he?"

"Heavy," said Morris. "The other was big."

Frank was standing in the doorway, watching.

Dectective Minogue turned to him. "Who're you?"

"He's my clerk," explained Morris.

The detective unbuttoned his overcoat and took a clean handkerchief out of his suit pocket. "Do me a favor," he said to Frank. "Tie this around his puss."

"I would rather not," Frank answered.

"As a favor. To save me the trouble of getting hit on the head with his cuffs."

Frank took the handkerchief, and though not liking to, tied it around the man's face, the suspect holding himself stiffly erect.

"How about it now, Morris?"

"I can't tell you," Morris said, embarrassed. He had to sit down.

"You want some water, Morris?" Frank asked.

"No."

"Take your time," said Detective Minogue, "look him over good."

"I don't recognize him. The other acted more rough. He had a rough voice—not nice."

"Say something, son," the detective said.

"I didn't hold this guy up," said the suspect in a dead voice.

"Is that the voice, Morris?"

"No."

"Does he look like the other one—the heavy guy's partner?"

"No, this is a different man."

"How are you so sure?"

"The helper was a nervous man. He was bigger than this one. Also this one has got small hands. The helper had big heavy hands."

"Are you positive? We grabbed him on a job last night. He held up a grocery with another guy who got away."

The detective pulled the handkerchief off the man's face.

"I don't know him," Morris said with finality.

Detective Minogue folded the handkerchief and tucked it into his pocket. He slipped his eyeglasses into a leather case. "Morris, I think I asked you already if you saw my son Ward Minogue around here. Have you yet?"

"No," said the grocer.

Frank went over to the sink and rinsed his mouth with a cup of water.

"Maybe you know him?" the detective asked him.

"No," said the clerk.

"Okay, then." The detective unbuttoned his overcoat. "By the way, Morris, did you ever find out who was stealing your milk that time?"

"Nobody steals any more," said Morris.

"Come on, son," said the detective to the suspect.

The handcuffed man went out of the store into the snow, the detective following him.

Frank watched them get into the police car, sorry for the guy. What if they arrested me now, he thought, although I am not the same guy I once was?

Morris, thinking of the stolen milk bottles, gazed guiltily at his assistant.

Frank happened to notice the size of his hands, then had to go to the toilet.

As he was lying in his bed after supper, thinking about his life, Frank heard footsteps coming up the stairs and someone banged on his door. For a minute his heart hammered with fear, but he got up and forced himself to open the door.

Grinning at him from under his fuzzy hat stood Ward Minogue, his eyes small and smeary. He had lost weight and looked worse.

Frank let him in and turned on the radio. Ward sat on the bed, his shoes dripping from the snow.

"Who told you I lived here?" Frank asked.

"I watched you go in the hall, opened the door and heard you go up the stairs," Ward said.

How am I ever going to get rid of this bastard, Frank thought.

"You better stay away from here," he said with a heavy heart. "If Morris recognizes you in that goddamned hat, we will both go to jail."

"I came to visit my popeyed friend, Louis Karp," said Ward. "I wanted a bottle but he wouldn't give it to me because I am short on cash, so I thought my good-looking friend Frank Alpine will lend me some. He's an honest, hard-working bastard."

"You picked the wrong guy. I am poor."

Ward eyed him craftily. "I was sure you'd have saved up a pile by now, stealing from the Jew."

Frank stared at him but didn't answer.

Ward's glance shifted. "Even if you are stealing his chicken feed, it ain't any skin off me. Why I came is this. I got a new job that we can do without any trouble."

"I told you I am not interested in your jobs, Ward."

"I thought you would like to get your gun back, otherwise it might accidentally get lost with your name on it."

Frank rubbed his hands.

"All you got to do is drive," Ward said amiably. "The job is a cinch, a big liquor joint in Bay Ridge. After nine o'clock they only keep one man on. The take will be over three hundred."

"Ward, you don't look to me in any kind of condition to do a stickup. You look more like you need to be in a hospital."

"All I got is a bad heartburn."

"You better take care of yourself."

"You are making me cry."

"Why don't you start going straight?"

"Why don't you?"

"I am trying to."

"Your Jew girl must be some inspiration."

"Don't talk about her, Ward."

"I tailed you last week when you took her in the park. She's a nice piece. How often do you get it?"

"Get the hell out of here."

Ward got up unsteadily. "Hand over fifty bucks or I will fix you good with your Jew boss and your Jew girl. I will write them a letter who did the stickup last November."

Frank rose, his face hard. Taking his wallet out of his pocket, he emptied it on the bed. There were eight single dollar bills. "That's all I have got."

Ward snatched up the money. "I'll be back for more."

"Ward," Frank said through tight teeth, "if you drag your ass up here any more to make trouble, or if you ever follow me and my girl again, or tell Morris anything, the first thing I will do is telephone your old man at the police station and tell him under which rock he can find you. He was in the grocery asking about you today, and if he ever meets up with you, he looks like he will bust your head off."

Ward with a moan spat at the clerk and missed, the gob of spit trickling down the wall.

"You stinking kike," he snarled. Rushing out into the hall, he all but fell down two flights of stairs.

The grocer and Ida ran out to see who was making the racket, but by then Ward was gone.

Frank lay in bed, his eyes closed.

One dark and windy night when Helen left the house late, Ida followed her through the cold streets and across the plaza into the interior of the deserted park, and saw her meet Frank Alpine. There, in an opening between a semicircle of tall lilac shrubs and a grove of dark maples, were a few benches, dimly lit and private, where they liked to come to be alone. Ida watched them sitting together on one of the benches, kissing. She dragged herself home and went upstairs, half-dead. Morris was asleep and she didn't want to wake him, so she sat in the kitchen, sobbing.

When Helen returned and saw her mother weeping at the kitchen table, she knew Ida knew, and Helen was both moved and frightened.

Out of pity she asked, "Mama, why are you crying?"

Ida at last raised her tear-stained face and said in despair, "Why do I cry? I cry for the world. I cry for my life that it went away wasted. I cry for you."

"What have I done?"

"You have killed me in my heart."

"I've done nothing that's wrong, nothing I'm ashamed of."

"You are not ashamed that you kissed a goy?"

Helen gasped. "Did you follow me, Mama?"

"Yes," Ida wept.

"How could you?"

"How could you kiss a goy?"

"I'm not ashamed that we kissed."

She still hoped to avoid an argument. Everything was unsettled, premature.

Ida said, "If you marry such a man your whole life will be poisoned."

"Mama, you'll have to be satisfied with what I now say. I have no plans to marry anybody."

"What kind plans you got then with a man that he kisses you alone in a place where nobody can find you in the park?"

"I've been kissed before."

"But a goy, Helen, an Italyener."

"A man, a human being like us."

"A man is not good enough. For a Jewish girl must be a Jew."

"Mama, it's very late. I don't wish to argue. Let's not wake Papa."

"Frank is not for you. I don't like him. His eyes don't look at a person when he talks to them."

"His eyes are sad. He's had a hard life."

"Let him go and fine someplace a shikse that he likes, not a Jewish girl."

"I have to work in the morning. I'm going to bed."

Ida quieted down. When Helen was undressing she came into her room. "Helen," she said, holding back her tears, "the only thing I want for you is the best. Don't make my mistake. Don't make worse and spoil your whole life, with a poor man that he is only a grocery clerk which we don't know about him nothing. Marry somebody who can give you a better life, a nice professional boy with a college education. Don't mix up now with a stranger. Helen, I know what I'm talking. Believe me, I know." She was crying again.

"I'll try my best," Helen said.

Ida dabbed at her eyes with a handkerchief. "Helen, darling, do me one favor."

"What is it? I am very tired."

"Please call up Nat tomorrow. Just to speak to him. Say hello, and if he asks you to go out with him, tell him yes. Give him a chance."

"I gave him one."

"Last summer you enjoyed so much with him. You went to the beach, to concerts. What happened?"

"Our tastes are different," Helen said wearily.

"In the summer you said your tastes were the same."

"I learned otherwise."

"He is a Jewish boy, Helen, a college graduate. Give him another chance."

"All right," said Helen, "now will you go to sleep?"

"Also don't go no more with Frank. Don't let him kiss you, it's not nice."

"I can't promise."

"Please, Helen."

"I said I'd call Nat. Let that be an end of it now. Good night, Mama."

"Good night," Ida said sadly.

Though her mother's suggestion depressed her, Helen called Nat from her office the next day. He was cordial, said he had bought a secondhand car from his future brother-in-law and invited her to go for a drive.

She said she would sometime.

"How about Friday night?" Nat asked.

She was seeing Frank on Friday. "Could you make it Saturday?"

"I happen to have an engagement Saturday, also Thursday —something doing at the law school."

"Then Friday is all right." She agreed reluctantly, thinking it would be best to change the date with Frank, to satisfy her mother.

When Morris came up for his nap that afternoon Ida desperately begged him to send Frank away at once.

"Leave me alone on this subject ten minutes."

"Morris," she said, "last night I went out when Helen went, and I saw she met Frank in the park, and they kissed each the other."

Morris frowned. "He kissed her?"

"Yes."

"She kissed him?"

"I saw with my eyes."

But the grocer, after thinking about it, said wearily, "So what is a kiss? A kiss is nothing."

Ida said furiously, "Are you crazy?"

"He will go away soon," he reminded her. "In the summer."

Tears sprang into her eyes. "By summer could happen here ten times a tragedy."

"What kind tragedy you expecting—murder?"

"Worse," she cried.

His heart turned cold, he lost his temper. "Leave me alone on this subject, for God's sakes."

"Wait," Ida bitterly warned.

On Thursday of that week Julius Karp left Louis in the liquor store and stepped outside to peek through the grocery window to see if Morris was alone. Karp had not set foot in Morris's store since the night of the holdup, and he uneasily considered the reception he might meet if he were to go in now. Usually, after a time of not speaking to one another, it was Morris Bober, by nature unable to hold a grudge, who gave in and spoke to Karp; but this time he had put out of his mind the possibility of seeking out the liquor dealer and re-establishing their fruitless relationship. While in bed during his last convalescence he had thought much of Karp—an unwilling and distasteful thinking—and had discovered he disliked him more than he had imagined. He resented him as a crass and stupid person who had fallen through luck into flowing prosperity. His every good fortune spattered others with misfortune, as if there was just so much luck in the world and what Karp left over wasn't fit to eat. Morris was incensed by thoughts of the long years he had toiled without just reward. Though this was not Karp's fault, it *was* that a delicatessen had moved in across the street to make a poor man poorer. Nor could the grocer forgive him the blow he had taken on the head in his place, who could in health and wealth better afford it. Therefore it gave him a certain satisfaction not to have anything to do with the liquor dealer, though he was every day next door.

Karp, on the other hand, had been content to wait for Morris to loosen up first. He pictured the grocer yielding his aloof silence while he enjoyed the signs of its dissolution, meanwhile pitying the poor Jew his hard luck life—in capital letters. Some were born that way. Whereas Karp in whatever he touched now coined pure gold, if Morris Bober found a rotten egg in the street, it was already cracked and leaking. Such a one needed someone with experience to advise him when to stay out of the rain. But Morris, whether he knew how Karp felt, or not, remained rigidly uncommunicative—offering not so much as a flicker of recognition when on his way to the corner for his daily *Forward*, he passed the liquor dealer standing in front of his store or caught his eye peeking into his front window. As a month passed, now, quickly, almost four, Karp came to the uncomfortable conclusion that although Ida was still friendly to him, he would this time get nothing for free from Morris; he wasn't going to give in. He reacted coldly to this insight, would give back what he got— so let it be indifference. But indifference was not a commodity he was pleased to exchange. For some reason that was not clear to him Karp liked Morris to like him, and it soon rankled that his down-at-the-heels neighbor continued to remain distant. So he had been hit on the head in a holdup, but was the fault Karp's? *He* had taken care—why hadn't Morris, the shlimozel? Why, when he had warned him there were two holdupniks across the street, hadn't he like a sensible person gone first to lock his door, then telephoned the police? Why? —because he was inept, unfortunate.

And because he was, his troubles grew like bananas in bunches. First, in another accident to his hard head, then through employing Frank Alpine. Karp, no fool, knew the makings of a bad situation when he saw it. Frank, whom he had got acquainted with and considered a fly-by-night rolling stone, would soon make trouble—of that he was certain. Morris's fly-specked, worm-eaten shop did not earn half enough to pay for a full-time helper, and it was idiotic extravagance for the grocer, after he was better, to keep the clerk working for him. Karp soon learned from Louis that his estimate of a bad situation was correct. He found out that Frank every so often invested in a bottle of the best stuff, paying, naturally, cash—but whose? Furthermore Sam Pearl, another waster, had mentioned that the clerk would now and then paste a two-dollar bill on some nag's useless nose, from which it blew off in the breeze. This done by a man who was no doubt paid in peanuts added up to only one thing —he stole. Who did he steal from? Naturally from M. Bober, who had anyway nothing—who else? Rockefeller knew how to take care of his millions, but if Morris earned a dime he lost it before he could put it into his torn pocket. It was the nature of clerks to steal from those they were working for. Karp had, as a young man, privately peculated from his employer, a half-blind shoe wholesaler; and Louis, he knew, snitched from him, but by Louis he was not bothered. He was, after all, a son; he worked in the business and would someday—it shouldn't be too soon—own it. Also, by strict warnings and occasional surprise inventories he held Louis down to a bare minimum—beans. A stranger stealing money was another matter—slimy. It gave Karp gooseflesh to think of the Italian working for him.

And since misfortune was the grocer's lot, the stranger would shovel on more, not less, for it was always dangerous to have a young goy around where there was a Jewish girl. This worked out by an unchangeable law that Karp would gladly have explained to Morris had they been speaking, and saved him serious trouble. That *this* trouble, too, existed he had confirmed twice in the last week. Once he saw Helen and Frank walking on the Parkway under the trees, and another time while driving home past the local movie house, he had glimpsed them coming out after a show, holding hands. Since then he had often thought about them, indeed with anxiety, and felt he would in some way like to assist the luckless Bober.

Without doubt Morris kept Frank on to make his life easier, and probably, being Bober, he had no idea what was happening behind his back. Well, Julius Karp would warn him of his daughter's danger. Tactfully he would explain him what was what. After, he would put in a plug for Louis, who, Karp was aware, had long liked Helen but was not sure enough of himself to be successful with her. Swat Louis down and he retreated to tenderize his fingernails with his teeth. In some things he needed a push. Karp felt he could ease his son's way to Helen by making Morris a proposition he had had in the back of his head for almost a year. He would describe Louis' prospects after marriage in terms of cold cash and other advantages, and suggest that Morris speak to Helen on the subject of going with him seriously. If they went together a couple of months—Louis would give her an extravagant good time—and the combination worked out, it would benefit not only the daughter, but the grocer as well, for then Karp would take over Morris's sad gesheft and renovate and enlarge it into a self-service market with the latest fixtures and goods. His tenant around the corner he would eliminate when his lease expired—a sacrifice, but worthwhile. After that, with himself as the silent partner giving practical advice, it would take a marvelous catastrophe to keep the grocer from earning a decent living in his old age.

Karp foresaw that the main problem of this matter would

be Helen, whom he knew as a strictly independent yet not unworthy girl, even if she had pretensions to marriage with a professional—although she had got no place with Nat Pearl. To be successful, Nat needed what Louis Karp would have plenty of, not a poor girl. So he had acted in his best interests in gently shooing Helen away when her thoughts got too warm—a fact Karp had picked up from Sam Pearl. Louis, on the other hand, could afford a girl like Helen, and Helen, independent and intelligent, would be good for Louis. The liquor store owner decided that when the opportunity came he would talk turkey to her like a Dutch uncle. He would patiently explain that her only future with Frank would be as an outcast, poorer even than her father and sharing his foolish fate; whereas with Louis she could have what she wanted and more—leave it to her father-in-law. Karp felt that once Frank had gone she would listen to reason and appreciate the good life he was offering her. Twenty-three or four was a dangerous age for a single girl. At that age she would not get younger; at that age even a goy looked good.

Having observed that Frank had gone into Sam Pearl's place, and that Morris was for the moment alone in the back of his store, Karp coughed clear his throat and stepped inside the grocery. When Morris, emerging from the rear, saw who it after all was, he experienced a moment of vindictive triumph, but this was followed by annoyance that the pest was once more present, and at the same time by an uncomfortable remembrance that Karp never entered unaccompanied by bad news. Therefore he stayed silent, waiting for the liquor dealer, in prosperous sport jacket and gabardine slacks which could not camouflage his protrusive belly nor subtract from the foolishness of his face, to speak; but for once Karp's active tongue lay flat on its back as, embarrassed in recalling the results of his very last visit here, he stared at the visible scar on Morris's head.

In pity for him, the grocer spoke, his tone friendlier than he would have guessed. "So how are you, Karp?"

"Thanks. What have I got to complain?" Beaming, he thrust a pudgy hand across the counter and Morris found himself unwillingly weighing the heavy diamond ring that pressed his fingers.

Since it did not seem sensible to Karp, one minute after their reconciliation, to blurt out news of a calamity concerning Morris's daughter, he fiddled around for words to say and came up with, "How's business?"

Morris had hoped he would ask. "Fine, and every day gets better."

Karp contracted his brows; yet it occurred to him that Morris's business might have improved more than he had guessed, when peering at odd moments through the grocery window, he had discovered a customer or two instead of the usual dense emptiness. Now on the inside after several months, he noticed the store seemed better taken care of, the shelves solidly packed with stock. But if business was better he at once knew why.

Yet he casually asked, "How is this possible? You are maybe advertising in the paper?"

Morris smiled at the sad joke. Where there was no wit money couldn't buy it. "By word of mouth," he remarked, "is the best advertising."

"This is according to what the mouth says."

"It says," Morris answered without shame, "that I got a fine clerk who has pepped me up the business. Instead going down in the winter, every day goes up."

"Your clerk did this?" Karp said, thoughtfully scratching under one buttock.

"The customers like him. A goy brings in goyim."

"New customers?"

"New, old."

"Something else helps you also?"

"Also helps a little the new apartment house that it opened in December."

"Hmm," said Karp, "nothing more?"

Morris shrugged. "I don't think so. I hear your Schmitz don't feel so good and he don't give service like he used to give. Came back a few customers from him, but the most important help to me is Frank."

Karp was astonished. Could it be that the man didn't know what had happened practically under his nose? He then and there saw a God-given opportunity to boot the clerk out of the place forever. "That wasn't Frank Alpine who improved you your business," he said decisively. "That was something else."

Morris smiled slightly. As usual the sage knew every reason for every happening.

But Karp persisted. "How long does he work here?"

"You know when he came—in November."

"And right away the business started to pick up?"

"Little by little."

"This happened," Karp announced with excitement, "not because this goy came here. What did he know about the grocery business? Nothing. Your store improved because my tenant Schmitz got sick and had to close his store part of the day. Didn't you know that?"

"I heard he was sick," Morris answered, his throat tightening, "but the drivers said his old father came to give him a help."

"That's right," Karp said, "but in the middle December he went every morning to the hospital for treatments. First the father stayed in the store, then he got too tired so Schmitz didn't open till maybe nine, ten o'clock, instead of seven. And instead of closing ten o'clock at night, he closed eight. This went on like this till last month, then he couldn't open till eleven o'clock in the morning, and so he lost half a day's business. He tried to sell the store but nobody would buy then. Yesterday he closed up altogether. Didn't somebody mention that to you?"

"One of the customers said," Morris answered, distressed, "but I thought it was temporary."

"He's very sick," said Karp solemnly. "He won't open again."

My God, thought Morris. For months he had watched the store when it was empty and while it was being altered, but never since its opening had he gone past Sam Pearl's corner to look at it. He hadn't the heart to. But why had no one told him that the place had been closing part of the day for more than two months—Ida, Helen? Probably they had gone past it without noticing the door was sometimes closed. In their minds, as in his, it was always open for *his* business.

"I don't say," Karp was saying, "that your clerk didn't help your income, but the real reason things got better is when Schmitz couldn't stay open, some of his customers came here. Naturally, Frank wouldn't tell you that."

Filled with foreboding, Morris reflected on what the liquor dealer had said. "What happened to Schmitz?"

"He has a bad blood disease and lays now in the hospital."

"Poor man," the grocer sighed. Hope wrestled shame as he asked, "Will he give the store in auction?"

Karp was devastating. "What do you mean give in auction? It's a good store. He sold it Wednesday to two up-to-date Norwegian partners and they will open next week a modern fancy grocery and delicatessen. You will see where your business will go."

Morris, with clouded eyes, died slowly.

Karp, to his horror, realized he had shot at the clerk and wounded the grocer. He remarked hastily, "What could I do? I couldn't tell him to go in auction if he had a chance to sell."

The grocer wasn't listening. He was thinking of Frank with a violent sense of outrage, of having been deceived.

"Listen, Morris," Karp said quickly, "I got a proposition for you about your gesheft. Throw out first on his ass this Italy-ener that he fooled you, then tell Helen that my Louis—"

But when the ghost behind the counter cursed him in a strange tongue for the tidings he had brought, Karp backed out of the store and was swallowed in his own.

After a perilous night at the hands of ancient enemies, Morris escaped from his bed and appeared in the store at five A.M. There he faced the burdensome day alone. The grocer had struggled all night with Karp's terrible news—had tossed around like a red coal why nobody had told him before how sick the German was—maybe one of the salesmen, or Breit-

bart, or a customer. Probably no one had thought it too important, seeing that Schmitz's store was until yesterday open
daily. Sure he was sick, but somebody had already mentioned
that, and why should they tell him again if they figured that
people got sick but then they got better? Hadn't he himself
been sick, but who had talked of it in the neighborhood?
Probably nobody. People had their own worries to worry
about. As for the news that Schmitz had sold his store, the
grocer felt that here he had nothing to complain of—he had
been informed at once, like a rock dropped on his skull.

As for what he would do with Frank, after long pondering
the situation, thinking how the clerk had acted concerning
their increase in business—as if he alone had created their
better times—Morris at length decided that Frank had not—as
he had assumed when Karp told him the news—tried to trick
him into believing that he was responsible for the store's
change for the better. The grocer supposed that the clerk,
like himself, was probably ignorant of the true reason for their
change of luck. Maybe he shouldn't have been, since he at
least got out during the day, visited other places on the
block, heard news, gossip—maybe he should have known,
but Morris felt he didn't, possibly because he wanted to believe he was their benefactor. Maybe that was why he had
been too blind to see what he should have seen, too deaf to
have heard what he had heard. It was possible.

After his first confusion and fright, Morris had decided he
must sell the store—he had by eight o'clock already told a
couple of drivers to pass the word around—but he must under no circumstances part with Frank and must keep him
here to do all he could to prevent the Norwegian partners,
after they had reopened the store, from quickly calling back
the customers of Schmitz who were with him now. He
couldn't believe that Frank hadn't helped. It had not been
proved in the Supreme Court that the German's sickness was
the only source of their recent good fortune. Karp said so but
since when did Karp speak the word of God? Of course
Frank had helped the business—only not so much as they had
thought. Ida was not so wrong about that. But maybe

Frank could hold onto a few people; the grocer doubted he himself could. He hadn't the energy, the nerve to be alone in the store during another time of change for the worse. The years had eaten away his strength.

When Frank came down he at once noticed that the grocer was not himself, but the clerk was too concerned with his own problems to ask Morris what ailed him. Often since the time Helen had been in his room he had recalled her remark that he must discipline himself and wondered why he had been so moved by the word, why it should now bang around in his head like a stick against a drum. With the idea of self-control came the feeling of the beauty of it—the beauty of a person being able to do things the way he wanted to, to do good if he wanted; and this feeling was followed by regret—of the slow dribbling away, starting long ago, of his character, without him lifting a finger to stop it. But today, as he scraped at his hard beard with a safety razor, he made up his mind to return, bit by bit until all paid up, the hundred and forty-odd bucks he had filched from Morris in the months he had worked for him, the figure of which he had kept for this very purpose written on a card hidden in his shoe.

To clean up the slate in a single swipe, he thought again of telling Morris about his part in the holdup. A week ago he was on the point of getting it past his teeth, had even spoken aloud the grocer's name, but when Morris looked up Frank felt it was useless and said never mind. He was born, he thought, with a worrisome conscience that had never done him too much good, although at times he had liked having the acid weight of it in him because it had made him feel he was at least that different from other people. It made him want to set himself straight so he could build his love for Helen right, so it would stay right.

But when he pictured himself confessing, the Jew listening with a fat ear, he still could not stand the thought of it. Why should he make more trouble for himself than he could now handle, and end by defeating his purpose to fix things up and have a better life? The past was the past and the hell with it. He had unwillingly taken part in a holdup, but he was, like Morris, more of a victim of Ward Minogue. If alone, he wouldn't have done it. That didn't excuse him that he did, but it at least showed his true feelings. So what was there to confess if the whole thing had been sort of an accident? Let bygones be gone. He had no control over the past—could only shine it up here and there and shut up as to the rest. From now on he would keep his mind on tomorrow, and tomorrow take up the kind of life that he saw he valued more than how he had been living. He would change and live in a worthwhile way.

Impatient to begin, he waited to empty the contents of his wallet into the cash drawer. He thought he could try it when Morris was napping; but then for some cockeyed reason, although there was nothing for her to do in the store today, Ida came down and sat in the back with him. She was heavy-faced, dispirited; she sighed often but said nothing, although she acted as if she couldn't stand the sight of him. He knew why, Helen had told him, and he felt uncomfortable, as if he were wearing wet clothes she wouldn't let him take off; but the best thing was to keep his trap shut and let Helen handle her end of it.

Ida wouldn't leave, so he couldn't put the dough back although his itch to do so had grown into impatience. Whenever somebody went into the store Ida insisted on waiting on them, but this last time after she came back she said to Frank, stretched out on the couch with a butt in his mouth, that she wasn't feeling so well and was going up.

"Feel better," he said sitting up, but she didn't reply and at last left. He went quickly into the store, once he was sure she was upstairs. His wallet contained a five-dollar bill and a single, and he planned to put it all back in the register, which would leave him only with a few coins in his pocket but tomorrow was payday anyway. After ringing up the six bucks, to erase the evidence of an unlikely sale he rang up "no sale." Frank then felt a surge of joy at what he had done and his eyes misted. In the back he drew off his shoe, got out the card, and subtracted six dollars from the total amount he owed. He figured he could pay it all up in a couple-three months, by taking out of the bank the money—about eighty bucks—that was left there, returning it bit by bit, and when that was all used up, giving back part of his weekly salary till he had the debt squared. The trick was to get the money back without arousing anybody's suspicion he was putting in the drawer more than the business was earning.

While he was still in a good mood over what he had done, Helen called up.

"Frank," she said, "are you alone? If not say wrong number and hang up."

"I am alone."

"Have you seen how nice it is today? I went for a walk at lunchtime and it feels like spring has arrived."

"It's still in February. Don't take your coat off too soon."

"After Washington's Birthday winter loses its heart. Do you smell the wonderful air?"

"Not right now."

"Get outside in the sun," she said, "it's warm and wonderful."

"Why did you call me for?" he asked.

"Must I have an excuse to call?" she said softly.

"You never do."

"I called because I wished I were seeing you tonight instead of Nat."

"You don't have to go out with him if you don't want to."

"I'd better, because of my mother."

"Change it to some other time."

She thought a minute then said she had better to get it over with.

"Do it any way you like."

"Frank, do you think we could meet after I see Nat—maybe at half past eleven, or twelve at the latest? Would you like to meet me then?"

"Sure, but what's it all about?"

"I'll tell you when I see you," she said with a little laugh. "Should we meet on the Parkway or our regular place in front of the lilac trees?"

"Wherever you say. The park is okay."

"I really hate to go there since my mother followed us."

"Don't worry about that, honey." He said, "Have you got something nice to tell me?"

"Very nice," Helen said.

He thought he knew what it was. He thought he would carry her like a bride up to his room, then when it was over carry her down so she could go up alone without fear her mother suspected where she had been.

Just then Morris came into the store so he hung up.

The grocer inspected the figure in the cash register and the satisfying sum there set him sighing. By Saturday they would surely have two-forty or fifty, but it wouldn't be that high any more once the Norwegians opened up.

Noticing Morris peering at the register under the yellow flame of his match, Frank remembered that all he had left on him was about seventy cents. He wished Helen had called him before he had put back the six bucks in the drawer. If it rained tonight they might need a cab to get home from the park, or maybe if they went up in his room she would be hungry after and want a pizza or something. Anyway, he could borrow a buck from her if he needed it. He also thought of asking Louis Karp for a little loan but didn't like to.

Morris went out for his *Forward* and spread it before him on the table, but he wasn't reading. He was thinking how distracted he was about the future. While he was upstairs, he had lain in bed trying to think of ways to cut down his expenses. He had thought of the fifteen dollars weekly he paid Frank and had worried over how large the sum was. He had also thought of Helen being kissed by the clerk, and of Ida's warnings, and all this had worked on his nerves. He seriously considered telling Frank to go but couldn't make the decision to. He wished he had let him go long ago.

Frank had decided he didn't like to ask Helen for any money—it wasn't a nice thing to do with a girl you liked. He thought it was better to take a buck out of the register drawer, out of the amount he had just put back. He wished he had paid back the five and kept himself the one-buck bill.

Morris sneaked a glance at his clerk sitting on the couch. Recalling the time he had sat in the barber's chair, watching the customers coming out of the grocery with big bags, he felt uneasy. I wonder if he steals from me, he thought. The question filled him with dread because he had asked it of himself many times yet had never answered it with certainty.

He saw through the window in the wall that a woman had come into the store. Frank got up from the couch. "I'll take this one, Morris."

Morris spoke to his newspaper. "I got anyway something to clean up in the cellar."

"What have you got there?"

"Something."

When Frank walked behind the counter, Morris went down into the cellar but didn't stay there. He stole up the stairs and stationed himself behind the hall door. Peering through a crack in the wood, he clearly saw the woman and heard her ordering. He added up the prices of the items as she ordered them.

The bill came to $1.81. When Frank rang up the money, the grocer held his breath for a painful second, then stepped inside the store.

The customer, hugging her bag of groceries, was on her way out of the front door. Frank had his hand under his apron, in his pants pocket. He gazed at the grocer with a startled expression. The amount rung up on the cash register was eighty-one cents.

Morris groaned within himself.

Frank, though tense with shame, pretended nothing was wrong. This enraged Morris. "The bill was a dollar more, why did you ring a dollar less?"

The clerk, after a time of long agony, heard himself say, "It's just a mistake, Morris."

"No," thundered the grocer. "I heard behind the hall door how much you sold her. Don't think I don't know you did many times the same thing before."

Frank could say nothing.

"Give it here the dollar," Morris ordered, extending his trembling hand.

Anguished, the clerk tried lying. "You're making a mistake. The register owes me a buck. I ran short on nickels so I got twenty from Sam Pearl with my own dough. After, I accidentally rang up one buck instead of 'no sale.' That's why I took it back this way. No harm done, I tell you."

"This is a lie," cried Morris. "I left inside a roll nickels in case anybody needed." He strode behind the counter, rang "no sale" and held up the roll of nickels. "Tell the truth."

Frank thought, This shouldn't be happening to me, for I am a different person now.

"I was short, Morris," he admitted, "that's the truth of it. I figured I would pay you back tomorrow after I got my pay." He took the crumpled dollar out of his pants pocket and Morris snatched it from his hand.

"Why didn't you ask me to lend you a dollar instead to steal it?"

The clerk realized it hadn't occurred to him to borrow from the grocer. The reason was simple—he had never borrowed, he had always stolen.

"I didn't think about it. I made a mistake."

"Always mistakes," the grocer said wrathfully.

"All my life," sighed Frank.

"You stole from me since the day I saw you."

"I confess to it," Frank said, "but for God's sake, Morris, I swear I was paying it back to you. Even today I put back six bucks. That's why you got so much in the drawer from the time you went up to snooze until now. Ask the Mrs if we took in more than two bucks while you were upstairs. The rest I put in."

He thought of taking off his shoe and showing Morris how carefully he had kept track of the money he had taken, but he didn't want to do that because the amount was so large it might anger the grocer more.

"You put it in," Morris cried, "but it belongs to me. I don't want a thief here." He counted fifteen dollars out of the register. "Here's your week's pay—the last. Please leave now the store."

His anger was gone. He spoke in sadness and fear of tomorrow.

"Give me one last chance," Frank begged, "Morris, please." His face was gaunt, his eyes haunted, his beard like night.

Morris, though moved by the man, thought of Helen.

"No."

Frank stared at the gray and broken Jew and seeing, despite tears in his eyes, that he would not yield, hung up his apron on a hook and left.

The night's new beauty struck Helen with the anguish of loss as she hurried into the lamplit park a half-hour after midnight. That morning as she had stepped into the street, wearing a new dress under her old coat, the fragrant day had moved her to tears and she felt then she was truly in love with Frank. Whatever the future held it couldn't deny her the sense of release and fulfillment she had felt then. Hours later, when she was with Nat Pearl, as they stopped off for a drink at a roadside tavern, then at his insistence drove into Long Island, her thoughts were still on Frank and she was impatient to be with him.

Nat was Nat. He exerted himself tonight, giving out with charm. He talked with charm and was hurt with charm. Unchanged after all the months she hadn't been with him, as they were parked on the dark shore overlooking the starlit Sound, after a few charming preliminaries he had put his arms around her. "Helen, how can we forget what pleasure we had in the past?"

She pushed him away, angered. "It's gone, I've forgotten. If you're so much of a gentleman, Nat, you ought to forget it too. Was a couple of times in bed a mortgage on my future?"

"Helen, don't talk like a stranger. For Pete's sake, be human."

"I *am* human, please remember."

"We were once good friends. My plea is for friendship again."

"Why don't you admit by friendship you mean something different?"

"Helen . . ."

"No."

He sat back at the wheel. "Christ, you have become a suspicious character."

She said, "Things have changed—you must realize."

"Who have they changed for," he asked sullenly, "that dago I hear you go with?"

Her answer was ice.

On the way home he tried to unsay what he had said, but Helen yielded him only a quick good-by. She left him with relief and a poignant sense of all she had wasted of the night.

Worried that Frank had had to wait so long, she hurried across the lit plaza and along a gravel path bordered by tall lilac shrubs, toward their meeting place. As she approached their bench, although she was troubled by a foreboding he would not be there, she couldn't believe it, then was painfully disappointed to find that though others were present—it was true, he wasn't.

Could he have been and gone already? It didn't seem possible; he had always waited before, no matter how late she was. And since she had told him she had something important to say, nothing less than that she now knew she loved him, surely he would want to hear what. She sat down, fearing he had had an accident.

Usually they were alone at this spot, but the almost warmish late-February night had brought out company. On a bench diagonally opposite Helen, in the dark under budding branches, sat two young lovers locked in a long kiss. The bench at her left was empty, but on the one beyond that a man was sleeping under a dim lamp. A cat nosed at his shadow and departed. The man woke with a grunt, squinted at Helen, yawned and went back to sleep. The lovers at last broke apart and left in silence, the boy awkwardly trailing the happy girl. Helen deeply envied her, an awful feeling to end the day with.

Glancing at her watch she saw it was already past one. Shivering, she rose, then sat down to wait five last minutes. She felt the stars clustered like a distant weight above her head. Utterly lonely, she regretted the spring-like loveliness of the night; it had gone, in her hands, to waste. She was tired of anticipation, of waiting for nothing.

A man was standing unsteadily before her, heavy, dirty, stinking of whiskey. Helen half-rose, struck with fright.

He flipped off his hat and said huskily, "Don't be afraid of me, Helen. I'm personally a fine guy—son of a cop. You remember me, don't you—Ward Minogue that went to your school? My old man beat me up once in the girls' yard."

Though it was years since she had seen him she recognized Ward, at once recalling the incident of his following a girl into a lavatory. Instinctively Helen raised her arm to protect herself. She kept herself from screaming, or he might grab her. How stupid, she thought, to wait for this.

"I remember you, Ward."

"Could I sit down?"

She hesitated. "All right."

Helen edged as far away from him as she could. He looked half-stupefied. If he made a move she would run, screaming.

"How did you recognize me in the dark?" she asked, pretending to be casual as she glanced stealthily around to see how best to escape. If she could get past the trees, it was then another twenty feet along the shrub-lined path before she could be out in the open. Once on the plaza there would be people around she could appeal to.

God only help me, she thought.

"I saw you a couple of times lately," Ward answered, rubbing his hand slowly across his chest.

"Where?"

"Around. Once I saw you come out of your old man's grocery and I figured it was you. You have still kept your looks," he grinned.

"Thanks. Don't you feel so well?"

"I got gas pains in my chest and a goddam headache."

"In case you want one I have a box of aspirins in my purse."

"No, they make me puke." She noticed that he was glancing toward the trees. She grew more anxious, thought of offering him her purse if he only wouldn't touch her.

"How's your boy friend, Frank Alpine?" Ward asked, with a wet wink.

She said in surprise, "Do you know Frank?"

"He's an old friend of mine," he answered. "He was here lookin' for you."

"Is—he all right?"

"Not so hot," said Ward. "He had to go home."

She got up. "I have to leave now."

But he was standing.

"Good night." Helen walked away from him.

"He told me to give you this paper." Ward thrust his hand into his coat pocket.

She didn't believe him but paused long enough for him to move forward. He grabbed her with astonishing swiftness, smothering her scream with his smelly hand, as he dragged her toward the trees.

"All I want is what you give that wop," Ward grunted.

She kicked, clawed, bit his hand, broke loose. He caught her by her coat collar, ripped it off. She screamed again and ran forward but he pounced upon her and got his arm over her mouth. Ward shoved her hard against a tree, knocking the breath out of her. He held her tightly by the throat as with his other hand he ripped open her coat and tore her dress off the shoulder, exposing her brassière.

Struggling, kicking wildly, she caught him between the legs with her knee. He cried out and cracked her across the face. She felt the strength go out of her and fought not to faint. She screamed but heard no sound.

Helen felt his body shuddering against her. I am disgraced, she thought, yet felt curiously freed of his stinking presence, as if he had dissolved into a can of filth and she had kicked it away. Her legs buckled and she slid to the ground. I've fainted, went through her mind, although she felt she was still fighting him.

Dimly she realized that a struggle was going on near her. She heard the noise of a blow, and Ward Minogue cried out in great pain and staggered away.

Frank, she thought with tremulous joy. Helen felt herself gently lifted and knew she was in his arms. She sobbed in relief. He kissed her eyes and lips and he kissed her half-naked breast. She held him tightly with both arms, weeping, laughing, murmuring she had come to tell him she loved him.

He put her down and they kissed under the dark trees. She tasted whiskey on his tongue and was momentarily afraid.

"I love you, Helen," he murmured, attempting clumsily to cover her breast with the torn dress as he drew her deeper into the dark, and from under the trees onto the star-dark field.

They sank to their knees on the winter earth, Helen urgently whispering, "Please not now, darling," but he spoke of his starved and passionate love, and all the endless heartbreaking waiting. Even as he spoke he thought of her as beyond his reach, forever in the bathroom as he spied, so he stopped her pleas with kisses. . . .

Afterward, she cried, "Dog—uncircumcised dog!"

While Morris was sitting alone in the back the next morning, a boy brought in a pink handbill and left it on the counter. When the grocer picked it

up he saw it announced the change of management and re-
opening on Monday, by Taast and Pederson, of the grocery
and fancy delicatessen around the corner. There followed, in
large print, a list of specials they were offering during their
first week, bargains Morris could never hope to match, because he couldn't afford the loss the Norwegians were
planning to take. The grocer felt he was standing in an icy
draft blowing from some hidden hole in the store. In the
kitchen, though he stood with his legs and buttocks pressed
against the gas radiator, it took an age to diminish the chill
that had penetrated his bones.

All morning he scanned the crumpled handbill, muttering to himself; he sipped cold coffee, thinking of the future, and off and on, of Frank Alpine. The clerk had left last
night without taking his fifteen dollars' wages. Morris thought
he would come in for it this morning but, as the hours
passed, knew he wouldn't, maybe having left it to make up
some of the money he had stolen; yet maybe not. For the
thousandth time the grocer wondered if he had done right
in ordering Frank to go. True, he had stolen from him, but
also true, he was paying it back. His story that he had put six
dollars into the register and then found he had left himself
without a penny in his pocket was probably the truth, because the sum in the register, when Morris counted it, was
more than they usually took in during the dead part of the
afternoon when he napped. The clerk was an unfortunate
man; yet the grocer was alternately glad and sorry the incident had occurred. He was glad he had finally let him go.
For Helen's sake it had had to be done, and for Ida's peace of
mind, as well as his own. Still, he felt unhappy to lose his
assistant and be by himself when the Norwegians opened up.

Ida came down, puffy-eyed from poor sleep. She felt a
hopeless rage against the world. What will become of Helen?
she asked herself, and cracked her knuckles against her chest.
But when Morris looked up to listen to her complaints, she
was afraid to say anything. A half-hour later, aware that
something had changed in the store, she thought of the clerk.

"Where is he?" she asked.

"He left," Morris answered.

"Where did he leave?" she said in astonishment.

"He left for good."

She gazed at him. "Morris, what happened, tell me?"

"Nothing," he said, embarrassed. "I told him to leave."

"Why, all of a sudden?"

"Didn't you say you didn't want him here no more?"

"From the first day I saw him, but you always said no."

"Now I said yes."

"A stone falls off my heart." But she was not satisfied. "Did he move out of the house yet?"

"I don't know."

"I will go and ask the upstairske."

"Leave her alone. We will know when he moves."

"When did you tell him to leave?"

"Last night."

"So why didn't you tell me last night?" she said angrily. "Why you told me he went early to the movies?"

"I was nervous."

"Morris," she asked in fright. "Did something else happen? Did Helen—"

"Nothing happened."

"Does she know he left?"

"I didn't tell her. Why she went so early to work this morning?"

"She went early?"

"Yes."

"I don't know," Ida said uneasily.

He produced the handbill. "This is why I feel bad."

She glanced at it, not comprehending.

"The German," he explained. "They bought him out, two Norwegians."

She gasped. "When?"

"This week. Schmitz is sick. He lays now in the hospital."

"I told you," Ida said.

"You told me?"

"Vey is mir. I told you after Christmas—when improved more the business. I told you the drivers said the German was losing customers. You said no, Frank improved the business. A goy brings in goyim, you said. How much strength I had to argue with you?"

"Did you tell me he kept closed in the morning his store?"

"Who said? I didn't know this."

"Karp told me."

"Karp was here?"

"He came on Thursday to tell me the good news."

"What good news?"

"That Schmitz sold out."

"Is this good news?" she asked.

"Maybe to him but not to me."

"You didn't tell me he came."

"I tell you now," he said irritably. "Schmitz sold out. Monday will open two Norwegians. Our business will go to hell again. We will starve here."

"Some helper you had," she said with bitterness. "Why didn't you listen to me when I said let him go?"

"I listened," he said wearily.

She was silent, then asked, "So when Karp told you Schmitz sold his store you told Frank to leave?"

"The next day."

"Thank God."

"See if you say next week 'Thank God.'"

"What is this got to do with Frank? Did he help us?"

"I don't know."

"You don't know," she said shrilly. "You just told me you said he should leave when you found out where came our business."

"I don't know," he said miserably, "I don't know where it came."

"It didn't come from him."

"Where it came I don't worry any more. Where will it come next week I worry." He read aloud the specials the Norwegians were offering.

She squeezed her hands white. "Morris, we must sell the store."

"So sell." Sighing, Morris removed his apron. "I will take my rest."

"It's only half past eleven."

"I feel cold." He looked depressed.

"Eat something first—your soup."

"Who can eat?"

"Drink a hot glass tea."

"No."

"Morris," she said quietly, "don't worry so much. Something will happen. We will always have to eat."

He made no reply, folded the handbill into a small square and took it upstairs with him.

The rooms were cold. Ida always shut off the radiators when she went down and lit them again in the late afternoon about an hour before Helen returned. Now the house was too cold. Morris turned on the stopcock of the bedroom radiator, then found he had no match in his pocket. He got one in the kitchen.

Under the covers he felt shivery. He lay under two blankets and a quilt yet shivered. He wondered if he was sick but soon fell asleep. He was glad when he felt sleep come over him, although it brought night too quickly. But if you slept it was night, that's how things were. Looking, that same night, from the street into his store, he beheld Taast and Pederson —one with a small blond mustache, the other half-bald, a light shining on his head—standing behind *his* counter, poking into *his* cash register. The grocer rushed in but they were gabbing in German and paid no attention to his gibbering Yiddish. At that moment Frank came out of the back with Helen. Though the clerk spoke a musical Italian, Morris recognized a dirty word. He struck his assistant across the face and they wrestled furiously on the floor, Helen screaming mutely. Frank dumped him heavily on his back and sat on his poor chest. He thought his lungs would burst. He tried hard to cry out but his voice cracked his throat and no one would help. He considered the possibility of dying and would have liked to.

.   .   .

Tessie Fuso dreamed of a tree hit by thunder and knocked over; she dreamed she heard someone groan terribly and awoke in fright, listened, then went back to sleep. Frank Alpine, at the dirty end of a long night, awoke groaning. He awoke with a shout—awake, he thought, forever. His impulse was to leap out of bed and rush down to the store; then he remembered that Morris had thrown him out. It was a gray, dreary winter morning. Nick had gone to work and Tessie, in her bathrobe, was sitting in the kitchen, drinking coffee. She heard Frank cry out again but had just discovered that she was pregnant, so did nothing more than wonder at his nightmare.

He lay in bed with the blankets pulled over his head, trying to smother his thoughts but they escaped and stank. The more he smothered them the more they stank. He smelled garbage in the bed and couldn't move out of it. He couldn't because he was it—the stink in his own broken nose. What you did was how bad you smelled. Unable to stand it he flung the covers aside and struggled to dress but couldn't make it. The sight of his bare feet utterly disgusted him. He thirsted for a cigarette but couldn't light one for fear of seeing his hand. He shut his eyes and lit a match. The match burned his nose. He stepped on the lit match with his bare feet and danced in pain.

Oh my God, why did I do it? Why did I ever do it? Why did I do it?

His thoughts were killing him. He couldn't stand them. He sat on the edge of the twisted bed, his thoughtful head ready to bust in his hands. He wanted to run. Part of him was already in flight, he didn't know where. He just wanted to run. But while he was running, he wanted to be back. He wanted to be back with Helen, to be forgiven. It wasn't asking too much. People forgave people—who else? He could explain if she would listen. Explaining was a way of getting close to somebody you had hurt; as if in hurting them you were giving them a reason to love you. He had come, he would say, to the park to wait for her, to hear what she had to tell him. He felt he knew she would say she loved him; it meant they would soon sleep together. This stayed in his mind and he sat there waiting to hear her say it, at the same time in an agony that she never would, that he would lose her the minute she found out why her father had kicked him out of the grocery. What could he tell her about that? He sat for hours trying to think what to say, at last growing famished. At midnight he left to get a pizza but stopped instead in a bar. Then when he saw his face in the mirror he felt a nose-thumbing revulsion. Where have you ever been, he asked the one in the glass, except on the inside of a circle? What have you ever done but always the wrong thing? When he returned to the park, there was Ward Minoque hurting her. He just about killed Ward. Then when he had Helen in his arms, crying saying at last that she loved him, he had this hopeless feeling it was the end and now he would never see her again. He thought he must love her before she was lost to him. She said no, not to, but he couldn't believe it the same minute she was saying she loved him. He thought, Once I start she will come along with me. So then he did it. He loved her with his love. She should have known that. She should not have gone wild, beat his face with her fists, called him dirty names, run from him, his apologies, pleadings, sorrow.

Oh Jesus, what did I do?

He moaned; he got instead of a happy ending, a bad smell. If he could root out what he had done, smash and destroy it; but it was done, beyond him to undo. It was where he could never lay hands on it any more—in his stinking mind. His thoughts would forever suffocate him. He had failed once too often. He should somewhere have stopped and changed the way he was going, his luck, himself, stopped hating the world, got a decent education, a job, a nice girl. He had lived without will, betrayed every good intention. Had he ever confessed the holdup to Morris? Hadn't he stolen from the cash register till the minute he was canned? In a single terrible act in the park hadn't he murdered the last of his good hopes, the love he had so long waited for—his chance at a future? His goddamned life had pushed him wherever it went; he had led it nowhere. He was blown around in any breath that blew, owned nothing, not even experience to show for the years he had lived. If you had experience you knew at least when to start and where to quit; all he knew was how to mangle himself more. The self he had secretly considered valuable was, for all he could make of it, a dead rat. He stank.

This time his shout frightened Tessie. Frank got up on the run but he had run everywhere. There was no place left to escape to. The room shrank. The bed was flying up at him. He felt trapped—sick, wanted to cry but couldn't. He planned to kill himself, at the same minute had a terrifying insight: that all the while he was acting like he wasn't, he was really a man of stern morality.

Ida had awakened in the night and heard her daughter crying. Nat did something to her, she thought wildly, but was ashamed to go to Helen and beg her to say what. She guessed he had acted like a lout—it was no wonder Helen had stopped seeing him. All night she blamed herself for having urged her to go out with the law student. She fell into an unhappy sleep.

It was growing light when Morris left the flat. Helen dragged herself out of bed and sat with reddened eyes in the bathroom, sewing on her coat collar. Once near the office she would give it to a tailor to fix so the tear couldn't be seen. With her new dress she could do nothing. Rolling it into a hopeless ball, she hid it under some things in her bottom bureau drawer. Monday she would buy one exactly like it and hang it in her closet. Undressing for a shower—her third in hours—she burst into tears at the sight of her body. Every man she drew to her dirtied her. How could she have encouraged him? She felt a violent self-hatred for trusting him, when from the very beginning she had sensed he was untrustable. How could she have allowed herself to fall in love with anybody like him? She was filled with loathing at the fantasy she had created, of making him into what he couldn't be—educable, promising, kind and good, when he was no more than a bum. Where were her wits, her sense of elemental self-preservation?

Under the shower she soaped herself heavily, crying as she washed. At seven, before her mother awakened, she dressed and left the house, too sickened to eat. She would gladly have forgotten her life, in sleep, but dared not stay home, dared not be questioned. When she returned from her half-day of work, if he was still there, she would order him to leave or would scream him out of the house.

Coming home from the garage, Nick smelled gas in the hall. He inspected the radiators in his flat, saw they were both lit, then knocked on Frank's door.

After a minute the door opened a crack.

"Do you smell anything?" Nick said, staring at the eye in the crack.

"Mind your goddamned business."

"Are you nuts? I smell gas in the house, it's dangerous."

"Gas?" Frank flung open the door. He was in pajamas, haggard.

"What's the matter, you sick?"

"Where do you smell the gas?"

"Don't tell me you can't smell it."

"I got a bad cold," Frank said hoarsely.

"Maybe it's comin' from the cellar," said Nick.

They ran down a flight and then the odor hit Frank, an acrid stench thick enough to wade through.

"It's coming from this floor," Nick said.

Frank pounded on the door. "Helen, there's gas here, let me in. Helen," he cried.

"Shove it," said Nick.

Frank pushed his shoulder against the door. It was unlocked and he fell in. Nick quickly opened the kitchen window while Frank, in his bare feet, roamed through the house. Helen was not there but he found Morris in bed.

The clerk, coughing, dragged the grocer out of bed and carrying him to the living room, laid him on the floor. Nick closed the stopcock of the bedroom radiator and threw open every window. Frank got down on his knees, bent over Morris, clamped his hands to his sides and pumped.

Tessie ran in in fright, and Nick shouted to her to call Ida.

Ida came stumbling up the stairs, moaning, "Oh, my God, oh, my God."

Seeing Morris lying on the floor, his underwear soaked, his face the color of a cooked beet, flecks of foam in the corners of his mouth, she let out a piercing shriek.

Helen, coming dully into the hall, heard her mother's cry. She smelled the gas and ran in terror up the stairs, expecting death.

When she saw Frank in his pajamas bent over her father's back, her throat thickened in disgust. She screamed in fear and hatred.

Frank couldn't look at her, frightened to.

"His eyes just moved," Nick said.

Morris awoke with a massive ach in his chest. His head felt like corroded metal, his mouth horribly dry, his stomach crawling with pain. He was ashamed to find himself stretched out in his long underwear on the floor.

"Morris," cried Ida.

Frank got up, embarrassed at his bare feet and pajamas.

"Papa, Papa." Helen was on her knees.

"Why did you do it for?" Ida yelled in the grocer's ear.

"What happened?" he gasped.

"Why did you do it for?" she wept.

"Are you crazy?" he muttered. "I forgot to light the gas. A mistake."

Helen broke into sobbing, her lips twisted. Frank had to turn his head.

"The only thing that saved him was he got some air," Nick said. "You're lucky this flat ain't windproof, Morris."

Tessie shivered. "It's cold. Cover him, he's sweating."

"Put him in bed," Ida said.

Frank and Nick lifted the grocer and carried him in to his bed. Ida and Helen covered him with blankets and quilt.

"Thanks," Morris said to them. He stared at Frank. Frank looked at the floor.

"Shut the windows," Tessie said. "The smell is gone."

"Wait a little longer," said Frank. He glanced at Helen but her back was to him. She was still crying.

"Why did he do it?" Ida moaned.

Morris gazed long at her, then shut his eyes.

"Leave him rest," Nick advised.

"Don't light any matches for another hour," Frank told Ida.

Tessie closed all but one window and they left. Ida and Helen remained with Morris in the bedroom.

Frank lingered in Helen's room but nothing welcomed him there.

Later he dressed and went down to the store. Business was brisk. Ida came down, and though he begged her not to, shut the store.

That afternoon Morris developed a fever and the doctor said he had to go to the hospital. An ambulance came and took the grocer away, his wife and daughter riding with him.

From his window upstairs. Frank watched them go.

Sunday morning the store was still shut tight. Though he feared to, Frank considered knocking on Ida's door and asking for the key. But Helen might open the door, and since he would not know what to say to her over the doorsill, he went instead down the cellar, and mounting the dumb-waiter, wriggled through the little window in the air shaft, into the store toilet. Once in the back, the clerk shaved and had his coffee. He thought he would stay in the store till somebody told him to scram; and even if they did, he would try in some way to stay longer. That was his only hope left, if there was any. Turning the front door lock, he carried in the milk and rolls and was ready for business. The register was empty, so he borrowed five dollars in change from Sam Pearl, saying he would pay it back from what he took in. Sam wanted to know how Morris was and Frank said he didn't know.

Shortly after half past eight, the clerk was standing at the front window when Ida and her daughter left the house. Helen looked like last year's flower. Observing her, he felt a pang of loss, shame, regret. He felt an unbearable deprivation

—that yesterday he had almost had some wonderful thing but today it was gone, all but the misery of remembering it was. Whenever he thought of what he had almost had it made him frantic. He felt like rushing outside, drawing her into a doorway, and declaring the stupendous value of his love for her. But he did nothing. He didn't exactly hide but he didn't show himself, and they soon went away to the subway.

Later he thought he would also go and see Morris in the hospital, as soon as he knew which one he was in—after they got home; but they didn't return till midnight. The store was closed and he saw them from his room, two dark figures getting out of a cab. Monday, the day the Norwegians opened their store, Ida came down at seven A.M. to paste a piece of paper on the door saying Morris Bober was sick and the grocery would be closed till Tuesday or Wednesday. To her amazement, Frank Alpine was standing, in his apron, behind the counter. She entered in anger.

Frank was miserably nervous that Morris or Helen, either or both, had told her all the wrong he had done them, because if they had, he was finished.

"How did you get in here?" Ida asked wrathfully.

He said through the air shaft window. "Thinking of your trouble, I didn't want to bother you about the key, Mrs."

She vigorously forbade him ever to come in that way again. Her face was deeply lined, her eyes weary, mouth bitter, but he could tell that for some miraculous reason she didn't know what he had done.

Frank pulled a handful of dollar bills out of his pants pocket and a little bag of change, laying it all on the counter. "I took in forty-one bucks yesterday."

"You were here yesterday?"

"I got in how I explained you. There was a nice rush around four till about six. We are all out of potato salad."

Her eyes grew tears. He asked how Morris felt.

She touched her wet lids with a handkerchief. "Morris has pneumonia."

"Ah, too bad. Give him my sorrow if you can. How's he coming along out of it?"

"He's a very sick man, he has weak lungs."

"I think I'll go to see him in the hospital."

"Not now," Ida said.

"When he's better. How long do you think he'll be there?"

"I don't know. The doctor will telephone today."

"Look, Mrs," Frank said. "Why don't you stop worrying about the store while Morris is sick and let me take care of it? You know I make no demands."

"My husband told you to go out from the store."

He furtively studied her face but there was no sign of accusation.

"I won't stay very long," he answered. "You don't have to worry about that. I'll stay here till Morris gets better. You'll need every cent for the hospital bills. I don't ask a thing for myself."

"Did Morris tell you why you must leave?"

His heart galloped. Did she or didn't she know? If yes, he would say it was a mistake—deny he had touched a red cent in the register. Wasn't the proof of that in the pile of dough that lay right in front of her eyes on the counter? But he answered, "Sure, he didn't want me to hang around Helen any more."

"Yes, she is a Jewish girl. You should look for somebody else. But he also found out that Schmitz was sick since December and kept closed his store in the mornings, also earlier in the night. This was what improved our income, not you."

She then told Frank that the German had sold out and two Norwegians were opening up today.

Frank flushed. "I knew that Schmitz was sick and kept his store closed sometimes, but that isn't what made your business get better. What did that was how hard I worked building up the trade. And I bet I can keep this place in the same shape it is, even with two Norwegians around the corner or three Greeks. What's more, I bet I can raise the take-in higher."

Though she was half-inclined to believe him, she couldn't.

"Wait, you'll see how smart you are."

"Then let me have a chance to show you. Don't pay me anything, the room and meals are enough."

"What," she asked in desperation, "do you want from us?"

"Just to help out. I have my debt to Morris."

"You have no debt. He has a debt to you that you saved him from the gas."

"Nick smelled it first. Anyway I feel I have a debt to him for all the things he has done for me. That's my nature, when I'm thankful, I'm thankful."

"Please don't bother Helen. She is not for you."

"I won't."

She let him stay. If you were so poor where was your choice?

Taast and Pederson opened up with a horseshoe of spring flowers in their window. Their pink handbills brought them steady business and Frank had plenty of time on his hands. During the day only a few of the regulars came into the grocery. At night, after the Norwegians had closed, the grocery had a spurt of activity, but when Frank pulled the strings of the window lights around eleven, he had only fifteen dollars in the register. He didn't worry too much. Monday was a slow day anyway, and besides, people were entitled to grab off a few specials while they could get them. He figured nobody could tell what difference the Norwegians would make to the business until a couple of weeks had gone by, when the neighborhood was used to them and things settled back to normal. Nobody was going to give specials away that cheap every day. A store wasn't a charity, and when they stopped giving something for nothing, he would match them in service and also prices and get his customers back.

Tuesday was slow, also as usual. Wednesday picked up a little, but Thursday was slow again. Friday was better. Saturday was the best day of the week, although not so good as Saturdays lately. At the end of the week the grocery was close to a hundred short of its recent weekly average. Expecting something like this, Frank had closed up for a half hour on Thursday and taken the trolley to the bank. He withdrew twenty-five dollars from his savings account and put the money into the register, five on Thursday, ten on Friday and ten on Saturday, so that when Ida wrote the figures down in her book each night she wouldn't feel too bad. Seventy-five less for the week wasn't as bad as a hundred.

Morris, better after ten days in the hospital, was brought home in a cab by Ida and Helen and laid to bed to convalesce. Frank, gripping his courage, thought of going up to see him and this time starting out right, right off. He thought of bringing him some fresh baked goods to eat, maybe a piece of cheese cake that he knew the grocer liked, or some apple strudel; but the clerk was afraid it was still too soon and Morris might ask him where he had got the money to buy the cake. He might yell, "You thief, you, the only reason you stay here still is because I am sick upstairs." Yet if Morris felt this way he would already have told Ida what Frank had done. The clerk now was sure he hadn't mentioned it, because she wouldn't have waited this long to pitch him out on his ear. He thought a lot about the way Morris kept things to himself. It was a way a person had if he figured he could be wrong about how he sized up a situation. It could be that he might take a different view of Frank in time. The clerk tried to invent reasons why it might be worth the grocer's while, after he got on his feet again, to keep him on in the grocery. Frank felt he would promise anything to stay there. "Don't worry that I ever will steal from you or anybody else any more, Morris. If I do, I hope I drop dead on the spot." He hoped that this promise, and the favor he was doing him by keeping the store open, would convince Morris of his sincerity. Yet he thought he would wait a while longer before going up to see him.

Helen hadn't said anything to anybody about him either and it wasn't hard to understand why. The wrong he had done her was never out of his mind. He hadn't intended wrong but he had done it; now he intended right. He would do anything she wanted, and if she wanted nothing he would do something, what he should do; and he would do it all on his own will, nobody pushing him but himself. He would do it with discipline and with love.

All this time he had snatched only glimpses of her, though his heart was heavy with all he hoped to say. He saw her through the plate glass window—she on the undersea side. Through the green glass she looked drowned, yet never, God help him, lovelier. He felt a tender pity for her, mixed with shame for having made her pitiable. Once, as she came home from work, her eyes happened to look into his and showed disgust. Now I am finished, he thought, she will come in here and tell me to go die some place; but when she looked away she was never there. He was agonized to be so completely apart from her, left apologizing to her shadow, to the floral fragrance she left in the air. To himself he confessed his deed, but not to her. That was the curse of it, to have it to make but who would listen? At times he felt like crying but it made him feel too much like a kid to cry. He didn't like to, did it badly.

Once he met her in the hall. She was gone before he could move his lips. He felt for her a rush of love. He felt, after she had left, that hopelessness was his punishment. He had expected that punishment to be drastic, swift; instead it came slowly—it never came, yet was there.

There was no approach to her. What happened had put her in another world, no way in.

Early one morning, he stood in the hall till she came down the stairs.

"Helen," he said, snatching off the cloth cap he now wore in the store, "my heart is sorrowful. I want to apologize."

Her lips quivered. "Don't speak to me," she said, in a voice choked with contempt. "I don't want your apologies. I don't want to see you, and I don't want to know you. As soon as my father is better, please leave. You've helped him and my mother and I thank you for that, but you're no help to me. You make me sick."

The door banged behind her.

That night he dreamed he was standing in the snow outside her window. His feet were bare yet not cold. He had waited a long time in the falling snow, and some of it lay on his head and had all but frozen his face; but he waited longer until, moved by pity, she opened the window and flung something out. It floated down; he thought it was a piece of paper with writing on it but saw that it was a white flower, surprising to see in wintertime. Frank caught it in his hand. As she had tossed the flower out through the partly opened window he had glimpsed her fingers only, yet he saw the light of her room and even felt the warmth of it. Then when he looked again the window was shut tight, sealed with ice. Even as he dreamed, he knew it had never been open. There was no such window. He gazed down at his hand for the flower and before he could see it wasn't there, felt himself wake.

The next day he waited for her at the foot of the stairs, bareheaded in the light that fell on his head from the lamp.

She came down, her frozen face averted.

"Helen, nothing can kill the love I feel for you."

"In your mouth it's a dirty word."

"If a guy did wrong, must he suffer forever?"

"I personally don't care what happens to you."

Whenever he waited at the stairs, she passed without a word, as if he didn't exist. He didn't.

If the store blows away some dark night I might as well be dead, Frank thought. He tried every way to hang on. Business was terrible. He wasn't sure how long the grocery could last or how long the grocer and his wife would let him try to keep it alive. If the store collapsed everything would be gone. But if he kept it going there was always the chance that something might change, and if it did, maybe something else might. If he kept the grocery on its feet till Morris came down, at least he would have a couple of weeks to change how things were. Weeks were nothing but it might as well be nothing because to do what he had to do he needed years.

Taast and Pederson had the specials going week after week. They thought of one come-on after another to keep the customers buying. Frank's customers were disappearing. Some of them now passed him in the street without saying hello. One or two crossed the trolley tracks and walked on the other side of the street, not to have to see his stricken face at the window. He withdrew all he had left in the bank and each week padded the income a little, but Ida saw how bad things were. She was despondent and talked of giving the place over to the auctioneer. This made him frantic. He felt he had to try harder.

He tried out all sorts of schemes. He got specials on credit and sold half the stuff, but then the Norwegians began to sell it cheaper, and the rest remained on his shelves. Hs stayed open all night for a couple of nights but did not take in enough to pay for the light. Having nothing much to do, he thought he would fix up the store. With all but the last five dollars from the bank account, he bought a few gallons of cheap paint. Then removing the goods from one section of the shelves, he scraped away the mildewed paper on the walls and painted them a nice light yellow. When one section was painted he went to work on the next. After he had finished the walls he borrowed a tall ladder, scraped the ceiling bit by bit and painted it white. He also replaced a few shelves and neatly finished them in dime store varnish. In the end he had to admit that all his work hadn't brought back a single customer.

Though it seemed impossible the store got worse.

"What are you telling Morris about the business?" Frank asked Ida.

"He don't ask me so I don't tell him," she said dully.

"How is he now?"

"Weak yet. The doctor says his lungs are like paper. He reads or he sleeps. Sometimes he listens to the radio."

"Let him rest. It's good for him."

She said again, "Why do you work so hard for nothing? What do you stay here for?"

For love, he wanted to say, but hadn't the nerve. "For Morris."

But he didn't fool her. She would even then have told him to pack and go, although he kept them for the moment off the street, had she not known for a fact that Helen no longer bothered with him. He had probably through some stupidity fallen out of her good graces. Possibly her father's illness had made her more considerate of them. She had been a fool to worry. Yet she now worried because Helen, at her age, showed so little interest in men. Nat had called but she wouldn't go near the phone.

Frank scraped down on expenses. With Ida's permission he had the telephone removed. He hated to do it because he thought Helen might sometime come down to answer it. He also reduced the gas bill by lighting only one of the two radiators downstairs. He kept the one in the front lit so the customers wouldn't feel the cold, but he no longer used the one in the kitchen. He wore a heavy sweater, a vest and a flannel shirt under his apron, and his cap on his head. But Ida, even with her coat on, when she could no longer stand the emptiness of the front, or the freezing back, escaped upstairs. One day she came into the kitchen, and seeing him salting up a soup plate of boiled potatoes for lunch, began to cry.

He thought always of Helen. How could she know what was going on in him? If she ever looked at him again she would see the same guy on the outside. He could see out but nobody could see in.

When Betty Pearl got married Helen didn't go to the wedding. The day before she apologized embarrassedly, said she wasn't feeling too well—blamed her father's illness. Betty said she understood, thinking it had something to do with her brother. "Next time," she remarked with a little laugh, but Helen, seeing she was hurt, felt bad. She reconsidered facing the ceremony, rigmarole, relatives, Nat or no Nat— maybe she could still go; but couldn't bring herself to. She was no fixture for a wedding. They might say to her, "With such a face, go better to a funeral." Though she had many a night wept herself out, her memories kept a hard hold in her mind. Crazy woman, how could she have brought herself to love such a man? How could she have considered marrying someone not Jewish? A total, worthless stranger. Only God had saved her from a disastrous mistake. With such thoughts she lost all feeling for weddings.

Her sleep suffered. Every day she dreaded every night. From bedtime to dawn she eked out only a few wearisome unconscious hours. She dreamed she would soon awake and soon awoke. Awake, she felt sorry for herself, and sorrow, no soporific, induced sorrow. Her mind stamped out endless worries: her father's health, for instance; he showed little interest in recovery. The store, as ever. Ida wept in whispers in the kitchen. "Don't tell Papa." But they would sometime soon have to. She cursed all grocery stores. And worried at seeing nobody, planning no future. Each morning she crossed off the calendar the sleepless day to be. God forbid such days.

Though Helen turned over all but four dollars of her check to her mother and it went into the register, they were always hard up for cash to meet expenses. One day Frank got an idea about how he might lay hold of some dough. He thought he would collect an old bill from Carl, the Swedish painter. He knew the painter owed Morris over seventy bucks. He looked for the housepainter every day but Carl did not come in.

One morning Frank was standing at the window when he saw him leave Karp's with a wrapped bottle in his pocket.

Frank ran out and reminded Carl of his old bill. He asked him to pay something on the account.

"This is all fixed up with me and Morris," the painter answered. "Don't stick your dirty nose in."

"Morris is sick, he needs the dough," Frank said.

Carl shoved the clerk aside and went on his way.

Frank was sore. "I'll collect from that drunk bastard."

Ida was in the store, so Frank said he would be back soon. He hung up his apron, got his overcoat and followed Carl to his house. After getting the address, he returned to the grocery. He was still angered at the painter for the way he had acted when he had asked him to pay his bill.

That evening he returned to the shabby four-story tenement and climbed the creaking staircase to the top floor. A thin, dark-haired woman came wearily to the door. She was old until his eyes got used to her face, then he realized she was young but looked old.

"Are you Carl the painter's wife?"

"That's right."

"Could I talk to him?"

"On a job?" she said hopefully.

"No. Something different."

She looked old again. "He hasn't worked for months."

"I just want to talk to him."

She let him into a large room which was a kitchen and living room combined, the two halves separated by an undrawn curtain. In the middle of the living room part stood a kerosene heater that stank. This smell mixed with the sour smell of cabbage cooking. The four kids, a boy about twelve and three younger girls, were in the room, drawing on paper, cutting and pasting. They stared at Frank but silently went on with what what they were doing. The clerk didn't feel comfortable. He stood at the window, looking down on the dreary lamplit street. He now figured he would cut the bill in half if the painter would pay up the rest.

The painter's wife covered the sizzling frying pan with a pot lid and went into the bedroom. She came back and said her husband was sleeping.

"I'll wait a while," said Frank.

She went back to her frying. The oldest girl set the table, and they all sat down to eat. He noticed they had left a place for their old man. He would soon have to crawl out of his hole. The mother didn't sit down. Paying no attention to Frank, she poured skim milk out of a container into the kids' glasses, then served each one a frankfurter fried in dough. She also gave everybody a forkful of hot sauerkraut.

The kids ate hungrily, not talking. The oldest girl glanced at Frank then stared at her plate when he looked at her.

When the plates were empty she said, "Is there any more, Mama?"

"Go to bed," said the painter's wife.

Frank had a bad headache from the stink of the heater.

"I'll see Carl some other time," he said. His spit tasted like brass.

"I'm sorry he didn't wake up."

He ran back to the store. Under the mattress of his bed he had his last three bucks hidden. He took the bills and ran to Carl's house. But on the way he met Ward Minogue. His face was yellow and shrunken, as if he had escaped out of a morgue.

"I been looking for you," said Ward. He pulled Frank's revolver out of a paper bag. "How much is this worth to you?"

"Shit."

"I'm sick," sobbed Ward.

Frank gave the three bucks to him and later dropped the gun into a sewer.

He read a book about the Jews, a short history. He had many times seen this book on one of the library shelves and had never taken it down, but one day he checked it out to satisfy his curiosity. He read the first part with interest, but after the Crusades and the Inquisition, when the Jews were having it tough, he had to force himself to keep reading. He skimmed the bloody chapters but read slowly the ones about their civilization and accomplishments. He also read about the ghettos, where the half-starved, bearded prisoners spent their lives trying to figure it out why they were the Chosen People. He tried to figure out why but couldn't. He couldn't finish the book and brought it back to the library.

Some nights he spied on the Norwegians. He would go around the corner without his apron and stand on the step of Sam Pearl's hallway, looking across the street at the grocery and fancy delicatessen. The window was loaded with all kinds of shiny cans. Inside, the store was lit as bright as day. The shelves were tightly packed with appetizing goods that made him feel hungry. And there were always customers inside, although his place was generally empty. Sometimes after the partners locked up and went home, Frank crossed to their side of the street and peered through the window into the dark store, as if he might learn from what he saw in it the secret of all good fortune and so change his luck and his life.

One night after he had closed the store, he took a long walk and stepped into the Coffee Pot, an all-night joint he had been in once or twice.

Frank asked the owner if he needed a man for night work.

"I need a counterman for coffee, short orders, and to wash the few dishes," the owner answered.

"I am your boy," said Frank.

The work was from ten to six A.M. and paid thirty-five dollars. When he got home in the morning, Frank opened the grocery. At the end of a week's working, without ringing it up, he put the thirty-five into the cash register. This, and Helen's wages, kept them from going under.

The clerk slept on the couch in the back of the store during the day. He had rigged up a buzzer that waked him when somebody opened the front door. He did not suffer from lack of sleep.

He lived in his prison in a climate of regret that he had turned a good thing into a bad, and this thought, though ancient, renewed the pain in his heart. His dreams were bad, taking place in the park at night. The garbage smell stank in his nose. He groaned his life away, his mouth crammed with words he couldn't speak. Mornings, standing at the store window, he watched Helen go off to work. He was there when she came home. She walked, slightly bowlegged, toward the door, her eyes cast down, blind to his presence. A million things to say, some extraordinary, welled up in him, choked his throat; daily they died. He thought endlessly of escape, but that would be what he always did last—beat it. This time he would stay. They would carry him out in a box. When the walls caved in they could dig for him with shovels.

Once he found a two-by-four pine board in the cellar, sawed off a hunk, and with his jackknife began to carve it into something. To his surprise it turned into a bird flying. It was shaped off balance but with a certain beauty. He thought of offering it to Helen but it seemed too rough a thing—the first he had ever made. So he tried his hand at something else. He set out to carve her a flower and it came out a rose starting to bloom. When it was done it was delicate in the way its petals were opening yet firm as a real flower. He thought about painting it red and giving it to her but decided to leave off the paint. He wrapped the wooden flower in store paper, printed Helen's name on the outside, and a few minutes before she came home from work, taped the package onto the outside of the mailbox in the vestibule. He saw her enter, then heard her go up the stairs. Looking into the vestibule, he saw she had taken his flower.

The wooden flower reminded Helen of her unhappiness. She lived in hatred of herself for having loved the clerk against her better judgment. She had fallen in love, she thought, to escape her predicament. More than ever she felt herself a victim of circumstance—in a bad dream symbolized by the nightmarish store below, and the relentless, scheming presence in it of the clerk, whom she should have shouted out of the house but had selfishly spared.

In the morning, as he aimed a pail of garbage into the can at the curb, Frank saw at the bottom of it his wooden flower.

On the day he had returned from the hospital Morris felt the urge to jump into his pants and run down to the store, but the doctor, after listening to his lungs, then tapping his hairy knuckles across the grocer's chest, said, "You're coming along fine, so what's your big hurry?" To Ida he privately said, "He has to rest, I don't mean maybe." Seeing her fright he explained, "Sixty isn't sixteen." Morris, after arguing a bit, lay back in bed and after that didn't care if he ever stepped into the store again. His recovery was slow.

With reservations, spring was on its way. There was at least more light in the day; it burst through the bedroom windows. But a cold wind roared in the streets, giving him goose pimples in bed; and sometimes, after half a day of pure sunshine, the sky darkened and some rags of snow fell. He was filled with melancholy and spent hours dreaming of his boyhood. He remembered the green fields. Where a boy runs he never forgets. His father, his mother, his only sister whom he hadn't seen in years, gottenyu. The wailing wind cried to him . . .

The awning flapping below in the street awoke his dread of the grocery. He had not for a long time asked Ida what went on downstairs but he knew without thinking. He knew in his blood. When he consciously thought of it he remembered that the register rang rarely, so he knew again. He heard heavy silence below. What else can you hear from a graveyard whose noiseless tombstones hold down the sick earth? The smell of death seeped up through the cracks in the floor. He understood why Ida did not dare go downstairs but sought anything to do here. Who could stay in such a place but a goy whose heart was stone? The fate of his store floated like a black-feathered bird dimly in his mind; but as soon as he began to feel stronger, the thing grew lit eyes, worrying him no end. One morning as he sat up against a pillow, scanning yesterday's *Forward*, his thoughts grew so wretched that he broke into sweat and his heart beat erratically. Morris heaved aside his covers, strode crookedly out of bed and began hurriedly to dress.

Ida hastened into the bedroom. "What are you doing, Morris—a sick man?"

"I must go down."

"Who needs you? There is nothing there. Go rest some more."

He fought a greedy desire to get back into bed and live there but could not quiet his anxiety.

"I must go."

She begged him not to but he wouldn't listen.

"How much he takes in now?" Morris asked as he belted his trousers.

"Nothing. Maybe seventy-five."

"A week?"

"What else?"

It was terrible but he had feared worse. His head buzzed with schemes for saving the store. Once he was downstairs he felt he could make things better. His fear came from being here, not where he was needed.

"He keeps open all day?"

"From morning till night—why I don't know."

"Why he stays here?" he asked with sudden irritation.

"He stays," she shrugged.

"What do you pay him?"

"Nothing—he says he don't want."

"So what he wants—my bitter blood?"

"He says he wants to help you."

He muttered something to himself. "You watch him sometimes?"

"Why should I watch him?" she said, worried. "He took something from you?"

"I don't want him here no more. I don't want him near Helen."

"Helen don't talk to him."

He gazed at Ida. "What happened?"

"Go ask her. What happened with Nat? She's like you, she don't tell me anything."

"He's got to leave today. I don't want him here."

"Morris," she said hesitantly, "he gave you good help, be-lieve me. Keep him one more week till you feel stronger."

"No." He buttoned his sweater and despite her pleading went shakily down the stairs.

Frank heard him coming and grew cold.

The clerk had for weeks feared the time the grocer would leave his bed, although in a curious way he had also looked forward to it. He had spent many fruitless hours trying to construct a story that would make Morris relent and keep him on. He had planned to say, "Didn't I starve rather than to spend the money from the holdup, so I could put it back in the register—which I did, though I admit I took a couple of rolls and some milk to keep myself alive?" But he had no confidence in that. He could also proclaim his long serv-ice to the grocer, his long patient labor in the store; but the face that he had stolen from him during all this time spoiled his claim. He might mention that he had saved Morris after he had swallowed a bellyful of gas, but it was Nick who had saved him as much as he. The clerk felt he was without any good appeal to the grocer—that he had used up all his credit with him, but then he was struck by a strange and exciting idea, a possible if impossible ace in the hole. He figured that if he finally sincerely revealed his part in the holdup, he might in the telling of it arouse in Morris a true understanding of his nature, and a sympathy for his great struggle to overcome his past. Understanding his clerk's plight—the meaning of his long service to him—might make the grocer keep him on, so he would again have the chance to square everything with all concerned. As he pondered this idea, Frank realized it was a wild chance that might doom rather than redeem him. Yet he felt he would try it if Morris insisted he had to leave. What could he lose after that? But when the clerk pictured himself saying what he had done and had been forgiven by the grocer, and he tried to imagine the relief he would feel, he couldn't, because his overdue confession wouldn't be complete or satisfying so long as he kept hidden what he had done to his daughter. About that he knew he could never open his mouth, so he felt that no matter what he did manage to say there would always be some disgusting thing left unsaid, some further sin to confess, and this he found utterly depressing.

Frank was standing behind the counter near the cash register, paring his fingernails with his knife blade when the grocer, his face pale, the skin of it loose, his neck swimming in his shirt collar, his dark eyes unfriendly, entered the store through the hall door.

The clerk tipped his cap and edged away from the cash register.

"Glad to see you back again, Morris," he said, regretting he hadn't once gone up to see him in all the days the grocer had been upstairs. Morris nodded coldly and went into the rear. Frank followed him in, fell on one knee, and lit the radiator.

"It's pretty cold here, so I better light this up. I've been keeping it shut off to save on the gas bill."

"Frank," Morris said firmly, "I thank you that you helped me when I took in my lungs so much gas, also that you kept the store open when I was sick, but now you got to go."

"Morris," answered Frank, heavy-hearted, "I swear I never stole another red cent after that last time, and I hope God will strike me dead right here if it isn't the truth."

"This ain't why I want you to go," Morris answered.

"Then why do you?" asked the clerk, flushing.

"You know," the grocer said, his eyes downcast.

"Morris," Frank said, at agonizing last, "I have something important I want to tell you. I tried to tell you before only I couldn't work my nerve up. Morris, don't blame me now for what I once did, because I am now a changed man, but I was one of the guys that held you up that night. I swear to God I didn't want to once I got in here, but I couldn't get out of it. I tried to tell you about it—that's why I came back here in the first place, and the first chance I got I put my share of the money back in the register—but I didn't have the guts to say it. I couldn't look you in the eye. Even now I feel sick about what I am saying, but I'm telling it to you so you will know how much I suffered on account of what I did, and that I am very sorry you were hurt on your head—even though not by me. The thing you got to understand is I am not the same person I once was. I might look so to you, but if you could see what's been going on in my heart you would know I have changed. You can trust me now, I swear it, and that's why I am asking you to let me stay and help you."

Having said this, the clerk experienced a moment of extraordinary relief—a treeful of birds broke into song; but the song was silenced when Morris, his eyes heavy, said, "This I already know, you don't tell me nothing new."

The clerk groaned. "How do you know it?"

"I figured out when I was laying upstairs in bed. I had once a bad dream that you hurt me, then I remembered—"

"But I didn't hurt you," the clerk broke in emotionally. "I was the one that gave you the water to drink. Remember?"

"I remember. I remember your hands. I remember your eyes. This day when the detective brought in here the hold-upnik that he didn't hold me up I saw in your eyes that you did something wrong. Then when I stayed behind the hall door and you stole from me a dollar and put it in your pocket, I thought I saw you before in some place but I didn't know where. That day you saved me from the gas I almost recognized you; then when I was laying in bed I had nothing to think about, only my worries and how I threw away my life in this store, then I remembered when you first came here, when we sat at this table, you told me you always did the wrong thing in your life; this minute when I remembered this I said to myself, 'Frank is the one that made on me the holdup.'"

"Morris," Frank said hoarsely, "I am sorry."

Morris was too unhappy to speak. Though he pitied the clerk, he did not want a confessed criminal around. Even if he had reformed, what good would it do to keep him here— another mouth to feed, another pair of eyes to the death watch?

"Did you tell Helen what I did?" sighed Frank.

"Helen ain't interested in you."

"One last chance, Morris," the clerk pleaded.

"Who was the antisimeet that he hit me on the head?"

"Ward Minogue," Frank said after a minute. "He's sick now."

"Ah," sighed Morris, "the poor father."

"We meant to hold Karp up, not you. Please let me stay one more month. I'll pay for my own food and also my rent."

"With what will you pay if I don't pay you—with my debts?"

"I have a little job at night after the store closes. I make a few odd bucks."

"No," said the grocer.

"Morris, you need my help here. You don't know how bad everything is."

But the grocer had set his heart against his assistant and would not let him stay.

Frank hung up his apron and left the store. Later, he bought a suitcase and packed his few things. When he returned Nick's radio, he said good-by to Tessie.

"Where are you going now, Frank?"

"I don't know."

"Are you ever coming back?"

"I don't know. Say good-by to Nick."

Before leaving, Frank wrote a note to Helen, once more saying he was sorry for the wrong he had done her. He wrote she was the finest girl he had ever met. He had bitched up his life. Helen wept over the note but had no thought of answering.

Although Morris liked the improvements Frank had made in the store he saw at once that they had not the least effect on business. Business was terrible. And with Frank's going the income shrank impossibly lower, a loss of ten terrible dollars from the previous week. He thought he had seen the store at its worst but this brought him close to fainting.

"What will we do?" he desperately asked his wife and

daughter, huddled in their overcoats one Sunday night in the unheated back of the store.

"What else?" Ida said, "give right away in auction."

"The best thing is to sell even if we have to give away," Morris argued. "If we sell the store we can also make something on the house. Then I can pay my debts and have maybe a couple thousand dollars. But if we give in auction how can I sell the house?"

"So if we sell who will buy?" Ida snapped.

"Can't we auction off the store without going into bankruptcy?" Helen asked.

"If we auction we will get nothing. Then when the store is empty and it stays for rent, nobody will buy the house. There are already two places for rent on this block. If the wholesalers hear I went in auction they will force me in bankruptcy and take away the house also. But if we sell the store, then we can get a better price for the house."

"Nobody will buy," Ida said. "I told you when to sell but you wouldn't listen."

"Suppose you did sell the house and store," Helen asked, "what would you do then?"

"Maybe I could find a small place, maybe a candy store. If I could find a partner we could open up a store in a nice neighborhood."

Ida groaned. "Penny candy I won't sell. Also a partner we had already, he should drop dead."

"Couldn't you look for a job?" Helen said.

"Who will give me at my age a job?" Morris asked.

"You're acquainted with some people in the business," she answered. "Maybe somebody could get you a cashier's job in a supermarket."

"You want your father to stand all day on his feet with his varicose veins?" Ida asked.

"It would be better than sitting in the freezing back of an empty store."

"So what will we do?" Morris asked, but nobody answered.

Upstairs, Ida told Helen that things would be better if she got married.

"Who should I marry, Mama?"

"Louis Karp," said Ida.

The next evening she visited Karp when he was alone in the liquor store and told him their troubles. The liquor dealer whistled through his teeth.

Ida said, "You remember last November you wanted to send us a man by the name Podolsky, a refugee he was interested to go in the grocery business?"

"Yes. He said he would come here but he caught a cold in his chest."

"Did he buy some place a store?"

"Not yet," Karp said cautiously.

"He still wants to buy?"

"Maybe. But how could I recommend him a store like yours?"

"Don't recommend him the store, recommend him the price. Morris will sell now for two thousand cash. If he wants the house we will give him a good price. The refugee is young, he can fix up the business and give the goyim a good competition."

"Maybe I'll call him sometime," Karp remarked. He casually inquired about Helen. Surely she would be getting married soon?

Ida faced the way she hoped the wind was blowing. "Tell Louis not to be so bashful. Helen is lonely and wants to go out with somebody."

Karp coughed into his fist. "I don't see your clerk any more. How is that?" He spoke offhandedly, walking carefully, knowing the size of his big feet.

"Frank," Ida said solemnly, "don't work for us any more. Morris told him to leave, so he left last week."

Karp raised bushy brows. "Maybe," he said slowly, "I will call Podolsky and tell him to come tomorrow night. He works in the day."

"In the morning is the best time. Comes in then a few Morris's old customers."

"I will tell him to take off Wednesday morning," Karp said.

He later told Louis what Ida had said about Helen, but Louis, looking up from clipping his fingernails, said she wasn't his type.

"When you got gelt in your pocket any woman is your type," Karp said.

"Not her."

"We will see."

The next afternoon Karp came into Morris's and speaking as if they were the happiest of friends, advised the grocer: "Let Podolsky look around here but not too long. Also keep your mouth shut about the business. Don't try to sell him anything. When he finishes in here he will come to my house and I will explain him what's what."

Morris, hiding his feelings, nodded. He felt he had to get away from the store, from Karp, before he collapsed. Reluctantly he agreed to do as the liquor dealer suggested.

Early Wednesday morning Podolsky arrived, a shy young man in a thick greenish suit that looked as if it had been made out of a horse blanket. He wore a small foreign-looking hat and carried a loose umbrella. His face was innocent and his eyes glistened with good will.

Morris, uneasy at what he was engaged in, invited Podolsky into the back, where Ida nervously awaited him, but the refugee tipped his hat and said he would stay in the store. He slid into the corner near the door and nothing could drag him out. Luckily, a few customers dribbled in, and Podolsky watched with interest as Morris professionally handled them.

When the store was empty, the grocer tried to make casual talk from behind the counter, but Podolsky, though constantly clearing his throat, had little to say. Overwhelmed by pity for the poor refugee, at what he had in all probability lived through, a man who had sweated blood to save a few brutal dollars, Morris, unable to stand the planned dishonesty, came from behind the counter, and taking Podolsky by the coat lapels, told him earnestly that the store was run-down but that a boy with his health and strength, with modern methods and a little cash, could build it up in a reasonable time and make a decent living out of it.

Ida shrilly called from the kitchen she needed the grocer to help her peel potatoes, but Morris kept on talking till he was swimming in his sea of woes; then he recalled Karp's warning, and though he felt more than ever that the liquor dealer was thoroughly an ass, abruptly broke off the story he was telling. Yet before he could tear himself away from the refugee, he remarked, "I could sell for two thousand, but for fifteen-sixteen cash, anybody who wants it can take the store. The house we will talk about later. Is this reasonable?"

"Why not?" Podolsky murmured, then again clammed up.

Morris retreated into the kitchen. Ida looked at him as if he had committed murder but did not speak. Two or three more people appeared, then after ten-thirty the dry trickle of customers stopped. Ida grew fidgety and tried to think of ways to get Podolsky out of the place but he stayed on. She asked him to come into the back for a glass of tea; he courteously refused. She remarked that Karp must now be anxious to see him; Podolsky bobbed his head and stayed. He tightened the cloth around his umbrella stick. Not know-ing what else to say she absently promised to leave him all her recipes for salads. He thanked her, to her surprise, pro-fusely.

From half past ten to twelve nobody approached the store. Morris went down to the cellar and hid. Ida sat dully in the back. Podolsky waited in his corner. Nobody saw as he eased himself and his black umbrella out of the grocery and fled.

On Thursday morning Morris spat on his shoebrush and polished his shoes. He was wearing his suit. He rang the hall bell for Ida to come down, then put on his hat and coat, old but neat because he rarely used them. Dressed, he rang up "no sale" and hesitantly pocketed eight quarters.

He was on his way to Charlie Sobeloff, an old partner.

Years ago, Charlie, a cross-eyed but clever conniver, had come to the grocer with a meager thousand dollars in his pocket, borrowed money, and offered to go into partnership with him—Morris to furnish four thousand—to buy a grocery Charlie had in mind. The grocer disliked Charlie's nervousness and pale cross-eyes, one avoiding what the other looked at; but he was persuaded by the man's nagging enthusiasm and they bought the store. It was a good business, Morris thought, and he was satisfied. But Charlie, who had taken accountancy in night school, said he would handle the books, and Morris, in spite of Ida's warnings, consented, because, the grocer argued, the books were always in front of his eyes for inspection. But Charlie's talented nose had sniffed the right sucker. Morris never looked at the books until, two years after they had bought the place, the business collapsed.

The grocer, stunned, heartbroken, could not at first understand what had happened, but Charlie had figures to prove that the calamity had been bound to occur. The overhead was too high—they had paid themselves too high wages—his fault, Charlie admitted; also profits were low, the price of goods increasing. Morris now knew that his partner had, behind his back, cheated, manipulated, stolen whatever lay loose. They sold the place for a miserable price, Morris going out dazed, cleaned out, whereas Charlie in a short time was able to raise the cash to repurchase and restock the store, which he gradually worked into a thriving self-service business. For years the two had not met, but within the last four or five years, the ex-partner, when he returned from his winters in Miami, for reasons unknown to Morris, sought out the grocer and sat with him in the back, his eyes roving, his ringed fingers drumming on the table as he talked on about old times when they were young. Morris, through the years, had lost his hatred of the man, though Ida still could not stand him, and it was to Charlie Sobeloff that the grocer, with a growing sense of panic, had decided to run for help, a job—anything.

When Ida came down and saw Morris, in his hat and coat, standing moodily by the door, she said in surprise, "Morris, where you going?"

"I go to my grave," the grocer said.

Seeing he was overwrought, she cried out, clasping her hands to her bosom. "Where do you go, tell me?"

He had the door open. "I go for a job."

"Come back," she cried in anger. "Who will give you?"

But he knew what she would say and was already in the street.

As he went quickly past Karp's he noticed that Louis had five customers—drunkards all—lined up at the counter and was doing a thriving business in brown bottles. *He* had sold only two quarts of milk in four hours. Although it shamed him, Morris wished the liquor store would burn to the ground.

At the corner he paused, overwhelmed by the necessity of choosing a direction. He hadn't remembered that space provided so many ways to go. He chose without joy. The day, though breezy, was not bad—it promised better, but he had little love left for nature. It gave nothing to a Jew. The March wind hastened him along, prodding the shoulders. He felt weightless, unmanned, the victim in motion of whatever blew at his back; wind, worries, debts, Karp, holdupniks, ruin. He did not go, he was pushed. He had the will of a victim, no will to speak of.

"For what I worked so hard for? Where is my youth, where did it go?"

The years had passed without profit or pity. Who could he blame? What fate didn't do to him he had done to himself. The right thing was to make the right choice but he made the wrong. Even when it was right it was wrong. To understand why, you needed an education but he had none. All he knew was he wanted better but had not after all these years learned how to get it. Luck was a gift. Karp had it, a few of his old friends had it, well-to-do men with grandchildren already, while his poor daughter, made in his image,

faced—if not actively sought—old-maidhood. Life was meager, the world changed for the worse. America had become
too complicated. One man counted for nothing. There were
too many stores, depressions, anxieties. What had he escaped
to here?

The subway was crowded and he had to stand till a pregnant woman, getting off, signaled him to her seat. He was
ashamed to take it but nobody else moved, so he sat down.
After a while he began to feel at ease, thought he would be
satisfied to ride on like this, provided he never got to where
he was going. But he did. At Myrtle Avenue he groaned softly,
and left the train.

Arriving at Sobeloff's Self-Service Market, Morris, although
he had heard of the growth of the place from Al Marcus,
was amazed at its size. Charlie had tripled the original space
by buying the building next door and knocking out the wall
between the stores, later running an extension three-quarters
of the way into the back yards. The result was a huge market
with a large number of stalls and shelved sections loaded
with groceries. The supermarket was so crowded with people that to Morris, as he peered half-scared through the window, it looked like a department store. He felt a pang, thinking that part of this might now be his if he had taken care
of what he had once owned. He would not envy Charlie
Sobeloff his dishonest wealth, but when he thought of what
he could do for Helen with a little money his regret deepened that he had nothing.

He spied Charlie standing near the fruit stalls, the bala-
bos, surveying the busy scene with satisfaction. He wore a
gray Homburg and blue serge suit, but under the unbuttoned
suit jacket he had tied a folded apron around his silk-shirted
paunch, and wandered around, thus attired, overseeing. The
grocer, looking through the window, saw himself opening
the door and walking the long half block to where Charlie
was standing.

He tried to speak but was unable to, until after so much
silence the boss said he was busy, so say it.

"You got for me, Charlie," muttered the grocer, "a job?

Maybe a cashier or something? My business is bad, I am going in auction."

Charlie, still unable to look straight at him, smiled. "I got five steady cashiers but maybe I can use you part time. Hang up your coat in the locker downstairs and I'll give you directions what to do."

Morris saw himself putting on a white duck jacket with "Sobeloff's Self-Service" stitched in red over the region of the heart. He would stand several hours a day at the checking counter, packing, adding, ringing up the cash into one of Charlie's massive chromium registers. At quitting time, the boss would come over to check his money.

"You're short a dollar, Morris," Charlie said with a little chuckle, "but we will let it go."

"No," the grocer heard himself say. "I am short a dollar, so I will pay a dollar."

He took several quarters out of his pants pocket, counted four, and dropped them into his ex-partner's palm. Then he announced he was through, hung up his starched jacket, slipped on his coat and walked with dignity to the door. He joined the one at the window and soon went away.

Morris clung to the edge of a silent knot of men who drifted along Sixth Avenue, stopping at the employment agency doors to read impassively the list of jobs chalked up on the blackboard signs. There were openings for cooks, bakers, waiters, porters, handymen. Once in a while one of the men would secretly detach himself from the others and go into the agency. Morris followed along with them to Forty-fourth Street, where he noted a job listed for countermen behind a steam counter in a cafeteria. He went one flight up a narrow staircase and into a room that smelled of tobacco smoke. The grocer stood there, uncomfortable, until the big-faced owner of the agency happened to look up over the roll-top desk he was sitting at.

"You looking for something, mister?"

"Counterman," Morris said.

"You got experience?"

"Thirty years."

The owner laughed. "You're the champ but they want a kid they can pay twenty a week."

"You got something for a man my experience?"

"Can you slice sandwich meat nice and thin?"

"The best."

"Come back next week, I might have something for you."

The grocer continued along with the crowd. At Forty-seventh Street he applied for a waiter's job in a kosher restaurant but the agency had filled the job and forgotten to erase it from their sign.

"So what else you got for me?" Morris asked the manager.

"What work do you do?"

"I had my own store, grocery and delicatessen."

"So why do you ask for waiter?"

"I didn't see for counterman anything."

"How old are you?"

"Fifty-five."

"I should live so long till you see fifty-five again," said the manager. As Morris turned to go the man offered him a cigarette but the grocer said his cough kept him from smoking.

At Fiftieth he went up a dark staircase and sat on a wooden bench at the far end of a long room.

The boss of the agency, a man with a broad back and a fat rear, holding a dead cigar butt between stubby fingers, had his heavy foot on a chair as he talked in a low voice to two gray-hatted Filipinos.

Seeing Morris on the bench he called out, "Whaddye want, pop?"

"Nothing. I sit on account I am tired."

"Go home," said the boss.

He went downstairs and had coffee at a dish-laden table in the Automat.

America.

Morris rode the bus to East Thirteenth Street, where Breit-bard lived. He hoped the peddler would be home but only his son Hymie was. The boy was sitting in the kitchen, eating cornflakes with milk and reading the comics.

"What time comes home papa?" Morris asked.

"About seven, maybe eight," Hymie mumbled.

Morris sat down to rest. Hymie ate, and read the comics. He had big restless eyes.

"How old are you?"

"Fourteen."

The grocer got up. He found two quarters in his pocket and left them on the table. "Be a good boy. Your father loves you."

He got into the subway at Union Square and rode to the Bronx, to the apartment house where Al Marcus lived. He felt sure Al would help him find something. He would be satisfied, he thought, with little, maybe a night watchman's job.

When he rang Al's bell, a well-dressed woman with sad eyes came to the door.

"Excuse me," said Morris. "My name is Mr. Bober. I am an old-time customer Al Marcus's. I came to see him."

"I am Mrs. Margolies, his sister-in-law."

"If he ain't home I will wait."

"You'll wait a long time," she said, "they took him to the hospital yesterday."

Though he knew why he couldn't help asking.

"Can you go on living if you're already dead?"

When the grocer got home in the cold twilight Ida took one look at him and began to cry.

"What did I tell you?"

That night Morris, alone in the store after Ida had gone up to soak her poor feet, felt an uncontrollable craving for some heavy sweet cream. He remembered the delicious taste of bread dipped in rich milk when he was a boy. He found a half-pint bottle of whipping cream in the refrigerator and took it, guiltily, with a loaf of stale white bread, into the back. Pouring some cream into a saucer, he soaked it up with bread, greedily wolfing the cream-laden bread.

A noise in the store startled him. He hid the cream and bread in the gas range.

At the counter stood a skinny man in an old hat and a dark overcoat down to his ankles. His nose was long, throat gaunt, and he wore a whisp of red beard on his bony chin.

"A gut shabos," said the scarecrow.

"A gut shabos," Morris answered, though shabos was a day away.

"It smells here," said the skinny stranger, his small eyes shrewd, "like a open grave."

"Business is bad."

The man wet his lips and whispered, "Insurinks you got —fire insurinks?"

Morris was frightened. "What is your business?"

"How much?"

"How much what?"

"A smart man hears one word but he understand two. How much you got insurinks?"

"Two thousand for the store."

"Feh."

"Five thousand for the house."

"A shame. Should be ten."

"Who needs ten for this house?"

"Nobody knows."

"What do you want here?" Morris asked, irritated.

The man rubbed his skinny, red-haired hands. "What does a macher want?"

"What kind of a macher? What do you make?"

He shrugged slyly. "I make a living." The macher spoke soundlessly. "I make fires."

Morris drew back.

The macher waited with downcast eyes. "We are poor people," he murmured.

"What do you want from me?"

"We are poor people," the macher said, apologetically. "God loves the poor people but he helps the rich. The insurinks companies are rich. They take away your money and what they give you? Nothing. Don't feel sorry for the in-surinks companies."

He proposed a fire. He would make it swiftly, safely, eco-nomically—guaranteed to collect.

From his coat pocket he produced a strip of celluloid. "You know what is this?"

Morris, staring at it, preferred not to say.

"Celluloy," hissed the macher. He struck a large yellow match and lit the celluloid. It flared instantly. He held it a second then let it fall to the counter, where it quickly burned itself out. With a *poof* he blew away nothing. Only the stench remained, floating in air.

"Magic," he hoarsely announced. "No ashes. This is why we use celluloy, not paper, not rags. You push a piece in a crack, and the fire burns in a minute. Then when comes the fire marshal and insurinks investigator, what they find?—nothing. For nothing they pay cash—two thousand for the store, five for the house." A smile crawled over his face.

Morris shivered. "You want me I should burn down my house and my store to collect the insurance?"

"I want," said the macher slyly, "tsu you want?"

The grocer fell silent.

"Take," said the macher persuasively, "your family and go for a ride to Cunyiland. When you come back is the job finished. Cost—five hundred." He lightly dusted his fingers.

"Upstairs lives two people," muttered the grocer.

"When they go out?"

"Sometimes to the movies, Friday night." He spoke dully, not sure why he was revealing secrets to a total stranger.

"So let be Friday night. I am not kosher."

"But who's got five hundred dollars?"

The macher's face fell. He sighed deeply. "I will make for two hundred. I will do a good job. You will get six—seven thousand. After, pay me another three hundred."

But Morris had decided. "Impossible."

"You don't like the price?"

"I don't like fires. I don't like monkey business."

The macher argued another half hour and departed reluctantly.

The next night a car pulled up in front of the door, and the grocer watched Nick and Tessie, dressed for a party, get in and drive off. Twenty minutes later Ida and Helen came down to go to a movie. Helen had asked her mother to go with her, and Ida said yes, seeing how restless her daughter was. When he realized that the house was deserted, Morris felt suddenly agitated.

After ten minutes, he went up the stairs, and searched in a camphor-smelling trunk in the small room for a celluloid collar he had once worn. Ida saved everything, but he couldn't locate it. He searched in Helen's bureau drawer and found an envelope full of picture negatives. Discarding several of her as a school girl, Morris took some of boys in bathing suits, nobody he recognized. Hurrying down, he found matches and went into the cellar. He thought that one of the bins would be a good place to start the fire but settled instead on the air shaft. The flames would shoot up in an instant, and through the open toilet window into the store. Gooseflesh crept over him. He figured he could start the fire and wait in the hall. Once the flames had got a good start, he would rush into the street and ring the alarm. He could later say he had fallen asleep on the couch and had been awakened by the smoke. By the time the fire engines came, the house would be badly damaged. The hoses and axes would do the rest.

Morris inserted the celluloid strips into a crack between two boards, on the inside of the dumb-waiter. His hand shook and he whispered to himself as he touched the match to the negatives. Then the flame shot up in a stupefying stench and at once crawled up the wall of the dumb-waiter. Morris watched, hypnotized, then let out a terrible cry. Slapping frantically at the burning negatives, he knocked them to the cellar floor. As he hunted for something with which to beat out the fire in the dumb-waiter, he discovered that the bottom of his apron was burning. He smacked the flames with both hands and then his sweater sleeves began to blaze. He sobbed for God's mercy, and was at once roughly seized from behind and flung to the ground.

Frank Alpine smothered the grocer's burning clothes with his overcoat. He banged out the fire in the dumb-waiter with his shoe.

Morris moaned.

"For Christ sake," Frank pleaded, "take me back here."

But the grocer ordered him out of the house.

aturday night, about one A.M. Karp's store began to burn.

In the early evening, Ward Minogue had knocked on Frank's door and learned from Tessie that the clerk had moved.

"Where to?"

"I don't know. Ask Mr. Bober," Tessie said, anxious to get rid of him.

Downstairs, Ward peered through the grocery window and seeing Morris, hurriedly withdrew. Though alcohol nauseated him lately, his thirst for a drink was killing him. He thought if he could get a couple of swigs past the nausea he would feel better. But all he had in his pocket was a dime, so he went into Karp's and begged Louis to trust him to a cheap fifth of anything.

"I wouldn't trust you for a fifth of sewer water," Louis said.

Ward grabbed a bottle of wine from the counter and flung it at Louis' head. He ducked but the wine smashed some bottles on the shelf. As Louis, yelling murder, rushed into the street, Ward snatched a bottle of whiskey and ran out of the store and up the block. He had gone past the butcher's when the bottle slipped from under his arm and broke on the sidewalk. Ward looked back with anguish but kept on running.

By the time the cops came Ward had disappeared. After supper that night, Detective Minogue, roaming the cold streets, saw his son in Earl's bar, standing over a beer. The detective went in by the side door but Ward saw him in the mirror and bolted out the front. Although short of breath, driven by great fear, he ran toward the coal yard. Hearing his father behind him, Ward leaped across the rusted chain stretched in front of the loading platform and sped over the cobblestones toward the back of the yard. He scrambled under one of the trucks in the shed.

The detective, calling him filthy names, hunted him in the dark for fifteen minutes. Then he took out his pistol and fired a shot into the shed. Ward, thinking he would be killed, crawled out from under the truck and ran into his father's arms.

Though he pleaded with the detective not to hurt him, crying he had diabetes and would surely get gangrene, his father beat him mercilessly with his billy until Ward collapsed.

Bending over him, the detective yelled, "I told you to stay the hell out of this neighborhood. This is my last warning to you. If I ever see you again, I'll murder you." He dusted his coat and left the coal yard.

Ward lay on the cobblestones. His nose had been gushing blood but it soon stopped. Getting up, he felt so dizzy he wept. He staggered into the shed and climbed into the cab of one of the coal trucks, thinking he would sleep there. But when he lit a cigarette he was overcome with nausea. Ward threw the butt out and waited for the nausea to leave him. When it did he was thirsty again. If he could climb the coal yard fence, then some of the smaller ones beyond it, he would land up in Karp's back yard. He knew from having cased the place once that the liquor store had a barred window in the back, but that the rusty iron bars were old and loose. He thought that if he got his strength back he could force them apart.

He dragged himself over the coal yard fence, then more slowly over the others until he stood at last in Karp's weedy back yard. The liquor store had been closed since midnight and there were no lights burning in the house. Above the dark grocery one of Bober's windows was lit, so he had to be careful or the Jew might hear him.

Twice, at intervals of ten minutes, he tried to bend the bars but failed. The third time, straining till he shook, he slowly forced the inside two apart. The window was unlocked. Ward got his fingertips under it and lifted it with care because it squeaked. When it was open, he squeezed through the bent bars, squirming into the back of the liquor store. Once in there he laughed a little to himself and moved around freely, knowing Karp was too cheap to have a burglar alarm. From the stock in the rear Ward sampled and spat out three different brands of whiskey. Forcing himself, he gurgled down a third of a bottle of gin. In a couple of minutes he forgot his aches and pains and lost the sorrow he had been feeling for himself. He snickered when he imagined Louis' comic puss as he found the empty bottles all over the floor in the morning. Remembering the cash register, Ward staggered out front and rang it open. It was empty. He angrily smashed a whiskey bottle on it. A feeling of nausea gagged him and with a croak he threw up over Karp's counter. Feeling better, he began by the light of the street lamp to smash the whiskey bottles against the cash register.

Mike Papadopolous, whose bedroom was right above the front part of the liquor store, was awakened by the noise. After five minutes he figured something was wrong so he got up and dressed. Ward had, in the meantime, destroyed a whole shelf of bottles, when he felt a hunger to smoke. It took him two minutes to get a match struck and the light touching his butt. He tasted the smoke with pleasure as the flame briefly lit his face, then he shook the match and flipped it over his shoulder. It landed, still burning, in a puddle of alcohol. The fire flew up with a zoom. Ward, lit like a flaming tree, flailed at himself. Screaming, he ran through the back and tried to get out of the window but was caught between the bars and, exhausted, died.

Smelling smoke, Mike came down in a rush and seeing fire in the store, raced to the drugstore corner to turn in the alarm. As he was running back, the plate glass window of the liquor store exploded and a roaring flame boiled up in the place. After Mike had got his mother and the upstairs tenants out of the house, he ran into Bober's hall, shouting there was a fire next door. They were all up—Helen, who had been reading when the window crashed, had run up to call Nick and Tessie. They left the house, bundled in sweaters and overcoats, and stood across the street, huddled together with some passers-by, watching the fire destroy Karp's once prosperous business, then devour the house. Despite the heavy streams of water the firemen poured into the flames, the fire, fed by the blazing alcohol, rose to the roof, and when it was at last smothered, all that was left of Karp's property was a gutted, dripping shell.

As the firemen began with grappling hooks to tear out the burned fixtures and heave them onto the sidewalk, everybody fell silent. Ida moaned softly, with shut eyes thinking of Morris's burned sweater that she had found in the cellar, and the singed hair she had noticed on his hands. Sam Pearl, lost without his bifocals, mumbled to himself. Nat, hatless, an overcoat on over pajamas, edged close to Helen until he stood by her side. Morris was fighting a tormenting emotion.

A car drew up and parked beyond the drugstore. Karp got out with Louis and they crossed the hose-filled street to their store. Karp took one unbearable look at his former gesheft, and though it was for the most part insured, tottered forward and collapsed. Louis yelled at him to wake up. Two of the firemen carried the stricken liquor dealer to his car, and Louis frantically drove him home.

Afterward Morris couldn't sleep. He stood at his bedroom window in his long underwear, looking down at the pile of burned and broken fixtures on the sidewalk. With a frozen hand the grocer clawed at a live pain in his breast. He felt an overwhelming hatred of himself. He had wished it on Karp—just this. His anguish was terrible.

Sunday, the last of March, was overcast at eight A.M., and there were snow flurries in the air. Winter still spits in my face, thought the weary grocer. He watched the fat wet flakes melt as they touched the ground. It's too warm for snow, he thought, tomorrow will come April. Maybe. He had awakened with a wound, a gap in his side, a hole in the ground he might fall through if he stepped outside where the liquor store had been. But the earth held him up and the odd feeling wore off. It went as he reflected it was no use mourning Karp's loss; his pocketbook would protect him from too much pain. Pain was for poor people. For Karp's tenants the fire was a tragedy, and for Ward Minogue, dead young; maybe also for the detective, but not for Julius Karp. Morris could have used the fire, so Karp had got it for free. Everything to him who has.

As the grocer was thinking this, the liquor dealer, apparently the victim of a sleepless night, appeared in the falling snow and entered the grocery. He wore a narrow-brimmed hat with a foolish little feather in the band and a double-breasted overcoat, but despite his stylish appearance, his eyes, with dark bags under them, were filled with gloom, his complexion pasty, lips blue. Where his forehead had smacked the sidewalk last night he wore a plaster patch—an unhappy figure, the loss of his business the worst that could happen to him. He couldn't stand the vision of dollars he might be taking in, flying daily away. Karp seemed embarrassed, ill. The grocer, his shame awakened, invited him into the back for tea. Ida, also up early, made a fuss over him.

Karp took a hot sip or two of tea, but after setting the cup down, hadn't the strength to lift it from the saucer. After a fidgety silence he spoke. "Morris, I want to buy your house. Also the store." He drew a deep, trembly breath.

Ida let out a stifled cry. Morris was stupefied.

"What for? The business is terrible."

"Not so terrible," cried Ida.

"Don't interest me the grocery business," Karp gloomily

replied. "Only the location. Next door," he said, but couldn't go on.

They understood.

He explained it would take months to rebuild his house and place of business. But if he took over Morris's store he could have it refixtured, painted, stocked in a couple of weeks, thus keeping to a minimum his loss of trade.

Morris couldn't believe his ears. He was filled with excitement and dread that somebody would tell him he had just dreamed a dream, or that Karp, fat fish, would turn into a fat bird and fly away, screeching, "Don't you believe me," or in some heartbreaking way change his mind.

So he put his foot on anticipation and kept his mouth shut, but when Karp asked him to name his price the grocer had one ready. "Nine thousand for the house—three down, my equity—and for the store twenty-five hundred cash." After all, bad as it was, the grocery was a going business, and for the refrigerator alone he had paid nine hundred dollars. With trepidation he figured a fair fifty-five hundred in cash in his hands, enough after he had paid his debts to look for a new business. Seeing Ida's astonished expression, he was surprised at his nerve and thought Karp would surely laugh him in the face and offer less—which he would grab anyway; but the liquor dealer listlessly nodded. "I will give you twenty-five hundred for the store, less the auction price of stock and fixtures."

"This is your business," Morris replied.

Karp could not bear to discuss the terms any further. "My lawyer will draw the contract."

When he left the grocery, the liquor dealer vanished in the swirling snow. Ida wept joyfully, while Morris, still stunned, reflected that his luck had changed. So had Karp's, for what Karp had lost he had in a sense gained, as if to make up for the misery the man had caused him in the past. Yesterday he wouldn't have believed how things would balance out today.

The spring snow moved Morris profoundly. He watched it falling, seeing in it scenes of his childhood, remembering things he thought he had forgotten. All morning he watched the shifting snow. He thought of himself, a boy running in it, whooping at blackbirds as they flew from the snowy trees; he felt an irresistible thirst to be out in the open.

"I think I will shovel the snow," he told Ida at lunchtime.

"Go better to sleep."

"It ain't nice for the customers."

"What customers—who needs them?"

"People can't walk in such high snow," he argued.

"Wait, tomorrow it will be melted."

"It's Sunday, it don't look so nice for the goyim that they go to church."

Her voice had an edge to it. "You want to catch pneumonia, Morris?"

"It's spring," he murmured.

"It's winter."

"I will wear my hat and coat."

"Your feet will get wet. You have no galoshes."

"Only five minutes."

"No," she said flatly.

Later, he thought.

All afternoon the snow came softly down and by evening it had reached a depth of six inches. When the snowing stopped, a wind rose and blew clouds of it through the streets. He watched at the front window.

Ida hung over him all day. He didn't get out till late. After closing he had sat relentlessly over a piece of store paper, writing a long list, until she grew impatient.

"Why do you stay so late?"

"I figure the stock for the auctioneer."

"This is Karp's business."

"I must help, he don't know the prices."

Talk of the store's sale relieved her. "Come up soon," she yawned.

He waited until he felt she was asleep, then went down to the cellar for the shovel. He put on his hat and a pair of old gloves and stepped out into the street. To his surprise the wind wrapped him in an icy jacket, his apron flapping noisily.

He had expected, the last of March, a milder night. The surprise lingered in his mind but the shoveling warmed him. He kept his back to Karp's burned hole, though with the black turned white it wasn't too hard to look at.

Scooping up a shovelful of snow he heaved it into the street. It turned to dust in mid-air and whirled whitely away.

He recalled the hard winters when he had first come to America. After about fifteen years they turned mild but now they were hard again. It had been a hard life, but now with God's help he would have an easier time.

He flung another load of snow into the street. "A better life," he muttered.

Nick and Tessie came home from somewhere.

"At least put something warm on, Mr. Bober," advised Tessie.

"I'm almost finished," Morris grunted.

"It's your health," said Nick.

The first floor window shot up. Ida stood there in her flannel nightgown, her hair down.

"Are you crazy?" she shouted to the grocer.

"Finished," he answered.

"Without a coat—are you crazy?"

"Took me ten minutes."

Nick and Tessie went into the house.

"Come up now," Ida shouted.

"Finished," Morris cried. He heaved a last angry shovelful into the gutter. A little of the sidewalk remained to be cleaned but now that she was nagging he felt too tired to do it.

Morris dragged the wet shovel into the store. The warmth struck him across the head. He felt himself reeling and had a momentary fright but after a glass of hot tea with lemon felt rested.

As he was drinking the tea it began to snow again. He watched a thousand flakes push at the window, as if they wanted to snow through the glass and in the kitchen. He saw the snow as a moving curtain, and then he saw it in lit single flakes, not touching each other.

Ida banged hard on the floor, so he finally closed and went upstairs.

She was sitting in her bathrobe with Helen in the living room, her eyes dark with anger. "Are you a baby you had to go out in the snow? What's the matter with such a man?"

"I had my hat on. What am I, tissue paper?"

"You had pneumonia," she shouted.

"Mama, lower your voice," Helen said, "they'll hear upstairs."

"Who asked him to shovel snow, for God's sakes?"

"For twenty-two years stinks in my nose this store. I wanted to smell in my lungs some fresh air."

"Not in the ice cold."

"Tomorrow is April."

"Anyway," Helen said, "don't tempt fate, Papa."

"What kind of winter can be in April?"

"Come to sleep." Ida marched off to bed.

He sat with Helen on the couch. Since hearing of Karp's visit that morning she had lost her moodiness, looked again like a happy girl. He thought with sadness how pretty she was. He wanted to give her something—only good.

"How do you feel that I am selling the house and store?" he asked her.

"You know how I feel."

"Tell me anyway."

"Refreshed."

"We will move to a better neighborhood like you like. I will find a better parnusseh. You will keep your wages."

She smiled at him.

"I remember when you were a little baby," Morris said.

She kissed his hand.

"I want the most you should be happy."

"I will be." Her eyes grew wet. "If you only knew all the good things I'd like to give you, Papa."

"You gave me."

"I'll give you better."

"Look how it snows," said Morris.

They watched the snow through the moving windows, then Morris said good night.

"Sleep well," Helen said.

But he lay in bed restless, almost dejected. There was so much to do, so many changes to make and get used to. To-morrow was the day Karp would bring the deposit. Tuesday the auctioneer would come and they would go over the goods and fixtures. Wednesday they could hold the auction. Thurs-day, for the first time in almost a generation, he would be without a place of business. Such a long time. After so many years in one place he hated the thought of having to get used to another. He disliked leaving the neighborhood though he hadn't liked it. It made him uncomfortable to be in a strange place. He thought uneasily of having to locate, appraise, and buy a new store. He would prefer to live above the store, but Helen wanted them to take a small apartment, so let it be a small apartment. Once he had the store he would let them look for a place to live. But the store he would have to find himself. What he feared most was that he would make an-other mistake and again settle in a prison. The possibility of this worried him intensely. Why would the owner want to sell? Would he be an honest man or, underneath, a thief? And once he had bought the place, would business keep up or go down? Would times stay good? Would he make a living? His thoughts exhausted him. He could feel his poor heart running a race against the merciless future.

He fell heavily asleep but awoke in a couple of hours, drenched in hot sweat. Yet his feet were freezing and he knew that if he kept his thoughts on them he would break into shivering. Then his right shoulder began to hurt, and when he forced himself to take a deep breath, his left side pained him. He knew he was sick and was miserably disappointed. He lay in the dark, trying not to think how stupid it had been to shovel the snow. He must have caught a chill. He thought he would not. He thought he was entitled, after twenty-two years, to a few minutes of freedom. Now his plans would have to wait, although Ida could finish the business with Karp and make arrangements with the auctioneer. Gradually he accepted the thought that he had a cold—maybe flu. He considered waking her to call a doctor but who could they call without a telephone? And if Helen got dressed and used Sam Pearl's phone, what an embarrassment that would be, waking up a whole family when she rang their bell; also arousing a doctor out of his precious sleep, who would say after examining him, "Mister, what's all the excitement? You got the flu, so stay in bed." For such advice he didn't need to call a doctor in his nightshirt. He could wait a few hours till morning. Morris dozed but felt fever shake him in his sleep. He awoke with his hair stiff. Maybe he had pneumonia? After a while he grew calmer. He was sick but sickness was nothing new to him. Probably if he hadn't shoveled snow he would have got sick anyway. In the last few days he hadn't felt so well—headachy, weak in the knees. Yet though he tried to resign himself to what had happened, he felt enormously bitter that he had become ill. So he had shoveled snow in the street, but did it have to snow in April? And if it did, did he have to get sick the minute he stepped out into the open air? It frustrated him hopelessly that every move he made seemed to turn into an inevitable thing.

He dreamed of Ephraim. He had recognized him when the dream began by his brown eyes, clearly his father's. Ephraim wore a beanie cut from the crown of an old hat of Morris's, covered with buttons and shiny pins, but the rest of him was in rags. Though he did not for some reason expect otherwise, this and that the boy looked hungry shocked the grocer.

"I gave you to eat three times a day, Ephraim," he explained, "so why did you leave so soon your father?"

Ephraim was too shy to answer, but Morris, in a rush of love for him—a child was so small at that age—promised him a good start in life.

"Don't worry, I'll give you a fine college education."

Ephraim—a gentleman—averted his face as he snickered.

"I give you my word . . ."

The boy disappeared in the wake of laughter.

"Stay alive," his father cried after him.

When the grocer felt himself awaking, he tried to get back into the dream but it easily evaded him. His eyes were wet. He thought of his life with sadness. For his family he had not provided, the poor man's disgrace. Ida was asleep at his side. He wanted to awaken her and apologize. He thought of Helen. It would be terrible if she became an old maid. He moaned a little, thinking of Frank. His mood was of regret. I gave away my life for nothing. It was the thunderous truth.

Was the snow still falling?

Morris died in the hospital, three days later, and was buried the day after in an enormous cemetery—it went on for miles —in Queens. He had been a member of a burial society since coming to America and the services took place in the Society's funeral parlor on the Lower East Side, where the grocer had lived as a young man. At noon in the chapel's antechamber, Ida, gray-faced and in mourning, every minute on the edge of fainting, sat in a high-backed tapestried chair, rocking her head. At her side, wasted, red-eyed from weeping, sat Helen. Landsleit, old friends, drawn by funeral notices in the Jewish mourning papers, lamented aloud as they bent to kiss her, dropping pulpy tears on her hands. They sat on folding chairs facing the bereaved and talked in whispers. Frank Alpine stood for a moment, his hat uncomfortably on, in a corner of the room. When the place grew crowded he left and seated himself among the handful of mourners already assembled in the long narrow chapel, dimly lit by thick, yellow wall lamps. The rows of benches were dark and heavy. In the front of the chapel, on a metal stand, lay the grocer's plain wooden coffin.

At one P.M., the gray-haired undertaker, breathing heavily, escorted the widow and her daughter to the front row on the left, not far from the coffin. A wailing began among the mourners. The chapel was a little more than half-full of old friends of the grocer, a few distant relatives, burial society acquaintances, and one or two customers. Breitbart, the bulb peddler, sat, stricken, against the right wall. Charlie Sobeloff, grown heavy-faced and stout, appeared, with Florida tan and sad crossed eye, together with his stylish wife, who sat staring at Ida. The entire Pearl family was present, Betty with her new husband, and Nat, sober, concerned for Helen, wearing a black skull cap. A few rows behind them was Louis Karp, alone and ill at ease among strangers. Also Witzig, the baker, who had served Morris bread and rolls for twenty years. And Mr. Giannola, the barber, and Nick and Tessie Fuso, behind whom Frank Alpine sat. When the bearded rabbi entered the chapel through a side door, Frank took off his hat but quickly put it on again.

The secretary of the Society appeared, a soft-voiced man with little hair, his glasses lit with reflections of the wall lamps, and read from a handwritten paper praise for Morris Bober and lamentation for his loss. When he announced the body could be seen, the undertaker and his assistant, a man in a chauffeur's cap, lifted the coffin lid and a few people came forward. Helen wept profusely at her father's waxen, berouged image, the head wrapped in a prayer shawl, the thin mouth slightly twisted.

Ida flung up both arms, crying in Yiddish at the corpse, "Morris, why didn't you listen to me? You went away and left me with a child, alone in the world. Why did you do it?" She broke into racking sobs and was gently escorted by Helen and the breathless undertaker to her seat, where she pressed her wet face against her daughter's shoulder. Frank went up last. He could see, where the prayer shawl fell back a little, the scar on the grocer's head, but outside of that it wasn't Morris. He felt a loss but it was an old one.

The rabbi then prayed, a stocky man with a pointed black beard. He stood on the podium near the coffin, wearing an old Homburg, a faded black frock coat over brown trousers, and bulbous shoes. After his prayer in Hebrew, when the mourners were seated, in a voice laden with sorrow he spoke of the dead man.

"My dear friends, I never had the pleasure to meet this good grocery man that he now lays in his coffin. He lived in a neighborhood where I didn't come in. Still and all I talked this morning to people that knew him and I am now sorry I didn't know him also. I would enjoy to speak to such a man. I talked to the bereaved widow, who lost her dear husband. I talked to his poor beloved daughter Helen, who is now without a father to guide her. To them I talked, also to landsleit and old friends, and each and all told me the same, that Morris Bober, who passed away so untimely—he caught double pneumonia from shoveling snow in front of his place of business so people could pass by on the sidewalk—was a man who couldn't be more honest. Such a person I am sorry I didn't meet sometime in my life. If I met him somewhere, maybe when he went to visit in a Jewish neighborhood— maybe at Rosh Hashana or Pesach—I would say to him, 'God bless you, Morris Bober.' Helen, his dear daughter, remembers from when she was a small girl that her father ran two blocks in the snow to give back to a poor Italian lady a nickel that she forgot on the counter. Who runs in wintertime without hat or coat, without rubbers to protect his feet, two blocks in the snow to give back five cents that a customer forgot? Couldn't he wait till she comes in tomorrow? Not Morris Bober, let him rest in peace. He didn't want the poor woman to worry, so he ran after her in the snow. This is why the grocer had so many friends who admir-ed him."

The rabbi paused and gazed over the heads of the mourners.

"He was also a very hard worker, a man that never stopped working. How many mornings he got up in the dark and dressed himself in the cold, I can't count. After, he went downstairs to stay all day in the grocery. He worked long long hours. Six o'clock every morning he opened and he closed after ten every night, sometimes later. Fifteen, sixteen hours a day he was in the store, seven days a week, to make a living for his family. His dear wife Ida told me she will never forget his steps going down the stairs each morning, and also in the night when he came up so tired for his few hours' sleep before he will open again the next day the store. This went on for twenty-two years in this store alone, day after day, except the few days when he was too sick. And for this reason that he worked so hard and bitter, in his house, on his table, was always something to eat. So besides honest he was a good provider."

The rabbi gazed down at his prayer book, then looked up. "When a Jew dies, who asks if he is a Jew? He is a Jew, we don't ask. There are many ways to be a Jew. So if somebody comes to me and says, 'Rabbi, shall we call such a man Jewish who lived and worked among the gentiles and sold them pig meat, trayfe, that we don't eat it, and not once in twenty years comes inside a synagogue, is such a man a Jew, rabbi?' To him I will say, 'Yes, Morris Bober was to me a true Jew because he lived in the Jewish experience, which he remembered, and with the Jewish heart.' Maybe not to our formal tradition—for this I don't excuse him—but he was true to the spirit of our life—to want for others that which he wants also for himself. He followed the Law which God gave to Moses on Sinai and told him to bring to the people. He suffered, he endu-red, but with hope. Who told me this? I know. He asked for himself little—nothing, but he wanted for his beloved child a better existence than he had. For such reasons he was a Jew. What more does our sweet God ask his poor people? So let Him now take care of the widow, to comfort and protect her, and give to the fatherless child what her father wanted her to have. 'Yaskadal v'yiskadash shmey, rabo. B'olmo divro . . .'

The mourners rose and prayed with the rabbi.

Helen, in her grief, grew restless. He's overdone it, she thought. I said Papa was honest but what was the good of such honesty if he couldn't exist in this world? Yes, he ran after this poor woman to give her back a nickel but he also trusted cheaters who took away what belonged to him. Poor Papa; being naturally honest, he didn't believe that others come by their dishonesty naturally. And he couldn't hold onto those things he had worked so hard to get. He gave away, in a sense, more that he owned. He was no saint; he was in a way weak, his only true strength in his sweet nature and his understanding. He knew, at least, what was good. And I didn't say he had many friends who admired him. That's the rabbi's invention. People liked him, but who can admire a man passing his life in such a store? He buried himself in it; he didn't have the imagination to know what he was missing. He made himself a victim. He could, with a little more courage, have been more than he was.

Helen prayed for peace on the soul of her dead father.

Ida, holding a wet handkerchief to her eyes, thought, So what if we had to eat? When you eat you don't want to worry whose money you are eating—yours or the wholesalers'. If he had money he had bills; and when he had more money he had more bills. A person doesn't always want to worry if she will be in the street tomorrow. She wants sometimes a minute's peace. But maybe it's my fault, because I didn't let him be a druggist.

She wept because her judgment of the grocer was harsh although she loved him. Helen, she thought, must marry a professional.

When the prayer was done the rabbi left the chapel through the side door, and the coffin was lifted by some of the Society members and the undertaker's assistant, carried on their shoulders outside, and placed in the hearse. The people in the chapel filed out and went home, except Frank Alpine, who sat alone in the funeral parlor.

Suffering, he thought, is like a piece of goods. I bet the Jews could make a suit of clothes out of it. The other funny thing is that there are more of them around than anybody knows about.

In the cemetery it was spring. The snow had melted on all but a few graves, the air was warm, fragrant. The small group of mourners following the grocer's coffin were hot in their overcoats. At the Society's plot, crowded with tombstones, two gravediggers had dug a fresh pit in the earth and were standing back, holding their shovels. As the rabbi prayed over the empty grave—from up close his beard was thick with gray— Helen rested her head against the coffin held by the pallbearers.

"Good-by, Papa."

Then the rabbi prayed aloud over the coffin as the gravediggers lowered it to the bottom of the grave.

"Gently . . . gently."

Ida, supported by Sam Pearl and the secretary of the Society, sobbed uncontrollably. She bent forward, shouting into the grave, "Morris, take care of Helen, you hear me, Morris?"

The rabbi, blessing it, tossed in the first shovelful of earth. "Gently."

Then the diggers began to push in the loose earth around the grave and as it fell on the coffin the mourners wept aloud.

Helen tossed in a rose.

Frank, standing close to the edge of the grave, leaned forward to see where the flower fell. He lost his balance, and though flailing his arms, landed feet first on the coffin.

Helen turned her head away.

Ida wailed.

"Get the hell out of there," Nat Pearl said.

Frank scrambled out of the grave, helped by the diggers. I spoiled the funeral, he thought. He felt pity on the world for harboring him.

At last the coffin was covered, the grave full, running over. The rabbi said a last short Kaddish. Nat took Helen by the arm and led her away.

She gazed back once, with grief, then went with him.

Louis Karp was waiting for them in the dark hallway when Ida and Helen returned from the cemetery.

"Excuse me for bothering you on this sad occasion," he said, holding his hat in his hand, "but I wanna tell you why my father couldn't get to the funeral. He's sick and has to lay flat on his back for the next six weeks or so. The other night when he passed out at the fire, we found out later he had a heart attack. He's lucky he's still alive."

"Vey is mir," muttered Ida.

"The doctor says he's gonna have to retire from here on in," Louis said, with a shrug, "so I don't think he'll wanna buy your house any more. Myself," he added, "I got a job of salesman for a liquor concern."

He said good-by and left them.

"Your father is better off dead," said Ida.

As they toiled up the stairs they heard the dull cling of the register in the store and knew the grocer was the one who had danced on the grocer's coffin.

Frank lived in the back, his clothes hung in a bought closet, sleeping under his overcoat on the couch. He had used their week of mourning, when mother and daughter were confined upstairs, to get the store going. Staying open kept it breathing, but beyond that things were rocky. If not for his thirty-five weekly dollars in the register he would have had to close up. Seeing he paid his little bills, the wholesalers extended credit. People stopped in to say they were sorry Morris was dead. One man said the grocer was the only storekeeper that had ever trusted him for anything. He paid Frank back eleven dollars that he owed Morris. Frank told anybody who asked that he was keeping the business going for the widow. They approved of that.

He gave Ida twelve dollars a week rent and promised her more when times got better. He said when they did, he might buy the store from her, but it would have to be on small installments because he had no money for a down payment. She didn't answer him. She was worried about the future and feared she might starve. She lived on the rent he paid her, plus Nick's rent, and Helen's salary. Ida now had a little job sewing epaulettes for military uniforms, a bag of which Abe Rubin, a landsman of Morris's, delivered in his car every Monday morning. That brought in another twenty-eight to thirty a month. She rarely went down to the store. To speak to her, Frank had to go upstairs and knock on her door. Once, through Rubin, someone came to look at the grocery and Frank was worried, but the man soon left.

He lived in the future, to be forgiven. On the stairs one morning he said to Helen, "Things are changed. I am not the same guy I was."

"Always," she answered, "you remind me of everything I want to forget."

"Those books you once gave me to read," he said, "did you understand them yourself?"

Helen waked from a bad dream. In the dream she had got up to leave the house in the middle of the night to escape Frank waiting on the stairs; but there he stood under the yellow lamp, fondling his lascivious cap. As she approached, his lips formed, "I love you."

"I'll scream if you say it."

She screamed and woke.

At a quarter to seven she forced herself out of bed, shut off the alarm before it rang and drew off her nightgown. The sight of her body mortified her. What a waste, she thought. She wanted to be a virgin again and at the same time a mother.

Ida was still asleep in the half-empty bed that had for a lifetime served two. Helen brushed her hair, washed, and put on coffee. Standing at the kitchen window, she gazed out at the back yards in flower, feeling sorrow for her father lying in his immovable grave. What had she ever given him, ever done to make his poor life better? She wept for Morris, thinking of his compromises and surrenders. She felt she must do something for herself, accomplish some worthwhile thing or suffer his fate. Only by growing in value as a person could she make Morris's life meaningful, in the sense that she was of him. She must, she thought, in some way eventually earn her degree. It would take years—but was the only way.

Frank stopped waiting for her in the hall. She had cried out one morning, "Why do you force yourself on me?" and it had struck him that his penitence was a hammer, so he withdrew. But he watched her when he could, through an opening in the tissue paper backing of the store window. He watched as if he were seeing for the first time her slender figure, high small breasts, the slim roundness of her hips and the exciting quality of her slightly bowed legs. She always looked lonely. He tried to think what he could ever do for her and all he could think of was to give her something she had no use for, that would end up in the garbage.

The idea of doing something for her seemed as futile as his other thoughts till one day, the tissue paper held a little aside as he watched her impassively entering the house, he had a thought so extraordinary it made the hair on the back of his neck stiffen. He figured the best thing he could do was help her get the college education she had always wanted. There was nothing she wanted more. But where, if she agreed to let him—he doubted it every minute it was in his mind—could he get the money unless he stole it? The more he pondered this plan, the more it excited him until he couldn't stand the possibility it might be impossible.

He carried in his wallet the note Helen had once written him, that she would come up to his room if Nick and Tessie went to the movies, and he read it often.

One day he got another idea. He pasted a sign in the window: "Hot Sandwiches And Hot Soups To Go." He figured he could use his short-order cooking experience to advantage in the grocery. He had some handbills printed, advertising these new things and paid a kid half a buck to deliver them to places where there were working men. He followed the boy for a couple of blocks to see that he didn't dump the papers into a sewer. Before the end of the week a few new people were coming in at lunch and suppertime. They said this was the first time you could get any hot food to take out in the neighborhood. Frank also tried his hand at ravioli and lasagna once a week, making them from recipes he got out of a cookbook in the library. He experimented with baking small pizzas in the gas stove, which he sold for two bits apiece. The pasta and pizzas sold better than the hot sandwiches. People came in for them. He considered putting a table or two in the grocery but there was no room, so all the food had to go.

He got another little break. The milkman told him the two Norwegians had taken to yelling at each other in front of their customers. He said they were making less than they had expected. The store was fine for one man but not for two, so they each wanted to buy the other out. Pederson's nerves couldn't stand the fighting, and Taast bought him out at the end of May and had the place all to himself. But he found that the long hours alone were killing his feet. His wife came in to help out around suppertime; however Taast couldn't stand being away from his family every night, when everyone else was free and at home, so he decided to close at seven-thirty and stop fighting Frank until almost ten. These couple of hours all to himself at night helped Frank. He got back some of the customers who came home from work late, and also the housewives who at the last minute needed something for breakfast. And Frank noticed, from peering into Taast's window after he was closed, that he was no longer so generous with the specials.

The weather turned hot in July. People cooked less, lived more on delicatessen, canned goods, bottled drinks. He sold a lot of beer. His pastas and pizzas went very well. He heard that Taast had tried making pizzas but they were too doughy. Also, instead of using canned soups, Frank made a minestrone of his own that everybody praised; it took time to cook up, but the profit was better. And the new things he was selling pushed other goods along. He now paid Ida ninety a month for rent and the use of her store. She was earning more money on her epaulettes, and did not think so often that she would starve.

"Why do you give me so much?" she asked him when he raised the money to ninety.

"Maybe Helen could keep some of her wages?" he suggested.

"Helen isn't interested any more in you," she said sternly.
He didn't answer her.

But that night after supper—he had treated himself to ham
and eggs and now smoked a cigar—Frank cleared the table
and sat down to figure out how much it would cost to support
Helen in college if she would quit her job and give all her
time to education. When he had figured out the tuition from
the college catalogues he had collected, he saw he couldn't
do it. His heart was heavy. Later he thought maybe he could
work it if she went to a free college. He could give her enough
for her daily expenses and also to make up whatever money
she now gave her mother. He figured that to do it would be a
rocky load on his head, but he *had* to do it, is was his only
hope; he could think of no other. All he asked for himself was
the privilege of giving her something she couldn't give back.

The big thing, exciting yet frightening, was to talk to her, say
what he hoped to do. He always had it in mind to say but
found it very hard. To speak to her, after all that had happened to them, seemed impossible—opening on peril, disgrace,
physical pain. What was the magic word to begin with? He
despaired he could ever convince her. She was remote, sinned
against, unfeeling, or if she felt, it was disgust of him. He
cursed himself for having conceived this mess he couldn't now
bring himself to speak of.

One August night after he had seen her come home from
work in the company of Nat Pearl, sick of the misery of un-
motion, Frank made himself move. He was standing behind
the counter piling bottles of beer into a woman's market bag
when he caught sight of Helen going by with some books on
her arm. She was wearing a new summer dress, red trimmed
with black, and the sight of her struck him with renewed
hunger. All summer she had wandered at night alone in the
neighborhood, trying to outwalk her loneliness. He had been
tempted to close up and follow her, but until he had his new
idea he could not think what he dared say that she wouldn't
run from. Hurrying the customer out of the store, Frank
washed, slicked back his hair and quickly changed into a fresh

sport shirt. He locked the store and hurried in the direction Helen had gone. The day had been hot but was cooling now and still. The sky was golden green, though below the light was dark. After running a block he remembered something and trudged back to the store. He sat in the back listening to his heart hammering in his ears. In ten minutes he lit a lamp in the store window. The globe drew a ragged moth. Knowing how long she lingered among books, he shaved. Then locking the front door again, he went toward the library. He figured he would wait across the street till she came out. He would cross over and catch up with her on her way home. Before she could even see him, he would speak his piece and be done with it. Yes or no, she could say, and if no, he would shut the joint tomorrow and skiddoo.

He was nearing the library when he glanced up and saw her. She was about half a block away and walking toward him. He stood there not knowing which way to go, dreading to be met by her as lovely as she looked, standing like a crippled dog as she passed him. He thought of running back the way he had come, but she saw him, turned and went in haste the other way; so, reviving an old habit, he was after her, and before she could deny him, had touched her arm. They shivered. Giving her no time to focus her contempt, he blurted out what he had so long saved to say but could not now stand to hear himself speak.

When Helen realized what he was offering her, her heart moved violently. She had known he would follow and speak, but she could never in a thousand years have guessed he would say *this*. Considering the conditions of his existence, she was startled by his continuing ability to surprise her, make God-knows-what-next-move. His staying power mystified and frightened her, because she felt in herself, since the death of Ward Minogue, a waning of outrage. Although she detested the memory of her experience in the park, lately it had come back to her how she had desired that night to give herself to Frank, and might have if Ward hadn't touched her. She had wanted him. If there had been no Ward Minogue, there would have been no assault. If he had made his starved leap in bed she would have returned passion. She had hated him, she thought, to divert hatred from herself.

But her response to his offer was an instantaneous no. She said it almost savagely, to escape any possibility of being directly obligated to him, of another entrapment, nausea.

"I couldn't think of it."

He was astonished to have got this far, to be walking at her side—only it was a night in a different season, and her summer face was gentler than her winter one, her body more womanly; yet it all added up to loss, the more he wanted her the more he had lost.

"In your father's name," he said. "If not for you, then for him."

"What has my father got to do with it?"

"It's his store. Let it support you to go to college like he wanted you to."

"It can't without you. I don't want your help."

"Morris did me a big favor. I can't return it to him but I might to you. Also because I lost myself that night—"

"For God's sake, don't say it."

He didn't, was dumb. They walked dumbly on. To her horror they were coming to the park. Abruptly she went the other way.

He caught up with her. "You could graduate in three years. You wouldn't have any worry about expenses. You could study all you want."

"What would you expect to get from this—virtue?"

"I already said why—I owe something to Morris."

"For what? Taking you into his stinking store and making a prisoner out of you?"

What more could he say? To his misery, what he had done to her father rose in his mind. He had often imagined he would someday tell her, but not now. Yet the wish to say it overwhelmed him. He tried wildly to escape it. His throat hurt, his stomach heaved. He clamped his teeth tight but the words came up in blobs, in a repulsive stream.

He spoke with pain. "I was the one that held him up that time. Minogue and me. Ward picked on him after Karp ran away, but it was my fault too on account of I went in with him."

She screamed and might have gone on screaming but strangers were staring.

"Helen, I swear—"

"You criminal. How could you hit such a gentle person? What harm did he ever do you?"

"I didn't hit him, Ward did. I gave him a drink of water. He saw I didn't want to hurt him. After, I came to work for him to square up what I did wrong. For Christ's sake, Helen, try to understand me."

With contorted face she ran from him.

"I confessed it to him," he shouted after her.

He had managed well in the summer and fall, but after Christmas business dragged, and though his night salary had been raised five bucks, he found it impossible to meet all his expenses. Every penny looked as big as the moon. Once he spent an hour searching for a two-bit piece he had dropped behind the counter. He tore up a loose floor board and was elated to recover more than three dollars in green and grimy coins that Morris had lost during the years.

For himself he spent only for the barest necessities, though his clothes were falling apart. When he could no longer sew up the holes in his undershirts he threw them away and wore none. He soaked his laundry in the sink and hung it to dry in the kitchen. He was, as a rule, prompt in his payment of jobbers and wholesalers, but during the winter he kept them waiting. One man he held off his neck by threatening to go bankrupt. Another he promised tomorrow. He slipped a couple of bucks to his most important salesman, to calm them at the office. Thus he kept going. But he never missed a payment of rent to Ida. He valued his payments to her because Helen had returned to night college in the fall, and if he didn't give the ninety to Ida, Helen wouldn't have enough for her own needs.

He was always tired. His spine ached as if it had been twisted like a cat's tail. On his night off from the Coffee Pot he slept without moving, dreaming of sleep. In the dead hours at the Coffee Pot, he sat with his head on his arms at the counter, and during the day in the grocery he took catnaps whenever he could, trusting the buzzer to rouse him, although other noises did not. When he awoke, his eyes were hot and watery, his head like porous lead. He grew thin, his neck scrawny, face bones prominent, his broken nose sharp. He saw life from a continual wet-eyed yawn. He drank black coffee till his stomach turned sour. In the evening he did nothing—read a little. Or he sat in the back with the lights out, smoking, listening to the blues on the radio.

He had other worries, had noticed Nat was hanging around Helen more. A couples of times a week the law student drove her home from work. Now and then, over the week end, they went for a ride at night. Nat would toot his horn in front of the door and she came out dressed up and smiling, neither of them noticing Frank, in open sight. And she had had a new telephone put in upstairs, and once or twice a week he heard it ring. The phone made him jumpy, jealous of Nat. Once on his night off from the Coffee Pot, Frank woke abruptly when Helen and somebody came into the hall. Sneaking into the store and listening at the side door, he could hear them whispering; then they were quiet and he imagined them necking. For hours after, he couldn't get back to sleep, desiring her so. The next week, listening at the door, he discovered the guy she was kissing was Nat. His jealousy ate him good.

She never entered the store. To see her he had to stand at the front window.

"Jesus," he said, "why am I killing myself so?" He gave himself many unhappy answers, the best being that while he was doing this he was doing nothing worse.

But then he took to doing things he had promised himself he never would again. He did them with dread of what he would do next. He climbed up the air shaft to spy on Helen in the bathroom. Twice he saw her disrobe. He ached for her, for the flesh he had lived in a moment. Yet he hated her for having loved him, for to desire what he had once had, and hadn't now, was torture. He swore to himself that he would never spy on her again, but he did. And in the store he took to cheating customers. When they weren't watching the scale he short-weighted them. A couple of times he short-changed an old dame who never knew how much she had in her purse.

Then one day, for no reason he could give, though the reason felt familiar, he stopped climbing up the air shaft to peek at Helen, and he was honest in the store.

One night in January Helen was waiting at the curb for a trolley. She had been studying with a girl in her class and afterward had listened to some records, so she had left later than she had planned. The trolley was late in coming, and though she was cold, she was considering walking home, when she began to feel she was being watched. Looking into the store before which she was standing, she saw nobody there but the counterman resting his head on his arms. As she observed him, trying to figure out why she felt so strange, he raised his sleepy head and she saw in surprise that it was Frank Alpine. He gazed with burning eyes in a bony face, with sad regret, at his reflection in the window, then went drunkenly back to sleep. It took her a minute to realize he hadn't seen her. She felt the momentary return of an old misery, yet the winter night seemed clear and beautiful.

When the trolley came, she took a seat in the rear. Her thoughts were heavy. She remembered Ida saying Frank worked some place at night but the news had meant nothing to her. Now that she had seen him there, groggy from over-work, thin, unhappy, a burden lay on her, because it was no mystery who he was working for. He had kept them alive. Because of him she had enough to go to school at night.

In bed, half-asleep, she watched the watcher. It came to her that he had changed. It's true, he's not the same man, she said to herself. I should have known by now. She had despised him for the evil he had done, without understanding the why or aftermath, or admitting there could be an end to the bad and a beginning of good.

It was a strange thing about people—they could look the

same but be different. He had been one thing, low, dirty, but because of something in himself—something she couldn't define, a memory perhaps, an ideal he might have forgotten and then remembered—he had changed into somebody else, no longer what he had been. She should have recognized it before. What he did to me he did wrong, she thought, but since he has changed in his heart he owes me nothing.

On her way to work one morning a week later, Helen, carrying her brief case, entered the grocery and found Frank hidden behind the tissue paper of the window, watching her. He was embarrassed, and she was curiously moved by the sight of his face.

"I came in to thank you for the help you're giving us," she explained.

"Don't thank me," he said.

"You owe us nothing."

"It's just my way."

They were silent, then he mentioned his idea of her going to day college. It would be more satisfying to her than at night.

"No, thank you," Helen said, blushing. "I couldn't think of it, especially not with you working so hard."

"It's no extra trouble."

"No, please."

"Maybe the store might get better, then I could do it on what we take in here?"

"I'd rather not."

"Think about it," Frank said.

She hesitated, then answered she would.

He wanted to ask her if he still had any chance with her but decided to let that wait till a later time.

Before she left, Helen, balancing the brief case on her knee, unsnapped it and took out a leather-bound book. "I wanted you to know I'm still using your Shakespeare."

He watched her walk to the corner, a good-looking girl, carrying his book in her brief case. She was wearing flat-heeled shoes, making her legs slightly more bowed, which for some reason he found satisfying.

The next night, listening at the side door, he heard a scuffle in the hall and wanted to break in and assist her but held himself back. He heard Nat say something harsh, then Helen slapped him and he heard her run upstairs.

"You bitch," Nat called after her.

One morning in the middle of March the grocer was sleeping heavily after a night off from the Coffee Pot, when he was awakened by a pounding on the front door. It was the Polish nut wanting her three-cent roll. She came later these days but still too early. The hell with all that, he thought, I need my sleep. But after a few minutes he grew restless and began to dress. Business still wasn't so hot. Frank washed his face before the cracked mirror. His thick hair needed cutting but it could wait one more week. He thought of growing himself a beard but was afraid it would scare some of the customers away, so he settled for a mustache. He had been letting one grow for two weeks and was surprised at the amount of red in it. He sometimes wondered if his old lady had been a redhead.

Unlocking the door, he let her in. The Polish dame complained he had kept her waiting too long in the cold. He sliced a roll for her, wrapped it, and rang up three cents.

At seven, standing by the window, he saw Nick, a new father, come out of the hall and run around the corner. Frank hid behind the paper and soon saw him return, carrying a bag of groceries he had bought in Taast's store. Nick ducked into the hallway and Frank felt bad.

"I think I will make this joint into a restaurant."

After he had mopped the kitchen floor and swept the store, Breitbart appeared, dragging his heavy boxes. Lowering the cartons of bulbs to the floor, the peddler took off his derby and wiped his brow with a yellowed handkerchief.

"How's it going?" Frank asked.

"Schwer."

Breitbart drank the tea and lemon that Frank cooked up for him, meanwhile reading his *Forward*. After about ten minutes he folded the newspaper into a small, thick square and pushed it into his coat pocket. He lifted the bulbs onto his itchy shoulders and left.

Frank had only six customers all morning. To keep from getting nervous he took out a book he was reading. It was the Bible and he sometimes thought there were parts of it he could have written himself.

As he was reading he had this pleasant thought. He saw St. Francis come dancing out of the woods in his brown rags, a couple of scrawny birds flying around over his head. St. F. stopped in front of the grocery, and reaching into the garbage can, plucked the wooden rose out of it. He tossed it into the air and it turned into a real flower that he caught in his hand. With a bow he gave it to Helen, who had just come out of the house. "Little sister, here is your little sister the rose." From him she took it, although it was with the love and best wishes of Frank Alpine.

One day in April Frank went to the hospital and had himself circumcised. For a couple of days he dragged himself around with a pain between his legs. The pain enraged and inspired him. After Passover he became a Jew.

MODERN LIBRARY GIANTS

A series of sturdily bound and handsomely printed, full-sized library editions of books formerly available only in expensive sets. These volumes contain from 600 to 1,400 pages each.

THE MODERN LIBRARY GIANTS REPRESENT A
SELECTION OF THE WORLD'S GREATEST BOOKS

G76 ANDERSEN & GRIMM: *Tales*
G74 AUGUSTINE, ST.: *The City of God*
G58 AUSTEN, JANE: *Complete Novels*
G70 BLAKE, WILLIAM & DONNE, JOHN: *Complete Poetry*
G2 BOSWELL, JAMES: *Life of Samuel Johnson*
G17 BROWNING, ROBERT: *Poems and Plays*
G14 BULFINCH: *Mythology* (Illustrated)
G35 BURY, J. B.: *A History of Greece*
G13 CARLYLE, THOMAS: *The French Revolution*
G28 CARROLL, LEWIS: *Complete Works*
G15 CERVANTES: *Don Quixote* (Illustrated)
G33 COLLINS, WILKIE: *The Moonstone* and *The Woman in White*
G27 DARWIN, CHARLES: *Origin of Species* and *The Descent of Man*
G43 DEWEY, JOHN: *Intelligence in the Modern World: John Dewey's Philosophy*
G70 DONNE, JOHN & BLAKE, WILLIAM: *Complete Poetry*
G36 DOSTOYEVSKY, FYODOR: *The Brothers Karamazov*
G60 DOSTOYEVSKY, FYODOR: *The Idiot*
G51 ELIOT, GEORGE: *Best-Known Novels*
G41 FARRELL, JAMES T.: *Studs Lonigan*
G82 FAULKNER, WILLIAM: *The Faulkner Reader*
G39 FREUD, SIGMUND: *The Basic Writings*
G6 ⎫
G7 ⎬ GIBBON, EDWARD: *The Decline and Fall of the Roman Empire*
G8 ⎭ (Complete in three volumes)
G25 GILBERT & SULLIVAN: *Complete Plays*
G76 GRIMM & ANDERSEN: *Tales*
G37 HAWTHORNE, NATHANIEL: *Complete Novels and Selected Tales*
G78 HOLMES, OLIVER WENDELL: *The Mind and Faith of Justice Holmes*
G19 HOMER: *Complete Works*
G3 HUGO, VICTOR: *Les Miserables*
G18 IBSEN, HENRIK: *Eleven Plays*
G11 JAMES, HENRY: *Short Stories*
G52 JOYCE, JAMES: *Ulysses*
G4 KEATS & SHELLEY: *Complete Poems*
G24 LAMB, CHARLES: *The Complete Works and Letters*
G20 LINCOLN, ABRAHAM: *The Life and Writings of Abraham Lincoln*
G84 MANN, THOMAS: *Stories of Three Decades*
G26 MARX, KARL: *Capital*
G57 MELVILLE, HERMAN: *Selected Writings*

G38   Murasaka, Lady: *The Tale of Genji*
G30   Myers, Gustavus: *History of the Great American Fortunes*
G34   Nietzsche, Friedrich: *The Philosophy of Nietzsche*
G88   O'Hara, John: *49 Stories*
G55   O'Neill, Eugene: *Nine Plays*
G68   Paine, Tom: *Selected Work*
G86   Pasternak, Boris: *Doctor Zhivago*
G5   Plutarch: *Lives* (The Dryden Translation)
G40   Poe, Edgar Allan: *Complete Tales and Poems*
G29   Prescott, William H.: *The Conquest of Mexico* and *The Conquest of Peru*
G62   Pushkin: *Poems, Prose and Plays*
G65   Rabelais: *Complete Works*
G12   Scott, Sir Walter: *The Most Popular Novels* (Quentin Durward, Ivanhoe & Kenilworth)
G4   Shelley & Keats: *Complete Poems*
G32   Smith, Adam: *The Wealth of Nations*
G61   Spaeth, Sigmund: *A Guide to Great Orchestral Music*
G75   Stevenson, Robert Louis: *Selected Writings*
G53   Sue, Eugene: *The Wandering Jew*
G42   Tennyson: *The Poems and Plays*
G23   Tolstoy, Leo: *Anna Karenina*
G1   Tolstoy, Leo: *War and Peace*
G49   Twain, Mark: *Tom Sawyer* and *Huckleberry Finn*
G50   Whitman, Walt: *Leaves of Grass*
G83   Wilson, Edmund: *The Shock of Recognition*

MISCELLANEOUS

G77   *An Anthology of Famous American Stories*
G54   *An Anthology of Famous British Stories*
G67   *Anthology of Famous English and American Poetry*
G81   *An Encyclopedia of Modern American Humor*
G47   *The English Philosophers from Bacon to Mill*
G16   *The European Philosophers from Descartes to Nietzsche*
G31   *Famous Science-Fiction Stories: Adventures in Time and Space*
G85   *Great Ages and Ideas of the Jewish People*
G89   *Great Classical Myths*
G72   *Great Tales of Terror and the Supernatural*
G9   *Great Voices of the Reformation*
G87   *Medieval Epics*
G48   *The Metropolitan Opera Guide*
G46   *A New Anthology of Modern Poetry*
G69   *One Hundred and One Years' Entertainment*
G21   *Sixteen Famous American Plays*
G63   *Sixteen Famous British Plays*
G71   *Sixteen Famous European Plays*
G45   *Stoic and Epicurean Philosophers*
G22   *Thirty Famous One-Act Plays*
G66   *Three Famous Murder Novels*
      Before the Fact, Francis Iles
      Trent's Last Case, E. C. Bentley
      The House of the Arrow, A. E. W. Mason
G10   *Twelve Famous Plays of the Restoration and Eighteenth Century* (1660–1820)
      (Congreve, Wycherley, Gay, Goldsmith, Sheridan, etc.)
G56   *The Wisdom of Catholicism*
G59   *The Wisdom of China and India*
G79   *The Wisdom of Israel*